W9-BUY-768

ONLY THE DEAD KNOW BROOKLYN

ALSO BY CHRIS VOLA

Monkeytown

How to Find a Flock

ONLY THE DEAD KNOW BROOKLYN

A NOVEL

CHRIS VOLA

THOMAS DUNNE BOOKS
ST. MARTIN'S PRESS
NEW YORK

THOMAS DUNNE BOOKS.
An imprint of St. Martin's Press.

ONLY THE DEAD KNOW BROOKLYN. Copyright © 2017 by St. Martin's Press. All rights reserved. Printed in the United States of America. For information, address St. Martin's Press, 175 Fifth Avenue, New York, N.Y. 10010.

www.thomasdunnebooks.com
www.stmartins.com

Designed by Omar Chapa

The Library of Congress Cataloging-in-Publication Data
is available upon request.

ISBN 978-1-250-07907-7 (hardcover)
ISBN 978-1-4668-9162-3 (e-book)

Our books may be purchased in bulk for promotional, educational, or business use. Please contact your local bookseller or the Macmillan Corporate and Premium Sales Department at 1-800-221-7945, extension 5442, or by e-mail at MacmillanSpecialMarkets@macmillan.com.

First Edition: May 2017

10 9 8 7 6 5 4 3 2 1

For my parents

ONLY THE DEAD
KNOW
BROOKLYN

1

Ryan Driggs hated when he was hungry.

Even though the pangs didn't come as often as they did the first few decades after he turned, and never as strong, they were still a reminder of weakness. Of what you needed to take from another in order to survive. That you still wanted to survive.

But as he walked west on North 7th Street toward the Bedford Avenue L train station in Williamsburg on a sun-drenched, late-spring afternoon, he wasn't thinking about the meal that was waiting for him in the subway. Or about the fight with Jennifer the previous night, how he was going to try to convince her that they could still make things work.

Instead, he felt oddly reflective.

Maybe it was because he rarely visited the Brooklyn neighborhood where he'd been born almost 128 years earlier—normally he felt uncomfortable being this close to the East River and the border with Queens. Or maybe it was because many of the two- and three-story row houses and decaying industrial buildings on this part of the street remained intact from the first years of his second life, when immigrants from every depressed corner of Europe swarmed the tenements and the horse-dung avenues, when his "mentor," Frank, would roll back the curtain a little more each day, revealing the seemingly endless possibilities in what they were, what they could become.

When the bodies piled up faster and higher than he could count, or wanted to.

In his mind he saw the drab, woolen-coated workers jostling
and shouting in a dozen different languages on their way to jobs at
the docks, shipyards, and refineries that lined the nearby waterfront. The Polish and Russian Jews fleeing fascism and later an
increasingly hostile Manhattan, across the Williamsburg Bridge.
The original tenements decaying. The housing projects rising and
welcoming waves of Puerto Ricans and Dominicans to work on
new highways and in new industrial spaces. The racial and political
tensions, vacant squalor and violent degeneration, the dark years of
the sixties and seventies. The artists seeking cheap rents and long-
abandoned factory lofts. The galleries, shops, and restaurants cater-
ing to condo-dwelling yuppies who didn't worry about rent as long
as their neighborhood was still considered "trendy yet accessible."
The grid of streets that, like him, had remained visibly unchanged
for as long as anyone alive could remember, longer than any of the
city's architects would have imagined. Maybe it had been *too* long.

The scent of fresh sweat and the sound of a relentless, beckon-
ing pulse under the skin of every self-absorbed pedestrian he passed
brought him back to the present, reminded him why he was here.
His stomach lurched.

He crossed Bedford Avenue, passed a crowded Swedish espresso
bar and a Dunkin' Donuts, and saw the subway entrance—a small
sign above a nondescript staircase flanked by a green railing that
took up about half of the sidewalk; it wasn't a major commuter hub.
Ryan descended the stairs that led to a small, dim lobby that had seen
better days. Dull orange paint peeled from the steel-bar rafters and
the chipped-tile walls. There was a ticket and information booth,
a MetroCard kiosk, and a single, doodle-scarred bench where a man
in an unseasonal wool beanie and a T-shirt featuring the logo of an
obscure punk trio was seated and fiddling with a harmonica.

Ryan opened an e-mail on his phone to look at the picture Zoe
had sent him after they'd exchanged first names and numbers and
decided to meet at the closest subway station to Manhattan. She'd
recently moved to Harlem to be close to Columbia University where
she was going to graduate school, and the commute was already
going to be outrageous for her, apparently, without the extra twenty-
five minutes or so to a hole-in-the-wall fried chicken and pizza

place near his apartment in Crown Heights, where he'd originally suggested they meet.

He'd found her on the "Strictly Platonic" section of the Craigslist personals pages, where Frank said he'd find something. Her ad was the first he'd clicked on, and it seemed legitimate, all of the necessary information in the correct order without any extra details:

B negative

Female

22 years old

5'4"

110 pounds

Ashkenazi (mother) / Irish-Italian (father)

Brooklyn Native

He didn't like having to rely on contacts he'd never met or knew anything about, but his last two regular donors had moved out of the borough, the last one a month ago, and Frank had said that Craigslist was generally reliable, that it was how things were heading. Plus, Ryan hadn't had any B negative from someone in their twenties since before 9/11. A full meal would mean not having to eat again for six weeks, maybe longer. It was worth the risk.

Zoe's head shot—pale skin, long wavy black hair with side-swept bangs, thick-rimmed glasses, dark lipstick, earth-tone cardigan— looked like it had been taken on a crappy low-resolution webcam, but it was probably good enough for him to figure out if she was in the station or not.

His initial scan of the lobby wasn't very promising. Besides the harmonica guy, an older Hasidic man buying a MetroCard, and the dozing booth attendant, the only other person he saw was a girl leaning against the far wall, earbuds in, staring at the floor. She didn't look exactly like Zoe, but she didn't *not* look like her either. Vintage-store-frayed jeans, sleeveless collared shirt, a beanie cocked at an ironic angle over the same style of bangs. It had always been like this, he thought as he walked over to her. The more everyone tried to preach individualism, the more everyone managed to look the same.

"Zoe?" he said, trying to get her attention.

No response.

"Zoe!"

She looked up, and for a second he thought he saw a look of recognition, but that quickly turned into a scowl.

"B negative?"

She mouthed *Fuck off*, turned, and started walking toward the turnstiles and the train tracks beyond them.

Shit, Ryan thought. Maybe Zoe had seen him and run off, gotten cold feet. At a toned six foot one and 185 pounds, with short, dirty-blond hair, hazel eyes, and a perpetual thirty-two-year-old face, he didn't think of himself as particularly intimidating, but she was young for a donor, and it wouldn't be the first time one had flaked on him. He could feel his muscles ache, an intense pounding reverberating through his skull.

He needed to eat, fast.

As he headed back toward the stairs, his phone buzzed. A long text message.

From: B-

Hey I'm super sorry I should have let you know sooner but I'm not going to be able to make it to BK like we planned. I definitely need the money but I had a bunch of crazy stuff come up for school, finals next week, etc. I sent my roommate Nicki instead. I told her mostly what to expect and she's totally down and into it. And is also B-Neg!! She's waiting for you at the Starbucks on N 7th. I showed her your pic. Sorry again!

5:03PM

He didn't like it, but at this point his only other immediate option was messy and outdated, regardless of how good the booth attendant had begun to smell. He jogged up the stairs and reemerged into the fading sunlight and the buzz of early-evening foot and bicycle traffic.

The Starbucks was a block away, occupying the first floor of a reclaimed brick warehouse, painted off-white with an all-glass façade. Inside, it was nearly silent besides the trendy ambient music flowing from hidden speakers, and the keystrokes of student types and faux-bohemians seated in front of laptops on the long wooden tables that occupied most of the space. A woman in a black tank top with full tattoo sleeves on both arms sat in a chair near the front windows next to a sleeping baby in a stroller, reading something on an iPad. They made eye contact as Ryan approached and for a second he thought she recognized him before looking back down at the screen.

He was about to say something when a bird-pitched voice shouted his name from across the room. The girl was sitting in a green pleather armchair holding a half-eaten yogurt parfait. Olive-colored skin, attractively curvy in most of the right places, wearing a plaid button-down shirt and distressed jeans, without the bangs but with the same thick-rimmed glasses. She smiled and motioned for him to come over.

"Nicki?" he asked, sitting in the vacant chair adjacent to her.

She nodded. "I'm sorry about Zoe," she said, nervously twisting her hair with her free hand. "She told me to tell you that she doesn't normally do this, that she's usually not this, like, unprofessional." She looked around, lowered her voice. "But can I just tell you how crazy this is? I always thought she was like an escort or something, I mean she's definitely hot enough. I didn't believe her at first when she asked me to fill in, but then I saw the e-mails she sent to you and other clients of your uh, species, and I was like holy shit, this is for real. I'm sorry, I talk too much when I'm on edge."

This is going to be painful, Ryan thought. But the hunger knives relentlessly stabbing his gut were worse. "Are you sure you're B negative?" he asked.

"Yeah!" she beamed. "I just found out last week after I broke up with this loser and went to get tested because he was getting blown by a girl he knew from home in Nebraska or somewhere equally negligible. I asked the doctor at the clinic what my type was because I figured as an adult it's probably something you should know. Oh, and for the record I'm totally clean. Disease free."

"It doesn't matter," he said, wondering if Frank had just been fucking with him by suggesting the kind of ordeal this was turning out to be.

"Okay, good," she said. "I hope it's kosher I'm eating before we do this. I thought Zoe told me to get to the Bedford station by four, but then I remembered that she said that you guys had agreed on five, and I got bored and hungry. Then Zoe just texted me and told me that you would just meet me. So."

"It's fine." He scanned the room. The laptop jockeys, the cashier, and the woman with the stroller were all oblivious, immersed in their electronic devices. The location wasn't ideal, but the girl was here and he didn't want to risk upsetting her. Having to go through the process of finding another donor might mean not surviving the next twenty-four hours. He motioned toward the restroom in the back.

"Whoa, we're doing this here?" she asked tensely, her eyes searching the walls for—he assumed—a security camera. "When Zoe said to meet you in the subway, I didn't think it would actually go down *in* the subway. I assumed you had an apartment around here that you used."

He grinned, in spite of himself. "A lair?"

"I mean, yeah. I guess."

"This is fine," he repeated. "Let's go."

She shrugged. "Well, so much for the foreplay." She stood up and he followed her past the counter where the teenaged cashier unconsciously poked at his phone. She dropped her yogurt container into a garbage receptacle and opened the restroom door. He locked it behind them, pausing and listening for a few moments to make sure no one was outside. When he turned around, Nicki was standing next to the toilet, her shirt halfway unbuttoned, lacy yellow bra exposed, neck tilted back, eyes closed.

"I'm ready," she whispered, fearful and excited.

He shook his head. Rookies. "Didn't your friend explain how this works?"

"You mean like the actual process? I assumed it was pretty straightforward. You suck and I hopefully get a weird lady boner and you hopefully don't get all insatiable and kill me. If you prefer thighs, that's cool too." She started unzipping her jeans.

"Stop," he said. "Just relax." First-timers, even those who had been minimally educated about the process, were beyond irritating. If he wanted to, he could spend hours explaining how he didn't sleep in a coffin. How he couldn't get sunburned if he wanted to.

How he couldn't fly. How he hadn't used what she would call his fangs since transfusion bags and anticoagulants became easily accessible after the Second World War. Or, he could extract her heart through her throat easily and quickly enough, take what he needed, and leave a gory surprise for the next customer or crackhead who needed to pee. But either way, what would be the point? In the seventy years or so since it had become revolting to him to simply drain a body dry and leave, it was always safer—and easier—to say little while maintaining as many stereotypes as possible.

And he was starving.

"Sit down and roll up your right sleeve," he growled.

"Uh, okay?" Her face flushed with embarrassment, she rebuttoned her shirt, sat on the closed toilet lid, and extended a trembling arm.

He placed the leather satchel he'd been carrying on the floor, opened it, and took out a plastic collection bag attached to a tube and a syringe, a rubber tourniquet, and a small package of cotton balls and alcohol wipes. He leaned over and started tying the tourniquet around her bicep.

Nicki's eyes widened, then deflated. She stopped shaking.

"How long is this going to take?" she asked, more annoyed now than nervous, an impatient child at a Frappuccino-scented doctor's office. "I'm really not that cool with needles. I'm also antivaccination, even though my parents didn't give me a choice."

He snickered. "But you were cool with me piercing a vein that supplies most of the blood to your brain, with my teeth, no questions asked?"

"I don't know, the idea of being overpowered seemed kind of sexy, and Zoe showed me the picture you sent to her and it was definitely hot in a moody-adjunct-professor kind of way, and I've watched enough trashy movies to assume that—"

"I know," he said, cutting her off. "This is way more efficient and safer for both of us, especially since I don't know your medical history. I want to maximize my investment. It won't take long."

"Ugh. Fine. Just hurry up because I'm supposed to meet this guy for drinks later at the new Japanese place on North 8th. I don't want to look pale or whatever."

In less than two seconds he finished securing the tourniquet, disinfected the puncture area, and inserted the needle. She gasped at the speed and the blood that was already flowing into the bag he was holding above her head.

"That was pretty dope," she said.

"Yeah," he mumbled, anxious for the bag to fill. He inhaled deeply. She was right. B negative, premium shit.

A familiar ringtone blared loudly from his pocket, a popular second-wave synth-pop song by a band Jennifer knew he couldn't stand, that she'd downloaded while helping him set up his phone. He sighed. He'd been putting off the conversation all day, weeks really, trying to figure out the best way to explain to her what he was, why he couldn't leave Brooklyn, all of the variations of what it might mean for them going forward.

"Ooh, I love this band," Nicki cooed. "Hey! I think they're playing at the Knitting Factory in a couple weeks, you should definitely get tickets now."

"Hold this for a second," Ryan said, handing her the bag.

"Gross," she muttered, lifting it with her nonpunctured arm.

He answered his phone without checking the caller ID. "Hey, babe, sorry for not getting back to you after last night. The market was crazy today and I had to monitor a bunch of stuff. I was just about to call you. What's going on?"

Nothing but the hum of static and dead space.

"Hello? You there?"

He heard a series of breaths, fast but labored, like something was gradually closing off airways, constricting. Then a loud metallic scrape, two or three choked gurgles, and a squeal that could have been either masculine or feminine, he couldn't tell.

The caller hung up.

A few seconds later he got two picture messages from the same number. The first was a painting of a cherry-red Old-English-style letter *M* on a black background, hovering above what looked like an upside-down crown bleeding onto a pile of decomposing limbs. He couldn't remember where he'd seen the image, but it awoke a twinge of discomfort, an ingrained resentment he couldn't quite place.

The second picture was a photograph. A naked figure facing the camera with his arms raised over his head, suspended, hands bound together and tied to a metallic pipe running parallel to a grime-covered ceiling. A large tube protruded from a festering incision below his rib cage to somewhere off the screen. The concrete wall behind him was bare except for a large graffiti version of the same Old English *M*. He had pale, milky skin; a taut, well-defined physique; long auburn hair tied into a bun that was protruding from the black cloth that had been placed over his head; a crude star-shaped tattoo above his left nipple.

Seamus.

He remembered what the *M* represented, who it belonged to. But this was something new, a game changer.

"Fuck," he whispered, stuffing the phone into his pocket.

"What's wrong?" Nicki asked. "You look sick. Now I'm sort of glad you didn't bite me. Do you need to sit down? Or is this like, normal?"

He took out his wallet and dropped a small rubber-banded wad of hundred-dollar bills onto her lap. The bag wasn't a third full yet, but he couldn't wait. He cinched the tube, removed the syringe from Nicki's arm, placed a bandage on the puncture area, and returned the bag to the satchel in less time than it had taken to set up the procedure.

As he moved toward the bathroom door, Nicki was stuffing the money into her purse, trying hard not to grin. "So how does this work for next time?" she asked. "Do I call you or—"

He didn't stay for her to finish the sentence.

He needed to make it to Prospect Park before dusk. He had to talk to Frank.

Ryan walked out of Starbucks, took the collection bag out of his satchel, and ripped it open with his teeth. He chugged as much as he could, feeling some excess blood running down his cheek and neck. He wiped his mouth, not caring if the tattooed woman in the window or anyone else on the street was watching.

He stuffed the bag in his satchel and ran.

2

Moving south on Washington Avenue through the tree-lined, gen-trified enclaves of Clinton Hill and Prospect Heights, Ryan didn't slow down to consider the brownstones that had remained more or less unchanged since his childhood—those once-mysterious castles of the ruling class whose air-conditioner-filled windows now looked down on locked Vespas and fixed-gear Schwinns instead of surly carriage drivers. But the time for nostalgia, both pleasant and painful, had passed.

He was running at a speed that could only be reached in the first few hours after eating, floating on effortless bursts. Normally, he would try to savor the feeling of the world moving in slow motion around him, a sprinter in the zone letting his mind immerse itself in pure, energized focus, but now his thoughts moved in time with his feet, maybe faster.

The stylized *M* was an old letterhead used by members of the Manhattan tribe, that much was obvious. But as far as he knew, it hadn't been used since the telephone and all of its faster, electronic offspring had made stationery obsolete. And, as far as he knew, an act of aggression between boroughs was not only unprecedented but physically impossible.

The simple fact was that you couldn't cross the boundaries of the area where you'd been turned without sacrificing all that being turned meant, without returning your body to its original dying condition. Sure, you could send humans across the river, but unless they knew exactly what they were looking for, had the element of surprise and an insane amount of military-level training, the odds of their survival, let alone success, would be close to zero. Especially against Seamus, a cauliflower-eared, bare-knuckle boxer from Windsor Terrace in an era when the Irish fought for much more than money, whose early feeding sprees on Protestants were epic, as well as his predilection for using future meals as training bags, regardless of their denomination.

For a moment an almost-forgotten image appeared in Ryan's mind. It was the early twenties, a putrid tenement in Brownsville cramped with five or six families, fresh off the boat and screaming in Yiddish and German, unable to comprehend what had happened to them, what was going to happen. While Frank and the others were gorging themselves on the meals they'd rounded up on the ground floor, Ryan had gone up a rickety wooden staircase to forage. The first one-room apartment he entered—unlit, poorly ventilated, and clogged with the stench of sweat, human waste, and too-old meat—seemed empty until he felt a small body rush past him and crash against the stained floorboards before escaping out the door. She was maybe six or seven, wild brown hair, a dirty gingham dress, her mouth frozen and gaping in terror. As he approached she lifted both of her shaking hands, palms facing him and fingers splayed, a plea for him to stop, maybe a prayer, or maybe she thought he was there to help. Before he could do anything Seamus was on top of her, tearing her apart from belly to neck, burying his face in the wetness, a red smile for Ryan when he paused to take a breath. The hands stayed open, still trembling, reaching for something they'd never touch.

A second later the hands were gone and Ryan was back in the present, trying to process the pictures he'd been sent. How were they able to find Seamus, he wondered, and how was he connected? *How did they get my number?* And most importantly, why?

Any further self-questioning was interrupted by a ringtone from the phone he was still clutching in his hand. He slowed his pace and looked at the name on the screen. Jennifer. As much as it frustrated him, as much as he felt the sudden urge to see her now, to tell her everything, she would have to wait.

He silenced the phone, put it on vibrate, and scanned the major intersection that opened up just ahead of him, the crunch and hiss of traffic. Across Eastern Parkway loomed the classical Beaux Arts pillars and modernist glass pavilion that composed the Brooklyn Museum's main façade. Clusters of people were posted up in front of the large building taking selfies and group shots while joggers, skateboarders, and hand-holding couples entered and exited the leaf-shaded paths that formed the northern boundary of Prospect Park to the right.

Ryan had always found it intriguing that for the past few decades, Frank had insisted on working either in or adjacent to the park. Maybe it was because the manicured meadows, hills, ponds, and groves of chestnuts and oaks reminded Frank of a time that only he could recall, when most of the borough consisted of bucolic villages and long stretches of uninterrupted farmland. But then why, with more than 580 acres to choose from, did he always seem to set up shop in the park's most high-traffic area, where you were far more likely to hear the incessant bass thumps of a soon-to-be-archaic sound system or the incomprehensible hum of ten different languages spoken at once than the piercing cry of a hawk making its first kill of the day? With Frank, nothing was ever easy to figure out. And unless you wanted a far-from-simple answer, it was better to keep your theories to yourself.

But any hopes for simple answers had already been extinguished, which was why Ryan was here. He crossed the parkway, continuing down Washington Avenue where it bisected then paralleled the park's eastern border. Half a dozen brightly painted food trucks were idling in a row on the street, swarmed by the last of the postmuseum crowds, offering a standard selection of tourist-trap fare: vegan ice cream, gluten-free Belgian waffles, fair-trade coffee, Korean-Mexican barbecue.

"Now I *know* this motherfucker wants a kimchee burrito!" boomed a familiar voice from the Seoul Survivor truck's service window as Ryan approached. Raj was in his late thirties but looked younger, jovially plump, his jowls concealed by a formidable black beard that would have made him look like an aspiring guru from the Sri Lankan province where his parents had been born, if he hadn't been wearing a grease-stained apron and matching baseball cap. He handed his lone waiting customer a paper bag, took the cash from her, and extended a latex-gloved fist for Ryan to bump.

"Looks like you've been eating enough burritos for both of us," Ryan said.

"Damn, that's cold," Raj replied, grinning. "But for real, these bulgogi tacos are like meth, man. Can't get enough of them."

As Raj turned to put the money in an unseen register, Arianna appeared in the service window, wearing the same grimy uniform, her long black curls reined in by a hairnet. "That's why Frank won't let him near the grill anymore," she said, big green eyes reflecting the last dying rays of sunlight. "Profit margins are shitty enough with the way this tank soaks up gas."

A portly South Asian and a cute Venezuelan toiling in a failing multiethnic food truck sounded like the start of a bad joke or a soon-to-be-canceled sitcom, but Ryan knew there was nothing intentionally funny or random about it. Raj and Arianna were both AB negative, the rarest blood type after B negative, and Frank's beverage of choice. For years they'd been his donors, employees, drug mules, roommates, factotums, whatever you wanted to call it, the only two sentient beings—mortal or otherwise—that he fully trusted. Hiding the truth about yourself and what you valued in plain sight was more than a cliché, it was how you stayed alive. In that respect, Raj and Arianna were the perfect extensions of Frank.

"I was in the area and figured I'd stop by and pay my respects to your boss," Ryan said. "It's not a big deal, but I have something I wanted to ask him about before you all went home for the night. You know where I can find him?"

"Ooh," Arianna cooed, faux-dramatically. "Mysterious. If he's not heading back this way already he's probably still hanging out at that lawn a couple blocks south of here in the park. There's a bunch of benches and a jogging path."

"You know," Raj added, "where the hipsters are always playing their guitars and bongos and shit." He started banging his palms on the service counter and doing a dance that looked more like a minor seizure. Arianna rolled her eyes.

"Thanks, guys," Ryan said as he turned to leave, not in the mood for Raj's usual brand of bullshit. "Always a pleasure."

Raj stopped gyrating and fiddled with something under the counter. "Hey, wait," he said. He tossed Ryan a packet of sanitary wipes and added, with what sounded to Ryan like the faintest hint of condescension, "Looks like you got something on your neck, bro."

Ryan reached up and ran his fingers across a few small streaks of Nicki's crusted blood. *Embarrassing*, he thought, *and potentially dangerous.* But he didn't have time to be patronized by someone whose facial hair reeked of cabbage. He waved at Raj and Arianna and left.

A few seconds later, wiping the blood off as he walked, he felt a sudden tremor shoot down his spine, sort of a chill, though he couldn't exactly remember what it was like to be cold. And a strange gripping, something magnetic and shapeless trying to pull him back toward the trucks. He stopped and turned around. A thin, pale man with a shaved head, wearing aviator sunglasses and a midnight-blue European-cut suit, was hoisting what looked like a small duffel bag onto the Seoul Survivor's service counter. He said something to Arianna, who unzipped the bag and inspected its contents. She nodded and Raj handed the man a thick, bill-sized envelope. Raj said something and the three of them laughed.

The truck's real purpose. Hiding in plain sight.

The chill he'd felt was gone. He picked up the pace in the direction he'd been going, not looking back again.

Ryan entered Prospect Park just east of the Botanic Garden's main ticket kiosk. He followed a winding, slightly uphill trail for a few yards, passing a mostly vacant playground and public restrooms. The trees on either side began to thin, the ground leveled, and he found himself at the edge of a large grassy space that was ringed by several long, semicircular benches. It was past dusk and the streetlights had been turned on, illuminating the remaining inhabitants of the lawn—a few teenagers tossing a Frisbee, a pair of dozing brown-baggers sitting cross-legged on a blanket of garbage bags—in a synthetic orange glow. Frank reclined alone on the bench closest to the path, wearing jeans and a black tank top and smoking what looked like an e-cigarette. His shoulder-length, salt-and-pepper dreadlocks framed his angular, mahogany-toned face and rested on wide, muscular shoulders. His skin was smooth, almost glistening except for a small X that had been branded onto his left cheek and the gouge marks crisscrossing his back and arms that would look like shrapnel wounds to the casual observer but were actually whip scars. That complexion, and the unblinking gold eyes that were staring straight into nothing, made Frank look as ageless as he actually was, a permanence that had once been a source of comfort and a goal for Ryan when he'd been interested in discovering what he had become, when he'd considered Frank much more of a father figure than Jonah, the gin-rotted bricklayer who caught tuberculosis when Ryan was nine.

But during the few instances that Ryan had made physical contact with Frank in the last couple of years, those eyes always seemed increasingly predatory and desperate, confirmation that the exile's life Ryan had chosen had been the right one, or at least a little more stable than Frank's version.

"Raj says you aren't a fan of my burritos," Frank said, stone-faced, a whiff of cannabis vapor exiting his mouth as Ryan sat next to him.

"How did he—"

Frank motioned at the blinking phone on his lap. "It's the future now, get with it or die," he hissed.

"That's probably what you told everyone when the telegraph came out," Ryan said, repeating the beginning of a very bad and very old joke.

"More or less, the vernacular might have been a little different," Frank said, unable to hold back a smile. He handed Ryan the vaporizer pen. "You have to admit, though, there's some pretty cool shit out there now, like this. It uses butane wax, far more concentrated than your standard hydroponics or hash and without the impurities, totally portable and easy to refill. You charge it with a USB cable. Push the chrome button halfway down the stem, try a hit."

"No thanks, not really my thing," Ryan said, handing the pen back to Frank. "Does it even do anything for you?"

"I don't think so, not really, I just like the taste. Arianna says it knocks her out. Takes her to outer space or somewhere equally unimaginative." Frank took another hit, long and deep, closing his eyes.

"Is that what was in the gym bag that wannabe Reservoir Dog

handed over to your minions a couple minutes ago?" Ryan asked. "The suit's a cute touch, Frank, but not the most subtle wardrobe choice for a, what is he, a wholesaler or something?"

Frank was silent for a few seconds, then chuckled. "Tony," he said. "He's a forensic chemist. Works in a medical lab in Bushwick that has a contract with the DEA. He hooks us up with a few pounds of levamisole every three months. I'm not sure what's going on with the suit, but if it makes him feel a little more badass, so be it."

"Levamisole. There was an article about that in the *Times*. It's a cutting agent in cocaine, really nasty stuff. Destroys the immune system. It's supposed to be used as a cow dewormer or something. Jesus, Frank, is your blow really that bad?"

"I'm impressed you're keeping up so well with current events," Frank said sardonically. "It also causes a significant spike and later a major crash in dopamine levels, which basically guarantees repeat customers in the short term."

"And in the long term?"

"It's not hard to find new customers."

Though Ryan was focusing on the dimly lit lawn and the hills and rock formations fading to gray in the distance, he could feel Frank's stare, really sizing him up for the first time. "You didn't come here for my food or my drugs," Frank said, "and you didn't come to ask me to find you another donor because I can tell by the glow you've got going that you've enjoyed a satisfying meal today. You're welcome. And you're also not here because you were in the neighborhood and felt the urge to sit with a dear friend and reminisce about old times, because that's definitely not your style. Do you want to change your name again? It's been what, seven or eight years now? Ryan Driggs—it has such a nice ring to it, alliteration that doesn't sound forced, WASPy and unassuming, strong masculine consonants."

"I think you need to look up the definition of *alliteration*," Ryan said. "I was born on Driggs Avenue. I wasn't going for style points."

"Oh well. I can get you a new driver's license and the necessary documents, but it's going to take longer this time. And it's expensive. The new security features—holograms, embedded cryptoprocessor chips, RFID tags—they're a real pain in the ass to replicate. I have a guy, but . . . the impatience you're trying to hide under that pretty-boy face tells me you aren't interested. So, why *are* you here?"

"Because we're living in the future," Ryan said dryly, taking his phone out of his pocket. He pulled up the picture messages on the screen and handed the phone to Frank. "Someone sent me these less than an hour ago."

Frank studied the images for a few seconds, then sighed. "God-damn it, Seamus," he whispered, his voice tinged with more disap-pointment than concern.

"What is this shit, Frank?" Ryan asked. "The *M* is Manhattan, that much I get, but how could they—"

"It's not Manhattan," Frank said, cutting him off. "At least not directly. It looks like someone trying to impress them. Or maybe a few people, groupies from one of the message boards."

"Message boards?"

Frank handed Ryan his phone. "How would you describe your level of curiosity when you're on the Internet? And I'm not talking about foot fetishes or amputee porn."

Ryan shrugged. "I'm curious about my stock portfolio, any potential subway delays, who's pitching for the Dodgers. I don't know. I go into Wikipedia black holes, I play Call of Duty, and I read the news. I check my e-mail." *And Jennifer's social media pages and her work's website and the pages that come up when I Google her name.*

"But not about the tribes, the people who know about them. Your tribe."

Ryan shook his head.

"You've done your own thing for a long time, had stretches of isolation longer than any one of us that I can remember, and that's fine, I respect that," Frank said. "You outgrew the old way of doing business before we did, found yourself a consistent source of food and a way to make and save money when most of us were still tak-ing what we needed when we needed it and burying the remains. In a way, most of us still are. But you need to understand how things have changed. Our world's gotten bigger."

Ryan let out a sarcastic snort, louder than he'd meant to. He braced himself for another of Frank's crackpot philosophy sessions, another argument without a point.

"Obviously I'm not talking geography," Frank continued. "The G train still sucks. What I mean is that there are underground web forums, off-the-grid chat apps, subreddits, blogs that no one reads anymore, all dedicated to us, to those like us. You're already familiar with the Craigslist personals section."

"Come on, man," Ryan sneered. "Nerds who have read too many comic books in their moms' basements come up with some pretty entertaining stuff, I'm sure, but you're telling me you actually pay attention to that garbage?"

"You're right, a lot of these places are bogus, the products of nutjobs looking for Bigfoot and interdimensional wormholes, but a few are legit. They're great for finding donors, people who want to be donors, people who think they want to be turned. I've been in contact with members of tribes—or what's left of them—in Connecticut, Delaware, Quebec. You'd be surprised how much accurate information is available to anyone who knows where and how to look. It's really kind of fascinating. But like anything else, you have to be careful. We have a higher profile than ever before."

"So you're saying that someone Seamus met on one of these sites was somehow able to organize a full-on kidnapping and torture session, gang-initiation style, hoping that Manhattan would notice them. That Seamus was stupid enough to allow himself to be caught out in the open. I don't care how hungry he was, he should have been strong enough to—"

"I don't know anything for sure." Frank cut Ryan off, sounding annoyed. "Maybe it was someone who'd been feeding him for a long time, enough for him to let his guard down. Whoever it was got greedy, wanted a raise, figured our compatriots across the water would respond to a visual aid. Maybe it was personal, maybe Seamus was talking shit to someone who got pissed off enough to trace an IP address to his apartment and make him pay for it. Found some other like-minded keyboard jockeys to help out. He's one of us, but Seamus is also an ignorant dick."

Ryan nodded in agreement. There was no arguing that. "But how did they get my number? I'm about as far off the grid as can be, according to you."

"I'd assume they got it from the contact list on Seamus's phone."

"I haven't seen him in at least fifteen years," Ryan said. "How would he have my number?"

"I gave it to him." Frank put his phone and the vaporizer pen in his pocket, stood up, and joined his forearms over his head, stretching.

"You what?"

"Yeah, a couple weeks ago I bumped into him on the way back from a delivery in Bed-Stuy. We talked for a while. He said he was feeling lonely or something, wanted to reconnect with his friends. He specifically asked about you."

Frank started walking in the direction of the street. Ryan got up and followed. "Okay, but that still doesn't explain why they would send me the pictures. You didn't get them, right?"

Frank shook his head. "They could have picked out random numbers from his phone. Or gone down the list alphabetically until they got the response they wanted. We don't know what name Seamus used when he entered you into his contacts."

"Do you think they killed him?"

"If they're smart."

"Should we be worried?"

Frank stopped walking and focused another eerie glare on Ryan's face. They were standing a few feet from the sidewalk where Ryan had entered the park, in the darkness between the path's last lamppost and the kaleidoscopic glimmer of neon-hued bodegas, traffic signals, and scurrying headlights. "No," he said, "not yet. I'm going to get in touch with some contacts, make a few house calls, rule out the possibility that this is just some kind of messed-up prank. Are you currently involved with anyone?"

"Involved?"

"Fucking. A human. You've been known to do that from time to time."

"Yeah, but she doesn't have any idea that I'm—"

"It doesn't matter. Cut it off until this situation sorts itself out. How long has it been since you've slept?"

"Four, maybe five weeks. The hunger was bad this time."

"That's too long. Go home and try to relax, let the food settle. I'll figure everything out, what the next step is, and I'll call you in the morning. And regardless of the circumstances, it's good to see you again, Ryan."

They shook hands without speaking, and Frank headed north to find Raj and Arianna. Ryan felt his phone vibrate in his pocket and for a second felt the urge to fling it into oncoming traffic, to watch it shatter into a thousand unrecoverable shards. Instead he ignored it, turned in the opposite direction, and headed home.

3

"*¡Que pasa, primo!*" Luis shouted from his folding chair as Ryan turned onto the corner of Nostrand Avenue and Union Street just after 8:30 P.M. The elderly Dominican, wearing a pink guayabera and a Yankees hat, was seated with three of his similarly dressed friends in front of the entrance to the four-story redbrick building where Ryan lived and where Luis was the superintendent, bathed in the neon façade of a Crown Fried Chicken restaurant. They were outside most nights around this time, weather permitting. Shooting the shit, drinking tallboys of Modelo, catcalling, blasting merengue tunes on an ancient CD boom box.

"Nada, man," Ryan said, forcing a smile, "just coming back from work."

Luis scowled. "Always work, work, work with you, man. You got to chill out more, too much stress is *no bueno*. Where's that *chica* you've been bringing around?"

"Not anywhere you need to know about."

"Oh ha ha, no need to worry about me, boss. Maybe twenty years ago, but now . . ." Luis clutched his bowling-ball stomach and jiggled it to prove his point. He reached into the small plastic cooler near his feet and pulled out a beer, holding it out for Ryan. "Come hang out for a little bit, take a load off."

Ryan shook his head. "Busy day tomorrow, maybe some other time."

Luis shrugged and cracked open the beer for himself. One of his friends started berating him in rapid-fire Spanish, something about the size of his wife's ears, from what little Ryan could make out. Luis barked something back and the men started laughing.

Normally, Ryan liked to find a new apartment every eight or nine years, usually coinciding with a name change and a new set of forged identification documents courtesy of Frank. He tried to find buildings in neighborhoods that were on the cusp of gentrification, where the established ethnic communities had grudgingly accepted the influx of police activity, demands for rezoning, and newly hip "wine and spirit" shops. Crown Heights, with its deeply rooted enclaves of West Indians and ultra-Orthodox Jews, had been an ideal place for Ryan to disappear for the past half decade. To the locals he was just another crazy *blanquito*, slaving away at a boring office job somewhere far away and paying far too much rent for what his apartment was actually worth.

Pausing at the building's front door, Ryan dug through his satchel for his keys. They weren't there. Assuming he had forgotten them during his earlier preoccupation with finding food, he called out to Luis and motioned for him to come over. "You mind opening this for me?" he asked the super. "Left my keys inside."

"For you, anything." Luis unclipped his key ring from his belt after three fumbling attempts but immediately found the correct key out of the dozens that were in his possession and opened the door. "You need me to go with you to open your apartment?"

"I'll be fine," Ryan said.

The old man looked relieved. "Okay, *papi*. You know where to find me if you do."

Ryan thanked him and headed through the narrow, poorly lit lobby and up three flights of stairs. He stopped for a moment in front of 4F's faded beige door and listened for signs of activity in the other three apartments on his floor. Besides the televised squawking of a French soccer commentator, everything was quiet. He thrust one palm against the door and it flew open, shattering whatever locking mechanism was in place, relieving some of the tension that had been building since he'd left Williamsburg. The strength he felt surging through his muscles was also a reminder of the quality of Nicki's blood, the best he'd had in years, so that he would have to get a full night's sleep in order to let his body fully acclimate to it.

As Ryan entered his apartment he caught a whiff of what he thought was fresh B negative, as if Nicki were somewhere close by. But the scent began to fade as soon as it appeared, probably just the drops that had spilled on his shirt or the fumes from the transfusion bag when he'd opened his satchel. He closed the broken door and turned on the overhead track lighting, reminding himself that he would have to call Luis in the morning to fix the lock. He tossed the satchel onto the hardwood floor, next to the black leather couch that took up most of the length of one side of the main living area. The only other pieces of furniture, besides a glass coffee table, were three iron bar stools tucked against a black granite island countertop that separated the kitchen and its stainless-steel appliances from the rest of the twelve-foot-by-twenty-foot space. Except for a large flat-screen television mounted opposite the couch and a bay window that took up most of the space between the kitchen and the door to Ryan's bedroom and bathroom, the walls were off-white and bare.

Ryan's minimalist aesthetic had been a point of contention for Jennifer the first time she'd spent the night. He'd tried to make a few halfhearted excuses, claiming he'd only moved in recently and had ordered a rug and several posters online, but there had been a framing issue. And his former roommate had won all of their previous apartment's artwork in a coin toss or rock-paper-scissors, he couldn't remember. But Jennifer wouldn't let him off the hook. "Well, looks like I'll have to tell my friends I'm sleeping with another serial killer," she'd said, giggling, a little tipsy from the wine they'd been drinking (and he'd been expelling periodically in the bathroom of the bar where they'd met). "That is, if I survive until the morning."

She'd made similar jokes during the first two or three months they'd been dating, probably only stopping when she realized she wouldn't ever be able to get a rise out of him, chalking up his apartment's blandness to a minor character flaw that was a little weird, but one she could live with.

For Ryan, the choice represented another part of himself that he wasn't ready to reveal to her just yet. Yes, people decorated their surroundings with objects that reflected their unique personalities. But those objects also provided them with a sense of security and permanence, in opposition to lives that were constantly changing and ending. When you were incapable of physical change, those objects—and plenty of other things—quickly lost their meaning. And it wasn't like he didn't have storage units.

He sat down at the kitchen island and opened the laptop that he'd left there. A blinking tab at the bottom of the screen announced an e-mail from James Van Doren III, Ryan's financial advisor and his last full-time donor before moving to Manhattan to start a family in the late nineties. James had stopped selling his blood to Ryan the week after he got married, on the grounds that he didn't want his wife to think he was sneaking around with a new girlfriend in Brooklyn, and that his doctor had told him he was anemic. It was a weak excuse on both fronts. James's blood tasted fine, even if it was O positive, and the rotund former middle linebacker had begun to more closely resemble a throbbing bowl of mashed potatoes than a heartthrob.

Ryan still valued James's knowledge of the stock market and how he had managed the sizable portfolio Ryan had developed for the last sixty or so years. But whatever James wanted tonight could wait.

There were two open windows on the laptop's screen—the last few days of instant-message exchanges with Jennifer and a press release on a food-and-drink-industry website announcing her recent promotion to assistant director of nutritional marketing at FreshInsights, where she provided consulting services to restaurants and healthcare institutions interested in local, organic, and farm-to-table meal options for their clientele.

She had corralled her wavy chocolate-brown hair into a businesslike low braid with side-swept bangs for the head shot that accompanied the press release, but her blue eyes and full-lipped smile shone with the wild intensity Ryan still found impossible to resist after six months of wanting to push her away. The genuine kindness and strength—rare enough in anyone, let alone a twenty-seven-year-old child of the Internet and Fairfield County corporate lawyers—that elevated her above the swarms of valueless human lives from which he had distanced himself until they were only a minor annoyance, like flies buzzing outside a window.

But with every unanswered call and text message, every excuse to avoid Manhattan, Ryan knew he was losing her. It had happened to him once before, forty years earlier, with the last woman he'd tried to let into his life. He needed to tell Jennifer who he was, as honestly as he could, but how would that be possible? It wasn't like dealing with donors, who for the most part knew what they were getting themselves into, who weren't overly curious as long as they got paid on time. In a best-case scenario, Jennifer would think he was fucking around, showcasing an offbeat sense of humor previously unknown to her. At worst, she would start filing the necessary paperwork to get a restraining order.

So, just wanted to let you know, my name isn't Ryan. I mean, it is now, but I've had to change it eighteen times to avoid the obvious attention that comes with not physically aging in ninety-six years. The only thing time has done to me is make me tougher, sharpen my senses, eliminate any chance of disease and most injuries. Oh, and I don't eat, at least not the seared scallops and truffle fries I pretended to like when you took me to that eco-friendly seafood place last week. I can stomach alcohol, but I can't process it, meaning I can't get drunk, which is why you think I have such a high tolerance. I can only digest blood, specifically human blood, once every few weeks when the need for nutrition becomes unbearable.

That sounds pretty messed up, I get it, borderline cannibalistic even. But it's not, because I'm not human, at least not anymore. I'm Ànkëlëk-ila—which loosely translates as "dead warrior" in the extinct language of the tribes that lived in New York for thousands of years before colonists arrived—the last of my family line. Our original purpose, as far as anyone can tell, was to protect our home villages—the chiefs, shamans, women, children, crops, and livestock. More than glorified bodyguards, we were super soldiers, able to stay awake and alert for days at a time, able to smell invaders from an enemy tribe before they set foot on our soil.

But whatever genetic loophole was exploited to create us only extends as far as the original boundaries of our tribe's land. For me, that's Brooklyn. When one of us crosses one of those boundaries, they return to their original human state, alone, a mortal outcast.

Back in the day, becoming Ànkëlëk-ila was the highest honor you could receive. You wouldn't give it up unless you'd done something shameful like failing in battle. Or if your heart just wasn't in it. Maybe you felt a profound weariness, or maybe you fell in love. My maker, Arthur, left the tribe for a woman only a few days after he turned me, according to what I've been told. And even though I think I'm starting to feel the same way about you, the way I felt in 1975 for a girl named Vanessa (which is a story I should probably bring up at a much later date, if ever), that I'd give up what I am for us, I can't leave, even if I wanted to.

When Arthur turned me, I had been working for years at the shipyards in Red Hook (near the Ikea store you told me not to buy furniture from because the company clear-cuts old-growth forests in Russia), hauling coal and shoveling it into the boilers of the ships that needed to be refueled. You can imagine what that did to my lungs, or maybe you can't, Miss E-Cigarette-on-the-Weekends. One day a freighter on its way from Mexico to the Erie Canal dropped anchor, carrying limes, bananas, and a particularly nasty strain of a South American virus that might have been related to bubonic plague, maybe something equally aggressive. Another invisible, incurable killer from the third world, which is basically what Brooklyn was in the 1910s. Arthur found me in the hospital a few days later. I was the last person who had gone on that ship that was still alive, just barely. If I leave Brooklyn I'll go back to the way I was: dying, lungs black, extremely contagious.

Maybe it would be a gradual process, weeks before I felt any symptoms, enough time to get treatment. Or maybe everything accelerates once I cross the boundary and I'm dead before I make it across the East River. That's why I can't make it to your friend's party tonight that you've been asking me about, why I can't go swimming with you if we still go to Coney Island next month like we've been planning. Because of what I might be carrying with me when I step out of that subway station, or back onto that beach. I'm sorry.

Any questions?

The bitter, choked laughter that had begun to rise from Ryan's gut was cut off by the buzzing of his phone. Regardless of whether he was ready to talk, he couldn't ignore her anymore.

"Hey Jen," he said. If he had a pulse, he knew it would be increasing rapidly. "I'm so sorry for not getting back to you sooner, not even a text or an instant message, but the market was going crazy this morning. I've been going back and forth on the phone with James all day. Not that you probably care."

"You're right," she said flatly. "I don't."

"Listen, I didn't mean to—"

"It's okay, seriously," she said, a hint of lightheartedness creeping into her voice. "I'm messing around. Busy days at the office are obviously understandable. As long as you aren't going to flake on me tonight. I promise we don't have to stay very long if it gets more than a little weird and, um, fashion-y. I just want you to meet a couple of my friends so I prove to them that I haven't just been Photoshopping you into all my pictures. Plus Erica's new collection is really cool. She has a pair of brass cuff links that look like bulls' skulls. For some reason I think you'd be into them."

Erica Guilford, one of Jennifer's closest friends from boarding school, was an up-and-coming jewelry designer whose pieces had been described as "dangerous yet delicate" with "a penchant for the esoteric" by a fashion blogger whose writings Ryan had recently skimmed. Erica's latest collection consisted almost entirely of metallic rings, brooches, and cuff links shaped into the skeletal remains of livestock, a statement about the inevitable end of sustainable agriculture or something equally morbid and trite, possibly the last thing Ryan could think of himself ever "being into." The launch party for the collection was going to be held at a cocktail bar in Manhattan's East Village in two hours, making his artistic opinions irrelevant.

He hoped that the happiness that had overwhelmed Jennifer the previous week, when she'd found out about her promotion, was still flowing through her. Otherwise this conversation was going to get ugly. "I'm sorry," he said, those two words almost automatic reflex at this point, "but I'm not going to be able to make it to Erica's thing. It isn't just that I've been so busy. Something crazy has come up and I—"

"No, *I'm* sorry," she snarled, cutting him off. "The only crazy thing is that I keep wanting you to be a part of my life, that I keep thinking you could be something more than just a random hookup after I finish with my Brooklyn clients. I hope you have fun with your fucking day-trading or whatever you do, because it sure as hell seems like the only thing you're capable of caring about."

"I'm not just a random hookup."

"Oh yeah?" she snapped, her voice rising steadily. "How many of my friends have you met? What can you tell me about my apartment that isn't in any of the pictures I've shown you? When do I normally do my laundry? Where do I do my grocery shopping? Why do you think I get upset that every time we hang out it has to be within walking distance of your creepy apartment? Go ahead, answer any of those."

Ryan exhaled. "I met Lindsay that night we got pizza at Rosemary's, but other than that, I don't . . ." He paused, trying to think of something he could say to stop the attack.

"You know what? Just stop. I don't even care anymore. When we first started seeing each other I thought that the reason you didn't want to come over was that you were married, that you were a player with a stable of other girls on speed dial, which is fine. That's New York, I can deal with assholes. But you're worse than that. You're a weird, lonely coward, afraid of commitment, afraid to step outside what you know, to take the next step. I've never met someone who I wanted to be with as much as I do with you, someone who seemed genuine, chill, and fun, but now I can see it was all a waste of time. Unless you can make it to the bar tonight, it's over. I don't want to see you again."

Scrolling unconsciously through his e-mails while Jennifer talked, Ryan came across an automated reply, a confirmation of the brunch reservation he had made for them at two P.M. the following afternoon in DUMBO, near the Brooklyn end of the Manhattan Bridge.

"I've been a shithead to you," he said, "and you don't deserve any of it. Just let me finish what I need to say and you can do whatever you want, delete my number, forget the last six months ever happened."

She sighed. "Fine. Go ahead."

"No, I'm not going to make it tonight. As much as I want to, I can't help it. But if you meet me for brunch tomorrow, I promise I'll tell you everything, the whole truth about me, why I can be so evasive, why I haven't been able to go to your apartment. If you still don't believe that I sincerely care about you, then that's it, and I've earned that. At least give me this one last chance."

There was a long pause followed by a painful groan. "I guess I can be there," she said, "but don't be surprised if something *crazy* comes up at the last second."

He could feel her sarcasm drip through the speaker.

"Thanks so much, you won't regret this," he said, but she had already hung up.

Ryan slammed the phone onto the kitchen island, screen side down, heard the crunch of glass that was less satisfying than he'd imagined. He closed his eyes, waited a few seconds, and turned the phone over to inspect the damage.

Through the spiderweb of cracks the image of Seamus glowed up at him, leering.

He closed the laptop, left the phone on the table, walked to the couch, and dimmed the track lighting before slumping down, the weight of the day's chaos pressing him into submission, immobilizing him. He turned on the TV. The head and shoulders of a police spokesperson filled the screen, her taut lips moving, reading a statement. Something about a young man in Gowanus who had been shot in the stomach by an undercover officer a few steps from the housing projects where he lived: "Paramedics rushed the twenty-one-year-old to Lutheran Medical Center, but doctors were unable to . . ."

Ryan was asleep before she finished the sentence.

4

The rain was tapping against the window, blown sideways from the constant bursts of wind, relentless as always. From the rocking chair where he was sitting, he could hear the babble of the street below: squawking taxis, church bells, the bellowing of a ship's horn. Everything faint and removed from the calmness of the tiny room on Grand Street that smelled of wood smoke, tobacco, and something sweeter. A Fred Astaire song was playing softly on the small RCA radio perched on the mantel above the fireplace, its slow tempo offset by the staccato punches of a sewing machine coming from across the room. He sighed contentedly, got up, and walked over to where she was sitting at the dining table, facing away from him, hemming a red and gold evening dress, her dark hair draped down past her nightgown-clad shoulders. She was singing softly along with the song, absorbed in her work. He moved behind her, ran his hands through her hair, pressed her shoulders gently. He leaned down to kiss her and Jennifer stopped sewing, turned her head to meet his, smiling until the skin and muscle suddenly started melting off her once-high cheekbones, pooling on the table and the dress in front of her until all that remained of her jaw was bone and cartilage, rotten and crawling with maggots and cockroaches, the hole that used to be her mouth still gargling out the lyrics in time with the radio—*And I seem to find the happiness I seek, when we're out dancing together cheek to cheek . . .*

"Wake the fuck up, man! Come on!"

The first thing Ryan noticed after he opened his eyes, as Frank prodded his chest with the barrel of a Glock 20 ten-millimeter pistol, was the blood. The fresh splatter stains that coated Frank's neck and arms, interspersed with the bits of skull and brain matter that were plastered to his shirt like sticky kernels of pink and gray popcorn. And the overwhelming smell that filled the apartment—AB negative, all from the same person.

As Ryan sprang up from the couch, fully alert and ready to defend himself, he saw something in the dim light that disturbed him far more than Frank's clothing: the deeply furrowed lines that crisscrossed Frank's forehead, his sunken but wide-open eyes darting crazily, the expression of a caged animal backed into a corner, coiling itself for one last desperate blitz before the inevitable slaughter.

It was a level of fear that Ryan had never seen before, had never thought possible.

Frank took off his gun's safety catch. He started moving slowly around the apartment, pausing at the window. Shaken by a sudden tremor, he steadied himself on the ledge. "Jesus," he muttered softly, after pulling himself together and peeking between the window blind's slats. "When I came up and saw your door busted open, I thought they'd gotten to you already. And then when you were on the couch, sort of writhing around, I . . . this is bad, man."

"I'm fine," Ryan said, walking past Frank into the kitchen, glancing at the microwave's clock, which read 1:07 A.M. "I'm pretty sure I left my keys in my bedroom when I went to meet the donor, had to break in when I came back. I was going to have the super fix the door tomorrow. But more importantly, what the hell happened, Frank? And whose blood is that, Raj's or Arianna's?"

"Raj," Frank spat. "After I talked to you, the three of us went back to my place. I did some research, sent a few e-mails and found out some truly alarming stuff, made me believe that whatever's happening is much bigger than I originally thought, much more than just Seamus, a chain reaction I didn't think was even possible. I figured it would be best to talk to Natalia first, in person, see what she thought about it, and then call you and the others in for a council. It would be the first real one in what, forty-five years?"

"Fifty-two," Ryan said as he removed a tray of silverware from a drawer next to the stove and began prying the drawer's false bottom open with a butter knife.

Frank nodded, wiping a chunk of something off his arm and onto the floor. "Yeah, well, regardless, it's been a while, probably too long. I called Natalia, made sure she was home, told Raj and Arianna to come with me because I figured it would be safer that way. We took the Beemer, Arianna driving, Raj riding shotgun, me in the back. They fired on us before we got out of the parking garage's driveway. Two shots from two different angles, one bullet through the passenger-side window, one through the windshield. The first bullet passed through my neck, just a graze; it's already healed. The second one hit Raj. A perfect head shot. This was some serious high-powered sniper shit, Ryan. These weren't groupies. They were professionals."

"Who is 'they'?" Ryan asked, lifting a Beretta M9 nine-millimeter pistol from the drawer, checking the ammo clip, "and do you think they're trying to take us all out?"

"I'm not completely sure," Frank said, moving toward the apartment's front door, "but I have some theories. What I do know is that it's not safe here. We have to move now, and move fast. Arianna's parked two blocks away. Natalia might be able to tell us something, if they haven't gotten to her already. Grab whatever you need and let's go."

"I'm good," Ryan said.

Frank was leaning against the wall next to the doorway, gun raised, craning his head to check for movement outside. He motioned for Ryan to follow and darted for the stairs.

Ryan tucked the pistol under his belt and scanned the apartment, wondering for a second if it was the last time he would see it, what he was going to tell Jennifer if he did make it back. He shook the thoughts off, cleared his mind, and followed Frank into the hallway.

5

Arianna was waiting for them in the lobby near the bottom of the stairs, partially concealed in the poorly lit alcove reserved for the building's mailboxes, her right hand hidden under a black Nets hoodie, clutching what looked, from its outline, like a large carving knife. When she stepped entirely under the lobby's flickering tube lights, Ryan noticed the same distress boiling under her eyeliner-stained cheeks that Frank had shown earlier, but also more than a little relief that he and Frank were okay.

"I'm sorry about Raj," Ryan whispered while tucking the pistol under his belt, not knowing what else to say, not knowing if she and Raj had been anything more than just coworkers.

Arianna nodded, let go of her weapon, and wiped most of the smudged makeup off her face. "Thanks. I'll be fine. Better when we find the assholes that did this. I'm glad they didn't get to you."

Frank was already at the lobby's entrance, gun lowered at his side below the glass part of the door, scanning the street.

"Looks quiet," he said, his voice low, almost cracking. "The car's parked east on Union, less than a block. We need to move fast."

Outside the building, the intersection of Nostrand Avenue and Union Street was mostly still, nothing out of the ordinary. A black restricted-license cab drove slowly by and a pair of men wearing white Muslim tunics walked into Crown Fried Chicken where a sleepy employee was reading a copy of *AM New York*, the free paper that was distributed on street corners and in subway stations. Luis and his folding-chair mafia had retired for the night. The nearest pedestrians were walking in the opposite direction, at least a block and a half away. First Frank, then Arianna and Ryan, turned onto Union Street in single file, speed-walking in the shadows formed by the sidewalk's maple trees.

Ryan could just make out the hood of Frank's black BMW 7 Series sedan, parked a few dozen yards away, in the darkest midpoint between two streetlights. He remembered giving Frank a bunch of crap about the car when Frank had bought it a few years earlier, how gaudy and obvious it was for someone with Frank's current business interests, the potential irony in getting detained not for being a 345-year-old freak of nature but for being a dreadlocked black dude getting chauffeured in a ninety-thousand-dollar car with twenty-four-inch black chrome rims and tinted windows only a rapper, athlete, or DEA agent could love, how Frank could barely even drive.

The vehicle, as Ryan approached it, actually did look like a case of unmistaken identity, a drug deal gone horribly wrong. Bullet holes through the windshield, rear window, and rear passenger-side window, heavy scarring along the entire passenger side from a recent collision, the black outline of a body slumped against the rear driver's-side window, as if sleeping.

"A bit of a mess," Frank said, stating the obvious, standing next to Ryan at the front passenger-side door as Arianna circled around to the driver's side. "We didn't want to leave him on the street. Ryan, you sit up front. Ari, do you remember how to get to Natalia's?"

Arianna fished a key fob out of her pocket and pressed a button that caused the headlights to flash. "Head south on Nostrand, then a left on Linden Boulevard, right?"

Before Frank could respond, a gunshot rang out from across the street and Arianna's body immediately slammed into the side of the car as if she'd been shoved, causing Raj's corpse to topple on its side in the backseat. Mouth agape in shock, she let out a sound halfway between a gurgle and a wail and collapsed onto the concrete.

The bullet from a second shot tore into the skin beneath Ryan's neck and settled in his left shoulder blade, knocking him back a few feet. From the way the metal expanded after penetrating the muscle, he assumed it was a hollow-point bullet, probably fired from a

.45 caliber cartridge. It had been almost eighty years since he'd been shot, when the owner of a drugstore had found him crouching over a nearly drained counter girl in the back room of the shop. But the shrapnel from the pharmacist's pocket-sized pistol had been like a bee sting compared to the ammunition that was currently lodged in his body, being attacked and dissolved by whatever regenerative processes had kept him young for so long, faster than usual because of his recent feeding.

Ryan didn't feel any pain. He barely heard Frank—squatting next to him, yelling at him to duck down behind the car. Instead, he was consumed by an animal-like rage that caused his entire body to throb, that sharpened and focused his senses. He quickly scanned the area and pinpointed a dark figure sprinting on the sidewalk across the street almost two blocks away, running in the opposite direction.

Ryan kicked away Frank's hands, which were trying to pull him down, and bolted down the street after the shooter. In a few seconds he was running parallel with a pale, flabby kid with a wispy goatee who couldn't have been older than nineteen or twenty, wearing a black tracksuit and red baseball cap, separated from Ryan only by the row of parked cars. Noticeably winded, the kid fired several desperate shots at Ryan while trying to maintain his pace, until his foot caught on the wire of an empty tree planter and he crashed onto the sidewalk, sprawled out on his back. Not breaking stride, Ryan leapt over a Honda Accord and was on top of his prey in a moment. The kid fired one last shot into Ryan's stomach and Ryan ripped the gun away, taking most of the kid's trigger finger with it.

A part of Ryan knew he should stop, that he should let the kid live, at least until he and Frank could figure out what his motives were, who he was working for, but the all-consuming anger, the immediate and uncontrollable desire to eliminate any threat, was far too powerful.

"Don't, don't, don't . . ." the kid kept repeating, convulsing, his soft, double-chinned face frozen in the same grimace of shock and horror as Arianna's.

Ryan plunged two fingers and a thumb, bowling-ball-style, into the kid's eye sockets and mouth and rearranged them in one brutal twist.

Ryan stood up, wiped his hand on his pants, looked down at the face that was no longer a face, and listened to the night that, besides a distant horn blare and a few other less distinct traffic noises, had gone completely silent. Whatever primal instinct had taken over after he'd been shot was now leaving his body in a powerful gush, leaving only a throbbing soreness in his gut and shoulder, an intense dizziness, and a liquid warmth expanding across the front of his shirt.

As he reached out to steady himself against the Honda, his vision narrowed, then blurred; his knees gave out and he crumpled to the ground, suddenly paralyzed by exhaustion. He heard a woman's screams coming from one of the upper floors of the nearest building, the squeals of multiple sets of brakes. A fast-approaching siren.

But as he stared up at the light-polluted sky, none of it mattered.

Not the swirl of neon blue and red that would soon be surrounding him, the frantic voices demanding answers. Not the missed calls and texts from Jennifer that would trickle to nothing once she made herself stop caring about him. Not Frank, who was shaking him, then pleading for him to get up, then finally dragging him across the pavement toward the battered BMW.

There was only the night air, pulsing auburn and purple in time with the energy exiting his pores, lifting him up and calling him home.

It was the closest he'd felt to being alive in almost a century.

6

They sat in silence for a long time, absorbed in their thoughts, in the heaviness of the moment.

Frank drove south for about two miles on Nostrand Avenue before turning onto Church Avenue, a mostly nondescript intersection flanked by a Walgreens and a McDonald's in what might have been the northern end of Ditmas Park or the western end of East Flatbush, depending on the latest real estate trends.

Ryan was staring at the hole in the windshield that was on a level with his forehead, reflexively rubbing the hole in his shirt just below his sternum where the bullet had entered his abdominal cavity. Where there was now only smooth skin. He could tell from every swerve of the car that Frank was constantly taking his eyes off the road, checking the rearview and side-view mirrors, Ryan assumed, for any indication that they were being followed. But there was nothing to suggest that the shooter had been a part of a team, and if he had been, his collaborators were doing an expert job of remaining invisible. And attracting any police attention seemed unlikely at this point. Every cruiser in the vicinity had most likely been summoned to Crown Heights as backup in the aftermath of the shooting, creating roadblocks that they had somehow evaded, though Ryan couldn't exactly say how; the immediate details were still more than a little fuzzy.

One clear sequence of images kept repeating itself through the last hour's haze—Frank's emotionless poise as he lifted Ryan into the passenger seat, as he opened the rear driver's-side door and pulled out Raj like a piece of luggage, dropping the corpse so that its one remaining ear rested against Arianna's chest, arms splayed, a grotesque approximation of an embrace, the two or three seconds Frank stared down at them before jumping in the car and pressing the ignition.

The once-bright sky fading to nothing.

"Do you think it was smart to leave the bodies on the street?" Ryan asked, breaking the silence that had become unbearable. "By now the police have probably made positive IDs of their prints, figured out where Raj and Arianna lived and worked. Unless you had their identities forged, too."

"Do you think it was smart to turn that asshole's face into a fucking Jackson Pollock painting?" Frank snarled.

"Probably not," Ryan mumbled, swiveling his neck to focus on the closed businesses and restaurants they passed, most of their entrances and front windows shuttered by metal rolling gates.

Frank was right. In order to survive, especially in a new century of credible forensic science, DNA testing, and ubiquitous hidden surveillance, you had to be as hands-off as possible, literally. When you had to kill, you did it quickly and discreetly, avoiding as much messiness as you could, making sure you already had an efficient disposal plan in place. If you were stupid enough to let yourself get arrested, you had two options: fight your way out and become a highly sought-after, caged-in fugitive who couldn't hide more than twelve miles in any direction, or allow yourself to become the world's most important science project and in doing so, jeopardize the survival of your tribe and the anonymity of however many other tribes still existed. It was why you had to take precautions with donors, keep the interactions as short and sterile as possible, deny them any plausibility in case they tried to go public. All it would take was one fallen strand of hair or one carelessly flicked piece of fingernail for someone to go from conspiracy theorist of the week to biological whistle-blower of the decade.

Leaving Raj and Arianna's bodies on the street was a cold-blooded move, but it didn't look that different from your run-of-the-mill gang- or drug-related assassination. The shooter's body was different. There would be fingerprints in places where they shouldn't be, at least one witness and probably more. Although it was nearly impossible for the small amount of fluid that flowed in his veins to bleed out because of how fast it coagulated when exposed to the air, Ryan had felt a wet discharge from the point-blank second bullet. He couldn't be sure that all of it had soaked into his shirt and hadn't dripped onto the sidewalk.

"You weren't thinking and you'd been shot," Frank said, lowering his voice. "It was a natural reaction, the fight response that's programmed into us. I'm actually surprised you didn't black out."

"I'm not sure I didn't," Ryan replied, trying to slow the roller coaster of his mind, recall what the shooter had looked like, how he'd managed to pull himself into the car and fasten his seat belt, but all that kept coming back to him, reverberating around his head on constant repeat, was a guttural shriek that might have come from someone watching the scene on the street from an apartment window, or maybe from the shooter in the second or two before Ryan snuffed his life out.

"The last time I got hit hard like that, point-blank, it must have been about 1705 or so," Frank said, taking a left turn onto Ocean Avenue. "I'd already been freed by my master and turned, it might have been two or three years later, I was still living in the woods like a feral beast, no clothes, jumping travelers on the King's Highway at night when I needed to eat, trying to figure out what to do with myself, how to control my urges. One day I was resting in some undergrowth next to Newtown Creek, the boundary with Queens in an area that today would be Greenpoint, and heard a woman's voice singing something in Dutch. Johanna. She was young, blond, must have been AB negative, smelled unbelievable. When I stood up a few feet from where she was washing her clothes in the creek, she was scared shitless, of course. But that didn't last long. She was what you would call, um, open-minded for that time period. If I remember correctly, she thought I was a runaway, and for the next few mornings she would invite me to the kitchen of the farmhouse where she lived while everyone else was out working. It was obvious what she wanted from me, but the craziest thing was that she would cut her wrists, let me drink from her, like she knew what I was, had been with others like me, or could sense it. She also gave

me clothes and shoes, washed me and cut my hair. A real sadomas-
ochistic sweetheart.

"One day I walked into the kitchen and was greeted by a very
angry farmer pointing the barrel of a loaded blunderbuss at my
chest. Whatever projectiles he shot tore through my insides like fire,
instantly knocked me out. When I woke up, it could have been days
later, I was at the bottom of Newtown Creek, my wrists and ankles
tied and attached to stone weights. There was another body next to
mine. I broke free and lifted her onto the bank and when I saw her,
gray skin turning green, fish-chewed lips and tongue, I lost it.
Within an hour there was no one left alive on that farm. But that was
a different time, you could get away with losing it once in a while.
They'd blame it on Indians or witches or something."

"Seems like you haven't had the best of luck with donors," Ryan
said, looking at Frank after the car skidded a little too noticeably to
a stop at a red light.

Frank chuckled dryly, then scowled. "True, but that's not the
point. Things could have gotten way more fucked up tonight."

Ryan rolled his eyes. He'd had more than enough of Frank's
rambling faux-fatherly advice and was wondering if it had been a
good idea to have shown his old (*former*, if he was being honest with
himself) friend the picture of Seamus. "Congratulations on keeping
yourself alive for so long," he said, grinning sarcastically. "I can only
hope to be half as wise when I'm your age." He took his phone out
of his pocket to see if he'd missed any calls or texts, but the battery
was dead.

"How many of us are left, not counting Seamus?" Frank asked,
rhetorically.

"You, me, Natalia, Asher, and what's she calling herself now,
Fiona? That's it, unless someone's been turning people and hasn't
told me."

"You know that hasn't happened. You would have felt it. And
they would have called us to help, otherwise there would have been
deaths, ugly ones; it would have been a media sensation. Do you
remember what you did to that cop near the Gowanus Canal the
first night Arthur and I let you out on your own? It would be al-

most impossible to bury something like that now. One of the main reasons why only two others have been turned since you."

"I always just thought you guys broke the mold with me, realized it couldn't get any better after that," Ryan replied, the bad joke falling flat before it exited his mouth.

Frank turned onto Tennis Court, a quiet two-block stretch of stunted row houses and larger redbrick housing projects with no actual tennis courts in sight, then took a quick left onto East 18th Street and slowed down, looking for a place to park. He continued talking as if Ryan hadn't spoken. "We've always kept our numbers low; makes sense from a visibility standpoint, easier to stay off the radar. But before the last century, there was way more turnover. People left the tribe because they wanted to experience a world they could only read about in less-than-accurate books and newspapers; maybe the idea of living immortally on blood and denial didn't sound all that appealing to those who had been raised to believe that a clouds-and-haloes eternity with a white-bearded old man was possible for anyone who tricked himself into feeling like he could be forgiven and went to church. Sometimes before leaving the tribe they'd turn someone to continue the family line, so to speak, but a lot of times they wouldn't. When I was turned there were close to thirty of us."

At the next intersection, Frank turned right onto Albemarle Road, in the opposite direction of the ONE WAY signs that lined the empty street. A block later, Albemarle came to an abrupt end: a graffiti-covered concrete wall and a chain-link fence, rust-colored train tracks beyond. Frank put the car in park and turned off the ignition.

Ryan's annoyance with Frank suddenly turned to anger. "What does any of this—shit I already know—have to do with me eliminating a threat, who happened to be the murderer of your favorite pets?" he asked. "What does this have to do with Seamus, with all of us now somehow exposed and being hunted down? Why did you stop here? Am I a threat now, too?"

Frank opened the driver's-side door and motioned for Ryan to follow him out of the car.

"We've always been good at adapting," he said as he walked around to the back of the BMW, pushing the button on the key fob that popped the trunk. "We've had to be. But it's not just adjusting how we talk, how we dress, the names we choose, and the ways we make money. It goes deeper. We've become totally individualistic, self-serving. We no longer need to worry about boredom, about not seeing the world because we can turn on a screen and everything we'd wondered about is right there, in high definition or on Google Maps. The air is cleaner than it has been in two hundred years, and besides an overabundance of prescription drugs, our food is healthier than it's ever been. Why jeopardize that by turning someone? Or worse, go on a killing spree that, by its very nature, threatens to expose what we've always managed to hide from the authorities with the power to end us. Which is why a coordinated assault from Manhattan is so strange to me, why it doesn't make sense."

Frank hoisted two large, opaque plastic containers from the trunk, placed one on the ground, and unscrewed the other's cap. Ryan instinctively backed away from the car when he smelled the gasoline that Frank began pouring over the car's roof, windows, doors, and tires.

"Maybe they were feeling retro and wanted to get belligerent like an actual tribe?" Ryan asked, half joking, trying to lighten the disturbing scowl that seemed to have been permanently plastered onto Frank's face as he opened the car's back doors, as he mechanically splashed gas around the interior before leaving the nearly empty container on the backseat. "But seriously, I thought you said that the people coming for us aren't soldiers. They're Internet geeks who figured out how to track us and spent a few hours at the gun range. They got lucky with Seamus and now have the balls to try to come after the rest of us. Regardless of how tactless it might have been for me to kill that guy—and he made it easy—you have to admit that now they'll think twice before trying any more home invasions."

Frank picked up the second container and started fiddling with the cap. "You're partially right, we *are* being hunted. And they are nerds, insofar as they know how to operate on channels that aren't readily available to the average couch surfer. After I saw you in the park I did a little looking around at some places I'd run into over the last couple years messing around on the deep web."

"Deep web," Ryan repeated, remembering the term from an episode of a popular crime drama that Jennifer had made him watch the previous week, forty-five minutes of child pornography, arms trafficking, drugs, hired assassins, prostitution, and terrorism all neatly wrapped up with an expectedly unbelievable twist ending. "It's where you buy guns and Bitcoins from pimply hacktivists hiding in their moms' basements. Right?"

Frank adjusted the bulge under his T-shirt with his free hand. "Yes, it's where I purchase my firearms," he said, "but it's way more than that, five hundred times larger than anything you can find through a regular search engine. Like the entire part of the iceberg that's underneath the water. Most of it's innocuous, just like the regular web, but I was able to download and unlock some encrypted files on a forum that had been set up recently by someone from Manhattan, or someone working with them. The language was complicated, a combination of binary code, English, Dutch, and two or three Lenape dialects. At first I thought it was a set of guidelines, donor qualifications, maybe even a résumé template."

"LinkedIn for prospective food-bags?"

"That's what it looked like, but the more I read, I realized it was a sort of blueprint, a game plan for an operation. There was a timeline, a list of targets and their—our—locations, an extraction protocol."

"So I was right," Ryan said. "These humans want to take Abu Ghraib porn pics, then cut us up and bring us back across the East River in trophy boxes so they can . . . what, prove that they're worthy of being donors, that they're worthy of being turned?"

Frank sighed, then tossed the gas container's cap over the fence and onto the train tracks. "This isn't about unprovoked assaults or groupie dick-measuring contests. Sending you those pictures wasn't a frivolous threat, it was a calculated move. They wanted you to make contact with what's left of the tribe, get us close enough together for a much more efficient and speedy elimination. Think of it from a business perspective. For a corporation to continue to be lucrative, it needs to keep expanding."

The scope of what was happening to them began to sink in. Ryan now understood the terror Frank had shown earlier in the apartment, hopelessly scanning the walls of his cage, nostrils choked with the scent of impending slaughter.

"I thought there had to be some kind of consent thing," Ryan said finally, searching for some way to invalidate what Frank had just told him, to rationalize it out of existence. "Like a bond between us and the person we're turning. One of the few things I remember Arthur telling me was that he'd felt some kind of emotional connection with me, an attraction he couldn't shake."

"I don't know, because I've never had the desire to turn anyone," Frank said as he poured gasoline from the second container onto the car's backseat and kept pouring as he moved to where Ryan was standing, creating a thin liquid trail on the pavement. He tossed the now-empty container and watched it tumble until it came to a stop against the car's back tire. "We just need to hope that Natalia hasn't been compromised."

Frank reached into one of his jeans pockets and took out a packet of matches. He lit several at once.

"Move."

As they quickly strode away from the BMW, Ryan saw the flames reflected in the rear windows of the cars that were parked on both sides of the street. A tiny, singular light expanding into a massive blaze that, ironically, seemed to be getting closer to him the farther away he got from it, impossible to escape.

Something told Ryan he would have to get used to that feeling.

7

The house at 183 Argyle Road was a large three-story English Tudor with a brown-shingled, steeply pitched roof, cream-colored stucco walls accented with wood trim set in a decorative crisscross style, intersecting gables, and two rows of stained-glass casement windows embellished by ornate metal latticework. A narrow walkway led from the sidewalk to a raised flagstone porch that wrapped around the front of the house, where a gangly, vaguely Middle Eastern woman with close-cropped hair and bad skin, wearing a dark-colored tracksuit, was pacing and periodically staring at her phone. To the right of the open main entrance loomed a large screened-in porch that was partially obscured by the mature, overgrown shrubbery that dotted most of the lawn, the intentionally ignored hedges and vine-choked rosebushes contributing to the sense of opulent decay Natalia was always trying to cultivate.

In any other Brooklyn neighborhood the house and its yard's distinctly suburban flavor would have been a curiosity, maybe even a tourist destination. But here, a few blocks south of Prospect Park in Victorian Flatbush, it was just one of the hundreds of homes that ran the gamut of early-twentieth-century architectural styles, from Queen Anne and Colonial Revival to Spanish Mission and Georgian.

Ryan had always appreciated the lush, quiet streets that had been developed as an enclave for the country-club set, conveniently separated from the summer throngs of Coney Island and the industrial commotion of places like Greenpoint, Williamsburg, and Red

Hook. Whenever he found himself walking or cabbing through the area, he often felt blissfully transported, like he was able to escape some of the restrictions of his condition and spend a few moments somewhere far away like Westchester or Connecticut.

The last thing on Ryan's mind, as he slowly approached Natalia's house and slipped through the waist-high, wrought-iron gate that separated her yard from the sidewalk, was an impossible jaunt in the countryside. The woman in the tracksuit—black with red Adidas stripes lining the arms and legs, similar to the gear worn by the shooter, Ryan noticed—was preoccupied with texting and didn't hear him as he closed in on her in the darkness between the street and the house. "Hey," he said quietly, stepping onto the part of the lawn that was illuminated by the front porch's hanging lights, two or three yards from the front steps. "I don't mean to bother you, but you're the first person I've seen in the last hour who doesn't look like they want to steal my shit or worse. I'm not from around here and my phone died and I was wondering if you might be able to point me in the direction of the nearest Q train stop. I know it's close by."

Startled by his voice, her shoulders stiffened and she dropped her phone. As she bent over to pick it up, she stared warily at Ryan, trying to size him up as he smiled back at her. She stood up, breathed deeply, and brushed her straight, jet-black hair back behind her ears, and even though the shadows cast by the porch light made her dark-hued facial features seem angular and weathered, he could tell she was once cute in a tomboyish kind of way. And younger than the shooter, probably just out of high school.

"I'm sorry," he said, lifting his arms in open-palmed apology, "I wasn't trying to scare you. Just looking for directions."

"It's okay," she said, regaining her composure. "I didn't hear you is all. Where did you say you were trying to . . ."

As she trailed off, Ryan watched her mouth go slack and her face darken with a combination of panic and recognition. She had seen him before, or at least a picture, knew who he was. She dropped her phone a second time and reached for something in the pocket of her jacket. Before she could pull it out, Frank, his clothes covered in organic sludge, appeared out of the shadows that dotted the more bush-heavy right side of the house and stepped behind her, snapping her neck in one clean motion before she could move or make a sound. He hoisted her limp body over his shoulder and headed up the steps and through the open front door.

"Looks clear in here," Ryan heard him call out a few seconds later. "They rearranged her art collection a little but no real signs of a struggle. And judging by the scents I'm picking up, Natalia hasn't been here in a while. Hopefully she's in Red Hook with everyone else."

The safe house in Red Hook was an abandoned dye factory that Frank and Natalia had purchased and refurbished in the early seventies. They'd hoped that the four thousand square feet of scorched and soot-covered walls, rows of gutted-out chemical drums, and laboratory nooks filled with random pipes, vials, and beakers would become a secret haven, a tribal gathering place in times of trouble and uncertainty. But in spite of their elders' altruism, the rest of the tribe's members, it turned out, weren't much into reunions, and one of the few aspects of being a dead warrior of which you could be certain was that if you were careful, there was very little to worry about. The last time Ryan had heard even a brief mention of the place was in the early years of the eighties crack epidemic, when base-heads and other assorted squatters apparently outnumbered the rats, and were dealt with similarly.

Before following Frank into the house, Ryan picked up the girl's phone and a small cylindrical object that had fallen out of her pocket. It was a metallic spray bottle, painted black with no markings and nearly full of liquid.

"I think she was going to try to pepper-spray us," he said as he closed the door and stepped into a large, open foyer.

Frank had laid the girl next to an ornate stone umbrella holder shaped like a pair of wrestling alligators and was bent over, brushing thorns, dirt, and flower petals from his pants. He turned and Ryan tossed him the bottle. He rolled it through his fingers and snickered. "Maybe it's holy water or garlic juice," he said, tossing the bottle back to Ryan.

"Or liquid silver," Ryan said, pretending to twist off the spray top's plastic cover, trying to prolong a moment of levity in a night where anything resembling genuine positivity—and a chance to relax for even a second—had been totally absent. "Open your eyes real wide and let's find out."

"I wouldn't recommend that at all," a distorted female voice crackled from the hidden speaker portion of a home-security touchscreen mounted on the wall next to the door. "And I could have used your help an hour ago. If you're done wanking around, follow the trail of destruction and meet me upstairs. Bring the girl."

Natalia was never one for small talk.

Frank and Ryan exchanged a perplexed glance. Frank shrugged and started moving across the circular, high-ceilinged room. Ryan reached around the girl's stick-figure waist, angled her torso against his hip, and carried her toward a set of slightly curving hardwood stairs, letting her wilted arms drag across a huge primary-colored, zigzag-patterned Navajo rug that was littered with bits of glass and other debris.

The walls of the room were made of the same material as the stairs and warmly lit by recessed ceiling lights, giving the space a distinctly rural, ski-lodge feel, if that ski lodge had recently been used as a holding cell for a freshly jacked-up amphetamine freak. The two identical, seven-foot-tall totem poles covered in birds, foxes, bears, and unidentifiable grotesque creatures that normally flanked the entranceway were knocked over, splintered and covered with what looked like axe marks. A giant glass display case, built into the wall that stretched from the front door to the stairs on the right side of the room, was shattered, and its contents—hand-painted lizard and animal figurines, decorative canoe paddles, whalebone pipes, flint daggers and arrowheads—were broken, displaced, or strewn about the floor. A handful of framed photographs were missing from their hooks, their contents torn and scattered across the wreckage.

"Okay, maybe it was more than a little rearranging," Frank said, leaning over the railing at the top of the stairs. "She must be pissed."

Unlike the nomadic existence that Ryan, Frank, and the other members of the tribe had always favored, Natalia had sunk her roots in deeply here—with the help of a sizable inheritance—as the house's sole owner for nearly one hundred years, purchasing it under the guise of a limited liability company. For the last few decades, she'd worn a series of increasingly wrinkled silicone masks in public to simulate a natural aging process, until it was no longer feasible or believable. Now she walked around sans makeup, telling the few people who asked that she was the great-niece of the house's original owner. Most of her neighbors, immersed in their worlds of earbuds and charter school application forms, didn't seem to notice or care.

In reality she'd journeyed across the Atlantic as a reluctant twelve-year-old in the 1840s with her father, a master engineer who'd been hired to help oversee the development of one of the fledgling railroads that had begun to expand its metal and wooden spiderwebs across the continent. After a decade roughing it in the American wilderness that included, if you believed her stories, being kidnapped by a band of Sioux raiders, the hanging of her father at the hands of ornery Mormons, and a broken engagement to a gout-riddled provincial governor, she found herself shipping into the same Brooklyn port that had briefly welcomed her as a girl. Her second stopover in the borough would last quite a bit longer.

A lack of any real sense of permanence during her tumultuous youth allowed Natalia to cherish aspects of being turned that others found cumbersome, or simply impossible to live with. Whereas most new initiates looked at their condition as an eternal prison—albeit one that was free of disease and deterioration—she saw an opportunity to finally settle down, to immerse herself in a community that was older and far more fascinating than anything she'd yet encountered. According to Frank, most of her collection of artifacts had been acquired not during her earlier travels but as the fruits of her research, her obsession with what she'd become, not only in a physical or biological sense but in a larger anthropological context.

If Frank, because of his age, was the tribe's de facto chief, Natalia was unquestionably its historian and high priestess, always with one foot firmly placed in the past, a past whose priceless mementos had been broken and strewn about by someone with the delicacy of a starving rat sifting through garbage.

Yes, she was probably pissed.

As Ryan joined him on the second floor, a loud hydraulic hiss emanated from behind an unremarkable section of the wall to their left. The hidden panic-room door opened soundlessly, revealing a dark steel-walled cubicle with just enough space for a desk that contained a dual-monitor Apple desktop computer and a medical examination table, on top of which a broad-shouldered, lifeless body in a black tracksuit was lying, its shaved head drooping sideways off the far end, its jacket and undershirt pulled up around its chest.

A plump, pale, freckle-faced woman wearing green pajamas, who couldn't be more than five feet tall and looked like she might be in her late thirties, was standing over the body, pumping an old brass hand crank that was attached to a double-ended rubber tube running from an incision in the body's hairy stomach to a large glass container on the floor nearby that was quickly filling with blood.

Ryan had seen this exact pump model once before, the last time he'd been a patient in a hospital, when the technology had been cutting-edge. He tried to suppress a shudder.

Natalia looked up from her work, brushing a few strands of dirty-blond hair away from her forehead. "Ah good," she said with an accent that, even after close to one hundred seventy-five years in the States, still clearly belied her London roots. She sniffed, nodding at the girl who was tucked under Ryan's arm. "Another O positive, but one can't always be picky. Thank you, Francis, for the clean kill, one less mess I'll need to worry about cleaning up in the morning."

"No problem," Frank said, still staring around the cubicle in disbelief. "This is really something, Nat."

"Where should I put it?" Ryan asked.

Natalia pulled firmly on the rubber tube, and it exited the gut of the corpse on the table with a soft slurp. "Just drop her there in the hallway," she said. "No use crowding the bunker up any more than it already is, especially if another round of idiots comes back to try to finish us off with their squirt guns."

She moved over to the computer monitors, whose screens were divided into quadrants showing live security feeds at various locations in and around the house. As she leaned over the keyboard and into the much brighter light of the screens, Ryan noticed that her neck and cheeks were covered in pink scar tissue shining with a clear pus, as if her skin had been melted off and then crudely glued back together.

Frank cleared his throat, a little uncomfortably. "Did they do that to your—"

"Like I said, I wouldn't recommend getting sprayed," Natalia hissed, cutting him off, eyes remaining fixated on the screens. "Honestly, I don't know what it is, but it burns like hell, and it's taking way too long to heal. After you called last night, Francis, I locked myself in here to do some research, check the usual forums and gossip rooms, as I'm sure you did. Then I began exploring some more, ah, esoteric avenues until I was interrupted"—she patted at her chin lightly and winced—"by these children and their toys."

"How bad does it hurt?" Frank asked, as he stared a little too hard at the container of blood resting a few feet away on the floor, like he hadn't eaten recently.

Natalia ignored him. She rewound the video feed of the yard until it showed two figures in matching tracksuits opening the front gate. She used a mouse cursor to manipulate the frozen image, zoomed in on the faces, and highlighted them. A box appeared on one side of the screen showing the area she'd marked with enhanced clarity, the vague pixels mostly smoothed away. If part of Natalia remained fixated on the past, the rest of her interests and talents pulled her in a completely opposite direction.

"Stupidly," she continued, "I unlocked the front door from up here because I wanted to see if I might be able to learn something by observing them, if I could remotely access their phones or something, I don't know. But then I saw this fat cunt destroying in two minutes what I've spent the last century and a half acquiring, and I'm afraid I lost my wits. He was at the railing over there taking a picture of something with his phone when I opened the door. Scared the hell out of him; he dropped his phone over the railing and it shattered. He had time to get one spray off before it was over. I was lucky he missed my eyes or you two might have walked into a much different scene. I waited for the girl to come inside, but either she lost her nerve or she was only supposed to be a lookout."

Ryan approached the desk and placed the girl's phone next to the keyboard. "This will probably help," he said.

Natalia snatched it up and scrolled around for a few moments. "Yes, it will," she murmured, the faintest hint of a smile framing the edges of her singed lips for the first time. "It certainly will." She moved away from the monitors, picked up the container of blood, and headed out of the room. "Let's talk somewhere that's a little more comfortable," she said.

Ryan and Frank stepped over the girl's body and followed Natalia down a long hallway lit by stylish chrome sconces. As they walked, Frank gave her a rundown of everything that had happened to them after they'd left Ryan's apartment. She remained silent, her face taut and emotionless, betraying none of her thoughts. The three of them turned a corner and entered a high-ceilinged room featuring the same hardwood flooring as the downstairs foyer. Several plush leather chairs were arranged in a semicircle around a rustic oak coffee table and facing a large brick fireplace. An enormous, pencil-thin television had been hung above the mantel, its screen divided into the same live security feeds Natalia had been studying earlier. The other three walls were completely covered by shelves containing thousands of old books and manuscripts in various stages of disintegration, their spines cracked and moldy.

Natalia motioned for them to sit and began pouring blood from the container into champagne flutes that were resting on a tray at the center of the coffee table. She filled one, handed it to Frank, and started pouring a second glass until Ryan stopped her. "I'm fine," he said, "still full from yesterday."

"Fair enough," she said. "This one's for me, then." She finished pouring, then sat down in the chair between Ryan and Frank. "Let me know how this tastes to you," she said to Frank before they both took a sip.

Frank's eyes narrowed as he pursed his lips into a sour contortion, swirling the remaining blood in his flute around like a wine connoisseur. "A ridiculously tart O with notes of methamphetamine, OxyContin, and low-grade cannabis, with more than a hint of anemia and early-onset kidney failure." He wiped his mouth with his hand. "All jokes aside, Nat, this is truly disgusting. If I weren't so hungry I would have spit it out."

Natalia took a sip and made a similar face. "Like I said before," she said, "one can't always be picky. If you were paying attention you would have noticed that the girl smelled just as rancid, if not worse. I doubt I'll even bother draining her."

"So they're just a couple of junkies," Ryan said, thankful that he had abstained from the impromptu tasting.

"Well, they certainly aren't Navy SEALs," Natalia scoffed as she placed her flute on the table, got up, and walked over to one of the bookshelves. "Which raises several interesting questions."

"Like how the fuck were they able to get to Seamus," Ryan said. "Also, it kind of throws a wrench in your theory about this being a military-grade operation." He looked at Frank, who was trying to choke down the rest of the blood in his flute. "If we're being hunted, why not send in real hunters? Either this is the worst strategy ever, or you need to brush up on your Dutch."

"Not necessarily," Natalia said as she returned to her chair, holding a small stack of crumbling papers tied together with a leather string. "I've read the same chatter as Francis, deciphered the same messages. I don't think that most or any of it was meant for my two houseguests or whoever came after you two earlier. Look at it more like deep-sea fishing than hunting. The tracksuited cretins we've dealt with tonight are simply chum, near-worthless pieces of meat used to lure the prize, not catch it."

"You're saying that Manhattan offered them some kind of deal, a lifetime of free dime bags and needles to what, scare us before they send in the real cavalry?" Ryan asked.

"Wouldn't be the worst strategy," Frank said, shrugging. "We're here now, aren't we?"

Neither Ryan nor Natalia needed to say anything to acknowledge that he was right. The three of them sat in silence for several moments, Natalia scrolling through the dead girl's phone while Frank fiddled with his own.

"Hold on," Natalia said, scrunching her broad, snubbed nose in befuddlement. "Maybe *chum* wasn't exactly the correct word. Her last two dozen or so received texts were from the same unknown number. First, there's a list of addresses, mine and four others in Brooklyn that mean nothing to me. The rest of the messages are either questions or interrogatory phrases, demands for updates— 'Provide your current location,' 'Is the house occupied?'—boring stuff, mostly. But there's also questions about artifacts, the contents of my collection, if there's anything to suggest that Arthur Harker has been here recently or is nearby. His name appears several times, and gathering information about 'Harker's lineage' seems to be a main priority. And finally there's something about a jaguar—'Status of search re: jaguar?' 'Evidence for jaguar's recent presence or current whereabouts?' "

Ryan perked up at the mention of his maker, whom he'd always considered to be the tribe's version of a deadbeat dad, whose self-imposed exile he initially resented, until he decided that it was pointless to resent a ghost. After that, Harker had been surprisingly easy to forget.

One thing that couldn't be denied, though, was that Ryan was all that remained of Arthur's lineage, however much he tried to negate it.

"One of Harker's magic statues he never bothered to show us?" Frank blurted out with an incredulous sneer. "As impressively ballsy an idea as that is, it doesn't make it any less stupid. If they think they can use it to come over here and—"

He was cut off by the vibrating phone in his lap. He picked it up and stared at the screen. "I think this is one of the burners we left at the safe house," he said. "I need to answer this." He got up and walked out of the room.

Natalia followed him with her eyes for a few seconds, a glimmer of curiosity dissolving almost as soon as it appeared. "What do you know about Arthur Harker?" she asked, turning back to Ryan, the quiet scratch of silk friction emanating from her chair as she crossed her rotund, pajama-clad legs.

"He was old," Ryan said, "older than Frank. One of the original Dutch colonists in New Amsterdam. He was a royal cartographer or something else to do with maps. Other than that, I don't know, he seemed nice, but distant, maybe because he was already in the process of checking out for good. A couple of weeks later he was gone. Frank's always felt more like my maker than him or anyone else."

Natalia nodded. "Did he ever tell you why he turned you?"

"Arthur? He said that before he found me in the hospital he was planning on killing me. That he wanted to eradicate whatever disease I'd contracted before it seeped into his—your—food supply. Maybe he'd started going soft in his old age and took pity on me. Or he knew he'd be leaving the tribe and realized he hadn't put any thought into finding a replacement. Maybe it was a perfect kill-two-birds-with-one-stone kind of scenario. Lucky for both of us."

Ryan flashed back to the night in 1919—twisting and sweating on a hard cot, listening to the low moans of other patients separated only by faded linen sheets, trying to avoid breathing in too deeply the unmistakable odor of death that permeated the ward. A tall, gaunt man with thinning, cottony-gold hair in a white doctor's coat appeared over him in the gray predawn light, exuding a calmness that Ryan had never felt before as he pulled up a sleeve and gouged into his arm with a scalpel, letting the black drops fall over Ryan's face and naked torso, causing Ryan to cry out as it burned into his flesh and blinded him for what seemed like a long time.

When he could see again the man was propping him up, holding a clay cup covered with strange symbols and stick-figure animal drawings, pressing it to Ryan's lips, telling Ryan to open his mouth, to drink the thick, corrosive liquid that didn't taste like any kind of medicine. And then a greater, spinning darkness, a feeling of being pulled apart, a loss of identity, of life, of everything, a cocoon of emptiness pried open with an electric shock, Arthur's palm pressed against his scalding forehead, and then . . .

"The one thing you could be certain about with Arthur was that he was never soft, right until the end," Natalia said, chuckling at a private memory Ryan hoped she wouldn't be sharing with him. "That's why he did most of the culling whenever an infectious disease reared its head, something, thankfully, we rarely have to worry about anymore. No, it's more likely that he saw a quality in you," she continued, "something in how you'd managed to survive an illness that had destroyed everyone else who'd come in contact with it. An inner strength, perhaps something more profound than that.

Arthur had a precise, mathematical mind. Nothing he did was ever random or arbitrary, but he wasn't cold, either."

"Besides abandoning the only person he'd ever turned, I'll take your word for it," Ryan said, his voice tinted with the petulance of his youth.

"Still riding the self-pity train after all this time," she said with a sigh. "I thought we'd taught you better than that."

"Just calling it like I see it."

"It's not like you ever asked about what happened."

"I didn't think I needed to."

Natalia began untying the knot in the leather strap that held together the stack of papers in her lap. "That's a conversation for another day. Now," she said, "let's get back to Arthur, before he left. Yes, he was originally a mapmaker for the Dutch West India Company in the early seventeenth century. But more than anything, he was a curious soul, an anthropologist before that word existed.

"He was fascinated by the local tribes that had been living and trading in New Amsterdam, the Lenape and the Canarsee, and when he wasn't working in any official capacity, he spent most of his time with them, both here and in Manhattan, learning their languages, their social customs, and their spiritual practices, all of which he documented on these pages."

Ryan flipped through the pile of yellow, disintegrating parchment. Most of the papers were covered with the same dense, italic script; he assumed the language was Dutch. There were also numerous sketches—the faded outlines of coasts, islands, hillscapes, and other vague geological features that composed a mapmaker's rough drafts, as well as detailed watercolor drawings of loincloth-wearing Native American men, women, and children performing a variety of activities. Hunting, fishing, carrying wooden canoes to an unknown body of water, dancing around a giant bonfire at the center of a large dome-shaped hut, weaving baskets, whittling arrowheads and baseball-bat-like clubs, eating and drinking from large clay-colored bowls, braiding each other's hair. Intimate, carefully crafted moments that would have been forbidden to any outsider.

"Neat," Ryan said, the sarcasm on full blast as he handed the stack of papers back to Natalia. "I'm so proud to be descended from a humanitarian so far ahead of his time."

She sighed. "I'm not interested on your opinions about Arthur's character. Frankly, I don't care about what you think. I care about what you know, what you need to know, so that we can figure out an endgame to a situation that, if you haven't noticed already, affects the well-being of your entire tribe. Or you can continue being an ass and end up like Seamus. Your choice."

Ryan stared straight ahead, unblinking.

"Good," she said. "Now, when Manhattan Island was sold to the Dutch in 1626 by the band of Canarsees who lived there, the chief of the Brooklyn Lenapes saw the writing on the wall and guessed correctly that it was only a matter of time before the Europeans would either pay them in beads and seashells to evict them from their ancestral lands or simply annihilate them. Yes, the chief had a handful of dead warriors, but from his perspective it would have been foolish to start a war against an enemy who controlled gunpowder, a powerful magic against which even the Ànkëlëk-ila might not survive. Of course we know that's not true, but you can see why they wouldn't want to risk it."

"Why not just turn everyone?" Ryan asked. "Surely they must have realized that an army of Ànkëlëk-ila would be pretty much unstoppable, even against an enemy with guns."

"Well for one thing, we're sterile," Natalia replied. "This was a people that put respect for nature above all else. Those who were chosen to become dead warriors knew that their immortality was only temporary, that they would eventually return to their original condition and live out their days in an ordinary manner. An entire village that was incapable of perpetuating the natural cycle of life would be far more offensive to the spirits than simply leaving the ancestral homeland and starting over elsewhere. In any case, the chief decided to pack up and move his tribe westward, somewhere far from Long Island.

"Before he left, Arthur and the few of his colleagues who had gained the respect and trust of the Lenape approached the chief and his shaman and asked them if they might be able to carry on some of the tribal traditions, to preserve a way of life they smartly thought of as being superior to the inherent misery of colonialism. The chief took this to mean that they wanted to be turned, and for whatever reason, he agreed to it. Arthur's maker was the oldest dead warrior at that time, apparently famous throughout the region for his strength and brutality in battle. Arthur received not only his blood, the same blood that flows in you, but also the weapons and totems of his order that had been passed down to each succeeding generation of *Ànkëlëk-ila* since a time before memory, as he told it to me. Take a look at this."

She removed a sheet of paper from the pile and handed it to Ryan. It was a drawing of three Lenape men, one of them much taller than the other two, wearing a crown of white and gold feathers and a large metallic disk attached to a silver necklace that covered his chest. His shorter companions were broad-shouldered, muscular, with shaved heads and no visible jewelry besides the long knives that hung from their waists. Their entire bodies were painted cobalt blue. The same three symbols appeared in black ink above the head of each man: two jagged, parallel strokes that might have been lightning bolts, a fish, and an X within a circle. In their hands they held what looked like small figurines, made of stone or painted wood, in the shape of monkeys or maybe bats' heads attached to human bodies. Below the image were two lines of text, written in the same foreign script that appeared on the rest of the papers.

The drawing awoke in Ryan a twinge of memory: a granite crucifix under a starless sky, a wooden vessel in the earth, Arthur's muddy fingers. He thought he knew where he'd seen something like the statues before, but he couldn't tell Natalia, or anyone, until he was sure.

"What does the writing say?" he asked, handing the sheet back to her.

"It says, more or less, 'King Yellow Tree reuniting with his soldiers after a diplomatic journey to Raritan,' which could be any of the tribes living in Staten Island or northern New Jersey at the time."

"His soldiers are dead warriors?"

"Correct," Natalia said. "And they're using the statues. I don't know exactly how they work, and I haven't seen one in person in at least a century, but it seems likely that's what Manhattan is looking for. What I want to know from you is, did Arthur ever give you anything before he left, any, shall we say, family heirlooms? Or any location where he might have stored them? Did he talk about anything like this with you?"

The southwest corner of the graveyard . . . the box underneath the earth . . . you'll know when to use it . . .

"No," Ryan said, "to all of the above. I can remember maybe three or four conversations between us and none of them had anything to do with totems, weapons, King Yellow-whatever, none of that. I didn't even know we had anything to do with the Lenape until years later."

"Believe me, you're better off for it," Frank said as he walked back into the room and sat down. "Arthur used to go on and on about those fucking creepy child's dolls, that they were older than the tribe itself, that they were controlled by some kind of dark sorcery or some such nonsense. I can't believe you're asking him about this, Nat."

Ryan had rarely seen Frank get as worked up about something as he was now, breathing heavy, brow creased, scowling. But after the last few hours, maybe *rarely* was par for the course.

"What about us?" Ryan asked. "How do you explain what controls us?"

Frank snorted in mild amusement. "Us? It's simple science. What happens when we turn someone? We introduce our blood into their body. Our blood acts like a virus, changing the chemistry of our so-called offspring's blood until it matches our own. The same transformation occurs every time, no exceptions. And one of the rules of the virus is that it can't survive outside a specific geographical area. It's like certain animal species in the Himalayas that can't survive below a specific altitude. Whatever's flowing inside us has designed itself to exist within an extremely limited set of environmental conditions, which just so happens to roughly coincide with the boundaries of Brooklyn. But instead of destroying us when we travel outside those boundaries, the virus dies, returning us to our original state. That's how it is and how it will be, until there aren't any of us left. You can't change the rules of biology."

"What about, like, magnetic fields?" Ryan asked. "I read an article recently that—"

"It's irrelevant," Natalia said, cutting him off, "because you don't have the statues and you don't know where Arthur might have stored them, if he didn't take them with him when he decided to return to the land of the living."

She placed the stack of papers and the girl's phone on the coffee table next to her half-drunk flute of now-coagulated blood. "Who were you talking to, Francis?" she asked.

"Fiona," he replied. "She and Asher are at the safe house. They got there a couple hours ago, apparently with no problems, no signs of anyone trailing them. They're waiting for us."

"I'm surprised they responded at all," Natalia said, with a slight air of disdain. "It's been decades since they bothered reaching out to me."

Fiona and Asher were the youngest members of the tribe, both in physical appearance and in actual age. They had both been students—she at Brooklyn College, he at St. Francis—when they were turned less than a year apart in the late 1940s, when the rest of the tribe had begun to separate, to explore and enjoy the fruits of a postwar era on a mostly singular basis. But a lack of camaraderie had never been a problem for them because they'd always had each other, always had been inseparable. Their penchant for doing their own thing made Ryan look like the tribe's mayor.

Frank used to say that it was a good thing that the two of them couldn't reproduce, otherwise they'd probably have had enough children by now to put a serious dent in the food supply. It was funny because it was true, but suddenly the idea of being able to fully share a life with someone else caused Ryan to experience an old pang, not quite jealousy, but a longing for something similar that he'd experienced long ago with Vanessa and now with Jennifer, a longing he knew would probably be impossible to extinguish a second time.

"I think it's clear that we need to stay together," Frank said as he stood up and put his phone in his pocket. "We'll head to the safe house, figure everything out from there. Do you still have a car, Nat?"

"Audi A3," she said, with a slightly mischievous grin. "Leased it last week. Not everything in this house is a relic. Give me a moment to change into some real clothes and find my keys and I'll meet you boys downstairs."

Ryan followed Frank out of the study, through the hallway, and down the main staircase. They zigzagged toward the front door, careful to avoid most of the foyer's wreckage.

"Frank, wait," Ryan said. "I can't go with you guys now."

Frank stared at him, eyebrows arched, looking like he'd heard the beginning of a joke and was waiting for a punch line.

"I need to talk to Jennifer. We're supposed to meet for brunch in a few hours. I'll go to the safe house directly afterward. But this is something I need to do."

"Mm-hm. Jennifer. Is that your fuck buddy?"

Frank's sarcastic smirk made Ryan suddenly want to impale him against the glass shards that littered the floor, to drive his brain through his spinal column as his shoulders smashed together and caved in. "It's more than that," Ryan said, trying to control the rage that had begun to flow as fast as when he'd been shot.

"I've heard that before."

"You're not going to stop me."

Frank held up his hands defensively, palms facing Ryan. The smirk vanished. "Easy, pal," he said. "I'm not going to do anything. Nat might try if she heard you. But it's only because she feels the same way I do. We've never had to deal with a real threat like this before, it's new territory for all of us. We need to stay together in order to protect each other, that's all."

"I understand that," Ryan said, "and I appreciate everything you've done for me tonight, coming to check on me at my place, dragging me into the car after I blacked out, bringing me here. I'd be fucked without you. But I won't feel right with myself unless I try to explain to her who I am, what I am, as honestly as I can. Especially if it's my last chance."

"It won't be," Frank said quietly, as he pulled out his pistol from under his shirt and handed it to Ryan. "The clip's full."

"Thanks," Ryan said. "I'll be at the safe house no later than four o'clock. If I'm not there by then . . ."

Frank shook his head, not letting Ryan finish, trying to ward off the possibility of further complications. "Get out of here," he said, "before Natalia comes down here and tries to change your mind. You know how persuasive she can be."

Ryan tucked the pistol against the small of his back, then fist-bumped his former mentor.

"Thanks," he repeated before opening the front door and bolting into the predawn mist.

8

He paused in front of the intricately carved, chapel-like double arches of Green-Wood Cemetery's main gate, listening and smelling the air for any signs of human activity. The sun was just beginning to rise over Battle Hill, Brooklyn's highest natural point, the thin beams of light cascading over trees and endless rows of tombstones, marking the direct path Ryan planned on taking once he scaled the gate's brownstone walls and landed on the other side.

As he started walking in the direction of the gathering brightness, the windows of the gatehouse were suddenly illuminated by interior artificial lights, meaning that at least some of the caretakers and grounds crew had already arrived for work, that it was later in the morning than he'd thought.

To get what he'd come for and remain unnoticed, Ryan would have to take a more roundabout route.

The oldest and largest private cemetery in New York City's five boroughs, located a few blocks southwest of Prospect Park, Green-Wood spanned nearly five hundred acres of valleys, hills, ponds, and paved paths, a rural oasis that was home to more than half a million permanent, decomposing residents, surrounded by a postindustrial wasteland of automotive shops, government-owned warehouses, crumbling commercial buildings, and the odd public housing behemoth. In an hour or two, the fenced-in grounds would be overrun with tourists looking to visit and later post pictures of the mausoleums of robber barons, Civil War generals, and baseball legends; marble sculpture gardens; monuments honoring the heroes of the

Revolutionary War and every war since; and granite tombstones featuring names like Tiffany, Roosevelt, and Ebbets.

For Ryan, Green-Wood was a repulsive place, filled with the sour reek of several generations of bodily decay, a stench that made it hard for him to breathe as he changed course and began walking southward on 5th Avenue, parallel with the eight-foot-tall cast-iron fence that separated the cemetery's manicured permanence from the borough's more familiar milieu of charred asphalt and car exhaust.

Ryan had, for many years (and especially after killing his food became unnecessary), put up his own mental fence around the idea of death, kept it at a respectable distance, a distance that until the previous evening had been easy to maintain. Yes, he could smell cancer and every other chronic and fatal condition afflicting the people he passed on the street and sat near in the subway, but for Ryan that information had been mostly impersonal and emotionless, the equivalent of seeing a rotten piece of fruit at the supermarket and knowing not to choose it. You let it sit there until someone else threw it away, without having to participate in the moment of its demise.

Now that there were forces at work that were actively trying to exterminate his tribe—and apparently possessed the ability and manpower to carry out that desire—the possibility of death had reentered the forefront of Ryan's life for the first time since he'd been turned. He thought about Jennifer and his emotional response to Frank's dismissal of her as nothing more than a casual hookup.

Maybe Frank was right. Maybe they shouldn't have shared anything more than a couple of hazy (from her perspective) fucks. Besides a handful of donors, the overwhelming majority of the humans who had come in contact with him over the years had had one thing in common: a quick and violent extermination.

The lives he had cut short now made their way into the forefront of his brain, not just as a brief and abstract feeling of guilt shelved away in a dark corner, the way they normally did. The taste of their blood and their fear lingered, fresh as ever in his mind. The polio-stunted seamstress in her tiny shop near Borough Hall begging him to just have his way with her and leave, begging even after he removed her vocal cords. The young Lithuanian priest on his knees, praying to a god that wouldn't save him. The insane cop laughing hysterically until he drowned in his own fluids. The dozens of clean kills, the ones who didn't see it coming, whose families or neighbors were left to bear all of the suffering.

It didn't help that of the fenced-in rows of buried bodies to his left, as he followed the cemetery's perimeter southward on 5th Avenue, there were probably dozens he'd either directly or indirectly had a hand in putting there.

A few minutes later, he turned onto 36th Street at Green-Wood's southwest corner, a section of the cemetery that faced the beige-and-brick, government-bland façade of an enormous MTA bus depot across the street. Ryan continued a little longer and stopped where a rectangular boulder sat a few feet from the fence, its top smooth and tablelike except for a large indentation near its center. A plaque attached to a stake that had been hammered into the ground nearby read, partially:

> Legend has it that, near this spot during our Colonial period, an African American named Joost dueled the Devil in a fiddling contest. When Joost triumphed, the Devil, in defeat, stomped his foot on a rock, leaving the impression of a hoof print. By the time of the American Revolution, the rock with the Devil's Hoof Print had become a local tourist attraction.

Arthur had shown Ryan the rock the last time they'd visited Green-Wood, saying something about how history had gotten the legend wrong, that Joost was actually Frank, exiting the woods covered in blood and carrying the violin that had belonged to a meal he'd just disposed of, when he ran into a hunting party. Though they seemed to believe the story Frank told them about a contest with Satan, in reality, and especially in the eyes of the traveling musician he'd eaten, Frank had far more in common with a demon than a fiddler.

Ryan took a quick look around to make sure the street was clear and leapt over the fence, landing softly on the grass on the other side. Not wasting any more time considering the Devil or his fake footprint, he headed for the nearest paved section of the cemetery, a winding thoroughfare that was called Oak Avenue, according to a street sign that had been nailed to a large maple tree. Ryan followed the path up a hill dotted with small white-stone military grave markers, each accompanied by a wreath of plastic flowers and a miniature American flag. On the downward slope he passed a collection of obelisks and small crypts surrounding a man-made pond, their peaks and roofs moss-covered and rain-eroded.

Before the next increase in elevation, he veered off the path and navigated a densely wooded area, the rows of stones getting older the farther he walked, their inscriptions becoming less clear. He stopped beside a cluster of crucifix-topped monuments that were permanently shaded by the branches of a horse chestnut tree, a behemoth that had wizened and gnarled considerably in the ninety-four years since he'd last stood under its limbs. The stone closest to his feet was the smallest of the group, its inscription devoid of everything but the most cursory details: LAURA JANE HARKER 1807–1852.

Ryan couldn't recall the precise wording of most of the conversation he'd had with Arthur at this exact spot, the night before his maker returned to the species he'd forsaken three hundred years earlier. The only part of the exchange he remembered word-for-word occurred after he asked if Arthur was related to the woman buried under the stone. After several moments of uproarious laughter, Arthur explained that *Harker* had been chosen in jest because it was the surname of a character in a recently published novel called *Dracula*. He might have laughed more at the idea of two seemingly supernatural beings lurking around a cemetery late at night, but this was still a few years before Hollywood and its tropes had completely invaded the cultural consciousness.

In any case, it was the first time Arthur had shared anything more than the faintest hint of emotion with Ryan, and it would be the last.

Once he regained his composure, Arthur's tone turned serious. He pointed to a spot on the ground, near where Laura Jane's coffin would have been placed. "In this location," he'd said, "I've returned all that's left of our family line back to the earth. Buried near a Harker, so that you will remember this place and perhaps remember me. What lies here, you will know when to use it. Before then, let it rest."

At the time, Ryan had had no clue what Arthur was talking about, and even if he'd been curious enough to find out, the hunger pains that consumed him during his first months of being turned took precedence over everything else, made all other desires irrelevant. After he'd settled into his new life, the night at the cemetery had receded into a deep corner of his memory, like so much that had happened to him before and after.

Now he had an idea of what the old man might have left for him.

He began to rip through the earth with his hands, piling the warm, dew-soaked soil against the tombstone. About two feet down, his nails scraped metal, in the exact spot that Arthur had shown him nearly a century earlier. He lifted the shoebox-size container out of the ground. It was rectangular and made of dent-scarred tin, its lid held on by a heavily rusted padlock. He could hear the faint rattling of several hard objects inside. He pulled off the lock and opened the lid, its hinges creaking with disuse. Whatever had made the noise was covered by a few sheets of moldy, crumbling paper filled with Arthur's unmistakable handwriting. Ryan pushed these aside to reveal a small flint dagger with a long, deer-antler handle, on which had been carved symbols resembling those that had appeared on the drawing of the dead warriors Natalia had shown him, and a figurine encased in a glass jar.

It was five or six inches long, a hollow ceramic sculpture in the shape of a body cut off at the waist, humanoid from its base to its neck, its arms crossed over its chest. The head was different. Two gaping slits for eye holes, a pushed-in bat's nose, tiny feline ears, and large, bared fangs. A dime-sized hole had been drilled into the back of the neck. The faded paint that covered the creature looked like it had originally been a dark shade of orange peppered with black and gray spots.

Arthur's jaguar.

Ryan removed it from the jar and placed it into the black plastic deli bag he'd picked up on his way to the cemetery from Natalia's. He was about to rebury the container when he felt an impulse, something instinctual he couldn't explain. He picked up the knife and gouged deeply into the vein that bisected his wrist. He held the jar's opening under his arm, guiding a thin stream of blood into it before the wound healed.

He capped the jar, placed it in the container, and closed the lid. Just as he finished covering the hole, he heard the well-rehearsed drone of a tour guide in the distance, getting closer. By the time the group turned onto Oak Avenue, phone cameras ablaze, Ryan was on the other side of the fence, heading north.

9

"Hey, buddy! HEY!"

Ryan ignored the voice as he made his way through the Saturday afternoon throngs of tank tops and genital-hugging legwear swarming the sidewalks of Front Street, until he felt something tap against his shoulder. He swiveled around, grabbed the offender's wrist, and forced the man to the ground.

The appendage he was about to crush belonged to a skinny waif in his early twenties, wearing black leather pants and a white T-shirt that said I'M ALLERGIC TO BASIC BITCHES across the front, gazing up at Ryan with a combination of terror and indignation.

"What do you want?" Ryan asked, relaxing his grip.

"I was just trying to let you know that the price tag was hanging off the back of your shirt," the kid muttered as he tore his arm free and picked up a clear plastic cup containing what looked like a thick green sludge. "Fucking dick."

Ryan apologized and plucked the tag off the gray short-sleeve button-down shirt he'd bought on the way to meet Jennifer. He felt around his waist to see if a label or sticker might be hanging from his new jeans, but he couldn't feel anything.

He dropped the tag in the Urban Outfitters bag where it settled alongside his blood-and-dirt-smeared clothes from the previous night, the phone charger he'd just purchased at a Verizon store on Court Street, the antler-handle knife, and the jaguar statue that was still glowing.

He'd noticed the change almost as soon as he'd rehopped the fence and left the cemetery. The statue had begun to vibrate slightly and to feel warm, not hot enough to melt the plastic bag that had contained it, but still more than noticeable, as if removing it from the earth had jump-started some kind of internal mechanism. And its color scheme had morphed from orange and black to an eerie, iridescent green, giving off its own light like a radioactive object. It seemed like the real deal. Frank and Natalia would probably flip out when they saw it, he thought, but they would have to wait.

He crossed the street and passed under the Manhattan Bridge Overpass, the landmark that gave the neighborhood its acronymic name. The area that was now called DUMBO—which Ryan remembered as a seedy ferry stop and an anonymous manufacturing shithole that wasn't worth his or anyone's time—had attracted almost the same progression of pioneers as nearby Williamsburg: artists, hipsters, foodies, and condo developers, with a healthy dose of the tech industry for good measure. The company that Jennifer worked for did a fair amount of business in the neighborhood, meaning that Ryan had been dragged to nearly every restaurant, gastropub, and wine bar in the vicinity. Superfine, just east of the bridge, was one of her favorites, a low-key, locals-heavy spot that occupied the bottom floor of a recycled industrial building, as good a place as any to pretend to enjoy a Bloody Mary before totally blowing away Jennifer's conception of reality.

He hadn't given much thought to how exactly he was going to tell her. It would be easy enough to prove what he was. He could stab himself with the knife the server would provide with her huevos rancheros and show her not only how quickly he could heal but how little blood flowed through his veins. He could show her the draft registration card from the First World War that he kept in his wallet—rejected because of his coal-blackened lungs—and its accompanying photograph. Or he could pull out the statue if it didn't seem like she would make too much of a scene.

Whatever was going to happen would happen, he told himself, regardless of how much he considered all of the possibilities. The time for figuring out a game plan was long gone. He was running several minutes late and was sure that if his phone hadn't died he'd be receiving more than a few *where the fuck are you* texts and calls. He hoped she hadn't already left.

He entered the rectangular, high-ceilinged former factory space that was reverberating with the upbeat twang of a bluegrass band playing somewhere in the back and was stopped by a petite, bubbly hostess he didn't recognize. He told her his name. "I have a reservation for two o'clock, but my friend is probably already here," he said.

"Uh . . . yup!" she beamed after consulting a list tacked to the host stand. "She's been here for a few minutes. Follow me."

Shit, Ryan thought, *something else to apologize for.* But at least she hadn't walked out yet. He followed the hostess past a long cherry-wood bar buzzing with patrons and diners waiting for a table, an unoccupied orange-felt pool table, and up a small set of stairs to the raised dining area in the rear.

"Right over there." The hostess motioned at a table in the back left corner of the space where Nicki was sitting alone, wearing a black spaghetti-string top and chunky, fire-engine-red hoop earrings, scrolling around on her phone. Ryan's apartment keys were lying in a ball on the table in front of her menu. She looked up, ran her hand through her side-swept bangs, and smiled.

For a moment he stood still, mouth agape, paralyzed by her presence—and her scent. It took a miracle of composure for him to move slowly toward the table, to act as if everything were normal.

"Aren't you a little old for Urban Outfitters?" she asked as he sat down and tucked the shopping bag between his legs. "I mean, it's not necessarily a bad thing. Those jeans fit great on you. And your skin looks way better than the last time I saw you. Must be that delicious and nutritious dinner you ate yesterday. You're welcome."

"What the fuck is this?" Ryan snarled. He quickly scanned the room, overcome by a surge of paranoia, preparing for an imminent, unseen assault.

"Apparently you aren't very good at checking your phone," she replied calmly. "And you definitely suck at holding on to important personal items. *Keys, wallet, phone*, it's the Holy Trinity, dude, come on." She slid his keys across the table. "I liked your place, a little bland, a little small—and in the wrong neighborhood—for someone in your tax bracket, but I'll give you some cool points for the discretion factor."

"My phone's dead," Ryan said.

"Ooh," Nicki chortled. "That makes total sense. No worries though, I can just show you on mine."

She looked back down at her phone and started clicking the screen until a youngish waiter sporting a man bun arrived to take their drink orders. "Give us a couple minutes here, hon," she said, hardly glancing at him.

Ryan's unblinking eyes remained focused on her neck, the barely perceptible twitching vein that was the only thing keeping her brain from suffocating. *Where was Jennifer?*

Nicki handed him her phone. On the screen was a photograph of a jaguar statue, identical to the one in Ryan's bag, except this one was in its original, nonglowing state.

"Look familiar?" she asked.

Ryan shook his head.

She sighed. "Okay, I really hoped it would, because the next part, no matter how I say it, is going to come out all lame and villain-y, but trust me, it's just business. Like most of your browsing history when you're not Facebook stalking. Bo-ring. I don't have like, an agenda or something. My employers do. You probably have a vague idea about the people I work for—do you guys call yourselves *people*? Never mind, I don't even care. My employers are super stoked about adding the statue that you claim to not recognize to their collection and are basically prepared to get real gnarly in their, um, quest for it."

Their collection? How many statues were there?

"I'm not really sure who you think I am or what I am," Ryan said. "You've been through my apartment. You've gone through my records. You've probably been to my storage units. You know I don't have whatever is in this picture. If you're done here, I'm going to go—"

"Charge your phone and call your girlfriend?"

Ryan watched her throat muscles tense as she swallowed too hard, even though she was still smiling, beads of sweat forming at her temples.

"Um, yeah," she said while clicking her tongue, her voice rising half an octave. "This is where you're going to hate me. Swipe to the next picture and keep swiping. There's a few of them."

The first picture was of what looked like the ground floor of an office building, a mostly glass and sand-colored façade and a chrome revolving door. Something about it seemed familiar to Ryan, but he couldn't figure out what it was. The next picture showed Jennifer exiting the same door, her hair in a ponytail, wearing a beige jacket that she'd left at Ryan's apartment on several occasions, a black skirt, and heels. The building, he now remembered, was 881 3rd Avenue, where the company where Jennifer worked, FreshInsights, occupied a portion of the fourteenth floor. He swiped to a shot of her getting into a taxi at 53rd Street, then another in the cab's backseat from the driver's point of view.

This is where you're going to hate me . . .

The next shot was from the same angle except Jennifer was lying in a fetal position across the backseat, facing the camera, her head covered by what looked like a black garbage bag, her wrists bound in front of her chest, her hands clasped as if in prayer. The two final images were variations of the same photograph. In the first one, Jennifer was seated, staring at the camera in what looked like a poorly lit concrete bunker, positioned in front of a naked and masked creature suspended from a metal pipe, its skin slick and waxy, like shrink wrap slowly peeling from slabs of rotting beef jerky.

Seamus.

The montage concluded with a close-up of her face, her forehead and cheeks covered with constellations of welts, her pupils dilated and empty, a translucent stream of snot running from her nostrils, cresting and spilling over her burgundy-smeared lips.

"It's basically, like, your standard, old-school, one-for-one trade," Nicki said a few moments later as she snatched up the phone he'd dropped on the table. Ryan was visibly trembling, avoiding eye contact for the first time since he'd sat down. "But I don't need to explain that to you," she continued. "You're old-school by nature, right? You get it. Shit, I'm sorry, that was super cheesy. Oh well, I tried."

She lifted a small purse from her lap and started rummaging

through it. She pulled out a crisp hundred-dollar bill and placed it on top of Ryan's unopened menu. A phone number with a Manhattan area code was scrawled across the front in permanent marker ink. Ryan recognized the serial number; it was one of the unmarked bills he had used to pay for Nicki's blood.

"My employers think that twenty-four hours is a reasonable amount of time for your memory to improve regarding the jaguar. We'll meet tomorrow, same time, at the Starbucks where you took advantage of me in the bathroom yesterday," she said as she stood up to leave, fluttering her eyelids mischievously, her facial perspiration the only remainder of a temporary lapse of confidence. "Remember, Jennifer for the statue. I mean, it won't be like a handoff, but we'll let you see her being released in real time. On an iPad. If you need to reach me for any reason, call the number that's written on the hundo. Oh, and have a Bloody Mary or three on me."

She walked past him in the direction of the front entrance, intentionally close, her left breast grazing the side of Ryan's face. He flinched, slightly, but kept staring straight ahead.

A minute later the waiter reappeared. "Dude," he said in the commiserating tone of a fellow bro, "breaking up sucks, am I right? Same thing happened to me last week, but at least she didn't drag me out to brunch to do it. Can I get you anything? A shot or something on the house?"

"I'm fine," Ryan mumbled. He handed him the bill Nicki had left.

The waiter ran it through his fingers, wide-eyed. "Whoa," he said, "I can't accept this. At least let me get you a—"

Before he could finish, Ryan flipped over the table that had been bolted to the floor, picked up the Urban Outfitters bag, and exited the building, oblivious to the other patrons' glares.

10

". . . NYPD spokesman says in a newly released statement that the police are pursuing all possible leads in connection with a grisly, possibly gang-related shooting that occurred early this morning on Nostrand Avenue in Crown Heights, leaving three dead. Two of the victims, Arianna Velasquez, twenty-six, and Rajakumaran Rupasinghe, thirty-seven, were both Brooklyn residents. A third victim was unable to be immediately identified due to the severity of his injuries and the absence of any identifying documents. Witnesses reported seeing two suspects, a white male of average build and height and a shorter black male, exiting the crime scene in a black BMW sedan shortly before officers arrived. DNA evidence has been collected and is currently undergoing analysis . . ."

"Can you turn the radio down?" Ryan asked the cabdriver as they turned onto Court Street and continued southward through Cobble Hill.

"Sure, boss, no problem," the driver said absentmindedly, ignoring his request, returning to the muted conversation—in what sounded like a patois of French and an indistinguishable African dialect—that he'd been having with his earpiece.

Though he was seated, Ryan felt like he was spinning blindly through a vast shadow world, a twisted fun-house distortion of the one he'd known. Any thoughts that managed to materialize in the fog were misshapen abortions of logic, ill-fitting puzzle pieces amounting to nothing.

The only thing he could be certain of, as he clutched the Urban

Outfitters bag to his chest, was that he couldn't hand over the statue to Nicki. Her guarantees about Jennifer's release were more than likely as hollow as the hole where his stomach used to be.

He needed to get to the safe house before he did something he would regret almost as much as digging up the jaguar.

As much as allowing Jennifer into his life.

". . . in another developing story, a ceramic Mayan artifact was stolen yesterday afternoon from the Brooklyn Museum. The effigy vessel, part of the museum's Arts of the Americas collection, depicts the head and torso of a human figure wearing a jaguar-skin costume. Security footage released by the NYPD shows a male suspect wearing a dark suit approaching the vessel's display case and using a small, laser-powered tool to cut through the glass. The suspect is described as being between five feet ten inches and six feet tall, of indeterminate race, and having a shaved head. If you have any information, please contact . . ."

A sudden wave of clarity washed over Ryan, almost jarring him out of his seat.

The man in the midnight-blue suit outside the Brooklyn Museum, handing off a package to Raj and Arianna in the food truck. Frank had said he was a scientist, delivering a chemical shipment, but Ryan had felt a force that had compelled him to stop, a magnetic energy that reminded him of the vibrations that were currently emanating from the bag on his lap. And it was Frank who had told him about Craigslist, had put him on the path to meeting Nicki.

Another distortion. Another set of mirrors nailed to the fun house wall.

Ryan leaned forward until his head was almost through the hole in the glass partition that separated the front and back seats. "Let me out," he said loudly.

"Huh?" The driver turned down the radio's volume.

"Pull over."

"But my friend, this is not Red Hook."

"I know."

Ryan paid the fare and emerged from the taxi onto a street that no longer looked like anywhere he'd ever been, utterly alone.

11

The buildings of Lower Manhattan—a jagged hodgepodge of residential and commercial structures showcasing more than a century's worth of architectural styles and upgrades, everything dwarfed by the Freedom Tower's glass-skinned middle finger to anyone foolish enough to challenge America's will a second time—shimmered in the brilliant, cloudless afternoon.

From the Bedford Avenue rooftop where he'd been waiting for the past two hours, Ryan tried to trace the evolution of the glistening skyline's metal teeth but found it to be an almost impossible exercise. Though the island had always been an inescapable presence, lurking less than a mile away across a narrow, polluted, and easily traversed river, it had remained as foreign to him as Pittsburgh or Europe. His visits to the city as a boy and a young man had been brief and mostly unremarkable, tainted by the claustrophobic stench of fermenting sweat and manure, the wearying slum life that seemed to be little more than a jacked-up version of his own upbringing.

Another murky portion of his memory, like so many others, that he'd decided wasn't worth keeping.

Since he'd been turned, and until he'd met Jennifer, his knowledge of his smaller, more famous neighbor had been gathered by watching movies and television clips, skimming newspaper—and later, Internet—headlines, and listening to people bitching and moaning about this politician or that cable provider, conversations that could have easily been between two Brooklynites if the proper nouns had been changed. Manhattan was inaccessible to him but far from exotic, only vaguely entertaining when viewed through the lens of a fictional zombie apocalypse or a gold-digging housewife's plot for revenge.

He'd only recently begun researching Manhattan's current state of affairs because he hadn't wanted Jennifer to think he was a totally uncultured recluse. But what he did know—where to find the best falafel in the East Village, which neighborhoods had the highest yuppie-to-hipster ratio, the economics of surviving as a Midtown psychic—was trivial, abstract, and opinion-based. Nothing close to resembling a genuine experience, and therefore totally unhelpful in quieting his unease about the trip he'd be making.

The nervous paranoia that had been vibrating nonstop since the previous evening when he'd tucked Arthur's statue into a crevice in the truss that supported the Brooklyn side of the Williamsburg Bridge gave the day's perfect weather a sinister tint, another trap he'd be letting himself walk into.

Ryan checked the time on his watch, lowered his gaze, and rested his palms on the rooftop's ledge. Nicki was thirty-two minutes late and counting. He looked down at the intersection of Bedford and North 7th, focusing on the foot traffic going in and out of the Starbucks across the street, his view of the shop's interior obscured by the rays of sun reflecting off the all-glass façade.

"Where the fuck is she?" he mumbled to himself, suppressing the urge to check his phone again.

Instead he reviewed, for the fourth time, a mental checklist of what he'd packed in the Patagonia hiking bag that was strapped to his back, making sure he hadn't forgotten anything. The pistol Frank had given him and six clips of ammo, the deer-antler knife from the cemetery, the spray bottle that had fallen out of the dead girl's pocket at Natalia's, an IV needle attached to a small collection pouch, a notebook containing several addresses that he'd also saved in his phone, his phone charger . . .

. . . and then he smelled her.

Coming up the subway stairs on the far side of the intersection and moving quickly in his direction. He saw her when she was about fifty yards from Starbucks, wearing Wayfarer sunglasses, a burgundy leather jacket, and a white and black party dress, carrying a small handbag and power-walking in a straight line on the sparsely populated sidewalk. Like she knew she was late. She tossed a half-finished cigarette onto the street and opened the coffee shop's door in one rushed motion, without slowing down or checking her surroundings before going inside.

Ryan watched the street for the next few minutes, looking for any signs that she might not be alone, looking for anyone wearing black, anyone randomly posted up and acting weird or nervous. But even with better-than-perfect vision and ears that could pick up every heartbeat in a quarter-mile radius, it was difficult to be one hundred percent certain about anything from four stories up. He put on sunglasses, adjusted his throwback Brooklyn Dodgers baseball cap, and headed for the roof's fire exit. Inside the building, he bypassed the stairs, hopping over the handrail and landing silently on the lobby's tiles, a few feet from where a woman was checking her mailbox, a leashed French bulldog by her side.

The dog tilted its head at Ryan in disbelief, then began yelping. The woman looked up, gasped, and dropped the letters she'd been holding. "Geez, you're quiet," she said sheepishly, as he squatted to pick up her mail.

"Not quiet enough, apparently," he said, reaching out to pet the dog, who immediately backed away until its nonwagging stub of a tail bumped against its owner's legs. It let out a low growl, baring its teeth at him.

"Careful," the woman said, "she doesn't like to feel like she's being forced into a corner."

"No one does," Ryan said, forcing a smile as he handed her the letters and walked out of the building.

Part of him wanted there to be an entire squad of assholes waiting for him on the street, one last opportunity for him to fight with the confidence of knowing they couldn't hurt him, that he might be slowed, but never brought down. Instead, North 7th Street was tranquil, its scarce pedestrians moving slowly and quietly in the midafternoon heat. The only abnormally fast heartbeat that Ryan could detect came from an old man passing by in spandex shorts, jogging on the sidewalk while carrying a five-pound dumbbell in each hand.

The calm before *something*, Ryan thought, but what?

He started walking in the direction of the subway station so that he wouldn't be directly across from the Starbucks and stopped in front of a building that was currently occupied by a massage therapy practice. He sat on a bench outside the office and took out his phone. Another four missed calls, all from an unknown number that had been steadily inundating his call history since he'd connected the charger.

The first image that came up, after he unlocked the screen, was one of the photos of Jennifer that he'd been sent. He scrolled through those, the original picture of Seamus, the red *M*, looking for something that might tie them together, any kind of clue as to their location, any identifying details of the kidnappers, anything at all, but the only thing he could be sure of was his increasingly uncontrollable desire to rip the condescending smirk from Nicki's face, to make her understand what it was like to truly suffer.

Fifteen minutes later, as she emerged from the Starbucks looking as tense as she had when she'd entered, he would have that opportunity. But he needed her alive, at least for a little while longer.

He tried to relax as she passed him on the other side of the street, unclenching the muscles that were poised to launch. He turned off his phone and stuffed it in his pocket. He took a deep breath, caught the unmistakable B-negative aroma, and held it, felt his trembling rage diffuse and change into pure, unbreakable focus. When she was a block away and out of sight in the sidewalk traffic, he got up, crossed the street, and followed her scent. When it suddenly weakened and disappeared, he knew she'd gone underground, en route to Manhattan.

As he approached the subway station's entrance, he paused for a second, expecting to be overcome by some kind of life-flashing-before-your-eyes mental slide show followed by a powerful moment of clarity, something that would either confirm that his sacrifice was the right course of action or cause him to reevaluate everything that had happened in the previous forty-eight hours, and by default, the last six months. But in that second, nothing changed. There was no doubt or anxiety, no increased fear at the prospect of sudden mortality, and likewise, no sense of encouraging, righteous certainty.

There was only Jennifer's dead, hopeless expression, the same one that had plastered itself onto the forefront of his brain since he'd opened the picture on his phone. And the same primal anger that had been surging through him since he'd been shot, coupled with the need to make things right, regardless of what happened to him.

Feeling the underground shudder from an approaching west-bound train, Ryan glanced up at the familiar buildings lining both sides of the street, took one last breath of the only air he'd ever really known, and jogged down the stairs.

12

He listened to the Metropolitan Transit Authority's automated announcement system—*This is a Manhattan-bound L train. The next stop is First Avenue. Stand clear of the closing doors please.*—that was followed by a chime and the pneumatic hiss of the train's doors. From where he was standing, clutching one of the three metal poles that bisected the aisle, Ryan had a mostly unobstructed view of the windows and doors that separated his car from the one ahead of him, where Nicki had taken a seat only a few feet away, already frantically scanning the pixilated confines of her phone, oblivious to her surroundings like most of the other passengers.

The doors closed and there was no going back. Ryan turned to face the side windows and took a last glance at the subway platform where he'd stood for the second time in nearly forty years. Besides the usual twenty-first-century accoutrements—advertisements for the latest superhero movies, small-batch whiskey, and designer grooming products, digital message boards and LED screens flashing train schedules and the time of day—the gloomy subterranean space looked almost the same as it had on the July morning in 1975 when he'd tried—and failed—to make Vanessa Hawkins stay with him in Brooklyn.

She had just finished her senior year at St. Francis when they'd met, when he was living in Brooklyn Heights and calling himself Charles Vincent and she was putting her creative writing degree to use by "waiting for the inspiration" to finish a collection of poems and crashing on a succession of increasingly seedy beds and couches.

The last of those temporary landlords was a pudgy, anemic record store owner named Enzo who lived across the hall from Ryan and whose natural stench was almost as bad as his collection of pineapple-shaped ice buckets that functioned as weed and Quaalude receptacles.

Whenever Ryan left his apartment, Vanessa always seemed to be there in the same faded white T-shirt and skintight jeans, reading a stolen library copy of Rimbaud or Ginsberg, smoking cigarettes with friends from the neighborhood, or screaming at Enzo to quit sniffing her laundry. She'd stop whatever she was doing, ask how his day was going, flirt with him to an extent that was excessive even for the tail end of the free-love era; Ryan rarely escaped without having his ass gently groped or hearing playfully vulgar commentary on that part of his anatomy's cuteness.

At first he found her advances childish and annoying, but he soon found himself looking forward to them. He couldn't exactly say why. Outwardly she was just like any other tri-state postadolescent who had listened to Patti Smith's first album and who had forsaken a God-fearing suburban upbringing—and her bras—for the no-consequence chaos of pre-HIV New York. Her poems all rhymed and had titles like "One Small Step for a Woman" and "Barbie Fucker."

But her persistence spoke to an outer confidence that was as appealing as it was refreshing, especially in someone so young. And once you scraped off the layer of affected grunge, she was as impressive physically as anyone Ryan had ever met. She was tall, a mane of wind-combed blond frizz, willow-slender with hips that whispered mischief and a dancer's soundless strut. Her laugh was as deep as the hazel eyes that, if he was being honest with himself now, bore a strong resemblance to Jennifer's. The first time they kissed, he remembered thinking that her lips were the softest he'd ever felt, nothing like the opium-chapped ones he'd tasted in Red Hook brothels as a young man.

And, though her strength and physical advantages were obvious turn-ons, Ryan was equally drawn to her vulnerabilities, the innocence that belied her tough exterior. One night she burst into his apartment, her thick mascara smudged and running, saying she'd caught Enzo dropping powder from a measuring cup into the glass of wine she'd left on the kitchen counter. She suspected he'd been doing it for months. The tears streaming onto Ryan's shirt and the surprisingly small fingers digging into his back awoke whatever protective instinct existed in the blood that had been passed down to him.

He told Vanessa she was safe with him, walked across the hallway, and removed her possessions from his neighbor's apartment— Enzo had left for the airport a few minutes earlier, on his way to San Diego to spend some time with a cousin, something about expanding his three-store empire into a bicoastal operation.

Ryan and Vanessa spent the next month in a shared peace that Ryan had never imagined would be possible. Her Lucky Strike butts and half-assed notepaper stanzas littered the nightstand next to the bed they hardly ever left. She seemed to need to eat less than he did. For the first time since he'd been turned, he could embrace someone who wouldn't pull back in revulsion, who wouldn't scream, who wouldn't freeze in terror. When she did moan (and that was frequently), it was never out of fear.

The day Enzo got back into town, he returned to the building and waited in the lobby, sullen and glaring and obviously aware of what had transpired between Ryan and Vanessa. When Ryan came downstairs to check his mail, Enzo shoved an eight-inch fillet knife into Ryan's abdomen as far as the blade would go, twisting it around a few times for good measure. Ryan flinched a little, removed the knife, and returned the favor.

By the time men in cheap suits who might as well have had the word *DETECTIVE* tattooed across their foreheads started coming around and asking questions, Vanessa had guessed, more or less correctly, what had happened, except for who had committed the act; Enzo wasn't exactly well liked. She pleaded with Ryan to leave Brooklyn with her. They could go to Manhattan, or to South Jersey to crash with her parents for a while. She could get him a job at her father's contracting business, laying roof tiles and digging in-ground pool foundations. Or they could go anywhere; as long as they were together it didn't matter.

For most of the next week he avoided giving her any semblance of a real answer. Maybe she took his near-total silence as being louder than any excuse he could try to stumble through. Or maybe she was just scared about a possible retaliation from one of Enzo's less-than-upstanding business associates. In any case, when Ryan came home from a meeting with his financial advisor on the sixth or seventh day after Enzo's disappearance, Vanessa—along with her threadbare duffel bag and dog-eared notebooks—was gone.

He tracked her to the Bedford Avenue subway station (this was when the L line was still being called the LL), where she had already purchased a token and was waiting on the Manhattan-bound platform, wearing one of Ryan's white undershirts and eyeliner that was thicker than her usual mascara. Ryan jumped the turnstile; he could feel the vibrations of a Manhattan-bound train, knew he would have at most two or three minutes to convince her to stay.

She nearly leapt away when he gently touched her arm, and she would have fallen onto the tracks if he hadn't held on tight. And though she was clearly shocked that he'd found her, he could tell by her flushed face and crooked half smile that part of her was impressed, flattered by his doggedness.

But after she'd calmed down and he had one last moment to state his case, he choked, literally. He couldn't tell her why he had to remain in Brooklyn, why she really would be safer with him than she could ever know. Maybe a part of him still couldn't believe that Vanessa had fallen into his life the way she had, that he didn't deserve the brief contentment she had brought him. As the train—one of the clunky, toasterlike R38 models with more rust stains and graffiti than bleary-eyed commuters—closed in on the station, Ryan managed to croak out a lame excuse for a good-bye.

Vanessa just stood there, eyes wet, smiling sadly, and he could see that she was confident in the choice she had made. He couldn't blame her.

In the seconds before the train doors opened, she leaned in, kissed his cheek, and thanked him for everything he'd done for her.

"You'll find me when you're ready," she whispered.

He knew as soon as she said it that he'd never find her, that their time together was always meant to be temporary, that he would slowly fade from her thoughts, an uncomfortable reminder of a careless—and nearly fatal—youth.

But four decades later he *had* found Jennifer, another lucky accident that brought back in a sudden rush everything he'd felt for Vanessa, but stronger, a more acute urge. Maybe it was because Jennifer was older and knew what she wanted; she and Ryan were closer to being on the same page.

Whatever the case, he'd failed Jennifer just like he'd failed Vanessa, except this time it was worse. Instead of revealing himself and letting her decide whether she believed him, whether she wanted to continue the relationship, he allowed his fear of rejection to take over, to cocoon himself in a silence that festered until it had reached a breaking point. And because of that he'd gotten her caught up in something terrible, something he didn't even fully understand.

He would go to Manhattan. He would return to humanity and suffer with the rest of them, probably more than most of them, if his disease continued to progress as it had before he was turned. He didn't care how long it would take his own body to weaken and rot. The only thing that mattered now was that he couldn't allow himself to be totally responsible for the destruction of one of the only two people he'd ever truly cared about.

And if she was already dead, the humans wouldn't be the only ones who would suffer.

The train began to lumber along the track and Ryan felt someone watching him. He turned to his left, where a postcard version of a Russian grandmother—her white hair mostly covered by a red-and-yellow floral headscarf—was staring up at him, her forehead creased in concern, the only other passenger in the car who wasn't asleep or immersed in a personal electronic world.

"Whatever it is that pains you, honey," she said with a thick Slavic accent, "it will pass."

Ryan loosened his death grip on the pole, unclenched his jaw, and relaxed his facial muscles, removing the stress furrows that he hadn't realized were plainly visible. He nodded at the woman, avoided eye contact, and took a vacant seat across the aisle as the train picked up speed and shot into the subterranean blackness where Brooklyn ended and Manhattan began.

13

Nicki stood up, placed her phone in the bag, and checked out her reflection in the glass portion of the car's doors as the train approached the Eighth Avenue station, its final westbound stop.

Ryan took a breath and prepared to do the same, half expecting to collapse before he could leave his seat. Maybe his previously damaged lungs wouldn't be able to handle the pressure, or the reappearance of old bad blood after so many years would shock his system to the point of no return, past consciousness and into the darkness that he'd imagined was tightening its grip around his throat since the train had crossed over into Manhattan and made four additional stops.

But as he slung his backpack over his shoulders, tested his still-steady legs, and glanced at his reflection that looked the same as it had for as long as he could remember, nothing happened. He could still easily read the fine print on the advertisement for an online food ordering service at the far end of the car. He knew that the sixtyish bald man wearing an unseasonal black leather jacket and standing to his left had been suffering from non-Hodgkin lymphoma for about five years and that the disease had recently progressed from stage two to stage three. And, as the train doors opened and he walked out onto the well-lit platform, he could single out Nicki's scent from the masses of jostling passengers, knew without seeing her that she was heading quickly toward the stairs that led to the station's upper mezzanine and eventually up to the street.

Maybe, Ryan thought, the rules that he'd been taught, the

boundaries that affected nearly every aspect of his existence, had been misinterpreted. No one he knew had ever returned—human or otherwise—to Brooklyn after leaving the tribe. Maybe it was all an outright lie.

It was only in the last few days that he'd begun to realize how much the tribe's so-called elders had withheld from him, even if he had never been the most curious initiate. It was more than a little shady that Natalia hadn't shown him the stacks of papers written by Arthur until the night her house was supposedly broken into, while Frank was conveniently (or strategically) out of the room. And what about Frank? Had their relationship always been one long sequence of manipulations? What did he stand to gain from working with the Manhattan tribe? And what would be the point of Manhattan exhausting a seemingly significant amount of resources to collect the statues unless they did possess uniquely powerful properties?

These were questions that could wait. Ryan needed to focus on the task at hand, while he still had the strength to correct his mistakes, while he could still track the prey that would lead him to Jennifer or, if she was already gone, whoever was responsible.

While he could still watch them die.

He walked up two levels of stairs and emerged into a midafternoon light—no less brilliant than when he'd left Williamsburg—that was partially obstructed by a massive beige HSBC bank building and a smaller, green, copper-domed repurposed bank that now housed a CVS. The traffic lanes and wide sidewalks that composed the corner of 14th Street and 8th Avenue swarmed with map-wielding Europeans, Citi Bikers, sweat-drenched power-walkers screaming into their phones, dog walkers, halal cart vendors wearing headscarves and vacant expressions, fresh-off-the-clock professionals chattering and streaming in and out of a deli/salad bar and a discount liquor store.

It was a density of sound and movement that rivaled some of Brooklyn's busiest avenues at rush hour, even though Ryan knew from his research that this borderland between the neighborhoods of Chelsea and the West Village wasn't especially high on the island's tourist or commercial hierarchies. The buildings in his immediate vicinity were on the smaller side, most of them six or seven stories, but Ryan had the weird sensation that he had tunneled out into a claustrophobic valley of Steve Madden and H&M-wearing insects surrounded by imposing giants, like the unmistakably stagnant and sweetly putrid air was being trapped by the silver reflective towers rising thirty blocks to the south in the Financial District and the similar ones that dotted the Midtown skyline to the north, the direction Nicki was currently heading.

Ryan shook himself free from the architecture's sinister spell, took a long breath, and zeroed in on Nicki's freshly ponytailed head and her bare upper back, watching her weave through the throngs on the west side of the street about a hundred yards away, passing a Banana Republic storefront.

As he crossed the street he briefly looked up to where the Empire State Building's needle point peeked out between two nearby water towers, then lowered his gaze to focus on his target.

He quickened his pace until he was about fifty yards behind her, what he considered an appropriate distance—close enough not to lose her in case she made any sudden changes in direction or decided to get back on the subway or hop in a cab, but far enough away that he wouldn't attract the attention of anyone else who might be watching Nicki's movements or accompanying her unseen. For the next several blocks she continued in the same direction, past banks, cafés, boutiques, art galleries, and gay bars, gaggles of fashion types strutting gingerly in four-figure footwear over the trash-strewn and gum-speckled pavement, bicycle delivery guys on their breaks cackling and sipping from paper-bagged beverages, and sickly hustlers who reeked of bad coke posted up in front of the occasional porn shop, the last vestiges of a seedier time that Ryan remembered well. Whether you were in Chelsea or Williamsburg or Cobble Hill, gentrification always looked more or less the same.

His familiarity with the environment gave Ryan some confidence, but he knew he had to stay alert and, more importantly, wary. When Nicki stopped at the corner where 21st Street intersected with 8th Avenue, he ducked out of her range of vision and leaned against a magazine kiosk until the pedestrian signal changed from an orange palm to a white silhouette and Nicki was well across the street, heading west. Her pace slowed as she continued on the tree-heavy block that was lined by neat row houses, chained bicycles, and a well-maintained playground, and Ryan hung a little farther back, not wanting to draw attention in the now sparsely trafficked residential area.

She continued west on 21st Street, across two more similarly quiet blocks before turning right on 10th Avenue. Ryan broke into a jog to catch up, turned the corner around the side of a three-story redbrick bookstore, and found her standing in front of the shop's entrance, facing him and intensely digging for something in her bag. Drops of perspiration were condensing on the bottom rim of her sunglasses, and Ryan detected a slight muscle twitch above her right eyelid. As he started to reach for the gun tucked under his belt, she took out her phone from her purse, pressed it to her ear, turned, and continued moving in the direction she'd originally been heading. Her heart rate hadn't increased when he'd turned the corner. She hadn't seen him.

He pretended to browse through the discount book cart next to the shop's front door for a few moments, letting Nicki create some distance between them. As he tried to stop the adrenaline flowing through his trembling hands, he wondered why he hadn't been able to sense that she'd stopped. Maybe it had only been a momentary lapse of concentration when he'd lost sight of her. Or maybe it was the start of something worse. Either way, he couldn't allow his mind to drift in that direction while Nicki was still in motion.

She walked uptown another eight blocks, phone plastered to the side of her face, before crossing 10th Avenue at the intersection with 29th Street, just south of the Lincoln Tunnel, where the shadows cast by a massive, prisonlike U.S. Postal Service processing facility darkened the sidewalk and most of the traffic area. She headed west on 29th for a few yards, passing a storefront with an awning that said NIGHTLINE DELI, and stopped at the entrance of an unassuming five-story brick building sandwiched against a much larger, under-construction luxury condominium complex. She fumbled around in her bag, found her keys, and entered the front door.

Ryan felt a minor jolt of anxiety, jogged across the avenue, and stopped on the side of the street opposite the building she'd disappeared into, where a fenced-off empty lot took up most of the block. He stood for several seconds, studying the building's rows of narrow windows and the rust-covered fire escape that connected half of them, trying to figure out his next move.

A light went on in an open third-floor window, one of the few that wasn't obscured by a curtain or an air conditioner. Ryan could see wooden kitchen cabinets, a wall calendar featuring a basket of golden retriever puppies, and a framed print of Salvador Dali's *Geopoliticus Child*. Nicki appeared behind the glass for a moment, her sunglasses off and her long dark hair flowing freely over her shoulders, and yanked down the shade.

Part of Ryan wanted to break into the building and the apartment immediately, to chain Nicki to the wall like what had been done to Jennifer, torture her until she told him what he wanted to hear, hate-drain her and leave her empty corpse to the large rodents that were scurrying back and forth between the vacant lot's wooden-slab-covered fence and an adjacent Dumpster. But even though he couldn't be sure how much time he had left, he knew that in this case, it would be smarter to exercise a little patience. The apartment might be wired to alert her or her employers the second he tried to break in, to destroy any sensitive information that might be available on her phone or a computer. And there were always cameras. You were always being watched by someone, regardless of whether the person at the other end of the tube had a motive for it—Big Brother was no longer a fictional concept, if it ever had been. He also had no real insight into how the Manhattan operation was structured. Nicki was more than likely a small pawn in a much larger game. Anything she thought she knew might actually turn out to be worthless.

He decided that the best move was to not make contact, to continue to follow her while his body showed no signs of deteriorating in the hopes that she would lead him to someone or something that would allow him to find Jennifer. If that didn't pan out, he could act on his original impulse.

The first order of business was to get away from the exposed sidewalk where he was currently standing and starting to look like a major stalker. The lot behind him—an apocalyptic graveyard of trash and rubble, from what he could see in the small gaps in the wood boards—might be a good place to camp out of sight (there didn't seem to be any active construction going on), but he couldn't jump the seven-foot fence without the possibility of attracting the attention of a pedestrian or a passing motorist.

To his left, at the far end of the block, an old elevated railway ran perpendicular over the street. From his ground-level vantage point Ryan could make out rows of vegetation lining the track on both sides, as well as the occasional human head passing by.

Ryan remembered it as the West Side Line, the primary route for bringing produce into and out of the numerous warehouses that had covered much of Chelsea, the Meatpacking District, and the West Village. Today, he'd read, most of the meat being exported came in the form of steroidal knuckleheads stumbling out of clubs at five in the morning and heading home to Jersey or Long Island. The abandoned railway was now called the High Line, a newly created park featuring quaint walkways and seasonal plantings and stretching from 34th Street in the north to Gansevoort Street in the south. Even though going into the park would provide the best views of the street and the immediate area, he couldn't risk losing sight of the building to find the nearest entrance, no matter how close it was. Nicki would need less than a minute to exit the apartment and be gone forever.

Scanning the shaded area under the High Line overpass, Ryan noticed a sizable—but not particularly obvious—opening where the construction fence ended and the structural support of the overpass began, less than a foot wide, barely enough space for him to squeeze through. He walked over to the spot, swiveling his neck to maintain visual contact with the building, and waited a few minutes until the sidewalk was free of pedestrians. He tossed his backpack over the fence and quickly shimmied through the opening, tearing his shirt and pants in the process. He reached down and felt where the fence's metal had deeply punctured his thigh, where the skin had already healed itself. There was no pain.

He fished a white plastic bucket from one of the debris piles that covered the entirety of the lot, flipped it upside down, and took a seat. From where he was sitting he had a direct view of Nicki's window, and through a gap in the fence he could see the building's front entrance. No one could enter the lot without ample warning and he was virtually invisible to anyone passing by on the street.

He took a breath, then rubbed his eyes with fingers that were no longer trembling. All he had to do now was wait.

14

The shade went up just before eleven the next morning.

Nicki appeared for a moment in the window, her hair pulled back into a tight knot on top of her head, wearing a loose gray T-shirt that was a far cry from the suggestive outfits she'd worn in Ryan's previous encounters with her. She moved out of sight and exited the building a minute later in gym shorts and running shoes, a hefty black North Face backpack slung over her shoulders. She went into the deli, came out carrying a small plastic bag, and headed west. She passed under the High Line a few feet from where Ryan had been sitting for the previous eighteen hours, unblinking, with no interruptions besides two huge rats that had gotten a little too curious during the night and were now lying stiff on a nearby pile of rotting *New York Post*s.

Ryan waited a moment, got up, and squeezed his body through the fence's opening. He looked down at the freshly ripped holes in his pants, at the concrete dust caking his shoes. He pulled the brim of his cap lower on his forehead, staining it with the rat gunk and other unidentifiable grime that had been collecting on his hands. It was better to look and smell this way, he told himself. The more disheveled you appeared, the more people would go out of their way to avoid you, to quickly look in a different direction.

You were just another crazy bum.

He followed Nicki as she walked along 29th Street toward the island's westernmost edge, past another hodgepodge of luxury housing, galleries, storage facilities, abandoned warehouses, vaguely industrial structures, and a commercial bus depot protected by a barbed-wire fence. As they approached the West Side Highway and the Hudson River, the buildings began to thin out and the cloudless sky seemed to open up, reflecting the vastness of the river that made the residential towers and marinas on the New Jersey side seem doll-sized and insignificant. Nicki waited for the traffic light to change, crossed the highway and a two-lane bike path, and entered a paved park area dotted with tree boxes, benches, a gazebo, and a small pier jutting out for several yards above the water. The only people in the vicinity were a pair of parks department employees lounging on a green-and-yellow John Deere utility vehicle and an elderly inline skater seated on the ground, stretching his legs. Nicki made a beeline for the pier and the lone bench at the end of it. She sat down, removed her backpack, and took out a large can of Red Bull and a sandwich from the bag she'd been carrying.

Ryan walked past the workers on the golf cart, both of whom ignored him. He sat down at the picnic table under the gazebo, placed his backpack on the table, and laid his head on it, resting at an angle that would be optimal for watching Nicki and would lead any passersby to believe that he was simply napping off a rough night.

Nicki finished eating, unzipped her backpack, and removed a laptop. She opened it and began typing in what looked like a Word document. Every few minutes she would stop to check something on her phone, sip from the Red Bull can, or stare out at the water. Occasionally a jogger or a couple would stroll out onto the pier to take a selfie or a picture of the Freedom Tower. Nicki maintained the zenlike focus of a Ph.D. student. After about three hours, she stood up, walked slowly in a circle around the bench, stopped, and bent over. She did a few yoga stretches, sat back down, and took another Red Bull out of the plastic bag. The typing resumed.

For the first time since he'd started tracking her, Ryan began to fidget, to waver in his concentration. This wasn't what he had anticipated happening. With every hour that passed, the chances of him finding Jennifer and the chances of him reverting to an incurable, disease-riddled state increased exponentially.

His only viable option to make things right was sitting a stone's throw away, oblivious and unguarded, surrounded by water on three sides. He could grab her phone and backpack and toss her computer into the river before she could do anything to stop him. He could sit soundlessly on the bench next to her and wrap his arm around her neck, muffle her screams and make it look like a gentle embrace. When he'd gotten the information he needed from her, he could tighten his grip and leave her lifeless and upright; it might be hours before anyone noticed. Even if she didn't know anything of value, there would be contacts in her phone, new leads he could act on immediately.

As Ryan reached in his backpack to retrieve Arthur's knife, two city-pale shaggy-haired kids, maybe thirteen or fourteen years old, shot by him on skateboards. They skidded to a halt at the pier. One of them took a packet of Skittles out of his pocket and began slinging the candies into the water, trying to skip them across the surface like tiny colored pebbles. The other kid fiddled with his phone, and an egg-shaped speaker in his other hand started blasting a hip-hop beat.

Nicki swiveled around sharply and gave them her best fuck-you glare. They ignored her and began rapping along to the music. She rolled her eyes, shut the laptop, packed up the rest of her stuff, and stood up to leave.

Ryan, still leaning over the picnic table, slid the knife out of his pack and slowly pressed it against his stomach, gripping the bone-smooth handle. He watched Nicki walk the length of the pier, scowl at the skateboarders, and head in a direct line back to the highway that would bring her only a foot or two away from the gazebo.

It would be so easy. All he had to do was reach out and grab her, pull her in and press the knife to her little liar's throat. The candy-chucking delinquents wouldn't have a clue as to what was happening. And if she was being watched over by the Manhattan tribe, he would at least have the satisfaction of seeing her eyes go blank before they could do anything about it.

But as she approached the gazebo—raising her smug chin to unknowingly provide an easy target—and walked within an arm's length of where Ryan was waiting for her, he didn't make a move. Not because he'd had a sudden change of heart, caught sight of any new potential witnesses, or lost his grip on the blade.

He sat frozen by a helpless panic that he hadn't felt since he'd seen the pictures of Jennifer for the first time.

He couldn't smell Nicki.

The coughing started at night. At first it was minor, a soft wheeze every minute or so, like a tiny piece of lint or food was caught in his throat and needed to be forced out. The spasms gradually increased their intensity until his entire body trembled with every half-stifled bark, with every massive wad of phlegm and blood that he spat onto the vacant lot's rubble-covered ground. Worse than the coughing was the pain that came with it.

The burning in his throat that made swallowing impossible and breathing a luxury.

The shocks of electricity running from his chest to the base of his spine that caused his jaw to clench to the point where he tasted tooth fragments along with the mucus.

And finally, the snap. The unbearable sizzle of every muscle in his body seizing at once as he plummeted to the dirt, writhing, clutching himself, still desperately trying to focus on the building where Nicki had returned after her trip to the park, as he slipped in and out of consciousness, closer than ever to the true darkness.

He watched Nicki leave the building, wearing the same pseudo-athletic gear as the day before. It might have been some time in the early afternoon, but he wasn't sure. She stopped at the deli, came out carrying a bulging plastic bag, and headed in the direction of the park.

Ryan tried to move from the fetal position he'd been in for hours—how long he couldn't be sure—but he was still too shattered to even feebly kick at the rats that periodically gnawed at his shoes and legs and were beginning to explore the holes in his pants. He could tell that the small bites one of them had made in his calf weren't going to heal, that they would fester and spread and might cause a serious infection that would take him out quicker than the illness that had returned and would completely overrun his system in the near future.

Paralyzed and feverish, Ryan had entered a place beyond time and physical trauma, where what had happened and what was going to happen fused into a waking nightmare that he could neither touch nor escape. He saw his mother sitting in a shadow-spun room lit by a single oil lamp on a distant mantel, her drawn face and pinched nose hunched over an industrial-size, wheel-driven sewing machine like the ones from the garment factory in Sunset Park where she'd sat for ten years, through four or five miscarriages and daily beatings from a jealous, pitiful man. A man who now appeared in a fleck of light behind her, who gathered the darkness of the room until he consumed it, a cackling specter, shattering the lamp with an empty quart bottle he held in his rough, blackened fist and stepping behind the woman at the sewing machine who still looked like his mother, but leather-skinned and white-haired, far older than the thirty-five years she'd actually lived. The man kissed the back of her head and her belly swelled until it exploded, submerging Ryan in a blinding sea of salt and blood and he was drowning and then being lifted up by two sets of hands and thrust out onto a mist-tinged valley the color of charcoal and gangrene. He looked up at the men who had saved him but there was only one, a towering figure with a sad expression whose shifting features were somehow a composite of Arthur and Frank, who disintegrated into a thick mist when Ryan reached out to grab the man's leg and use it to pull himself up. He stayed immobile and sightless on the sludgy ground for what seemed like years, lifetimes before finally gathering the strength to get upright, to lift his legs, to take in his surroundings. The mist began to clear and through it he saw dozens of bodies silently trudging toward him, men and women in drab wool coats and seersucker caps, cocktail dresses and smudged overalls, pastel bell-bottoms and black tracksuits. He saw slit necks, gouged-out chests, slick cavities where jaws should have been, all of the wounds he'd inflicted to satisfy his hunger, to prolong the solitary drudge of his life, to get what he wanted. And walking behind the corpses were taller, smooth-skinned men wielding spears and bows, naked except for animal-skin cloths around their waists and the feathers and seashells that were woven into the braids of hair that hung nearly to the ground. Their eyes were emerald pits of pure fire. They were the original tribe, coming to take back what he had stolen from them, to punish his failure. He turned to run and the ground morphed into an impassable jigsaw of pits and swamps bordered by two rocky hills that were rising in the distance, buoyed by some invisible force. At the summit of each stood a pale, beautiful woman, the same woman, one version young and wild-haired, the other older and withered, both of them holding a glowing stone object that shone with the intensity of a furnace. At first they were smiling, calling out to him in a language that he'd never heard before but one that pulled at him with its musicality, a song bathed in love. But when he tried to walk toward them, his feet snagged on an unseen root and he went tumbling into the slushy muck that had spread and was pouring over him like a chemical-choked river, boiling, burning through his skin. The women's faces distorted into grimaces of pain. Their words turned into guttural wails, pleas for him to continue, to rise and meet them above the gathering storm.

But weighed down and sinking lower into the muddy refuse—the foul mixture of everything that had come to define him, the painful glimpses of lives he might have had, and the possibilities he had yearned for but would never come to know—he was unable to crawl to either of them.

When he woke again it was night, orange-tinted but darker in the shadows under the overpass. He felt a cold wetness seeping down his forehead and pooling above his lips and wondered if it had rained, before realizing that the salty fluid was his own sweat.

His throat ached and his limbs felt like they were coated in rust, inside and out, but nevertheless, it was an improvement from the last time he had experienced anything close to a moment of clarity. He was able to wipe the crust out of his eyes and the foul-smelling residue that had congealed around his mouth and ease himself into a sitting position. When his vision cleared enough and his eyes adjusted to the monochromatic gloom, he saw his backpack resting on its side, the murky ground near his legs where puddles of dark liquid had dried and cracked, the constant scurrying of rodents along the base of the fence.

The building across the street was quiet, devoid of color and life. The deli was shuttered and the closest streetlight was broken, further obscuring Ryan's view. The only break in the monotony came from an open third-floor window where Nicki could be seen leaning against an unseen counter or table, naked, fondling one of her large, dark brown nipples and running the fingers of her other hand through the black, close-cropped hair of a head that was tucked firmly between her abundant thighs, bobbing in a slow, circular rhythm. She closed her eyes, tilted her own head back, allowed her tongue to escape the corner of her mouth, and let out a squeal of pleasure that was loud enough to shatter the silence of the slumbering block.

Ryan felt a sudden surge of adrenaline, a violent jolt of energy that allowed him to pull his backpack onto his lap, take out the pistol and tuck it against his waist, sling the pack over his shoulders, and crawl to the fence, causing the rats to scatter and his chest to heave with a series of wet, body-shaking coughs. Breathing heavily, spitting the remnants, he waited a few moments before gathering what little strength he had left and gripped the chain links, hoisting himself up into a standing position, trying not to scream at what felt like power drill bits boring into every inch of his feet when he tried to take a step.

He staggered along the edge of the lot, using the fence to support himself, until he reached the opening next to the overpass. Somehow he was able to slip through the gap without catching any more of his tattered clothing on the metal protrusions that had stabbed him during previous exits, or without face-planting onto the pavement. He leaned against the street-facing side of the fence as another coughing spell worked its way through his sunken frame, while his stomach tried to expel something that wasn't there.

He looked up at the window to see if Nicki or her fuck buddy had heard him. If they had, it hadn't stopped them.

She was facing the street, red-faced and smiling, bent over with her arms splayed outward and her hands resting on the window ledge, her chest heaving and her skin glistening with a wet red sheen as a bronze-skinned guy in his early twenties with the no-fat, hair-less physique and requisite chest tattoos of a mixed martial arts fighter thrust into her from behind, his hands clamped tightly on her shoulders, a thin line of red fluid dribbling from his mouth and pooling onto her back. Staring at an unknown point in the distance, his unblinking, straight-lipped expression exuded, even from where Ryan was standing, an uncanny amount of both calmness and in-timidation.

Exactly like the tribal elders whom he had seen pursuing him in his vision.

The tattoo on the man's right breast was a series of black swirls and dashes that extended over his shoulder and across his bicep, a design that reminded Ryan of several of the drawings from Arthur Harker's crumbling papers. On the other breast was a gleaming red *M*. The man was either a member of the tribe or going all out to do a convincing impersonation.

Maybe Nicki was his donor, or he was her human bodyguard, trying to earn enough respect from the tribe to be turned himself. A well-placed exit wound would answer those questions quickly. It would be a relatively straightforward shot, Ryan tried to convince himself, as long as he could keep his crippled arms from shaking for a few seconds.

He moved along the fence, pausing for a moment to listen to Nicki's choked grunts. He sized up the angle, visualized the trajec-tory the bullet would need to take while trying to steady the nerves that he hoped hadn't already been frayed to the point of uselessness.

"Relax," he said to himself, even though he knew that would be impossible. It was now or never. There was no benefit in waiting for a perfect moment he didn't have. This was his last and only real chance to enact some small measure of revenge, to make his death at least a little meaningful.

As he reached under his shirt and fumbled for the gun's handle, he heard footsteps quickly approaching from the east end of the block. "I'd think twice before you do anything else stupid," a bari-tone voice growled.

He turned to face a scowling, barrel-chested black man wear-ing a backward baseball cap and a lightweight black jacket. The man's softball-sized fists were clenched in a show of strength that was unnecessary for Ryan to realize that he would have no way of defending himself if things got physical.

Ryan's forefinger traced the pistol's magazine, clicked off the safety, and rested next to the trigger. "Fuck off," he heard himself mumble in a voice he barely recognized.

The man sighed, rubbed his stubbled jaw, and nodded at the window where Nicki had moved out of view even though her moans had increased in volume. "This ain't a peep show, dude," he said. "You can't just grab your shit and rub one out on the street every time you catch a glimpse of some freakiness. Those two should at least pull down the curtain, but until someone calls in to complain, there's nothing I can do about it. And it doesn't make what you're doing down here any less disgusting or illegal. Frankly, I'm surprised to see you walking around. Figured you'd still be in the dirt sleeping one off or hustling for another fix somewhere a little more, uh, economically viable."

"You can't—" Ryan sputtered before being cut off by another cough attack that ended with him doubled over and spitting blood on the sidewalk. Blood that didn't show any signs of dissolving.

The man reached into his back pocket, pulled out a wallet, and flipped it open to show Ryan an NYPD badge. "I could have taken you in for trespassing hours ago," he said, putting the wallet back into his pocket and brushing back his jacket to reveal a holstered sidearm. "But this site's been empty for months, some kind of zoning snafu between the city and Van Pelt or one of those other big construction companies. You weren't bothering anybody."

Ryan stared at him blankly, gasping for air.

"Not that you give a shit about that. Believe me, I know what withdrawal is like. I'm four years sober next Tuesday. And the only thing that I hate more than the fact that I'll always have the desire to get high is paperwork. So get out of here. Go to a shelter, your favorite trap house uptown, I don't care. Just don't make me think I wasted my goodwill on a fucking pervert."

Ryan stood for a moment, weighing his options. He stared at the unflinching cop, then up at the building, where Nicki's window shade had finally been pulled down. If he'd had any options, they no longer existed. "Thank you," he managed to croak out. "I'm . . . going now."

He brushed past the cop, who scrunched his nose and shook his head in revulsion at the odor wafting from Ryan's soiled clothing and oil-clogged pores, and limped slowly east toward the metallic hum of 10th Avenue's intermittent late-night traffic, not looking back.

As the adrenaline left his body, it was replaced by a fresh bout of crippling vertigo and muscle tremors, as well as an unshakable brain fog that made it impossible for him to comprehend where he was, where he was going. The buildings he passed became taller, denser, the older rectangular brick façades replaced by glass and chrome behemoths formed in irregular geometric patterns, their spires glimmering in the gathering dawn that seemed to become full-blown sunlight in an instant.

Above him lurked the neon swirl of Midtown advertising, the pixilated billboards featuring airbrushed models, unbeatable cell phone plans, hybrid vehicles, and starving children that swirled interchangeably in a revolving kaleidoscope of commerce. The leering eyes of fresh-out-of-work custodians and sanitation workers were replaced by the disinterested glances of men in suits and women in bland tops and knee-length skirts, entering and exiting the continuous stream of cabs that registered as darting yellow particles on the periphery of his vision.

After what seemed like hours, he felt himself spiraling totally out of control, losing what little balance he had left. At a busy intersection he thought he saw a pulse of white light from a traffic signal and stumbled into the street. He didn't see the car but he heard the screech of tires and a series of squalling horns and loud curses as someone grabbed him by his backpack and flung him sideways into a halal cart parked next to the sidewalk.

While the hairnet-clad woman manning the cart berated him in what he assumed was Arabic, he focused on the building he'd landed in front of, tried to clear his head enough to read the address plate above the double-door entrance. 469 SEVENTH AVENUE. Something about the address rang a bell, pushed its way through the garbled bits of memory that were reverberating randomly around his brain. He'd seen it on envelopes, letterheads, countless e-mails, bullshit tax statements. But the number he was thinking of was slightly different. 489? 499? 499 7th Avenue, Suite 5B. Van Doren & Associates, Financial Planners.

469 meant he was close. He moved away from the cart, staggered onto the sidewalk, and headed uptown, pushing his way through the rush-hour crowds, ignoring the angry and nauseated stares from the unsuspecting travelers he lumbered into, focusing on the numbers of the restaurants and stores he passed to make sure he was going in the right direction. Two blocks later, on the verge of another collapse, he found himself in front of the building he was looking for, its brown-and-red Art Deco façade looking exactly as it had in the images he'd Googled years ago.

He pushed through the revolving doors and into a sparsely decorated marble-tiled lobby where a bleary-eyed security guard was seated behind a large semicircular desk reading a newspaper and munching on a bagel. Ryan's knees buckled and he swerved right, then left, slamming into a wall where a directory of the building's business tenants was posted. His backpack slipped off his shoulders. The security guard snapped to attention, stood up, and rushed out from behind the desk, spilling a large mug of coffee onto the freshly polished floor.

"Hey, buddy, hey, hey!" the portly, balding man stammered in a European accent of unknown origin. "This is no good. You cannot—"

"Van Doren," Ryan mumbled, cutting him off. "5B."

The security guard hovered near him for a moment, eyes darting nervously from the building's entrance to the row of elevators at the back of the lobby, deciding what to do. "You must leave now," he said finally, "or I call police. Your choice."

He reached into the inner pocket of his navy sports jacket, took out his phone, and waited to see what Ryan would do.

"No, it's fine, just call . . . James," Ryan croaked before sliding down the wall into a sitting position and out of consciousness.

15

Beyond the open French windows, the waning sunlight drenched the heavily wooded park across the street in a golden glow as a light breeze caused the branches of the tallest trees to sway in an irregular, soothing rhythm. A child's happy squeal and the chatter of birdsong were the only noises louder than the perpetual buzz of the city that now seemed distant, removed from the calm that was radiating through Ryan.

He stretched his legs that no longer felt like anchors, ran his tongue over lips that were still chapped but no longer raw and peeling. He groggily sat up on the couch where he'd been lying and looked down at the clothes he was wearing: a Grateful Dead 1992 summer tour T-shirt and a pair of gray sweatpants drenched in blood. A needle was sticking into a vein in his forearm. It was connected to a tube that ran from where he was sitting to a nearby IV bag attached to a hospital-style metal pole and filled with a clear fluid that was being pumped into him.

He ripped the needle out of his arm and shot up from the couch. Overcome by a sudden rush of dizziness and nausea, he reached for the pole, grabbing it to support himself, accidentally ripping off the IV bag and spilling its contents onto the dull wooden floor. Trying to regain his balance, he noticed his backpack resting on a cherry-colored leather armchair adjacent to the couch, unopened and still caked in grime from the vacant lot near Nicki's building. He waited for the spinning in his head to stop, then snatched the backpack up and headed for a narrow hallway at the far end of what he assumed was the apartment's living room. Feeling a rapid trembling in his chest that he quickly realized was a heartbeat, he shuffled toward the bolted door at the end of the hallway, trying to move as silently as possible. On his right were two doors, each slightly ajar but not enough for him to see what was on the other side. On his left he passed the entrance to a walk-in kitchen that reeked of peanut oil and something older, putrid. Then a bathroom, the door flung open, what was left of the clothes he'd been wearing since leaving Brooklyn spread across the floor, his gun resting on the toilet tank next to a small pipe still smoldering with pungent weed.

A brief rustling came the room adjacent to the bathroom, followed by the creak of metal springs and a grunt. Footsteps.

Ryan grabbed the gun. The magazine clip was gone. He rushed to the door at the end of the hallway, tried to manipulate the deadbolt with fumbling fingers that seemed to have lost all of their previous dexterity.

"The old hit-it-and-quit-it," a distinctly crackly, familiar voice boomed as the door to the room where the sounds had originated was flung open. "Taking a play out of my book, dude!"

Ryan exhaled deeply, felt his heart rate slow and his shoulders go limp.

"Where are we?" he asked as he sat back down on the couch and James Van Doren III scrunched the massive ass and gut portion of his six-foot-four frame into the armchair. His financial advisor had always been a big guy, but Ryan found it hard to believe how puffy his face had gotten, his triple chin flecked with gray and black stubble, his pre-happy-hour tremble-fingers roving nervously over his swollen knees. He'd always lived the unapologetically degenerate lifestyle of a spoiled kid who never had to work for anything, who knew that when his old man finally collapsed from a clogged artery, a bum liver, or a diabetic seizure (or, as it turned out, a combination of the three), he would seamlessly take control of the business that was his birthright. Now that he was on the wrong side of forty-five, his exterior had caught up to the internal carnage that had been taking place since he'd been old enough to figure out how to pop the tab on a Budweiser can. He'd partied the shit out of himself.

"Oh," Ryan added, "sorry about the floor."

James, wearing baggy mesh shorts and a faded Knicks hoodie, rubbed his bald, sunburned head, squinted his bloodshot eyes, looked at the puddle the IV bag had created, and shrugged. "No worries," he said, "didn't even notice. To be honest, the only thing I'm a little pissed about is that I gave you that shirt to wear. It's pretty rare. Going to run you like three hundred to get a replacement on eBay but I know you're good for it." He chuckled. "To answer your question, we're at my place. Upper West Side, 87th and Central Park West. Land of the Jewish middle-aged yogi. Make yourself at home."

"Was your wife at work when you brought me here?" Ryan asked. "I can't imagine she'll be too happy to see the bathroom renovations when she gets back."

James's eyes grew wide in amused disbelief. "You don't remember anything from Tuesday, do you? I knew you were out of it, but oh man, wow. And I've been divorced since before the previous presidential administration. Did we not ever talk about that?"

"Tuesday," Ryan repeated, trying to make sense of any hours he might have lost. "What's today?"

"Thursday." James checked something on the phone in his lap for a few seconds, then looked back up. "You picked the right time to come all batshit-hobo into the office," he continued. "Normally I don't make it in until around ten thirty, but I was feeling ambitious. You should have seen Gustav standing over you, looking like he was about to puke. I couldn't tell which of you was closer to croaking!"

"Gustav?"

"The doorman at the office, older dude, kind of worthless when an actual emergency occurs, as you've seen, or sort of saw. His wife makes some amazing pierogis, though, brings them in a couple times a month, otherwise he'd have been canned years ago. Anyway, I finally got him to help me get you in to the car that had brought me in and was still idling outside the building. Peter, the driver—not happy, but he'll keep his mouth shut. You're going to be getting a cleaning bill in the next couple days. We brought you here, tried to get you comfortable, figure out what was wrong, what you needed, but you were wired, dude. Kept thrashing around even though you didn't have the strength to stand up. Telling me you needed to leave, then you needed to eat. Told me you'd sign over all your assets to me if I gave you my blood. Ha! That's how I knew you were totally off your gourd. You wouldn't shut up, so I fired up the old collection bag, gave you a vial, and you coughed it back out as soon as it touched your throat. Then I realized, duh, you're in Manhattan so you must be one of us again, probably forgot that you needed to eat solid food and drink water to, like, survive. My buddy at Mount Sinai gave me a few bags of electrolyte replacement solution for when I overimbibe and need to be semilucid the next morning. I've been pumping you full of that shit since yesterday. You're welcome."

"Thanks," Ryan managed, weakly, the reality of how stupid and reckless he'd been finally sinking in.

"Don't thank me yet," James said, "until you try the pad thai I got from this place around the corner. Figured your first real meal in however many years should be memorable. Sit tight. I'll be right back."

James hoisted himself out of the chair with no small amount of effort and disappeared into the kitchen.

Ryan looked around the room at the random assortment of crookedly slung, dust-covered objects hanging from the walls—a wooden fraternity paddle, a heavily scratched acoustic guitar, prints of generic cityscapes, a massive taxidermy of a striped bass—that made it clear that no self-respecting woman had spent any significant time in the apartment for years. At least not during the daylight hours. He noticed a large photograph hanging above the curved-screen, wall-mounted TV: a much younger (and thinner) James, his father and grandfather raising pints and flashing tipsy smiles at the camera.

Ryan had a clear memory of the first time he'd met Jimmy Sr. on a winter night in the early forties. Shitfaced, decked out in a plum-colored hound's-tooth jacket and matching fedora, weaving his way home from a squalid Brownsville pub, slipping and pinballing between the brown and gray snowdrifts, oblivious to everything, belting out the chorus to Sinatra's "Pale Moon" in a slurry brogue. Ryan, following him in the shadows of the otherwise empty street, waited until Jimmy slipped on a patch of black ice and landed stomach up in a gutter, still singing. The easiest of meals.

But Jimmy was an incomparable talker, especially after a dozen scotches. Ryan had dragged him onto the sidewalk and pinned him down in a telephone booth that was blocked from the street by a large snowbank and, consumed by his hunger, was ripping through his prey's scarf to get at the soft veins under the jowls.

Jimmy threw his hands up, not so much in fearful protest as in annoyance.

"Hold on, buddy, what's going on here?" he asked incredulously. "Let's talk about this like men and not savages from a John Ford picture. We can make a deal. What do you want from me, my wallet, my watch? They're yours."

"Your blood."

"Okay, that's a first," Jimmy replied without skipping a beat. "You some kind of mad scientist? A Bela Lugosi fanatic? But sure, no problem. I got plenty of it. Freshest around, no syphilis, and seven years ago I'm the backup quarterback at Fordham. But you don't need all of it, do you? How's about this. I got a nurse friend over in Bay Ridge. She'll drain a pint, a quart, whatever you need. I'll get it for you whenever you need it, within reason, of course."

Even in Ryan's haste to eat, Jimmy's alcohol-fueled boldness made him pause. There was something to be said about not having to risk exposing yourself every time you got the urge to feed. And Jimmy's blood, regardless of how much booze was flowing through it, smelled above average, maybe even great.

"And of course if you aren't going to change your mind and leach me into an early grave, I'll need to be properly compensated," Jimmy continued, speaking like the two of them were old acquaintances, eyeing the mink collar of the jacket Ryan had recently extracted from the still-warm corpse of an anesthesiologist. "I got a feeling you've been playing this game for a while, probably collected a few souvenirs in your line of work."

Jimmy was right. There were piles of cash, jewelry, silverware, and china, as well as dozens of pieces of art that Ryan had taken from his more affluent victims, all hidden in the stash house in Brighton Beach he shared with Frank and Seamus. A hoard that would soon be getting difficult to manage regardless of how much money Ryan spent on clothes and the swanky hotels in Brooklyn Heights, where he'd grown accustomed to staying.

The fifty dollars Jimmy requested for the first quart was a pittance to Ryan, even back then. When he came to collect what he was owed the following afternoon at the address printed on Jimmy's business card, Jimmy handed him the blood in a glass milk bottle, as well as three hundred dollars in crisp bills. "Had a good day at the market," Jimmy said nonchalantly. "Doubled what you gave me, plus this."

Whether or not Jimmy was bullshitting him (which, Ryan thought, now seemed more than likely), the transaction was the start of a long-term, mutually beneficial relationship that saw Ryan not only stop having to kill for his meals but also consolidate and expand his wealth in the most legitimate way possible, and saw Jimmy open a business that had fed his and his descendants' appetite for irresponsible consumption. Ryan never asked what percentage Jimmy, Jimmy Jr., or James took from him, as long as the numbers that he saw continued to grow. And they always did, through several minor scares and the 2008 bank collapse.

Even though they were no longer Ryan's donors, it behooved the Van Dorens to make sure their biggest and oldest private client remained happy. Ryan had trusted this family of alcoholic fuck-ups and womanizers for three generations. It had paid off so far, which was why he was here. It wasn't for the ambiance.

James returned from the kitchen, freshly stoned and giggling in weird triumphant bursts, a forty-seven-year-old child, cradling a plate of noodles, chicken, and tofu, a pint of Belgian chocolate Häagen-Dazs, and a can of barbecue-flavored Pringles. He set them on the scuffed coffee table in front of Ryan and handed him a fork. Ryan breathed in the steam coming off the pad thai, an aroma that would have made him gag a week ago but now smelled irresistible, better than any B-negative blood.

"Breakfast of champions," James said. He sat down in the armchair and stopped smiling for the first time since Ryan had seen him. "I figure I'll wait to ask you the obvious stuff," he said, taking a serious, businesslike tone. "Like, why did you show up at my door and almost blow a cover you've been maintaining since before my grandfather was born? What fucked-up set of circumstances led you to give up a gift that most people would probably kill to have? How can I get you out of whatever situation you're in? Just know now that whatever you're going through, I'll do anything in my power to help you. You can stay here as long as you want. I owe you that much, and more. Also, you might want to slow down a little there, bud."

Ryan nodded, even though he wasn't really listening, his mouth and chin stained with noodle grease and chocolate goo as he tore open the Pringles can, pulled out a fistful of chips, and shoved them down his throat. Everything that touched his tongue was the best thing he'd ever tasted. He could feel his grateful stomach expanding with each swallow, his seldom-used jaw muscles working off their rust, an unfamiliar warmth surging through him.

In spite of all that had happened and the future ugliness that was inevitable, he found himself totally absorbed in the moment, content in a singular, simple purpose. For now, he had everything he needed.

16

"So what you told me yesterday is for real? This whole thing is about a girl? Bro, you're even more messed up than I thought," James said, sipping his coffee and staring longingly at a woman smoking a cigarette on the corner of 95th and Broadway, a few yards from the diner where they were sitting in a window booth.

Ryan looked down at the bacon and cheese omelet, hash browns, and sausage links he was in the process of devouring, took a few more bites. "You left Brooklyn for a girl," he said.

James chuckled dryly. "Just because you leave a place," he said, "doesn't mean your personality magically changes. Did you think you were going to suddenly become a personable nonrecluse schooled in manipulating the fickle heartstrings of a member of the Tinder generation? Good luck with that. Oh, and one more small detail. You gave up your immortality! What the fuck, dude? In a hundred years you could probably have custom-ordered a robot that looks and feels exactly like, what's her name, Jessica? Plus, I was hoping that when I finally beat my insides up to the point of no return you'd be nice enough to bite me or whatever you guys do and let me join the club. Guess I'll have to settle for becoming a cyborg."

"Jessica," Ryan repeated. "Sucking down people's bodily fluids for an eternity isn't exactly everything it's cracked up to be. No offense, yours was pretty good. But it's got nothing on this omelet."

"This place is pretty dope, right?" James said, winking at the redheaded, college-aged waitress who had come to refill their waters. She groaned and sped away. "Well at least you're rich," he contin-

ued, "good looking, and technically still young. You can do whatever you want, go wherever you want to go. Which is why it's even
weirder to me that you're settling for this one chick, a chick who,
from what you've told me, might not even feel the same way about
you."

"So this Rhodes you were talking about last night," Ryan said,
changing the subject. "You're saying he can trace the location of
where a call came from, even if the number is private?"

"Derrick?" James shrugged. "The guy is legit, OG hacker status.
He could find a dick pic you took ten years ago on a digital camera, accidentally uploaded on MySpace, and deleted five seconds
later. He's that good. Not trying to burst your bubble—I don't know
how out of the loop you are when it comes to dating in the modern
world—but when a girl you've supposedly been in love with for an
extended period of time starts calling you from a private number
and then suddenly stops contacting you, it's not a good sign. Maybe
you should try sending her a Facebook message or an e-mail or
something. The last thing you need, now that you're like, fully back
in the world, is to get a stalker reputation right off the bat. Not a
great look, Ry."

"I think she might be in trouble," Ryan said, stabbing through
the last sausage with his fork. "Can you set up a meeting or not?"

James held up his hands. "Yeah, yeah sure. Take it easy. I got
you. I can probably set something up for this afternoon. But you
need to know a few things about Derrick Rhodes. First of all, he's
super strange, not the easiest person to get a read on, Asperger's to
the max. He'll want to meet somewhere relatively off the grid, probably Central Park."

"That's fine," Ryan said. "I can deal with it."

"Also," James continued, lowering his voice, "he's a fugitive.
Like, pretty high up on the Most Wanted list. Used to do some joint
contracting work with Homeland Security and the NSA, then decided to, um, borrow a hefty amount of money, as well as a hard
drive of sensitive information, some of which he's already leaked;
the rest he's planning on releasing to the Internet once he's out of
the country."

"What the hell is he doing in Manhattan of all places?" Ryan asked. "And how are you able to contact him if the feds don't even know where he is?"

James grinned, adjusted his crooked tie, swept croissant crumbs from the front of the wrinkled navy sports jacket that made him look like the overgrown boarding school brat he was, and signaled for the waitress to bring the check. "He's a client. Came to the city to get his financials in order before he continues up the coast, backpacking through the woods to Nova Scotia, where he's going to hop on a boat to Ireland or somewhere. Sounds pretty fucking ridiculous if you ask me, but it's not my problem. Plus, he owes me."

Ryan rolled his eyes. "Sounds like you guys have a great vetting process at Van Doren and Associates."

"We've never had a moral issue doing business with entities that aren't necessarily legitimate in the eyes of the federal government. Our company was founded on that very principle. You of all people should know that."

Ryan nodded. He didn't have a comeback for that.

James stood up to leave. "I've got to get to the office before my secretary starts scouring every rub-and-tug parlor on Canal Street for my corpse. Stay put at the apartment and I'll call you on the house phone when I hear from Derrick. The tab's on you today." He scooted out of the booth, making a point of brushing against the backside of the waitress, who had just arrived and was removing the check from the front pocket of her apron.

"What a dick," she murmured after James had exited the diner. "He a friend of yours?"

"Nope," Ryan said as he handed her some cash.

17

Ryan had never been religious, even before he was turned. Especially before.

He'd grown up in places that wouldn't be habitable by any stretch of the twenty-first-century, first-world imagination, seen the people around him governed by, at best, a kind of harmless pettiness, and at worst, an animalistic viciousness beaten into them by the unending drudgery of the coal-smeared industrial landscape. Words like *faith* and *salvation* were as useful to him as an empty plate or a worn-out boot heel; a prayer was the ultimate waste of breath. When he'd been given a reprieve from the death that so many self-proclaimed believers sought in vain to transcend, it wasn't because of divine intervention. The simple (if little understood) biological process would have been seen by Ryan's familiars only as a kind of savage witchcraft, the worst heresy.

But walking north along the leafy residential sprawl of Central Park West under the auspices of regal apartment buildings whose impressive towers rose skyward in an unbroken display of prewar opulence, he felt like an unseen hand had reached down and given him a second chance.

He couldn't smell the blood or the underlying medical conditions of the people he passed—the women pushing strollers in yoga pants or business-casual skirts, the elderly men snoozing on benches and against the low stone wall that separated Central Park from the sidewalk, the occasional soccer player or jogger—or read the numbers on any of the approaching street signs until they were almost directly overhead. And though he felt somewhat replenished by the seemingly endless supply of frozen burgers, Gatorades, and untouched fruits and vegetables in James's refrigerator, he still had a nagging cough that wasn't getting any better, and with each step he took, the invisible weights that seemed to be attached to both of his ankles got heavier, as if he'd spent the last century cheating not only death but also gravity.

But he was armed, not only with a firearm and a blade but with a renewed sense of purpose, a hope that he still had enough time to find Jennifer, as long as the lead that James had given him panned out.

Ryan had Googled Derrick Rhodes on the desktop in the extra bedroom in James's apartment while he waited for James to set up a meeting. There were hundreds of images of the lanky, bespectacled former computer professional (along with accompanying news articles), and in all of them he had the same close-cropped, blasé haircut, the same deer-in-the-headlights stare, looking at least a decade younger than his thirty-four years.

Rhodes had been busy during his four years as a government contractor. He'd gathered information about secret military expenditures and weapons projects, black ops orchestrated by privately held companies with no ostensible ties to any of the world's intelligence agencies, improper relationships between hedge fund managers and members of the judicial and executive branches. The files he'd sent to a handpicked selection of multinational journalists also included sinister memos regarding the Big Brother scope of government surveillance, the OxyContin and gambling habits of a posse of New Jersey police commissioners, hundreds of assassinations that had been carried out by spies but officially blamed on terrorist cells and other extremist groups.

As impressive as the sheer volume of data he was able to unload on the public over the fourteen months was Rhodes's ability to totally remove himself from the grid, to remain an at-large fugitive with no discernible trail to his whereabouts. Tracing a call sent to Ryan's phone to a physical location would be like child's play to someone like Derrick, he assumed, as long as the fugitive didn't spook first.

Ryan entered the park at 103rd Street, following a paved pathway to a grassy hillside that sloped down to a large, algae-covered pond ringed with weeping willows, oaks, and the occasional spruce tree. Continuing across a bridge that overlooked a small man-made waterfall, the path rose up a more heavily wooded hill and across a larger road being used by a few bicyclists and runners. After another section of forest, the landscape changed to an open expanse of baseball and soccer fields, handball courts, and glacial deposits in the form of massive rock formations. It was called the North Meadow, according to the map that Ryan had printed out from the desktop in James's apartment.

Over the years, Ryan had absorbed plenty of images and video footage of the park, enough to form what he thought was a fairly accurate sense of the place. But here, in the park's northern reaches, it was nothing like the ultra-crowded Great Lawn or the tourist-clogged path that circled the Jacqueline Kennedy Onassis Reservoir. There were no horse-drawn carriages, caricaturists, or meandering Shakespeare troupes dressed in period attire. Besides the occasional group of two or three pedestrians, a few couples with strollers and/ or dogs, and a handful of sunbathers lounging on the grass, the area was empty of humanity. The constant urban undercurrent of traffic and phone noises, the blare of secondhand music, and the drone of voices had been replaced by the quiet chatter of birdsong and the ripple of wind through the leaves. The only life form that could be said to be bustling was a gray squirrel barreling down a tree trunk, its cheeks fat with seeds. To Ryan, it seemed like he had been transported to a different time, one that might have been familiar to a young, pretribal Frank.

Whether it was the thought of his former friend or the sudden silence that surrounded him, Ryan paused for a moment as a shiver went down his spine. He had always felt most comfortable in the loudness of the city, swept up in the crowds, one anonymous face in a sea of millions. But the farther into the park he'd gotten, the more he felt trapped by nature, his inner self exposed to the trees that seemed to whisper and point to each other, like they were watching him.

Like they knew he didn't belong.

Ryan started moving again, told himself to shake off any further insane thoughts about malevolent plants. As he continued through the meadow, the trees receded and the buildings lining Central Park North loomed to his left, soothing him a little, reminding him that he was only a quick jog away from his native terrain.

He picked up the pace as he walked across a traffic overpass and onto a running path before turning north, through another series of rolling hills and rocky outcroppings, then down a steep decline that bottomed out at a black wrought-iron gate, only a few yards from 5th Avenue, the park's eastern border.

It was the entrance to the Conservatory Garden, a six-acre enclosure of impeccably manicured lawns, fountains, hedges, flowers, and sculptures that, to Ryan, looked like something straight out of *Alice in Wonderland*. It was fitting, he thought, that he was searching for someone who might be more than a little mad, in every sense of the word.

He passed a large lawn surrounded by yew bushes and bordered by two rows of crabapple trees and seasonal displays of tulips and chrysanthemums (there was a small plaque denoting the species of each particular plant), with a twelve-foot-high bronze jet fountain at its center. At the far end of the lawn, a bride and groom stood under a flower-covered pergola, posing while a photographer crouched in the foreground and barked out instructions. Ryan walked by a few more rows of trees and hedges, a small Victorian-style brick building, looking for Rhodes, who James had said would be sitting alone and wearing black. He came to a large circular section of the walkway that featured a smaller fountain containing a bronze sculpture of three dancing girls. Displays of sunflowers, daisies, and dozens of other plants formed concentric circles that expanded in size and height the farther they got from the fountain. There were also a few wooden benches scattered between the rows of plants. On one of them, partially concealed by a massive pink rhododendron bush, sat a solitary man, methodically chewing something.

Ryan thought he must have been mistaken, or James had given him the wrong location. The man—or more accurately, the creature—sitting on the bench devouring what Ryan now saw was a corn dog and slurping from a plastic soft drink container was anything but skinny. He belched softly every few seconds, wiping crumbs from his faded black jeans and the expansive gut portion of his black T-shirt that featured the demonic head shots of the Norwegian black metal band Gorgoroth. He had bleach-white skin and no trace of hair except for a pencil-thin, reddish-brown goatee. His eyes, unmoving and seemingly fixed on an unknown point in front of him, had white lenses surrounded by thin black circles, an effect created by contact lenses, Ryan assumed (and hoped).

A small ponytailed child wearing pink overalls skipped away from the adults she'd been walking with around the rows of shrubs surrounding the fountain and, not paying attention, crashed into the man's heavy-duty camouflage hiking bag that was resting on the ground next to the bench. He looked down at where she'd fallen with the same emotionless stare and opened his mouth slightly. The girl yelped, jumped up, and ran back to her group.

The man lifted his head and focused his gaze on a quickly approaching Ryan, who was trying to decide whether to stop or to make a U-turn and go back through the park to James's apartment.

Sit down, the man mouthed when Ryan was a couple of feet away.

"Derrick?" Ryan asked as he followed the command and noted an intense chemical aroma coming from the backpack, what he imagined a combination of Pine-Sol and formaldehyde might smell like.

"Let me see the phone," the man whispered in a dry, medium-pitched Midwestern accent, emphasizing every syllable just like he had on the YouTube video Ryan had watched hours earlier, a short clip about a new algorithm used for solving linear equations that Derrick had posted a month before he disappeared.

"Right now?" Ryan asked, scanning the area in front of them, trying to realign himself with the main path, which was obscured by flowering hedges and cherry trees. "Here?"

Derrick calmly extended an upturned palm. At first Ryan thought that the hand was covered in clay or some kind of hair wax, but then he realized it had been burned badly. Each of Derrick's fingers looked like it had been blowtorched into a leather-charred, shiny mess of rearranged flesh. His fingerprints were gone.

Mesmerized by the scar tissue, Ryan reached into his pocket and pulled out his phone, then handed it to Derrick. "You need my password? I can—"

"Not necessary." Derrick studied the phone for a moment, rolling it around in his ruined claw. He turned the phone on, somehow bypassed the security screen, and scrolled through the call history. His expression remained taut, indecipherable. He unzipped the top section of his pack, placed it inside, and resumed staring into space, as if Ryan were no longer sitting next to him. "When you look like a monster," he said, apropos of nothing, "you get treated like one. An unpleasant image that's cast aside and quickly forgotten. Compartmentalized. You're safe if you remain in the shadows with the other ghosts. When you have the heart of a monster, a real monster, that's when you're rewarded for it. You get to carve out the rules. Everyone else is sort of in between. And when you're caught in between . . . That's when it gets dangerous."

Derrick paused to observe a large white moth that had settled on his knee. He snatched it up and shoved it into his mouth in one lightning-quick motion.

"So, uh, how does this work?" Ryan asked after a few awkward moments of silence, trying to erase the what-the-fuck grimace he knew he was making. "Do you have the equipment you need with you, or should I come back later?"

"Right now's not ideal," Derrick said, swallowing the insect. "We'll need to meet again tomorrow. I'll be heading north, out of the city, following the greenways. Morningside Park, a little farther uptown near Columbia. That's as good a place as any. Does ten in the morning work for you?"

Ryan nodded. It worked great, in that it signified a concrete ending to whatever batshit universe he'd stumbled into.

Without warning, and with the same uncanny speed that he'd used to snare the moth, Derrick's hand shot out and caught Ryan's wrist in a sandpaper-like grip, which would have been an interesting sensation if Ryan hadn't been freaked out beyond belief. Derrick was studying him with a sudden intense interest that was almost as disconcerting. If Ryan tried to break free it might lead to a fight, which might attract attention. If he simply got up and ran from this Marilyn Manson protégé, his phone and his only real lead were as good as gone.

"You're one of them, or you were," Derrick whispered excitedly.

"One of what?"

"I'm sorry," he said with a hint of embarrassment, withdrawing his hand. "I don't want to presume anything, or be offensive. I'm not entirely sure about the in-group terminology you use—I didn't know there was still a Brooklyn faction until recently—but 'dead warrior' kept coming up in my research of your Manhattan cousins. A more literal translation from the original indigenous dialect would be 'those who walk in the changeless struggle.'"

"I don't know if I follow what you're . . ." Ryan trailed off, the skin on the back of his neck bristling, the fight-or-flight response kicking into a higher gear.

Derrick's lips stretched into the beginnings of the tiniest grin. "It's all right," he continued. "James gave me a concise rundown of your former business relationship with him, of your current situation. I wouldn't have agreed to meet with you otherwise. And I can't do anything to expose you, at least now that you're human again, out of the real game, so to speak."

"The real game?"

"I've been dying to get a few minutes of face time with someone who's been exposed to the ancient genetics, even if they were from one of the younger factions. What year were you born?"

"1887."

"Fascinating. Do you recall what it felt like when the virus entered your bloodstream? Were you able to stay conscious? I've heard that in an ideal environment it can open up your inner eye, give you a glimpse of things that no one remembers, things that don't want to be remembered. A place deeper than time. I apologize again. I'm prying. It's like Newton being able to actually see and communicate with the gravity that caused the apple to fall from the tree."

"I'd think that digging up enough dirt to make the entire military-industrial complex shit itself is a big enough achievement,"

Ryan said, no longer apprehensive, annoyed that James had outed him to a crackpot whistle-blower whose months of isolation had clearly sent him far out into the deep end. A place deeper than time? Younger factions?

Ryan had had his fill of nonsense. He needed to get out of Wonderland.

"If you really want to know what I was," he said, "I hear there are plenty of message boards for you to check out, other stuff on the deep web, if you haven't found that already. But I can't help you anymore. Good luck."

Derrick croaked out a chuckle that was as rough as his hands. "I only deal in the truth," he said, "and the truth is far bigger than anything you or I can fathom, bigger than anyone's psyche can reasonably handle. It goes beyond governments, beyond manufactured immortality. It's why I've released the information I have. I needed to sacrifice myself to establish credibility, send out the more easily digestible tidbits first. I hope it's enough for when I start dropping the real mind-bending knowledge, but the masses will believe what they want to believe. It's how we've been programmed."

Ryan just hoped that whatever synapses were still firing in Derrick's brain would be enough to figure out how to manipulate his phone. He felt a coughing fit rise in his chest, tried to clear his throat before it got too much worse, tried not to think about the migraine that was seeping into the space behind his temples.

"I can see you're tired," Derrick continued, zipping up the section of his pack where he'd stashed the phone. "You crave simpler things, you want to be a normal guy chasing girls. Or a girl. *The* girl, whatever. That's okay. I get it. You don't need to worry, you've already rejoined the flock. When I let the world know what's really going on, you'll have a choice, like everyone else, about whether to take a step forward on the path to the truth. Or you can stay in the dark. In the meantime, I'll find your pretty sheep."

Ryan waited out the silence that followed. It seemed like Derrick was finally done. He stood up to leave. "Ten o'clock tomorrow, Morningside Park?"

Derrick nodded. "You should probably head through the North

Woods on your way back. Switch it up. It's a little less conspicuous than the meadow."

Ryan walked briskly in the direction of the wrought-iron gate that separated the garden from the rest of the park, his head exploding in pain, not turning to ask Derrick how he'd known about the route he'd taken to get to the meeting. He'd heard and seen more than enough for one day.

18

He could hear the electronic dance music pulsing and vibrating off the asphalt before he turned onto 87th Street. It was just past dusk, but the ceiling's track lights were already blazing beyond the flung-open second-story French windows. A shadow-wreathed woman was perched near the ledge, smoking. Ash from her cigarette landed on Ryan's shoulder as he stepped to the building's front entrance and fumbled for James's spare key. He groaned.

As he exited the elevator and walked down the hallway, the ever-present odor of marijuana grew stronger and the bass thumps got wall-shaking loud. James's door was ajar. Ryan pushed through it and was greeted by a pair of butch girls who couldn't have been older than nineteen or twenty—one with a shaved head and a pierced septum, the other wearing a tank top stained by armpits that sprouted a robust amount of black fuzz—making out roughly in the entranceway to James's bedroom. They noticed him gawking, giggled, and entered the room, slamming the door behind them.

There were other people flitting around in the hallway and the living room, a few more youngish girls, a couple of sweat-gleaming guys in wrinkle-free shirts that were unbuttoned to their sternums. They looked like they could have been James's interns.

Ryan stopped in front of the entrance to the kitchen, where James was bent over a black granite countertop next to the stove, separating orange, pink, and white pills from a large Ziploc bag into three ceramic bowls, apparently based on which color they were. He seemed giddy, agitated, humming along to the repetitive drone of the song that was blasting from invisible speakers that were seemingly everywhere in the apartment. His thick, darting fingers were covered in a sherbet rainbow of dust.

He looked up, grinned, twisted off the cap of a bottle of Budweiser that had been perspiring nearby on the stove, and handed it to Ryan. "GHB, ketamine, and of course, some Molly that I think is actually Molly," he said, pointing at the pharmaceutical salad in front of him. "Never been a fan of the club stuff, get sweaty enough after a couple brews and a handful of key bumps. But you know me, can't help but be a gracious host."

Ryan slammed the beer down on the counter. "What the fuck were you thinking?" he hissed.

"About what?" James replied, wiping his hands on an off-white V-neck that accentuated his paleness and his love handles. "Did he not show up? Did he not want to help you? I made it more than clear that he wouldn't be able to cash out with me if he didn't. Do you need me to call him?"

"I needed you to not tell him anything about me, biologically. I've spent most of my life trying to avoid becoming a science project. It also would have helped if you had given me at least a minimal warning about Derrick's current choice of wardrobe and hairstyle. Also his tendency to ramble like a delusional cult groupie. Jesus, man."

James grinned, opened the fridge, pulled out another beer, and twisted the cap off. "Thought I told you he was weird," he said before taking a long swig. "But the skin stuff is fucking crazy, right? He used a chick's curling iron on his fingers. Feet look the same way, apparently. I guess it's one way to avoid getting caught. Hiding in plain sight. You know a thing or two about that. You guys might be more similar than you think."

James had always been an idiot and a scumbag, but at least he hadn't been reckless. The man Ryan knew might have had a little too much fun most nights of the week, but when it came to business, to his side gig as Ryan's donor, he had kept his shit together. And above all else, he had kept his mouth shut. But that part of the man seemed to no longer exist. Ryan had been a fool for thinking James could help him.

"You know what, this whole thing was a bad idea. I'm going to grab my bag—unless one of your friends has decided to sell it for a quick fix—and I'm going to ask you where Derrick is staying in case he doesn't show up tomorrow. And that's it. You won't hear from me in person again. Thanks for everything."

Ryan turned to walk out of the kitchen. A moist hand latched on to his shoulder, bullet-quick.

"That's not going to happen," James said, lowering his voice.

"Why?" Ryan whispered. His body tensed up, ready to spring in whatever direction he needed it to.

"Well, for one thing," James continued, relaxing his grip, "he isn't staying anywhere. He's been living in the park, sleeps there. Where, I can't say. He thinks it's safer that way. And for Derrick, it probably is. He's got the lay of the land down cold. Like some kind of urban ninja savant. You'd never find him, and if you somehow got close, he'd see you before you made contact and disappear again. If you haven't been paying attention to the news, he's pretty good at that. But you need to chill out because he can't leave, not until I deliver the funds he's invested with my company. His little hiking trip across the border and his insane plot to upset the fabric of society or whatever he's trying to do won't work without them. And guess what? He's not cashing out until he gets you what you want. It's what I told him. It's as simple as that."

"You're sure about that?"

Ryan turned back around to face James, who chugged from the Budweiser bottle until it was empty, wiped the backwash from his chin, and smiled. He picked up the beer Ryan had put down and handed it to him a second time. "I'm positive," he said. "So just relax tonight, enjoy my humble festivities, and tomorrow you'll be on your way. When's the last time you got wasted? You remember what beer tastes like?"

"Not really, but I'm sure this is better than the rotgut we used to swill at the shipyards." He put the bottle to his lips and took a long pull. It tasted bitter and slightly grating as it went down his throat, but the longer he drank, the more refreshed he felt. A forgotten fuzziness began to work its way into his stomach and radiate outward.

Maybe it was smarter for him to stay at the apartment over-night. He needed to rest before meeting with Derrick and obtaining whatever information the bleached oddball could find, wherever that might lead him. He couldn't get wasted, but he could afford to relax for a couple of hours. And he owed James as much. He took another pull, emptying the bottle.

"That's more like it!" James boomed. He took another beer out of the fridge and held the bowl of orange pills in front of Ryan.

"No way, man," Ryan said, holding up his arms, palms out. "I'm not even sure I can handle the booze."

James pressed the bowl into his hand. "Calm down, I know you're a pussy," he said. "They're for my other, slightly more hip guests. And by 'slightly' I mean 'significantly.' Be a pal and help me bring these into the living room. Oh, and I told everyone you were like, some kind of New Age monk just back from a five-year pilgrim-age to Nepal or Bangladesh or somewhere, totally ignorant of the ways of modern civilization. It's actually pretty accurate when you think about it. Don't worry about getting the story straight. Most of them probably won't even remember it."

"You what?"

"Just shut up and follow me!"

James scooped up the other two bowls, grabbed his beer, and plunged out of sight into the murky hallway.

Ryan looked down at the clothes James had lent him. An XXL gray T-shirt, baggy sweatpants that were almost the same color, and a white pair of gender-neutral tennis shoes that had belonged to a recent hookup (he hadn't asked James why they were still in his possession) and were the only footwear in the apartment that came close to fitting correctly. If he was going to have to play the role of a world-denying hermit, he at least looked the part.

He walked into the living room, where the couch, the window ledge, and two folding chairs he hadn't noticed the previous morn-ing were occupied by the finance bros he'd seen earlier, a young Hispanic guy with a ponytail rolling a joint on his lap, the lesbians from the hallway, and a pot-bellied burnout wearing a tie-dyed ban-dana who was dozing and drooling onto the lap of his corduroy overalls.

"I come bearing gifts!" James shouted over the music as he set the bowls on the coffee table, which was already occupied by various drink containers, a small rectangular mirror, two dusty credit cards, and several sections of a cut-up plastic straw. "Oh, and this is my good buddy Ryan I was telling you about."

Ryan did a wave-and-nod routine as he placed the bowl he'd been carrying next to the others and settled with his beer on the window ledge next to the semicomatose old-timer. Most of the group only gave him brief grunts of acknowledgment, as they were already fixated on the fresh batch of goodies.

One of the women scooped out pills from the bowls and placed them on the mirror, separating them by color. She began crushing and chopping them with a credit card until she'd formed multiple rows of neat, nail-sized lines. Buoyed by the prospect of killing more brain cells, the other party guests slurred along with a newish song by an Australian rapper that had just come on the stereo, with varying degrees of success.

James flitted back and forth from the kitchen, replacing empty bottles and glasses, distributing cigarettes, his forehead glistening, his perma-grin unbreakable.

When Ryan finished his beer, another appeared in front of him, then another. The woman who had taken on the role of drug dispenser wiped her hands on the slinky black dress that was riding up her orange-tinted thighs, revealing craters of cellulite and veins that would have once made Ryan salivate but now only caused him to shudder. Her drooping eyes found his and she motioned for him to come over to the mirror, to take his place in the giddy line that had formed, behind the guy with the ponytail. He smiled back, weakly, and shook his head. She shrugged and bent over, took a long snort.

Though a pleasant, hoppy numbness had begun to seep through him, allowing him to reach a level of relaxation he hadn't felt in weeks, he knew he shouldn't take it to the next level; he had to remain focused on the next day, to not lose the sense of urgency that gnawed at him, the image of Jennifer that had been grafted onto his brain.

At one point he noticed that James had been absent from the room for a few minutes. Ryan decided he would wait until his host returned, thank him for the beers, and crash in the room where he'd left his backpack, if it wasn't already being used as a fuck pad by more of James's esteemed colleagues. But his game plan was interrupted by the sudden coldness of metal against his forearm—a stainless-steel flask that was being offered to him by the grizzled hippie on the ledge next to him who had apparently just woken up.

"Don't bother with that stuff," the man rasped, his wet, cracked lips sputtering like a dying lawn mower as he motioned at the human vacuum cleaner convention across the room. "This is the real deal. All you'll ever need. Take off the edge you've got going there, son."

Ryan nodded, took the flask, and twisted off the cap. A small nightcap wouldn't be the worst idea; it might make him drowsy enough to block out the earsplitting racket that would probably be going strong for the next few hours. He'd done it plenty of times in the creaky, boisterous boardinghouse where he'd lived for the two years before he was turned, cradling quart bottles in the oil-lit gloom.

He tilted his head back and lifted the flask to his lips. The liquor came out much faster than he'd anticipated, a skull-bruising gush of fire that burned through his throat and sent his vestibular system into a spasm of vertigo. He coughed, drooled, tried not to gag, lowered his head between his knees as the laughter and music swirled and drowned him in a suddenly deafening sea of noise. When he finally lifted his head, tears streaming down his face, the hippie was massaging his shoulders and saying something he couldn't hear and everyone else was smirking, their expressions warped and ghoulish, applauding, but at a strange distance—he was outside himself.

The creatures on the couch beckoned to him, made a space for him, and he watched his body get up and join them, watched someone pass him an unmarked bottle of amber liquid, then a joint, then a burst of sour air and he was fully transported to a place beyond caring, beyond meaning and sound, that only existed as a series of increasingly disjointed snapshots—James materializing and holding him in a long bear hug, whispering something under his hot and spit-infused breath, another beer in his hand, one of the women passing out next to him, foam exiting her mouth, the other two taking pictures of her with their phones, snorting more lines, the beer falling out of his hand and shattering on the carpet, the finance bros dragging the passed-out woman somewhere else, another beer, the hippie straddling the ledge, cackling and flinging the flask and jumping out of the window and into the darkness, the girls who had been making out in the hallway earlier suddenly pressed against him on either side, flushed and sweaty, hands creeping up his thighs, laughing, licking, pleading, bending over the mirror while someone held a straw in his nostril, staring at a face he no longer recognized, a face that didn't want to be recognized, then no face at all.

He tried to scrunch the sun from his eyes, to return to the soothing blackness where nothing mattered, but it was impossible.

He was lying on the folded-out sofa in James's extra room. Of that much he could be certain, unlike the location of his shirt and backpack, and the last three or four or five hours of the previous night. He tried covering his face with his arm, and when that didn't work he flailed blindly at the curtain of the window that he hoped was an arm's length away, but all he came up with was a fistful of pillow-soft breast and a goose-pimpled areola.

Ryan pulled his hand back, opened his eyes, and was greeted by the smirking, squinting face of the girl with the shaved head and nose ring. "All night Isabel and I basically throw ourselves at you," she murmured, turning onto her back and rolling her eyes, "and now you want to play. Go figure." She reached for a crumpled bedsheet that was wrapped around her stomach, just below her pale, freckled chest, and began to pull it down over her slender waist, revealing a bellybutton piercing and several small tattoos depicting geometric shapes—pyramids, disks, spheres in chain formations.

"Oh shit," Ryan muttered as he jumped off the couch, head spinning, stomach twisted, trying to reconstruct the sequence of events that had led him to the situation he was currently in—naked except for the oversized Batman boxers James had lent him—and coming up with nothing. "Shit, shit, shit," he kept repeating while the girl rolled her eyes and pulled the sheet over herself, up to her neck.

"What time is it?" Ryan mumbled, half to himself. He scanned the room, past the dozens of half-empty beer bottles perched on a wooden desk, dresser, and bookshelf, many with cigarettes swimming in the leftover swill, a torn-open bag of Cheetos on the carpet, an old macroeconomics textbook on a bed stand, covered with powdery residue and several rolled-up dollar bills. The clothes he'd been wearing were lying in a heap in the corner of the room nearest the couch, accompanied by a red silk bra that he assumed was the girl's.

"Can you toss me that?" she asked. She had rolled onto her stomach and was watching Ryan intently. "We've probably got an hour or so to kill before you have to go and make things right with your girlfriend or whoever it was you kept gushing so, um, eloquently about last night. I promise I won't tell. It'll be our little secret."

Ryan picked up the bra and threw it at her. He extracted the tennis shoes from the clothes that smelled of a gag-inducing combination of sweat, spilled booze, and vomit. He walked across the room to an open closet and pulled out a pair of jeans and a light blue T-shirt that looked, surprisingly, like they'd fit him reasonably well. Probably leftovers from when James's metabolism could make up for his total lack of control. He put the clothes on and lifted his sunglasses, baseball cap, and backpack from the middle of the floor where they had been lying.

He glanced into the mirror that hung above the dresser. His skin was pale and splotchy, his eyes were ringed by black circles, and his lips were rough and cracking. The stubble that had covered his cheeks and neck had grown into an unkempt rat's nest of a beard. He looked away, bracing himself as a rush of nausea tore through his gut.

"Tell James that I thank him for his hospitality," he said after recovering enough. He headed for the room's partially open entryway.

"Tell Jennifer I say hi," the girl called out, coyly. Her laughter was cut short as Ryan slammed the door behind him.

19

Ryan washed down the last bite of the greasy, life-giving slice with the Mountain Dew he'd bought with it at a pizza place on Columbus Avenue, and walked into Morningside Park at its southwest entrance on 110th Street.

Located just to the north of the much larger Central Park, Morningside stretched for fifteen heavily wooded blocks along the ridge that separated Columbia University and the neighborhood surrounding it with low-lying West Harlem. As Ryan walked down several sets of wide, multi-tiered stone stairs bordered by dome-capped stone pillars, he felt a pang of anxiety. Derrick hadn't given him an exact place in the park to meet and he was already running twenty minutes late. At the bottom of the stairs the paved walkway split in two. To the right, it meandered downhill and eventually curved along a basketball court and a pair of softball fields where the only signs of movement came from a couple of kids kicking a soccer ball and a shirtless man sitting in one of the fenced-in dugouts next to a shopping cart filled with empty bottles and aluminum cans, rubbing his belly and howling the lyrics to Aretha Franklin's "Baby I Love You." To the right the path took an uphill slant, running parallel with the ridgeline, bending slightly for a hundred yards or so until it came to an ascending set of stairs that were partially obscured by trees.

After a few seconds of nervous deliberation, Ryan decided to head toward the stairs. From a higher vantage point, it might be easier to catch a glimpse of Derrick, if he wasn't concealing himself in the denser foliage.

Ryan didn't need to search for very long. As he came around the bend just before the stairs, he almost bumped into the man he was looking for, sitting out in the open on the rock ledge that lined the path, rapidly smoking, his eyes darting in sporadic bursts. His pack was resting at his feet. He glanced at Ryan and seemed startled, as if he wasn't expecting to meet anyone. He turned away and reached for the pack of Marlboros in his lap, taking one out and lighting it with the remnants of the one he'd been smoking. He flicked the butt onto the pavement and watched it simmer until it went out.

"I get the whole hiding-in-plain-sight thing," Ryan said as he sat next to Derrick on the ledge, "but don't you think that puffing on those in a park and blatantly littering might not be the smartest course of action?"

Derrick kept staring into space, as if Ryan didn't exist. He was sweating, trembling slightly. Flakes of white body paint were peeling off his arms. His clothes were stained with an entire spectrum of crud. The façade he had created was literally crumbling in real time. Ryan wondered what had brought about the abrupt change in demeanor, but he needed to play it cool and not say anything that would freak Derrick out more than he clearly already was.

But as they sat in silence, Derrick smoking and pretending the world didn't exist around him, Ryan couldn't take it anymore. "Did you find anything from the phone?" he asked, impatiently.

"You didn't tell me about the pictures," Derrick said in a low, monotone voice that seemed on the verge of cracking.

"What pictures?"

"The ones you deleted. The girl and the guy, tied up and blindfolded. You should have told me."

Ryan tried to maintain his composure. It was too late to try to deny anything. "I didn't think they would make a difference," he said, "as far as what I needed you to do for me."

Derrick looked at Ryan for the first time since the two of them had been sitting next to each other. His lips curled into an awkward, disturbing smile. "No," he said, "you didn't think. Neither did I. And now it's over. For me at least. You may come out of this slightly less fucked if you run away now."

"What's over? What are you—"

"I had this great idea," Derrick cut him off, reaching into the top section of his pack with his cigarette-free hand. "I was going to peel back the layers of what was really going on. I was going to give the conspiracy theorists a hard-on like they'd never felt before and wake everyone else up from a five-thousand-year sleep. If I sent everything into chaos and started a revolution, if no one cared, or if something in between happened, that would be fine. I'd be okay with any outcome because at least I wouldn't have sat by and watched things continue in the direction they'd been going. I wouldn't be complicit."

He pulled out a Ziploc bag from his pack. It contained an index card with something scribbled on it, a stapled packet of standard-size papers folded in half, a small flash drive, and Ryan's phone.

"And at first it was great," Derrick continued. "The first stuff I leaked, the results were better than I expected. Shit was beginning to hit the fan at the correct velocity. But that was never the end goal. I wanted to really blow people's minds. I wanted to break Roswell and JFK, the stuff everyone talks about and already accepts to a certain extent, but I also wanted to expose the tribes, revealing not just a previously unknown subspecies, but also their political ties, the military contacts."

"Political ties? Military contacts? Where did you find that information? How do you know it's not just message-board bullshit?"

"That's not important right now. It's all in here," he said, handing the Ziploc bag to Ryan, "though you probably won't have time to read it. What was important for me was that if I wanted to blow the lid on the tribes, I needed to leave the country. If Homeland Security truly knew the extent of the information I had, if I tried to send that information through a U.S. server, I'd be killed in minutes. The data wouldn't get out there. Everything would be lost."

He paused, lit another cigarette.

"To get out of the country I needed money. Money that I'd left in the possession of our good friend James Van Doren a few months before I went off the grid. I'd researched him extensively before we made contact. A misogynist and an addict, sure, but he was unfailingly loyal to his clients, exceptionally discreet. And he seemed like the kind of guy who would get off on holding the bankroll of the most famous criminal in the world. Something he could brag about to his drug buddies when they'd be too fucked up to remember it."

Ryan nodded. That much was true. A nearly forgotten image from the previous night returned to him—pounding three tequila body shots in quick succession off one of the lesbians' sweaty, salt-crusted bellies—and he tried not to gag.

"Normally I would have had him send me the funds electronically through a series of offshore transfers. He'd done it for me plenty of times before. But the people who were going to provide my transportation this time are the kind of Luddites who only accept cash. That's why I had to come to New York. There had to be a physical paper exchange with James or one of his employees. Then I could hike north, follow the railroad tracks, disappear into the woods upstate and ultimately out of the country, eventually to Iceland where I'd made arrangements to stay.

"When I got here and contacted James, he said that I was being paranoid for refusing to come in and discuss things in his office. I'd managed to avoid getting caught when I'd leaked things in the past. Why would this time be any different? He gave me some bullshit about always having to make sure he was acting in his clients' best interests, said he would give me the cash only if I could prove to him that what I had was legitimately groundbreaking."

It made sense, Ryan said to himself. James and an investment were not easily parted. Especially one with a less-than-reputable beneficiary.

Derrick sighed. "I told him that I had proof that vampires were real. I put two or three of the pages from the packet I gave you in his mailbox. Just a taste. The next time we talked he was surprised, but not in the way I'd thought he would be. He told me he was impressed at what I'd been able to find, that he had no idea that the intelligence community had been monitoring the tribes, or that tribal organizations even existed, but he did know someone from Brooklyn who he used to give his blood to, someone who also happened to be his company's oldest private client. He said you had recently given up your immortality and needed to trace the location of a phone call. He asked if I could help. If I did, he said he'd give me an extra five percent on top of what I was already owed. I could have said no. I could have walked away. I'm carrying enough cash on me to make it to Canada and probably could have bartered my way off the continent. I should have smelled the shadiness. But I was curious. I wanted to meet you. And now I'm fucked because of it."

"I don't understand," Ryan said, his still-hungover brain doing somersaults. "What do the pictures on my phone have to do with you? How would Manhattan know anything about you, unless James . . ."

"The calls and the pictures were sent by the same number," Derrick said. "They were sent from the same residential building in the Upper East Side. East 80th Street. The address is written on a note card in the bag. I couldn't find anything remarkable about the building, but the cell phone number was registered to Van Doren and Associates."

"Meaning what?"

"Meaning," Derrick said, turning to look at Ryan for the first time, "James is somehow connected to the Manhattan tribe. He set us both up. He took the pictures, or had someone close to him do it. Based on the volume and the substance of the texts between you and 'Jennifer,' I'm assuming that there was something going on with you and the woman in the picture. But maybe it was the man, or maybe both of them. I'm not judging. Either way, it was enough for you to leave Brooklyn and your old life behind for some long-shot rescue, even though part of you knew, still knows, that both of them are long dead. Maybe it was out of guilt, maybe love, maybe a little of both. Does that sound accurate?"

It was Ryan's turn to stare dead-eyed into the space in front of them. He felt worse than sick. Gutted.

"James knew you would get in touch with him. He dangled you in front of me and I took the bait. He might have had one of his employees, or someone from the Manhattan tribe, follow you into Central Park yesterday, even though at the time I didn't detect anything. We shook hands. Maybe that would have been enough to glean my scent from you. Regardless, they know where I am, or have a very good idea. Did you make direct contact with anyone after you left the park last night?"

"There was a party at James's apartment."

Derrick nodded, as if Ryan's statement had confirmed something that he'd already suspected. "It's too late to run," he said softly. There was a long silence while he fished in his pocket for another cigarette. "Or I could be wrong about all of this. About you. Maybe you're just here to kill me. In which case, I wish you wouldn't have let me waste so much time babbling on about things."

"I'm not going to kill you. I'm going to kill James. Then I'm going to kill everyone else."

"Which makes perfect sense. Revenge would be an appropriate response, regardless of the likelihood of you actually being able to pull it off. What doesn't make sense is why you're still alive if they were just using you to get to me. Unless you're Arthur Harker, or his heir."

Ryan flinched noticeably at the name. He turned and Derrick was studying him intently. The hacktivist looked curious but oddly relaxed, as calm as Ryan had ever seen him, in videos or in person. Like he'd gone through all the stages of grieving and finally come to terms with an inescapable reality.

"What if I were?" Ryan asked.

Derrick flashed a sad half smile. "Then we'd have to reevaluate who the bait is in this situation. What's certain is that you would clearly be the bigger catch. The information that I've obtained is nothing compared to what you allegedly have."

"And what is that?"

"The documents are vague about it, like whoever wrote them wasn't exactly sure. Whatever it is, it's beyond ancient. Pre-Egyptian. Some kind of artifact that might also be an energy source. The Manhattan tribe seems to want it primarily for experimentation on their own people, to see how it reacts when it's combined with their DNA. To what end, I'm not sure. Other organizations, contractors, institutions, and private individuals—both obscure and well known—are also very interested. That's all I know. Any of this ring a bell?"

Ryan debated for a moment about what he would say. The only

thought that kept running through his mind was that both of them were already fucked beyond hope.

"It doesn't matter anymore," Derrick said, echoing Ryan's inner monologue. "You need to leave. Get out of the city. Upload the flash drive. Do it now, while I'm giving you a window."

While Derrick was talking, a tall, thin woman wearing sunglasses, black tights, and a pink tank top sprinted by them on the path, her long blond ponytail flapping in time with her steps. Ryan watched her without much consideration as she leapt effortlessly up the stairs, two at once. She paused when she reached the top, inhaled quickly a few times, turned around, and headed back down. At the bottom she slowed to a trot, then a walk, hands on her hips, breathing hard.

Derrick finished speaking and lit another cigarette, the same terrifying look of resolute calmness washing over his face. As Ryan slung his backpack over his shoulders, getting ready to bolt as far away as possible from the park to figure out how he would confront James and then retrieve the statue from the Williamsburg Bridge, the jogger pulled up even with them on the path, seeming to notice them for the first time.

She stared for a moment as if she was trying to decide something, pursed her thin lips together, and crinkled her pinched nose, which looked like it had had some major work done on it. She reached into the fanny pack that was strapped around her waist and took out what looked like a loose cigarillo.

"Probably defeats the whole purpose of everything I've done today," she said as she approached the rock wall, smiling at Derrick, making the do-you-have-a-light gesture. "But when you've got a craving, there's not much you can do, am I right?"

Her voice was cheerful, a chirpy East Coast non-accent, outwardly indistinguishable from the average New York twenty-something. But there was something about it that Ryan found soothing, like a good memory from a simpler time.

Derrick fumbled in his pockets for a lighter, then stopped abruptly. He removed his hands from his pants and placed them on the rock wall on either side of him, bracing himself against the tremors that had started to surge through him, stronger than before. The cigarette he'd been smoking fell from his lips and landed on his backpack, burning a hole into the fabric. His eyes widened as the still-smiling woman placed her cigarillo between her lips.

"It's over?" he muttered in a child's frightened whisper.

"It's over," she repeated between clenched teeth.

She moved closer to Derrick until she was standing directly over him. Ryan noticed that she wasn't sweating. She had no body odor and her skin was taut, so devoid of moisture that it looked like she didn't have pores. The object in her mouth wasn't any kind of smoking apparatus Ryan had seen. It looked like a beige plastic tube with a hollowed-out tip.

Ryan suddenly realized that Derrick hadn't been chain-smoking because he'd been nervous. The smoke that he inhaled would circulate through his lungs, accumulating microscopic particles of blood and mucus that would be expelled into the air and travel intact, far enough so that any *Ànkëlëk-ila* in the area who had been familiarized with his scent would know exactly where to find him.

Derrick was done hiding. He was giving himself up, drawing the Manhattan tribe to him like a homing beacon. In doing so, he *had* given Ryan a brief window to escape.

A window that was now closed.

In one swift motion, Ryan pulled Arthur's knife out from under his shirt and lunged at the woman. The blade—still sharp after however many centuries—slashed into her shoulder, deep beneath the skin. She howled in pain and recoiled, taken by surprise. But in the moment before Ryan could raise the knife a second time she leapt at him, lightning-quick, and delivered a devastating blow to his solar plexus that dislodged the weapon from his grip and sent him crumpling to the ground, gasping for air, coughing up bloody phlegm.

As he struggled to lift himself off the pavement, Ryan watched helplessly as the woman bent over Derrick, who hadn't tried to flee and who had closed his eyes and tilted his chin skyward, no longer shaking. She adjusted the tube that was still sticking out of her mouth and blew into it, expelling a fine mist that settled on Derrick's face and clothes. Whatever chemicals it contained reacted almost immediately to the areas it had come in contact with, causing

Derrick's flesh to bubble, then peel, then disintegrate into a pink liquid sludge. Ryan saw yellow globules of fat and cartilage where Derrick's jawline should have been, then slabs of charred muscle, and finally shards of bone that collapsed and shrank until there was nothing left.

Ryan tried to shimmy the backpack off his shoulders so he could pull out the gun. But before he could make any real progress the woman was on top of him, pinning him to the ground, crushing his throat with her elbow. In her other hand she held Arthur's knife, still stained with her blood.

"Where the fuck did you get this?" she growled, waving the knife two inches in front of Ryan's face.

He didn't say anything as he tried to twist out from under her, but it felt like he was being smothered by a small pile of boulders.

"It doesn't make a difference now," she said. She dropped the knife, reached into her fanny pack, and retrieved the beige tube. She put it between her lips and lowered her face until it was a foot away from Ryan's.

He closed his eyes, waiting for the warm kiss of moisture that would send him into the true darkness.

Nothing happened.

He opened his eyes and looked up. The woman was studying him perplexedly, sniffing the air around his face. He could see the outline of her eyes widening behind her sunglasses as a flicker of recognition crossed her face.

Cringing in pain from—he assumed—the knife wound, she grunted disgustedly and pushed herself off him. She paused for another brief moment, then shot off down the path and out of sight.

After a long coughing spell, Ryan forced himself into a sitting position. When he finally was able to stand, he gathered up his backpack and the knife and stared at the steaming, fluorescent puddle that had once been Derrick and his hiking bag.

20

The first thing Ryan noticed after opening the unlocked door to James's apartment was the smell, or the lack of it. The rank post-party stench that he had woken up to had been replaced by a sterile hospital nonscent, the faintest chemical whiff.

He entered the hallway, gun cocked and pointed, and peered into the kitchen. The beer bottles, the dirty dishware, and the Campus Girls USA calendar James had tacked to the wall were gone. The cabinets were closed and the countertop and appliances were spotless, buffed clean. The room where he had slept and James's bedroom were both empty, with glistening hardwood floors and walls that looked freshly painted. Nothing in the closets. The armchair was the only piece of furniture left in the living room. It had been moved from its central location to a corner by the now-shuttered French windows.

Ryan lowered his gun, but his adrenaline remained as high as it had been since he'd sprinted back from the park. It would have been far less disturbing if the place had been totally ransacked, he thought, if all of James's stuff had been lying out on the floor, if the wall hangings and his desktop computer had been shattered and the kitchen drawers turned out. This was something else entirely, the cherry on top of the mindfuck sundae.

It looked as if James had never existed.

After making another fruitless sweep of the apartment, Ryan headed into the kitchen and peered out a narrow window that over-looked a vacant courtyard and lifeless adjacent building. He emptied his backpack's contents onto the countertop. Setting aside the items he'd brought with him from Brooklyn and the flash drive, he sifted quickly through the rest of the stuff in the plastic bag that Derrick had given him until he found a folded index card that had mixed in with the other papers. One line of text had been scribbled with a black ballpoint pen: *17 East 80th Street.*

Not wanting to spend a second longer than he had to in a place that was making him more and more uneasy, he attached the silencer to the gun, checked the magazine, and stuffed everything else into the backpack. He slipped silently into the hallway and out through the front door he'd left ajar, gun pressed inconspicuously against his side in case one of James's neighbors happened to pass by. It turned out to be a needless gesture; the floor was as empty as the apartment.

Part of Ryan wanted to remove the silencer and spray a few rounds into the wall, to wake the building from the silence that was strangling it, to jump-start whatever was coming to him, but ultimately he knew it wouldn't make a difference. This wasn't the calm before anything.

He was already in the storm.

21

"Come on," Ryan muttered under his breath as he paced along the sidewalk, repeating the words for the hundredth time, not quite sure of the response he was expecting.

He paused the next time he was directly across from the building—a five-story, gray-stone Georgian Revival embellished with ornate windows and Greek columns flanking the front entrance. While it was individually striking, the structure was just one of a hundred nearly identical ones in the ultra-posh Upper East Side enclave of residential buildings that formed the Metropolitan Museum Historic District, a stone's throw from the museum that gave the neighborhood its name.

Ryan didn't care about late-nineteenth-century architectural styles or old-money recluses wasting away in their crumbling gilded chambers. He was here to end the convoluted string of events that had started with a picture message, and to terminate as many of the lives of those who were responsible as he could.

In spite of the rage that had guided his most recent actions and was still surging through his bloodstream, he knew that it wouldn't be an ideal strategy to simply walk up to the door, break into the building, and start firing. But in the half hour or so that he'd been pacing the block, no alternative had presented itself.

He was done waiting. It was now or never.

"Fuck it," he said, loud enough that a postal worker pushing a letter cart stopped and stared at him curiously for a moment before continuing on her route. He waited for her to disappear into the lobby of a nearby podiatrist's office before turning his attention back to building number 17.

Just as he was about to cross the street, a metal door that had been built into the ground just to the right of the building's front entrance flew open. Ryan reached under his shirt and gripped his gun as a barrel-chested Hispanic man in a navy-blue superintendent's jumpsuit emerged from an unseen flight of stairs carrying a large cardboard box. He walked to a nearby pile of similar boxes and black plastic trash bags near the edge of the sidewalk and dropped it on top of them. He turned and went back down the stairs, leaving the door open to what Ryan assumed was a service entrance to the basement.

He strode quickly into the street, still gripping the gun under his shirt, and nearly collided with a passing taxi. The driver slammed on the brakes and let out a loud string of curses. Ryan ignored him, stepped over the curb and around the trash pile, paused, and looked down to see where the stairs led.

The man in the jumpsuit reemerged, carrying another box. He walked to the trash pile, then dumped the box and turned left on the sidewalk, heading toward Madison Avenue. Ryan watched him until he disappeared around the corner at the end of the block, then turned and approached the top of the stairs. They led to a narrow, concrete room lit by a series of partially burned-out halogen bulbs that ran along the ceiling. Dozens of metallic pipes crisscrossed the lights and the chipped and scarred walls that were covered in dust, grime, and numerous scribbles of graffiti.

Ryan drew the gun and headed down the stairs. The space was larger than it had seemed from the street, maybe twenty feet long with an eight- or nine-foot ceiling. There were dozens of cardboard boxes on the floor, lining the walls, filled with what looked like a random assortment of clothing, shoes, and lingerie. At the far end was an open doorway that led to a smaller, darker corridor. Three men stood in the passage. Two of them, facing away from Ryan, wore the same superintendent jumpsuits, and the other was dressed in a charcoal suit and a black shirt, the first few buttons undone to reveal a bronzed, hairless chest. His short black hair was gelled into an intentionally chunky faux-hawk and he was holding an iPad that the three of them were staring at, their faces illuminated, nodding and speaking in low voices.

Ryan recognized the man in the suit immediately. It was Nicki's bodyguard-slash-lover, the young man he'd seen fucking her when he'd approached her building for the last time.

Without hesitating, Ryan fired a series of shots. The first one missed but the second ripped through the temple of one of the jump-suited men, spraying the wall behind him with bits of bone and gleaming brain matter. The third bullet found its way into the torso of the other superintendent. He dabbed at the singed fabric around the hole in his gut, then looked up, confused. Ryan finished him off with a direct hit through the trachea. The man's eyes rolled back as he slumped to the ground, spewing fluid from his mouth and the hollow tangle of muscle where his neck had been.

The man in the suit hadn't flinched. He kept staring at Ryan with a clinical, emotionless interest as he used his shirt sleeve to wipe his colleagues' blood from his face and the iPad screen.

Ryan knew that if the man was a dead warrior, the bullets prob-ably wouldn't kill him. But a head shot would debilitate him, or at least slow him down enough for Ryan to try to do some serious damage with the knife.

The man took a step forward. Ryan aimed methodically and fired a shot that he thought would end up somewhere between the man's eyebrows, but the bullet didn't seem to reach its target. The man paused—not in shock or pain—his face unblemished, and scrunched up his nose as if he were trying to wrangle out an unco-operative sneeze. The wall behind him was free of any impact cra-ters from an errant blast.

That was because, Ryan realized, he hadn't missed. The skin that had absorbed the bullet had healed itself at a seemingly impos-sible rate, quicker than his eyes could process. He watched as the man gave a loud snort, spit out a square of metal that looked like it had gone through a miniature trash compactor, and smiled at him.

Ryan stood frozen by what he was seeing, unable to raise the gun for a second attempt or to reach in his pocket for the knife. Unable to process the sound of someone rushing down the stairs behind him.

Until it was too late.

22

The longer Ryan remained hanging, immobile in complete darkness, the less relevant the concept of time became. He subsisted only in terms of what he could feel was happening inside of him, the inevitable corrosion that he had tried to forget about, tried to contain, tried to reason out of existence.

The disease that had finally returned to claim him.

His coughing spells became more frequent and lung-racking, dousing the hood around his head with gobs of blood and phlegm. He could feel the lymph nodes in his neck swelling, his skin turning clammy and feverish, his throat muscles beginning to constrict. Sparks of light appeared in the corner of his vision, then flickered faster, then danced in the space between his face and the hood, then spun and clawed into eyes that might have been open or shut tightly; he couldn't be sure.

At some point he heard a door open, the sound of a muffled voice, voices. Then a series of loud grunts and the scrape of fabric. Someone was moving the superintendents' bodies. After another long period of silence, in which the room's temperature seemed to rise exponentially and sweat started to flow freely from his trembling, nearly dislocated limbs, a latex-gloved hand gripped the base of his neck, then lifted the bottom of the hood above his mouth. The opening of a plastic bottle was placed against his mouth, angled so that the cool water inside it engulfed his parched throat and swollen tongue and flowed down his neck and chest, mingling with the salty discharge from his pores. He bit down on the bottle, suckled on it until it was ripped away from him. Before he could close his mouth, a metal spoon containing a flavorless, peanut-butter-like paste was forced into it, then removed. Then the gloved hand clamped over his mouth and stayed there until he swallowed the substance. Then the hood was shoved back down into its original position and Ryan coughed hard, intentionally, trying to force himself to vomit, but nothing came up. He was left alone with the metallic hum of the pipes and the gurgling of his shrunken belly.

Much later he heard voices that seemed distant, as if carried on a far-flung breeze. There were shards of light beyond the hood, but these were intense and came in short, irregular bursts. He thought they might have been camera flashes, or a malfunction with the room's lighting, or the onset of a massive seizure.

But instead of being instantly torn apart from within, he felt the fullness in his throat trickle down in slow motion through his limbs, bringing with it a putrefying heat. Then a dizziness like when he was a child and would intentionally spin in a circle until falling to the ground, except now he was trying to stop himself, to fight the downward plummet.

Then a powerful liquid rush coursed through him and he was submerged in a milk-thick sludge, paralyzed, a vision flashing in his brain: an image of a naked figure at the bottom of a pool lying prone, dead, his own self dying.

Then there was only blackness.

He was thrust back into half consciousness—had he ever been awake at all?—by the voices. This time they were louder, angry, close enough for him to smell stale breath and body odor. And there was something fouler pooling around his suspended toes, something that had probably been of his own making.

He heard a few more indecipherable snippets of what sounded like an argument, then a dull thud, a shout, the squeak and scuffle of footwear, a childlike scream cut short. Another thud. A splash.

After a few moments of silence, the bungee cord connecting his hands was severed and Ryan fell to the ground, flailing in a warm puddle of sludge. His arms were blood-drained and useless, his legs soft rubber. Before he could try to gather the strength to move, someone threw a blanket over him, rolled him around in it until he was completely covered, lifted him off the ground as if he weighed little more than the filth he was caked in, and hoisted him horizontally onto a rock-hard shoulder blade. The hood fell off as they started to move and Ryan caught a brief glimpse of a freshly mutilated body slumped against the wall in a sitting position, its torso and neck split perfectly down the middle so that its ribs looked like the teeth of a Venus flytrap.

Then they were speeding up the stairs and into blinding sunlight and Ryan was tossed into the backseat of a silver SUV that was idling at the curb. A door slammed behind him and the vehicle sped off.

"Jesus, V, what septic tank did you drag this asshole from?" a man's voice asked from the driver's seat after a long, disgusted groan. "You're paying for the cleaning. I'm talking full detailing, upholstery, all that shit."

"Shut the fuck up, Karl," a woman in the passenger seat muttered.

Ryan struggled to break free of the blanket. He lifted his head from where it had been scrunched against the elbow rest of the rear driver's-side seat and looked at her. It was the blond jogger from Morningside Park, the woman who had melted Derrick. She was wearing a white V-neck T-shirt covered in mud and rust-colored stains. Her wavy hair was ponytail-free. The black Ray-Bans she had been wearing the previous day were perched above her forehead. She turned and looked at him with piercing hazel eyes that looked like something out of a once-recurring but nearly forgotten dream.

"Stay down, Charlie," she said in a reassuring voice. "Just try to relax."

No one had called him that since 1975. As far as he was concerned, Charles Vincent had died the day he sold the Brooklyn Heights apartment and bought the duplex in Borough Park, using fresh sets of documents that Frank and James's father had been able to fish up for him.

He kept staring at the woman. The structure of her cheeks was wrong, uneven. The lips were unnaturally full and the nose was a pencil-point disaster. But the hair was right. And the eyes were un-mistakable.

"Vanessa?"

She nodded.

The driver, in his midfifties and vaguely Mediterranean-looking with thick salt-and-pepper hair and a finely trimmed beard, rolled his eyes in the rearview mirror and gave another groan. "This is fucking stupid," he said.

Vanessa glared at him, twirling something between her fingers. The driver mumbled something Ryan couldn't hear and turned to focus on the road.

She lifted Arthur's dagger—coated in a thick layer of fresh blood—and licked it clean.

23

"This is completely unnecessary," Ryan said, flinching as Karl forced the needle into the vein in his left forearm. He eyed the IV bag—sitting nearby on top of a giant cat scratch post—that looked exactly like the one he'd been hooked up to in James's apartment.

He shuddered.

Karl ignored him and went back to work prepping the portable ultrasound equipment. He attached the wandlike device via USB cord to a laptop that he'd positioned on a massive cherrywood table. The gorgeous antique formed the centerpiece of the spacious apartment's kitchen-slash-dining area, where Ryan was lying on a hospital-style cot, shirtless and scrubbed clean.

Vanessa was seated on a black leather love seat on the opposite end of the large, high-ceilinged space whose walls were covered by bookshelves, swirling primary-colored abstract oil paintings, a row of antique kabuki-style theater masks, and a spiral staircase leading to an unseen upper level. She was wrapped in a white bathrobe, her hair limp from the shower she'd just taken. She looked up from the MacBook in her lap and shook her head. "It's just saline," she said. "If you could see how you look right now you wouldn't be arguing."

Ryan grunted, lay back, and stared at the cream-colored stucco ceiling, still trying to process the situation he'd found himself in. He went over what he already knew. Vanessa, his first real fling, had been turned. How long ago he couldn't be sure. What was clear was that she had carved up her face to the point of being nearly unrecognizable. She had a large enough role within the Manhattan tribe to be tasked with killing Derrick Rhodes, or maybe she'd taken the initiative herself. But why had she spared "Charlie," someone she knew for little more than a month in the 1970s? Nostalgia? She didn't seem surprised or shocked that he hadn't aged. Maybe she somehow knew about his lineage. Maybe she was a social climber and he was her ticket to the upper echelon of Manhattan tribal society.

But then why wouldn't she have taken him directly to her superiors? And why would she have this Karl guy pumping him with fluids and checking his vitals and internal organs? Who was Karl? He was human; that much had been made obvious when he'd struggled mightily trying to pull Ryan out of the SUV in the parking garage under Vanessa's building. He clearly had at least some medical training. Maybe Karl was Vanessa's donor, or maybe it was something more, closer to what Frank had had with Raj and Arianna.

Whatever the case was, Ryan didn't like the way the man stared at him, like Ryan was some kind of living cadaver. The way Karl had been pawing and prodding at him, timid yet eager, as if he couldn't wait to dig deeper and was only waiting for Vanessa's command to do so. The way the rotten breath seeped from his crooked sneer.

"You have a lot of questions," Vanessa said, making one of the most obvious statements of all time, Ryan thought. "And you're nervous. Your heart rate is going through the roof. Don't worry, it's not making me hungry. I find A positive to be absolutely vile."

Ryan had been turned before blood types became common knowledge. He'd never known what his had been. She was right about A positive—it tasted like fermented chalk.

He struggled to sit up. "Thanks for the confidence booster," he said after a minor coughing spell.

There was so much he wanted to find out, but in his still-groggy, adrenaline-addled state, he was drawn to the most glaring elephant in the room, one that was staring directly back at him. He was too far gone to be concerned with tactfulness. "I do have a few questions," he said. "Let's start with your face. What the hell happened?"

Vanessa shrugged. "I kept running into people I'd known from before I was turned. People who knew my parents and knew that they were looking for me. I was sick of having to pretend not to rec-ognize them or to shut them up for good, of having to eat people whose blood I didn't even like. I had to become someone else en-tirely, not just on the inside."

She stood up and walked over to a large wood-framed mirror hanging between two bookcases. She gently touched her trout lips, ran her fingers across her ruined plastic cheeks. She sighed. "It was the early eighties," she continued. "Karl is a great surgeon, was back then, but we were breaking new ground. No one understood the biology, how certain chemicals would react with the skin and tis-sues of someone who'd been turned. There was a period of trial and error. More than a few errors. But I'm okay with it. The change was what I needed."

Over the years, Ryan had occasionally fantasized about what it would be like to see Vanessa again, how she would look, what they would say to each other. But this wasn't a gracefully aged version of the fresh-faced poet-in-training who'd left him standing on the Bedford Avenue subway platform. This was something else entirely, far creepier than he could have ever imagined.

He started to ask her what she planned on doing with him but was interrupted by a series of muffled thuds and what sounded like moaning coming from somewhere nearby. Ryan looked across the room, opposite from where Vanessa was standing, past a leather couch and glass coffee table, and noticed, for the first time, a large but unassuming door in an undecorated corner. It was painted the same shade of banana yellow as the apartment's walls but was made of a different material, possibly metal. After another few seconds of louder pounding and sobbing noises, it became obvious that something was on the other side, trying to force its way into the apartment.

Vanessa turned and stared at the door. She sighed knowingly, as if she'd forgotten some basic part of her daily routine, like checking the mail or taking out the trash. "I have a newborn," she said, "whom I turned last week. And who's apparently hungry again."

Ryan shot up into a sitting position, nearly tearing the needle from his arm, his fight-or-flight response kicking in hard. He knew too well what a newborn was capable of. Even if his blood type was inferior, its appetite wouldn't allow it to discriminate.

Karl looked up from his laptop and glared disapprovingly, like Ryan was nothing more than an ignorant, misbehaving child.

"It's all right," Vanessa said, a grin creeping across her formerly serious face. "The chamber's solid concrete, half a foot thick, and the walls are reinforced with another quarter inch of steel. It was built to hold even the most rambunctious toddler, among other things. Though I never planned on becoming a mother so soon. But that's another story."

She turned and walked over to the spiral staircase that led to a loft area that Ryan couldn't quite see, his view blocked by a row of vaguely nautical hanging lights that formed the border between the kitchen and the living room. She paused at the bottom of the stairs. "We have a lot to talk about," she said, "but right now I need to go out and wrangle up some dinner for me and my, uh, progeny. In the meantime, let Karl take care of you, do a few more tests, figure out if there's anything more we can do for you. I'll see you both when I get back."

"Yes, master," Karl mumbled in a faux-dramatic, and possibly faux-Transylvanian, accent.

As Vanessa walked up the stairs, Ryan tried to tell her that he'd be fine to leave on his own, tried to ask her where his backpack was, tried to tell Karl—who was dutifully slathering an ultrasound wand with what looked like Vaseline—to fuck off. But he couldn't. He found that his body had been overtaken by a powerful fatigue that made it almost impossible to speak or to move. Ryan had a sinking feeling that whatever was being pumped into his bloodstream wasn't just saline, but the apprehension was brief, quickly replaced by a synthetic euphoria. He noticed that his limbs were pain-free and the coughing had stopped. The weight of the last few days—James's betrayal, the guilt about Jennifer, the guy from the Manhattan tribe who'd absorbed the head shot like it was nothing, the shock of seeing Vanessa—seemed to lift away from him, leaving him floating untethered on a zephyr, pushing him further and further away from himself, from the memories that now seemed like they were nothing more than scenes from a sad, half-forgotten movie about someone else.

Karl loomed over the cot, pressed the slime-covered wand

against Ryan's chest, and started moving it around, humming what sounded like the chorus to Fleetwood Mac's "Go Your Own Way." The pounding noises behind the metal door grew louder and became more violent, interspersed with bloodcurdling shrieks.

Ryan smiled and closed his eyes.

He didn't care about any of it.

24

Vanessa watched Ryan take a bite of the tuna melt he'd ordered with the slightest hint of envy flitting across her face.

"I hated you for so long," she said, pretending to pick at the side salad on the plate in front of her.

They were sitting at a table at the Grey Dog, a small eatery and coffeehouse on the corner of Bedford Street and Carmine Street in the West Village, a short walk from Vanessa's apartment on Sullivan Street. A walk they'd taken casually, as if Vanessa were totally unconcerned about the incident on East 80th Street, a sequence of events that was still mostly unclear to Ryan.

He was wearing a red St. John's hoodie and a pair of brown slacks that he'd found neatly folded on Vanessa's dining table when he'd woken up a couple of hours before, needle-less, on the cot. The contents of his backpack—the extra magazines for his gun, his phone, the Ziploc bag, the flash drive—had been spread out next to the clothes, along with Arthur's freshly cleaned knife and a sonogram printout of a pair of lungs.

The tumors were obvious, even to an untrained eye. Circular black splotches so numerous that the images looked like they could have been black-and-white close-ups of a leopard's hide. Looking at them, Ryan had felt almost nothing. They were simply confirmation of what he'd already felt happening inside himself before he'd been turned; calling it cancer didn't change the fact that he was dying.

"I got off the subway at Union Square," Vanessa continued, putting down her fork and absentmindedly tugging at the strands of her hair that were draped over her shoulders and the front of her black tank top. "I walked around for a while but I didn't know where to go. I thought about going back to you in Brooklyn, thought about taking the bus to Trenton and hitching it to my parents' place, thought about a dozen other options, but none of them felt right. I was sitting on a bench somewhere near Grand Central a few hours later, having a coffee when this guy came up to me. He was young, dressed in all black, ear pierced, a weirdly attractive cross between Paul Newman and Sid Vicious."

"You always were good at attracting the dangerous ones," Ryan said, not entirely sure if he was trying to be funny.

Vanessa chuckled dryly. "This guy—he said his name was Philip—approached me, fed me some lines about how I was like nothing he'd ever seen before, begged me to let him buy me dinner. I was in no position to refuse a free meal. Come to find out, he was a blood-eater, and he happened to be in the process of finding someone to turn."

"*Blood-eater?*" Ryan scoffed. "Is that what you call yourselves?"

"Among other things," she replied. "Why, what's wrong with that?"

"It's . . . I don't know, don't you think it's a little cheesy?"

Vanessa shrugged, mildly annoyed. "At least it's accurate, better than misappropriating and mangling a sacred but unpronounceable Native American word. Anyways, back to Philip. I later found out that the reason he had been drawn to me was that he smelled you on the clothes I was wearing, on my skin, knew that I'd recently been with one of his own kind. It made him curious. He had a million other options, but he chose me. And so here I am today. Mostly because of you."

"I'm really sorry?" Ryan mumbled after a few seconds, not knowing what else to say.

Vanessa reached across the table and placed her hand on Ryan's. "I'm over it," she said reassuringly. "I have been for years and years. It makes total sense why you didn't tell me who you were. I was just some idiot girl who you felt bad for and let shack up with you for a couple weeks. And even if you had told me, I definitely wouldn't have believed you."

"You aren't—*weren't*—just an idiot girl."

She snorted, rolled her eyes. "That's probably what you say to all of your conquests," she said sardonically. "You're right, though, I'm not, not anymore. It took six months of living with Philip, or Martin, or Oswald, whatever the hell his original Dutch name was, to beat the stupid out of me. Literally. He didn't want to raise a scared and confused child. He'd only procreated because the Committee had voted on it, had forced it on him for being a generally deviant fuck-up for three-hundred-plus years. Maybe they thought parenthood would change him. But the only thing he wanted from me—the only thing he ever wanted—was another submissive plaything that he could control. But I was stronger than the Vietnamese and Ukrainian girls he'd buy and ruin in a couple days. He fed me on their scraps, kept me locked in a titanium-reinforced cage on the top floor of his brownstone, naked, only brought me out when he wanted to try something that would have knocked out or killed a human too quickly. A baseball bat insertion, a high-voltage livestock prod. One week that stands out was when he got his hands on a few medieval devices after they'd been exhibited at the Met or somewhere. His favorite was something called an Iron Spider. Do you know what it feels like to have to regrow an entirely new set of breast tissue that's been torn off from the inside?"

Ryan winced in secondhand pain. "I was shot twice, but . . ." he said, trailing off. He put down his fork. His appetite was completely gone.

"But I healed fast," Vanessa continued, her voice resolute, unshaking. "Always have. Or at least faster than he expected. One night he'd left me on the floor for a few minutes while he sat in a chair, facing away, studying the flesh he'd pulled from my back, rubbing it between his fingers, rubbing it against his face. I grabbed the wire that he'd left near me in his haste to touch the skin he'd taken, the one he always used on me when I refused to play. It was three feet long, made of a flexible metal, the middle two feet coated in the same chemical you saw me spray on Derrick Rhodes. Real nasty shit. I crawled behind my maker, wrapped the wire around his neck while he was still drunk on torture, before he knew what was going on. It was over fast. No matter how old you are or how fast you can heal, no one's coming back without a head. I thought I was done, that when the Committee had been informed of what happened, I'd be the next to die. But when they found me and brought me in, it was like I was some kind of minor hero. Apparently my maker's, uh, appetites were drawing the wrong kind of attention and it wasn't like he was from one of the big families. If I hadn't taken him out, someone else would have. They respected what I'd done, trained me to do more of the same."

"The Committee?" Ryan whispered, lowering his voice as a group of stylishly scruffy twentysomethings walked by, laughing and speaking loudly in what sounded like French. "Should we even be talking about any of this here?"

"Relax," Vanessa said, suddenly irritated. "I'd smell it if something wasn't right. You're safe with me. That should be obvious."

Ryan immediately regretted questioning her judgment. If there was anyone to fear in the restaurant, it was the bona fide killer sitting across from him. "Sorry," he said. "This is just a lot to take in."

"Is it?" she asked. "It couldn't have been that different for you in Brooklyn? You had to have some kind of hierarchy, a governing body, tribal elders."

"Until a week ago, and for the last sixty years, there were only six of us left. One is older than the rest, but I've never considered him an authority. There were times when I'd go a year or more without seeing any of the others."

Vanessa's eyes widened in surprise. "Six?" she repeated in disbelief. "So, uh, you just kind of did whatever you wanted, no accountability?"

"Pretty much. As long as we kept a collectively low profile, there were no problems with keeping to ourselves. And all of us did, for the most part."

"Wow," she said, staring at Ryan as if he were from another planet. "It's different here. With all the newborns, there are probably more than a hundred of us now. We're governed by the Committee, sort of like a senate without elections. It includes some of the oldest members of the tribe, definitely the most powerful. For the most part they've got last names you see every day on street signs, museums, schools, hospitals, and monuments. The presumed-dead ancestors of the people who built New York. And are still building it today. They provide the rest of us with food, housing in buildings their families' companies own, money, anonymity, security, whatever we need. In return, we always have to be ready in case they want us to do something for them, depending on your individual personality and skill set. Usually it's small stuff, grunt work. Drive one of the higher-ups somewhere, transport a package or documents, oversee production at one of the food-processing facilities. Because of my accelerated healing and speed, quote-unquote antisocial tendencies, and what they considered a penchant for assassination, they decided to train me—firearms, jujitsu, Muay Thai, all that shit. My job is straightforward. They give me a target. I eliminate that target, regardless of species, no questions asked. Derrick Rhodes was just the latest, one of several hundred. It's what I've done, what I've always done, until they sent out the memo last month saying that everyone who wasn't a maker yet had to turn someone immediately. Not something that I would normally ever consider, at least for a couple hundred years. I mean, I already have Karl. When I first met him, fresh into his residency at NewYork-Presbyterian, he was like a little lost puppy. Had a decent bone to play with, too, which is why I kept him around. Now he's a sad old mutt who needs me more than ever. But like I said, when the Committee contacts you, you don't ask questions."

"I guess living forever always has a price," Ryan said, though he found it nearly impossible to identify with anything that Vanessa had lived through, anything she'd had to do to survive, the totalitarian bureaucracy she was apparently forced to serve.

Vanessa reached into her alligator-skin Givenchy purse, took some cash out, and put it on the table. She made no move to get up. "There is a price," she agreed. "One that you decided wasn't worth paying anymore, even though it seems like you had it pretty good in Brooklyn. Which is why I want to know why you gave it up, why you were working with Derrick Rhodes to expose us. That is what you were doing, isn't it? Don't tell me that you'd just been walking around and decided to randomly sit down and chat with that freak. Also, what's up with the knife? I've never felt anything like it."

"The knife was my maker's," Ryan said. "You'd have to ask him about it. The only problem is that he left Brooklyn a long time ago, decades before you were born and a week after I was turned. He wasn't the best at explaining, well, anything. And now he's gone for good."

Vanessa snickered. "At least we have one thing in common," she said. "Deadbeat dads."

Ryan nodded. "As for the papers," he said, "I didn't ask for them. I didn't know who Derrick Rhodes was until a couple days ago. I was meeting with him because we had a mutual friend who said that Derrick might be able to help me track someone by hacking into my phone."

He paused. Vanessa stared at him, unblinking, her lips pursed and skeptical.

"That doesn't explain anything, does it?" he asked, rhetorically.

She shook her head slowly. She pushed her salad away and folded her palms together on the table, waiting.

Ryan took a deep breath and weighed his options. He could continue being evasive or say nothing at all, but that would only continue to piss Vanessa off, something that didn't seem advisable under even the best circumstances.

But in the last two weeks he'd been manipulated by most of the people he'd ever trusted. What made her any different? She might be working with James and know everything about him, about Arthur, about the jaguar statue. Maybe she'd been handpicked to make contact with him because of their previous relationship. Cutting him loose and carrying him from the basement was just an elaborate ruse to get him to confide in her. Maybe there was no Committee. Maybe *she* was the Committee.

Death would be visiting him soon, one way or another. When it came down to it, lying to Vanessa would be no less dangerous to him than telling her the truth, and possibly much worse. If rescuing him hadn't been part of a larger strategy, it meant that a part of her still felt something for him, or at least she had enough pity—or possibly curiosity—to elevate him above the dozens of souls she'd ostensibly turned into meat without a second thought.

So he told her almost everything. His life in Brooklyn before he was turned, after, the years of gorging with Frank and Natalia and the rest of the tribe, the identity and apartment changes, the years of unbroken solitude, meeting Jennifer and loving her in spite of himself, in spite of what they never would become, finding Nicki on Craigslist and taking her blood at Starbucks, the shitstorm that came next, digging up Arthur's box in the cemetery, finding out about Frank's deception, hiding the statue (minus its location), most of what had happened once he'd crossed over into Manhattan, up to what Derrick had told him before Vanessa had interrupted them.

As he talked, he watched Vanessa to gauge her reaction. Her lips didn't twitch or purse and her brow remained smooth, but Ryan now understood that her seemingly constant lack of emotion was less a product of her occupational training and more to do with the surgeries she'd undergone. Her eyes told a different story. They seemed to shine, then to darken, the pupils expanding, not quite in fear, but with the wariness of someone who discovers that the reality they've taken for granted has gone badly askew. A discomfort that was impossible to hide, or to fake.

"We need to get back to my apartment," she said after he finished speaking, with a palpable sense of urgency in her voice. "We shouldn't be out here." She stood up and motioned for Ryan to follow her to the front of the restaurant, scanning the room that suddenly seemed to have gotten larger and gone silent, a tomblike sea of side-staring faces that now seemed anything but innocuous.

Ryan gripped the handle of the knife that he was carrying in his pocket. Vanessa didn't stop him.

"This will be a lot easier for you if you admit to yourself that Jennifer and Seamus are dead," Vanessa said, scanning the block as they crossed an intersection.

They were walking east at a brisk pace on Bleecker Street past a gaggle of dive bars that, even though it was only the middle of the afternoon, had already begun to reverberate with the bleating of buttoned-down yuppies and unabashedly crusty degenerates. "You should probably try to come to terms with that now," she continued.

"You're probably right," Ryan replied, spitting a gob of bright red blood onto the trash-soaked sidewalk. "I think I've known it since I saw the picture of her. The whole thing was probably always hopeless."

He could feel Vanessa's glare without looking over at her. The indecision he'd seen earlier in her eyes had been replaced by a harsh pragmatism, a distrust of weakness that he presumed was her standard mode of operation.

"There's no 'probably,'" she said as they turned onto Sullivan Street. "The basement you walked into was part of a processing plant, the largest on the east side."

"Processing for what?"

"Food. The harvests come in every couple weeks or so. They're separated by age, gender, health, blood type. I'm not exactly sure how the actual process works now, but it used to be that once the bodies were completely milked, the meals were pasteurized, cleared of any impurities, and packaged for distribution to the blood banks the tribe operates across the island. Very occasionally one of the selected—maybe one in five thousand—had blood that was so good they would be kept alive and healthy in a residential wing of the facility. A premium option for the Committee and other higher-ups until it died or their palates grew sick of it."

Jennifer's blood was O positive, nothing special. To Ryan, the type had always tasted like how he imagined eating an avocado would be: filling and nutritious, but lacking in flavor and texturally disgusting. It was one of the main reasons that he had thought a real relationship with her might be possible. The liquid flowing within her would never stir the urges that lurked just beneath the surface when he caught a whiff of B negative.

Now it appeared that her blood's commonness had been her death sentence. But *appeared* was wrong, he told himself, just like *probably*. He needed to banish the words from his thoughts. She was gone, plain and simple.

It was time to accept it.

"You're right," he said as they stopped in front of Vanessa's building, a nineteenth-century brick row house painted a light shade of violet with cream accents. "It's over."

He followed her down a short flight of stairs to a garden-level entrance and into the building's small, foyerlike lobby, where she turned back and stared at Ryan before entering the idling elevator. "It's not over," she said, a sense of urgency creeping into her voice that was little more than a whisper, even though they were on her home turf. "Not for me at least. I don't have answers for most of what you told me. The humans that attacked you and your tribe, the pictures, the statues, the girl who said she was working for us who you followed from the subway, the man you said she was with—none of it is like any kind of operation I've ever been a part of, like any I've heard about. I know you aren't lying. The mist your friend—what was her name, Natalia?—was sprayed with seems like it was a concentrated version of the substance I used to take out Derrick Rhodes. The lab where it's produced is part of a university that was founded by the grandson of two of the men on the Committee."

"You seem pretty well in the loop," Ryan said, wondering if she hadn't been playing coy with him the entire time just to verify his value. Maybe a few of her ruling-class friends would be waiting for him when they got out of the elevator he'd stepped into. "And very loyal to your superiors. What good did it do you to take me from the processing facility? That can't have made them too happy. Sentimentality or curiosity isn't an excuse, if things are as ruthless here as you're making them seem."

The elevator shot up to the top floor of the building. The doors opened and the entire length of the hallway that led to Vanessa's apartment was made visible. "Things are more complicated than I've been making it seem," she said, seemingly as relieved as Ryan that there was no one there to greet them.

He snorted in sarcastic amusement. "Try me," he said.

"The processing facility isn't operated by the Committee," she said. "At least not anymore. There's been a split in the leadership. The oldest member left a few months ago, fortified his uptown holdings, and took a few of our youngest people with him to the Upper East Side and Harlem, where they've stayed. There hasn't been any violence. As far as everyone knew, the separation was amicable. But some of the things you've told me have made me think about what I've been asked to do in the last few months, tasks I've had, targets I've eliminated. There's something happening, something that's been set in motion, but I don't know where it's heading, or why."

"I just want to find the people who killed my girlfriend before I die," Ryan said, repeating a mantra that was quickly becoming ingrained in his skull, the only thing that mattered. He couldn't care less about vague Manhattan politics.

"I stopped myself from turning you into liquid sludge and then saved you from becoming someone's dinner because I was curious," Vanessa replied, ignoring him. "Curious about why you'd left Brooklyn, why you were with Derrick Rhodes. I knew Derrick was important, it was why the Committee was nervous enough to need me to kill him. You are still a part of this, whether you like it or not. We need to find out how and why."

"What the fuck is *this*?" Ryan shouted, exasperated. "You sound exactly like Derrick. What difference do the motives for an elaborate plot make at this point? An elaborate plot we know nothing about? The only thing I want to know is *who* did this to me."

"Because *how* and *why* have a tendency of leading to *who*," Vanessa said, rummaging through her bag. "I'm going out, going to talk to some contacts who might have a better idea of the Committee's intentions."

"Do you trust them?"

"No, that's why I'm not using a phone. Face-to-face I can deal with. I can improvise if shit goes south. You should stay here, go through Derrick's packet, see what he had that he thought was worth more than his life. Oh, and I found this when you were passed out."

She handed him a rolled-up, crumbling piece of parchment, the same color as the papers from Arthur Harker that Natalia had preserved.

"It must have fallen out of the knife's handle when you were taken down in the basement," Vanessa said. "I found it lying on the ground next to your backpack."

Ryan reached in his pocket and felt the butt end of the knife. There did seem to be some kind of cap fused into the bone, so tightly wedged into the handle—and made of the same substance—that it was no surprise he hadn't noticed it before.

"Everything okay?"

Karl was standing in the open doorway to Vanessa's apartment, cradling an iPad, his jeans and Guns N' Roses T-shirt as rumpled as the mop of hair that was threatening to cover his bloodshot eyes.

"We're good," Vanessa said, unsurprised by his presence. "We're going for a ride. He needs to rest." She turned and looked at Ryan. "You going to be all right? You look way more tired than you did earlier."

"I'm fine," he said, pushing past Karl and into the apartment.

"We'll be back in a couple hours," Vanessa said, pausing for a moment before shutting the door.

Ryan listened to their footsteps in the hallway until they were gone. Then he ran to the kitchen and vomited into the sink.

25

Ryan took a fourth pull from the bottle of Old Grand-Dad 114-proof he'd found in a cabinet while looking for paper towels to clean up the mess he'd made.

Feeling himself relax a little as the liquor shot through his system, he cleared his throat and sat down at the dining table to start going through the pages Derrick had given him.

The silence in the room was interrupted by an extended period of sobbing and thrashing from Vanessa's newborn, its noises muffled by the concrete-and-titanium wall that separated the containment chamber from the rest of the apartment. Ryan looked at the chamber's door and visualized for a moment what would happen to him if it was flung open, and then he shuddered and tried to erase the images from his mind. He looked down and began to read.

The first thing that struck him was the sheer amount of data that Derrick had been able to obtain. There were fragments of financial reports, bank statements, screenshots from corporate websites, memos with Homeland Security and private contractor letterheads, e-mails, text messages, portraits of men and women from the eighteenth and nineteenth century juxtaposed with photographs of what appeared to be the same people walking the streets, getting into cars, and dining out in present-day New York. There were copies of documents handwritten in an unintelligible style similar to Arthur's; crude drawings of birds, deer, bears, and geometric patterns; and several pages of what looked like scientific and medical data that were beyond anything Ryan had ever tried to comprehend.

The only parts that were familiar to him were several images of jaguar figurines, identical to the one he'd dug up—the same hollowed eyes, mottled skin, and flared nostrils, the bared fangs—their pictures originally appearing in museum brochures, auction catalogs, and news stories that spanned decades. There were at least six different ones, scattered across the country until they'd been meticulously collected.

After briefly skimming through everything once and then starting over in earnest to try to make sense of the massive information junkyard staring up at him, Ryan noticed that the red-ink paragraphs filling the margins of most of the pages were more than just Derrick's random scribblings. They seemed to function as a sort of layman's guide, highlighting and explaining certain passages in a logical sequence, how they related to a larger narrative.

It seemed like the Manhattan tribe's origins were similar to those of its Brooklyn counterpart. The shamans and elders saw the writing on the wall and began moving their people west, but not before one of them turned a wealthy trapper and shipbuilder named Adriaen. He was the cousin of Peter Minnewit, the eventual governor of New Netherland who—possibly erroneously—was said to have purchased Manhattan for twenty-four dollars' worth of shells. What was certain was that the Minnewit (later Minuit) family flourished in their new home, as did the families of several other Dutch merchants and tradesmen. Once a patriarch had accumulated enough wealth and had sunk his claws deeply enough into the power structure of the era, he—or more commonly, one of his children—would be turned, ensuring a continuity of behind-the-scenes influence that endured through the Dutch and British colonial periods and the gilded age of brutal robber barons and the political pawns who served them, a kind of elite freemasonry for immortals, the only real empire in the Empire State.

As with any group whose net worth was greater than the gross domestic product of most countries, there was internal tension. At first it was arguments about fur quotas and shipping routes, disagreements over which sides to covertly support in various wars of independence, and finally, squabbles over northern real estate in the ever-expanding city that led to outright violence and the deaths of several of the tribe's oldest members—including Adriaen Minuit—during the 1863 draft riots. The survivors quickly made peace and formed the Committee, formalizing a system of government that appeared to still be in effect in the present day.

Derrick had compiled detailed profiles for each sitting member of the Committee, complete with information about their birthplaces, their education and upbringings, a timeline of their known addresses and professional lives, and speculation as to their rankings within the organizational hierarchy. These were the heaviest of hitters, with names like Van Pelt, Astor, Rockefeller, Gould, and Mellon, the owners of railroads, oil wells, arms factories, and public utilities, whose interests were synonymous with industrial growth that had raised America from its agricultural infancy.

At some point in the late 1800s, those interests had at least partially aligned and they had begun turning women, immigrants, and members of lower social classes, realizing that in order to maintain control of their growing and changing island kingdom, they need to expand their numbers, to infiltrate the ignorant masses from the bottom up, with faces that could blend in but also inspire an appropriate amount of terror if necessary. If any of the newly initiated refused to fulfill the roles for which they'd been chosen, there were others to eliminate them and take their places.

As the Manhattan tribe's membership increased and diversified, so did its business interests. During the first decades of the twentieth century, they formed mutually beneficial relationships with the police department, state senators, the precursors to the Italian and Jewish mobs, roughneck Irish gangsters, black heroin kingpins in Harlem, and bootleggers of any race and creed. When monopolies went out of fashion, the Committee's oligarchs expertly dispersed their legitimately earned wealth through shell corporations, trusts, offshore accounts, stock offerings, and charitable gifts to organizations they'd founded themselves. While their descendants publicly distanced themselves from the aggressive capitalism that had made their family names famous, becoming politicians or fading into the periphery as philanthropists, the Committee still pulled the strings that mattered, still kept a death grip on what they'd built.

That grip was tightened by an evolving public relations machine run by hired spin doctors and tech-savvy malcontents. These men and women were experts at maintaining their employers' anonymity, at manipulating the media with perfectly crafted lies and distortions, at feeding the message-board conspiracy theorists with enough seemingly plausible garbage to keep them looking in all the wrong places, at making anyone who'd stumbled onto something potentially threatening to the tribe look like such an unstable psychopath that any information they had wouldn't seem credible enough for the *Weekly World News*. The tribe was as safe as it had ever been.

It seemed that for the last thirty years or so, the real focus of the Committee members had been their own biology. There was evidence of extensive DNA and blood testing, as well as a wide variety of unnerving experiments on living tribe members and their newborns. These included amputations, immersions in liquid nitrogen and fire, exposure to substances that had previously been used as biological weapons and fertilizer, and forced removals from the island to test the limits of the virus that was responsible for creating the *Ànkëlëk-ila*.

The results of the experiments had been discussed extensively in e-mails and phone calls with high-ranking contacts in the military and the intelligence community, which made sense. If the virus could somehow be transported, if it could be dissected and its individual properties utilized for healing or combat, if American soldiers could somehow become dead warriors, it would represent the greatest technological advance—in certain government officials' eyes—since Hiroshima.

But any attempts to extract the virus, to replicate it or to transport it, had failed. The only real advance of any kind had come with the accidental discovery of DXT, the chemical that had been sprayed on Natalia and used to melt Derrick, a highly volatile and corrosive substance that was effective in both liquid and gas form, and was currently being studied in at least two Air Force bases in the Southwest. It was clearly the Committee's preferred method for executing would-be snitches and the crux of their scientific endeavors. Until they rediscovered the statues.

By Derrick's exhaustive standards, the information he had about them was fuzzy at best. They were made of basalt, Central American in origin, from a culture that predated the Mayans, possibly Olmec or Zapotec. Figuring out their exact age had been impossible because the substance with which they'd been painted resisted carbon dating. At some point in the last several thousand years, they had traveled from the place of their creation into what was now the United States and were scattered, reemerging much later in the possession of tribes in the Northeast and as far west as the Dakotas.

It was thought—based on a few photocopied documents and diagrams that looked similar to Arthur's drawings—that there were eight of them. Two of the jaguars had been in Manhattan since before the colonial period, and another four had been purchased by the tribe over the last decade from museums and private collections.

What would happen when all of the statues were brought together was anyone's guess. Individually they possessed a strange energy, the magnetic pull Ryan had felt outside the Brooklyn Museum and again when he'd removed Arthur's jaguar from the cemetery. The Manhattan tribe knew, as Arthur had, that the statues had been used by the Lenape to allow dead warriors to travel, that the statues also served a wartime purpose, but no one had been able to figure out what that was. And furthermore, it seemed that no one who had come in contact with one of them, whether human or *Ànkëlëk-ila*, had been able to touch it without extensive bodily damage. There were photographs of charred fingers, wrists with hands no longer attached to them. There had been more than a few casualties. Maybe Vanessa and other younger members of the tribe were being ordered to turn people simply so that there would be new fodder for experimentation. After everything Ryan had read so far, it didn't seem out of the question.

But regardless of the tribe's ultimate intentions, there was still the issue of obtaining the remaining two statues.

The Manhattan tribe knew about Arthur Harker, that much

was clear. The name had been mentioned in numerous cryptic e-mails with short, bullet-point paragraphs like "Last known Harker address (230 Frost Street) searched and scanned, new construction on lot, no promising ground radar results." It was clear that they knew he'd left Brooklyn. They also knew that he'd turned some-one before leaving, someone they'd been trying to find for at least the last few years—"Authorize status of probe re: Harker progeny location," "Re: transmission of file including likely age/gender/alias of Arthur Harker heir with composite photographs." If Frank had played a role in revealing Ryan's identity, as Ryan was sure he had, there was strangely no mention of him in any of the cor-respondence.

There was another name that kept coming up in the documents, one that was unfamiliar to him: *Xansati*, a word that, according to Derrick's handwritten notes, meant "older brother" in Lenape. There were notes confirming Skype calls with Xansati, making sure Xansati was being kept up to date about certain investigations or meetings with military officials, waiting for Xansati's guidance regarding how to proceed on a wide range of critical-sounding matters.

Maybe Xansati was another name for the Committee, what Derrick would have called "in-group terminology." Or maybe it was a smaller, older group within the Committee, or the group that had caused the split in leadership that Vanessa had talked about. The information Ryan had at his fingertips wasn't enough to make him feel confident in any guess.

The last page of the packet was bare except for a color photo-graph of a man getting out of a black Cadillac Escalade, phone pressed against his bronze-colored cheek. Ryan knew him. It was the dead warrior who had absorbed the bullet in the basement of the processing facility, the guy who he'd seen with Nicki. Below the picture was one word in all caps that had been underlined three times in Derrick's red ink: *XANSATI.*

Derrick had done his research. And now Ryan had a definitive target.

He closed the packet and flung it across the table. He took a deep breath and took another swig of bourbon. Besides the bottle, the only thing left in front of him was the scroll that Vanessa had allegedly taken from his knife.

He carefully unraveled the fragile piece of yellowed parchment. Spread out, it was a little smaller than a standard sheet of computer paper, its edges brown and crumbling. There were drawings of three humanlike figures in a row, encircled by a seemingly random assortment of circular and triangular shapes. The figure on the left looked exactly like the ones from Arthur's other drawing, a dead warrior holding a statue in his hand, his neck craning skyward, his face calm yet resolute. The figure in the center—most likely the same one—was depicted head-on, cradling the statue with both hands and pressing it against its chest. In the third and final image, the figure had raised both of its arms above its head but the statue was still affixed to its chest, surrounded by what appeared to be a halo of light. Smaller beams were shooting outward from the halo, most of them in the direction the figure was pointing.

"Finding out anything interesting?" a voice asked, softly. She was leaning over Ryan, her mouth inches from the back of his head.

Ryan shot out of the chair he'd been sitting in and lashed out, an automatic reflex, landing a direct elbow blow to her sternum. Vanessa didn't flinch; she smiled while he bent over the dining table and glared at her, trying to stop his heart from leaping out of his chest.

"Are you fucking kidding me?" he managed to stammer after a few moments of catching what little breath he had left, steadying his whiskey-wobbling legs. "How did you get in here? How long have you been watching me?"

"Long enough to know that you've been wading knee-deep in some serious shit for the last few hours," she replied. "Your jaw looked like it was going to explode. I'm sorry. I brought you dinner."

She placed a plastic bag on the table and walked into the kitchen. The aroma that assaulted his nostrils was mouthwatering, notes of soy and garlic, possibly something from the Korean place they'd passed earlier on Bleecker Street. He almost allowed himself to be consumed by the smell until Vanessa returned and sat across from him, gripping a blood-filled Evian bottle. She was wearing the same tank top she'd had on earlier at the restaurant, the same skintight distressed jeans, but something was different. Her hair looked like it had been combed and intentionally tossed to one side. She had on pink-tinted lip gloss and thick winged eyeliner that made her look like a 1950s pinup girl, minus the plastic that had reshaped her once-beautiful features.

"Cheers," she said, pushing the three-quarters-empty Old Grand-Dad bottle in his direction.

Ryan sat back down and took a long pull, and the worst part of his anger subsided. It was back to business, the only business that mattered. "Who is Xansati?" he asked.

Vanessa's eyes widened as she sipped from the bottle. "You *have* been doing your research," she said after she'd swallowed and wiped her lips. "He's the oldest member of the tribe, the oldest living thing in Manhattan, unless there's a tree somewhere that I don't know about. He was old before the Dutch came here."

"So he's Lenape?"

She nodded. "The son of a chief or the head shaman, or something like that. Royalty. I've only met him in person a couple of times. He stays uptown, way uptown, since the disagreement with the Committee. It's almost like he's started his own tribe."

"I've seen him twice," Ryan said. "I saw him in an apartment near the High Line, south of the Lincoln Tunnel, fucking the girl I was following, the one I told you about. Then I saw him at the processing facility. I shot him point-blank in the head and he shook it off like it was nothing."

"That's impossible," Vanessa said. "As far as I know, he hasn't left Harlem in months. He owns the processing facility, uses it to feed himself and the ones who decided to follow him, maybe twenty of them. The rest of us get our blood from donors now, we're trying to be as humane as possible. That's why I could take you from the facility without any repercussions from the Committee. They'd probably be happy if I burned it down."

Ryan rolled his eyes. "Apparently there's a lot you don't know. What about the military contracts? The experiments on humans? On your own kind? The jaguar statues you've been buying and stealing for years? You're going to tell me that this Xansati guy has been acting alone?"

"The ancient vessels?" she asked. "Of course I know about them. Everyone does. They're the relics of the original people. But the Committee stopped those experiments years ago. No one was able to figure out how to use them. They're with Xansati now. They were the only things besides the processing facility that he kept in the divorce."

"Why was there a divorce in the first place, especially after so many years?"

Vanessa gave Ryan an exasperated glare. "*I* wasn't in the room," she snarled. "I assume he was sick of having to share power with a bunch of white venture capitalists. Caucasian males can be insufferable, or so I hear. No, I don't know. Whatever the reason, it was stupid. As fascist as living under the Committee might seem, at least there's a safety net. There's a support network in place in case something like Derrick Rhodes happens. He's forfeited that."

Ryan took a pull from the bottle. "I'm sorry for the interrogation. I just need to know that Xansati is the one responsible for killing Jennifer. I need to be certain."

"If you're certain that the picture of Jennifer was taken in the processing facility in the last few weeks, then it's fairly obvious that he's the one who did it. Or more likely someone working for him. But you aren't going to be able to kill him by coming at him directly. You need to relax, clear your head. Take some time and figure out another way." She took a long sip from the water bottle, began to stroke her hair. "I have a mandatory one-on-one with a member of the Committee tomorrow. I think he's going to give me another assignment. He might also be able to help give us some answers, as long as I ask the right questions."

"I don't need any more help," Ryan muttered, starting to slur his words. "You've helped me enough."

Vanessa stood up and placed the now-empty water bottle on the table. She walked over to Ryan, a mischievous half smile flickering across her face. She pulled on the back of the chair he was sitting in, sliding it and him across the floor as if he were weightless. She moved in front of him and sat down, pressing her face against his, her legs straddling his lap. Ryan could smell the iron reek of blood on her lips. He tried to sit up, but he was paralyzed by her weight and the alcohol.

"I haven't forgotten that you saved my life," she said softly, rubbing his cheek with her fingers. "I didn't realize how much I missed you until I watched you sleeping yesterday. It brought back so many good memories, the good times we shared so long ago. I would do anything for you. I would even turn you, but I don't know if I'm mom enough to handle twins."

"I'd never let you," Ryan said, trying to hold back the coughing spell he knew was coming. "I'd kill myself first. I'm done with tribes. I'm done with all of it."

"I know you are," she cooed, "but I still want to try to make you happy, even if it's just for tonight, even if it's just for a few moments."

She kissed him with her unnaturally hard lips, silencing his protests. Whatever she was trying to do, he wasn't in the mood. He wasn't that kind of drunk. He tried to push her away and after a few seconds she let him, as if he were being a petulant child and she were humoring him temporarily. She started tugging at the straps of her tank top.

"You said you were going out to talk to people," Ryan said, trying to kill whatever passion had possessed her, as she ground her hips into him. "Did you figure anything out? Like, why you had to turn someone? Where's Karl?"

"Nothing worthwhile," she said. "Which is why it's good that they're calling me in. In the morning we'll find out everything you could ever want to know. But let's worry about tomorrow . . . tomorrow."

She pulled off the tank top and tossed it into the living room and guided Ryan's hands to the exposed part of her hips, then up her slim stomach and onto small, pert breasts that had surprisingly been spared the scalpel, or whatever Karl had used to carve into her face.

"I can't, I . . ." Ryan stammered. He was sweating, shivering, too weak and too intoxicated to stop her. Everything started moving in slow motion, then stop-motion, a series of dreamlike snapshots.

He saw her pulling him out of the chair, across the room, pushing him onto the couch. There were a few moments of sunken silence when he thought it might be over, but then she was on top of him again, pants removed, lifting his shirt over his head, kneading her face against his chest and neck, grating his back with her fingernails.

This isn't what I need right now. Ryan tried to form the words, but nothing came out. Instead, he arched his torso and sank deeper into the couch under Vanessa's weight, flinching as she bit the space between his neck and shoulder.

At some point he heard what sounded like a vague hydraulic hiss and assumed in his stupor that it was his own body liquefying, that maybe there had been some remnants of the DXT spray in Vanessa's mouth. But that was wrong. The sound had come from across the room. Vanessa paused and lifted her head, but before she could turn to look at what had caused it, something grabbed her by the hair, lifted her off Ryan, and flung her onto the floor, where she crumpled in a lanky, naked heap.

The sudden release of pressure sent Ryan into a fit of uncontrollable coughing. He closed his eyes and rode out the spell. When he opened them, a woman was standing over him in the dimmed track lighting, her mouth twisted in a scowl of pain and anger, her blue eyes wide in either terror or disgust. Her cheeks and neck and wavy chocolate-brown hair were covered in maroon patches of caked blood, her T-shirt was in tatters, and her fingers were pink and raw, as if the skin had just reclaimed them. Behind her, the door to the containment chamber had been flung open. Ryan could just make out what looked like the outline of two bodies piled, one on top of the other, in the chamber's darkness, could smell the sharp odor of decay that had suddenly seeped into the apartment.

The woman took a step forward. Ryan looked at her face again and this time his overnumb synapses began to fire in a surge of recognition, shocking him upright.

It was Jennifer.

She opened her mouth and released a prolonged, high-pitched cry that seemed to tear at Ryan's insides, stunning him further. He watched helplessly as she moved past the kitchen toward the apartment's main entrance, letting out a series of softer shrieks that were no less disturbing.

She opened the door and dashed into the hallway before Ryan could move from the couch and before Vanessa could pick herself up from the floor.

Then she was gone.

26

"Everything was a blur," Jennifer murmured as she paced back and forth from the spiral staircase to a few feet from the couch were Ryan was sitting. She clutched the belt of the bathrobe that Vanessa had given her to wear when she'd returned from her wandering. "It was like I was there the whole time, but I wasn't."

She paused to look at her reflection in the turned-off TV screen. She ran her hand through hair that was still wet from the shower she'd just taken, and over a face that looked, deceptively, like it always had, before the hood was placed over her head. Before she'd succumbed to a weeklong darkness she couldn't explain or piece together, the shards of an out-of-body nightmare, the pain and starvation that seemed too intense to be real. She muttered something to herself and resumed pacing.

"You sure you don't want to sit down?" Ryan asked; her frenetic movements were making him nervous. He wanted to embrace her, to tell her that the intensity of the changes she'd experienced would be decreasing, that soon she would begin to acclimate to her new life, but he knew it wouldn't do any good. He and Vanessa had spent the last two hours explaining to her what had happened to her, the inadvertent role he had played, and the basics of what it meant to be a dead warrior, what she could expect from here on out. But her turning had been so unbelievably different from his that it was difficult to relate to anything that she'd gone through.

Except for the hunger.

Jennifer continued pacing for another minute before sighing and collapsing in exasperation on the couch next to Ryan. She leaned forward, cupping her head in her palms. "I can't believe the door was unlocked the entire time," she said, briefly glancing up at the entrance to the containment chamber. "I just had to figure out how to use the handle, but all I wanted to do was—"

"Eat," Ryan said, finishing her sentence. He placed his hand on the small of her back and she flinched, violently. Her fists clenched. He let go of her, but not because he cared what happened to his own life. She had been operating from a place of pure aggression for long enough and needed to come back to reality, as completely fucked up as that reality now seemed to her. Attacking him would only prolong her metamorphosis.

Vanessa walked into the room from the kitchen, where she had been talking quietly with Karl, holding a glass filled with blood. "It's AB negative," she said, with an uncharacteristically cheerful lilt in her voice. Maybe, Ryan thought, she was trying to sound motherly. "Try it," Vanessa coaxed. "You'll love it." She handed the glass to Jennifer and took a seat on a chair across the room.

Jennifer sniffed the blood, took a sip, then another, her eyebrows arching in pleasant surprise. She put the glass down on the coffee table in front of her, turned, and stared at Ryan. "I don't think I've hated anyone more than when I came out of the room and saw you with *her*." She nodded in Vanessa's direction without looking at her. "The first person I recognized since I came out of the . . . fog, and I wanted to tear you apart. I needed to run out of here, immediately, or I would have done it. I could have kept running, maybe should have, but once I walked around the block a few times and calmed down a little, something drew me back here. Maybe it was curiosity. Or maybe—I can't believe I'm actually saying this—there's some kind of mind control thing going on that you guys haven't told me about yet, some kind of mystical, unbreakable bond between me and my, uh, maker."

Ryan chuckled. "This isn't some old B movie," he said. "I'd go with option A."

"No, it's not," Jennifer snarled, not joining in the levity. "I should still want to kill you, especially for not warning me about what you were. But when it comes down to it, I never would have believed you. I would have chalked it up as one more ridiculous, commitment-phobic excuse."

"I should have cut it off," Ryan said. "I shouldn't have let it get as serious as it did."

Jennifer sighed. "No, I'm too stubborn. I would have never let you give up that easily. And besides, it wasn't like we ever got *that* serious. I mean, it's not like you even spent a night at my place."

She watched Ryan try to hold back a grimace and put her hand on his thigh. "I'm kidding. I know you wanted to," she said softly. "I feel just as bad about you coming here. I mean, you were going to live forever. We do live forever, right?"

"As far as anyone can tell, as long as you stay in Manhattan. I knew a guy who was like three hundred years old."

"Wow. And I'll look the same?"

"I look pretty much how I did in 1919," Ryan said.

"Minus this stupid beard," Jennifer said playfully, as she ran her fingers through it. "I guess there are some positives to . . ."

She trailed off, let go of Ryan's face but kept staring at him, wrinkled her nose as if a curiously offensive scent had just entered the room. She inhaled again. "What am I smelling?" she asked, a look of concern flashing across her face. "Is that coming from inside you? Are you—"

"Dying? I am," Ryan nodded. "Advanced lung cancer. A hundred years ago I thought I was special, that I was wasting away from some kind of exotic disease I must have picked up on one of the South American freighters that came through the shipyard. But I'm not special and the diagnosis makes sense. I didn't exactly have the safest work environment before I was turned."

Jennifer sat silently for a few moments. Her eyes reddened. She swallowed hard. Ryan knew that she'd be crying if she were physically capable. If there had been any minuscule shred of doubt that he'd done the right thing by coming to Manhattan, it was erased in that moment. "You really did give up everything for me," she said after a while, smiling sadly. "And here I am talking about stupid shit like how I'm going to look. I'm flattered by everything you've done,

I really am. But I'm not worth throwing away a hundred and twenty-eight years of someone else's life. No one is."

Ryan locked his fingers with hers. Jennifer leaned into him, kissing his neck lightly.

Vanessa stood up and made a noise that sounded like she was groaning or clearing her throat, or a combination of the two. "I hate to break up the reunion, but you need to eat," she said to Jennifer in a businesslike monotone. "You may not feel like it, but you're still unstable; your body is still acclimating to the change. We need to prevent the hunger before you ever feel it coming. We don't want you reverting back to what you were when you were in that room."

Jennifer nodded, picked up the glass, and downed most of the blood in two long gulps. She looked down at the bathrobe she was wearing, as if noticing it for the first time. "I think I'm going to try on the clothes you bought for me," she said to Vanessa. "Are they upstairs?"

"On my bed," Vanessa said nonchalantly. "The green top with the white pants would make a pretty cute outfit for you."

Jennifer ran her hands through Ryan's hair one more time before standing and heading toward the spiral staircase. Vanessa walked into the kitchen. Ryan got up and followed her.

After the initial jolt of seeing Jennifer and seeing her run out of the apartment, worrying about whether she'd come back or not, and the relief he'd felt when she'd finally returned a few minutes before dawn and hadn't totally blamed him for everything that had happened to her, a slow rage began to work its way through him, bubbling closer to the surface with every second that passed.

A rage that found its target in Vanessa.

Karl was standing at the kitchen island, wearing the same pajamas he'd arrived in after Vanessa had called him about Jennifer's disappearance. He was flipping eggs from a skillet onto open-faced English muffin halves. "You want two or three?" he asked when he saw Ryan approach.

Ryan ignored him and walked to the open refrigerator, where Vanessa was studying several rows of blood-filled water bottles. He shut the door in her face and glared at her, watching her subtle, plastic-stunted expressions shift from surprise to mild annoyance to outright anger. Karl grabbed a fork and knife from a drawer in the island and took his breakfast into the living room without making eye contact.

"What?" Vanessa growled in a low voice after a few uncomfortable seconds. She raised her arms and gave an open-palm shrug. "How the fuck was I supposed to know she was your girlfriend?"

"Is that really how you're going to play this?" Ryan asked.

"How I'm going to play what? What do you want me to tell you?"

"I want you to tell me how you ended up with Jennifer," he said. "The last I knew she was being tortured near the service entrance of a building we're both familiar with, a building that allegedly isn't connected to your tribe anymore, a building that you say is controlled by a guy who's apparently so pissed at the elders of your tribe that he severed a multicentury relationship with them. You can stop lying now. If you want the statue for your masters, if that's what all of this is still about, you can have it. I'll bring it to the Committee myself, wherever the fuck they hang out, as long as you can guarantee that Jennifer doesn't become a lab monkey, as long as you can guarantee me that she'll be set up like you are. But who am I kidding? Guarantees are an ancient concept. You're progressive on this side of the river."

"The statues?" Vanessa looked genuinely confused. "What the hell do they have to do with anything? I'm as rattled by all of this as you are. None of it makes sense. I thought I'd been moving up the ladder the last few years, taking on important jobs, zero screwups. But the last couple days are making me think differently. Maybe I'm out of 'the loop,' as you called it. The only good thing is that Van Pelt is the one who called me in, and not some other board member. He's the only person on the Committee who knows me as more than just a soldier, the only one who I have anything close to a relationship with. I won't be able to ask him about you, obviously, but I'll try to find out what I can about Jennifer. Where they found her, who brought her in."

Ryan's lips curled in disgust. "You trust someone whose last name is Van Pelt?" he asked. "Really?"

"Do you trust me?" she asked.

"Not at all. I don't trust anyone. If you live long enough, you won't either. That's why I'm going with you to see this guy."

It was Vanessa's turn to let loose her own grating, sarcastic snicker. "That'll go over just great," she said. "Me bringing in a human to chat with Conrad Van Pelt in his private offices. Jesus Christ. You *are* hilarious."

"I wasn't always human. I wasn't human for eighty-five percent of my life."

"But you are now. And whatever you were, you were never in our tribe. Also there's the minor issue of you being a material witness to a murder I committed on orders and me not only letting you live, but also letting you crash at my place. Why? Because you were some guy I fucked a few times forty years ago and I felt bad for you. Excellent logic on my part. They'll probably ask me to join the Committee."

"You can tell them whatever you want," Ryan said, "as long as you mention that I'm Arthur Harker's heir. After that it won't matter."

"Arthur Harker? Your maker?"

"He had something that Xansati wants, something that I'm sure your bosses want, even if they don't act like it. Van Pelt will be interested enough to get me through the door."

Vanessa thought about this and sighed. "If you're wrong about this, it's both our asses. I should have killed you."

"I'm assuming that's a joke," Ryan said, though he wasn't sure it was. "If anything, you'll get a promotion for bringing me in. You can thank me later. Just make the call."

Vanessa was about to respond but stopped abruptly. Ryan followed her gaze as she turned to look at Jennifer, who was standing in front of the partial wall that separated the kitchen from the dining area, looking concerned.

She was wearing a vintage-looking forest-green peasant top and skintight white denim jeans. She'd brushed her hair and tucked it behind ears that were embellished with low-hanging gold-and-jade earrings that complemented the intensity of her sky-colored eyes. Besides her paler-than-usual skin—which was to be expected—she looked healthy, almost glowing.

"Everything okay in here?" Jennifer asked.

Vanessa opened the refrigerator, took out a bottle, and scowled. "You might want to ask *him*," she said, jabbing a finger in Ryan's direction without looking at him. "You should curl up on the couch for a nice long talk with your boyfriend, because it's probably going to be the last one you two have."

She walked up to Jennifer and shoved the bottle into her newborn's chest before storming out of the kitchen.

27

"'Conrad Jefferson Augustus Van Pelt, 1820 to 1858, was an American industrialist, tycoon, and entrepreneur. He invested in numerous business ventures and held executive leadership positions in the shipping, railroad, construction, and hotel businesses. By his early thirties, Van Pelt had already amassed a great fortune and founded the C.J.A. Van Pelt Company (later Van Pelt–Reinhardt International), which would become one of the largest commercial and residential building companies in the world. He was occasionally vilified in the press of his day as an archetypal robber baron, whose success at business—primarily the construction company he founded—made him the fourth richest U.S. citizen at the time of his untimely death at age 38 in a hotel fire.' Very impressive," Ryan said, looking up from the Wikipedia page he'd pulled up on his phone. "So how exactly did you come to be on friendly terms with this lovely gentleman?"

Vanessa, staring out the passenger-side window of the silver Range Rover at the postwork and touristy crowds that had begun to swarm along the sidewalks of Houston Street, didn't say anything. Ryan couldn't be sure if she was still angry at him for confronting her in the kitchen, or for convincing her to let him come to the meeting and what it might mean for her standing within the tribe, or if she was simply just apprehensive about what Van Pelt was going to ask her to do, or a combination of the three. Regardless, Ryan had been getting the silent treatment since they'd left Vanessa's apartment.

Karl took a right on Broadway and headed south through SoHo's cast-iron gauntlet of trendy boutiques and artists' lofts. "Don't want to toot my own horn, but I'm going to have to take the credit for that," he said. Ryan, from the backseat, watched Karl's smug smile in the rearview mirror. "It must have been what, eighty-eight, eighty-nine? There was a function to celebrate the orchestration of an East Asian banking crisis or something like that. V had made an attaché to the Japanese minister of trade disappear at a particularly crucial moment and was invited to the event. It was like her coming-out party. She had on this sapphire-blue gown—what was it, Dior?—that was just stunning, wasn't it, V?"

Vanessa rolled her eyes. She kept staring out the window.

"Anyway," Karl continued, "Van Pelt noticed more than the dress. He wanted to know how and where she'd gotten the work done on her face. He was impressed. V arranged for me to give him a consultation, which led to me performing several procedures over the next year, and led to V shooting right to the top of his list for when he needs something or someone taken care of in a prompt, professional manner. And he still calls me in every now and then for a touch-up. He got me my own place, this car, V's latest kitchen renovation. It's been a good deal for all of us."

The fawning self-satisfaction that dripped from Karl's mouth was more than a little creepy, but it didn't bother Ryan as much as it would have a few days earlier when they'd first met. Karl was less the menacingly jealous boyfriend type than a harmless middle-aged fanboy who would do anything to maintain the fantasyland existence he'd stumbled into. It was a little funny, a little sad, more pathetic than anything else.

They continued south on Broadway for a while, where the upscale cafés and chain store outlets gradually gave way to dozens of nearly identical tiny alcoves selling cheap luggage and knock-off perfume and sunglasses as they trudged along Chinatown's western border. Traffic was thick, more or less bumper-to-bumper. But Karl, ignoring the stink-eye Vanessa kept shooting in his direction, remained undaunted as he pointed out various buildings that were "friendly," controlled, at least partially, by the tribe—a nondescript former post office that housed a laboratory where DXT was produced, a Duane Reade pharmacy with a safe room in the basement, a blood bank that had recently been opened two floors above a GNC storefront.

The extent to which the Manhattan tribe was inextricably woven into the fabric of the island was impressive, but Ryan already knew that. This trip was about obtaining fresh information, about taking everything from whoever had taken the same from him, even if those people happened to be the most powerful and well-guarded he'd ever encountered.

It was about payback, plain and simple.

He could figure out the details later.

Ryan zoned out from Karl's tour guide spiel, which had gotten even more tiresome when they'd begun to pass some of Lower Manhattan's older landmarks. He didn't hear which members of the Committee had been present when City Hall's cornerstone had been laid, or who had been turned on All Saints' Day in the vestibule of St. Paul's Chapel. Instead, he decided to follow Vanessa's lead and focus on the increasingly narrow and jagged streets they passed, the rectangular green signs with Anglo and Dutch surnames, the buildings that had gotten taller, more imposing, their shadows casting a too-early gloom over the well-trampled pavement.

Karl pulled over to the curb near the intersection of Broadway and Fulton Street and put the SUV in park. Vanessa turned and looked directly at Ryan for the first time since they'd left her apartment. She wasn't wearing any makeup and her hair was tied in a neat ponytail, a look as conservative as the black long-sleeve top and matching slacks she was wearing. A sequence of images flashed through Ryan's brain: the young guy in the black-and-red tracksuit who had shot him in Crown Heights, the girl in the black tracksuit outside Natalia's house, Nicki in a black dress.

He told himself to remain objective, to try to disassociate Vanessa from everything that had happened to him before they'd run into each other, to not make connections before he knew in his gut that they existed. But it was nearly impossible. And his gut was on fire, rebelling against itself like the rest of his body, reminding him that whatever he was going to do, he needed to do it soon.

"Hey, are you all right?" Vanessa was asking when Ryan snapped back to reality. "You wanted to do this."

"I'm fine," he said. "I'm ready."

"Okay, then listen. You're going to follow me and do everything you're told. You're going to keep your mouth shut until you're asked to speak. Oh, and leave your phone in the car. I'm not sure why you turned it on again if you were so paranoid about us being able to track you."

Before he could respond, she opened the passenger-side door, slammed it shut, and crossed the street.

"See you in a bit," Karl said as Ryan was exiting the vehicle, though he didn't seem very confident.

Ryan caught up to Vanessa as she weaved under some sidewalk scaffolding, heading south. "There's one thing I forgot to tell you," she said as he pulled up even with her. "Something about Conrad. It's a little weird."

"Unless he looks like Derrick Rhodes's evil twin, I think I'm beyond being shocked."

Vanessa grunted in wry amusement. "Rhodes was something else, wasn't he? No, Conrad's, um, issues are a little different. He likes to listen to himself talk, a lot."

"Okay, so he's like every other high-ranking corporate executive."

"That's not the weird part. Have you ever seen those people who are big-time germaphobes, like they don't want to touch doorknobs or shake hands because they think they'll catch a deadly virus or get a major bacterial infection? He's like that, but worse."

"But he can't get sick," Ryan said.

"Things will go a lot smoother for both of us if you don't mention that. Okay, this is the place, straight ahead."

They crossed John Street where it intersected with Broadway and approached the Corbin Building. The narrow, brown-and-red structure, made of stone, cast iron, and terra-cotta in a Romanesque Revival style, was—according to one of Karl's earlier ramblings— built by Long Island Railroad president Austin Corbin in the late 1880s. He owned the building for a decade until he took a liking to the daughter of a popular haberdasher who also happened to be

Conrad Van Pelt's personal donor. Overnight, the building became Conrad's and Corbin left the city for an early retirement in New Hampshire, which ended a few months later when he was thrown from a carriage.

The building, at least on its Broadway-facing side, was connected by a glass wall to the sprawling Fulton Center, an ultra-modern, glass-windowed subway hub and shopping complex. The Corbin Building's arched front entrance was closed, the view of its lobby blocked by frosted-glass panes featuring the Fulton Center's logo. This apparent partnership between the city and the Committee seemed odd to Ryan.

"I thought Van Pelt owned this building," he said to Vanessa as she passed the entrance and took a left onto John Street. "Did he sell it to the Transit Authority? Are they connected to your tribe?"

"Not that I know of," she replied, glancing up at the longer side of the building that featured rows of windows with scalloped arches and vague floral patterns. "And he only sold part of it. The part you can see."

About halfway down the block, the Corbin ended and another, newer building butted against it. The bottom level of 15 John Street was primarily occupied by Brasserie Les Halles, an upscale French eatery, and a slender door made of dark, weathered wood with no handle or signage that Ryan wouldn't have noticed if Vanessa hadn't stopped in front of it and pressed an antique-looking brass doorbell near its center. There was a brief noise, a soft metallic hum, and the door opened inward, revealing a narrow, dimly lit, smoke-filled hallway. The entire threshold of the door began glowing with what looked like infrared metal detector sensors. Vanessa stepped through and motioned for Ryan to follow.

"What is this?" he asked, a little taken aback by the sudden presence of the strange technology.

"It's like a no-touch cavity search," she said impatiently, scanning the street to see if anyone was watching them. "Come on, you won't feel anything. It's too late to wuss out now. They don't like you to leave the door open for more than a couple seconds."

"Seems like an awful lot of radiation."

"Probably, but it's not like it'll do anything worse than what your body's already done to you."

He couldn't argue with that.

Ryan walked into the building and was assaulted by a thick wall of cigarette fumes. As his lungs barked out their discomfort, he squinted through the haze and saw a man in a tattered gray T-shirt, athletic shorts, and Birkenstock sandals sitting on a stool in front of a stainless-steel elevator door, smoking rapidly. He had a sallow complexion, long stringy hair that looked like it hadn't been properly washed or cut in a long time, and a grizzled beard similarly in need of attention.

"Jesus, Sean!" Vanessa exclaimed when she made it to the end of the hallway, stopping a couple of feet from the elevator.

The man scowled and let out a gasoline-soaked grunt. "What?" he muttered. "Ain't like any of it's getting down there." He nodded at the elevator door. "Not like there's anything else to do in here."

Vanessa groaned. "Read a book or something," she said. "Are you going to let us in or what? He's expecting me."

The man looked at Ryan, who was trying (and failing) to wave the smoke away from his face, to hold in the contents of his stomach.

"He your plus one?" the man asked.

"Yeah."

The man shrugged and flicked his cigarette onto the floor. He picked up a phone that had been resting on his lap and swiped at the screen. The elevator door opened. Vanessa gave the man one last disgusted grimace and walked inside. Ryan followed.

There was a loud vacuum hiss and the smoke-tainted air was sucked out through an unseen vent, much to Ryan's relief. Inside the elevator, there were no push buttons or screens to determine which floor they were on or where they were going. The walls, ceiling, and floor were made of an opaque, off-white material that glowed as if there were a powerful lighting system operating within it. The door shut behind Ryan and Vanessa and the car moved quickly downward.

"I'm surprised Van Pelt has a human watching the door," Ryan said after his chest had stopped heaving.

Vanessa laughed. "Sean? He's been around for almost two hundred years. And he's probably been an asshole for all of them."

"Then why does he smoke so much? I mean, I understand the whole oral fixation thing, but it's got to get old after a while."

"It's probably just some obtuse way of getting back at Conrad for making him sit there every day. A few decades ago he apparently got in trouble with the Committee, something about his side gig as a freak show performer. He was starting to get a lot of publicity for his seemingly impossible talents and he was told to stop, to disappear. He didn't want to, there was a squabble, and long story short, he's been sitting at that door ever since. I guess I'd be a grumpy old fuck, too."

The elevator door opened and they stepped into a long hallway that looked exactly like the elevator, its walls covered in the same kind of glowing tiles. Ryan scanned the expansive corridor for any signs of activity, but there were none. No people, and no visible cameras, even though it was certain that they were being watched. As Vanessa took a right and Ryan followed, the sound of their steps was almost totally muffled, dispersed by the floor's impressive insulating properties. The air was thick with a chemical sweetness, some kind of sterilizing agent, and cold, barely above freezing. The temperature wouldn't bother Vanessa, but Ryan was already shivering, his breath appearing in irregular bursts of steam when a sliding door opened in the wall about twenty yards away in the direction they were heading.

A man appeared in the entrance. He was tall, maybe six-four or six-five, with olive-colored skin and close-cropped black hair, built like a tight end. His thick shoulders and thicker biceps seemed like they were on the verge of busting through the black compression shirt he was wearing. When Vanessa approached him, he smiled and shook hands with her before stepping aside to let her pass through the opening. Ryan followed. The man briefly analyzed him without a trace of emotion, sniffed a little in Ryan's direction, scrunched his nose, and, satisfied, moved a few feet away from the door. He positioned himself against the wall, crossed his arms, and stared into space like a dead-eyed security guard.

The room that Ryan entered was slightly bigger than his last apartment, a frigid, undecorated cube that looked like a larger version of the hallway and the elevator. At the far end was a massive glass box containing a stainless-steel desk and a man sitting behind it, with no discernible entrance or exit hatch. Two smaller glass chambers had been installed a few yards away from the box, each one containing a stainless-steel chair.

The man in the box was eggshell-pale, clean-shaven with long dirty-blond hair that looked like it had been enhanced with plugs or extensions. He was wearing a black mock turtleneck that failed to fully cover two significant scars that ran horizontally below both sides of his jaw. His face had a stretched-out, rubbery appearance, unnaturally arched eyebrows, and a frozen-smooth forehead, and the same pinched nose as Vanessa.

Despite the modifications, Ryan recognized him immediately. It was Conrad Van Pelt.

As Vanessa moved toward the box, Van Pelt smiled at her. His lips began to move and a thin, saccharine voice boomed out from an invisible speaker somewhere in the ceiling. "Marvelous to see you again, Vanessa," he said. He spoke slowly, extending each syllable. His accent sounded vaguely British, but it was more likely indicative of the mid-nineteenth-century upper-crust society to which he had belonged. He looked at Ryan and nodded. "Please, both of you, would you be so kind as to take a seat?"

Vanessa approached one of the smaller chambers. When she was standing a foot away from it, the section in front of her slid down into the floor, allowing her to enter. She sat in the chair, facing Van Pelt, and the wall slid back up, trapping her inside. She motioned for Ryan to do the same. Ryan walked up to the other chamber, heard a faint hydraulic hiss, watched the glass disappear, and followed Vanessa's lead.

The temperature inside the chamber, once he was shut inside, was pleasant, maybe seventy degrees, and the chair was surprisingly comfortable. But the sudden and intense claustrophobia, the sensation of being helpless and caged, was more than enough to cancel out any positive emotions Ryan might have been able to extract from his current situation. He could feel the cold sweat dripping from his temples as his grip tightened on the chair's arms.

Van Pelt seemed to sense Ryan's unease. "I am truly sorry for the precautions," he said, his voice now emanating from a small speaker hidden somewhere in the chamber, "but I try to avoid all direct contact with, ah, humans, as well as any of my own people who may have had contact with them."

"No offense taken," Ryan said in a low, deadpan voice, assuming the speaker worked both ways. "It's a pleasure to meet you." He tried to remain calm, tried to silence the nervous twitching that seemed to stretch from his legs to his neck.

"A pleasure to finally meet you as well," Van Pelt said, "though I wish the circumstances were a bit different."

Finally? Ryan thought. So had the Committee—not just Xansati—known about him before he'd been reunited with Vanessa? Or was the word just a cloying exaggeration? Ryan looked over at Vanessa for a brief moment. She was stone-faced, staring straight ahead, barely blinking, giving away nothing in terms of her mental state or how she was going to spin her side of how she and Ryan had met.

"Vanessa has told me a bit about your unfortunate situation," Van Pelt continued, as if the three of them were having a relaxed chat on a café patio somewhere in Cobble Hill. "Unfortunate, and yet admirable. I can only imagine the courage it must have taken for you to give up the greatest gift any of us could ever hope to receive, to be forced to greet Death after being free from his grasp for so many years. All because of one antiquated fool's quest for another untamable relic."

Ryan assumed that Van Pelt was talking about Xansati and the jaguar statue that Arthur had buried. He also assumed that Vanessa hadn't told her boss about saving Derrick's papers and flash drive instead of destroying them like she'd been ordered to do. If that was the case, then Ryan could play ignorant, using Van Pelt's death-related paranoia and fear of contamination as a shield. With a pair of airtight glass walls separating them, Van Pelt would be unable to detect the obvious changes in Ryan's heart rate and the subtler changes in the scent of Ryan's sweat to determine whether he was lying.

Or so Ryan hoped.

"What fool would that be?" Ryan asked. "All I know is that I came to Manhattan because I received a series of messages leading me to believe that my . . . a human that was important to me was being tortured by members of your tribe, as I'm sure Vanessa told you. I was attacked, as were several others in my tribe, by humans who were operating on orders from someone in Manhattan. I was contacted by a woman who claimed to be working for the same employer, though she didn't say who it was, who told me that my human friend whom they'd taken would be killed unless I provided them with something, an artifact that had apparently been in the possession of my maker, whose name must have rung some kind of a bell because you decided to see me today."

"Not wasting any time with idle banter," Van Pelt said, his thin lips curling into a smile. "I like that. Did you give the woman what she wanted?" he asked.

"No," Ryan said, trying to remain calm. "I had no idea what she was talking about, which is why I ended up here. I felt like I had no other options if I wanted to make sure that my friend stayed alive. I tracked the woman across the river and eventually followed her to a building on the Upper East Side."

"East 80th Street," Vanessa interjected. "I noticed him outside the building while I was doing my regular surveillance."

Van Pelt nodded at her, his android-frozen features giving nothing away. "A happy coincidence," he said. "That must have been an interesting reunion." He turned his attention back to Ryan. "When Vanessa called and told me about what happened to you, I contacted the other board members, the elders who are responsible for the governing of our people, and I can tell you without any uncertainty that none of them had anything to do with it. Quite frankly, we've had our fill of artifacts, especially ones like what you were asked to procure."

"Then who's responsible?" Ryan asked, sharply. He didn't need to look at Vanessa to know that she was probably squirming in her seat.

"He calls himself our older brother, Xansati in the language of his people. He was part of the original tribe, the tribe whose chief and medicine men had the good foresight to realize that when the Dutch came, their time in Manhattan was over. Before they left, they gave the blood gift to a handful of Dutch settlers who they thought would be worthy of it, as a way to ensure that a part of the memory of the tribe would endure indefinitely. I am sure something similar took place in Brooklyn?"

"More or less, I suppose," Ryan said, "from what I've been told."

Van Pelt reached under the desk. He lifted the end of what looked like a clear plastic tube and placed it between his lips. The tube turned red as it filled with liquid from an unseen source. Van Pelt took a few sips and placed the tube back under the desk. He wiped his mouth with a white handkerchief that he had been holding in his other hand. He sighed audibly with pleasure. Even though Ryan could relate to the feeling, the cessation of hunger and the almost sensual thrill that went along with it, he hoped to never experience it firsthand again. The sound filled him with disgust.

"Xansati didn't want to leave," Van Pelt said. "He told his chief that he would stay behind, that he would help the colonists who had been turned, guide them through the transition and teach them how to live with the gift that they'd been given. But that wasn't quite how it panned out. Yes, he made himself available to those that sought him out, and would offer advice if it suited him, but he was no brother to any of us. He has never been concerned about the future, about the directions we have chosen to take as a business organization and as a species. His mind remains firmly entrenched in the past, clinging to the false possibilities of a six-hundred-year-old obsession."

"He's been searching for the statue," Ryan said. "The one he thinks I have."

"Statues," Van Pelt replied with disdain, spitting the word out. "There are eight that we know of, perhaps dozens more. He was entrusted with the two that had belonged to the Indians who once lived here, and he's been trying to collect the rest of them for a long time, since they started resurfacing. They're small, carved from stone and covered in painted patterns, or what's left of them. You might think they were toys or board game pieces if you didn't know what you were looking at. According to the indigenous traditions, they're supposed to resemble jaguars, but to me they look otherworldly, ghoulish, like the imps and goblins in the fairy tales my

Austrian governess would read to me as a small child. But what they look like is irrelevant. It is what they *do*, or what we *think* they do, that makes them fascinating and ultimately quite deadly. Are you familiar with the theory that there once existed a technologically advanced society that flourished before the last ice age, a society that was virtually wiped out by a cataclysm that came to be known as the Great Flood?"

"You mean like Atlantis?" Ryan asked. "Sure, I've been known to go on some *Ancient Aliens* binges every now and then." He snickered, looked over at Vanessa for her reaction to what was suddenly turning into the weirdest history lesson he'd ever had. She was staring at him, her eyes burning into his, looking even more serious than she had when she'd sat down, if that was possible.

"Atlantis," Van Pelt repeated. "Yes, that is a small part of it. There are also the remains of pyramids found on every continent, the interstellar flying machines mentioned numerous times in the ancient Hindu scriptures, the Ark of the Covenant, countless other mythological objects and enigmatic structures that were said to have been built by or were conduits for an unbelievably powerful energy, an energy whose origins predate the oldest sources, maybe even humanity itself.

"I can tell by both of your expressions that you're wondering where I'm going with this," he said. "You're thinking it sounds insane, and until recently I would have agreed with you. But I have seen how the statues function. Well, not the statues themselves. They are only vessels, carved in the Yucatán Peninsula by a culture whose name no longer exists, a culture who, for some reason, dispersed the objects across North America. The older magnetic properties inside of them are what react with the blood-eater virus, keeping the virus alive even when blood-eaters travel outside their infection zone. Xansati claimed to have journeyed several times in the past, though it has never been verified. He also claimed that the energy in the statues could be combined and harnessed to create a weapon with nuclear strength and the ability to be condensed and directed in a single, controllable beam, though he had never witnessed it during his own lifetime."

"You mean you can use one these things to cross the bound-

aries and still keep your, uh, gift?" Ryan asked, trying to subdue
the surprise in his voice.

"According to Xansati. The rest of the tribe had always dismissed
his ramblings as folklore, until early in the last century when Europe went to hell and it behooved us, from a business perspective,
to do what we could to help the war effort. We were willing to test
Xansati's hypotheses. He lent us the statues to conduct some trials,
many of which ended rather unfortunately. We learned that the
only people who could handle the statues directly, when they were
activated, were those who possessed the blood of the original tribe, or
those who had been turned by them. That meant Xansati and the two
oldest members of the Committee at the time, Jan Aertson—the
great-great-grandfather of Cornelius Vanderbilt—and Bram van den
Berg, who is no longer with us. Any other human or blood-eater
would not survive direct contact. We hired teams of scientists,
soldiers, doctors, and none of them made progress. They couldn't
figure out the activation protocols, how to turn the statues off once
they had been activated. The technology was beyond anything
they had seen. It still is. We stopped the trials, ended the pointless
deaths and our fascination with a substance we couldn't ever hope
to control."

Ryan thought back to Arthur's jaguar, glowing and vibrating
in the Urban Outfitters bag. It had been activated. If Van Pelt was
telling the truth, maybe he'd been able to hold it because Arthur
had been turned by a Lenape warrior. Ryan was only one generation removed from the original tribe.

"But Xansati wasn't done," Van Pelt continued. "He took back
the statues. He and Arthur Harker—who brought a statue with him
when he left Brooklyn and gifted it to Xansati—made it their primary objective to find the rest of them, to collect them for a purpose only they knew. Harker willingly gave up his gift and traveled
across the continent for decades. He found an additional three statues and brought them to Manhattan. When Xansati lost contact
with Arthur, he locked the statues in his personal vault at the Cloisters, where they've been for more than fifty years. When the seventh
statue resurfaced at the Brooklyn Museum earlier this year, we
asked Xansati to ignore it, to remember what had happened in the

past, to think about the difficulties we face in trying to remain hidden from the technologically enhanced eye of the modern public, to understand the kind of nightmare cover-up we would have to undertake if the statue decided to activate. Instead of disregarding us, as I thought he would, he said he would leave the statue alone, under several conditions. He told us he wanted to surrender his seat on the board of elders, to effectively cut himself off from the rest of the tribe. He asked to be granted complete control of several sections of northern Manhattan, including everything above 150th Street, and to allow anyone in the tribe who wished to follow him to be able to do so. We agreed without much deliberation. The museum contains a few heirlooms from my family and the families of my fellow elders, but really, in the scheme of things, the loss was not particularly great."

Ryan remembered having to research the Cloisters shortly after he and Jennifer had begun dating. She had wanted him to take her there, and he had to convince her that he'd already been there, that they should go to the first showing of a Civil War documentary at the Brooklyn Historical Society instead. The Cloisters was where the Metropolitan Museum of Art showcased its medieval art and artifacts, way uptown, in the middle of a large, hilly park near the northern tip of Manhattan. If he remembered correctly, it had been commissioned by a Rockefeller early in the twentieth century, and partially constructed using imported sections of European monasteries. Strategically, the Committee couldn't have picked a better place for a stronghold. It was as far out of the way as you could get on the island, not easily accessible from any direction, naturally fortified. But he hadn't come here to discuss strategic decisions.

"Why are you telling us all of this?" he said, cutting Van Pelt off. "You didn't call Vanessa in for a history lesson, and I couldn't care less about Xansati's relationship with the former head of a family I'm no longer a part of. What's the point?"

Van Pelt cleared his throat, then studied Ryan for a few moments before continuing. "What I am trying to do is to paint, for both of you, a picture of someone who has no respect for a gentlemen's agreement, and no regard for life, human or otherwise. Two weeks ago, going against everything he promised to the Committee, he set a plan in motion that resulted in the theft of the seventh statue. An intricate scheme that also seems to have involved seeking you out, Ryan, prying into your personal life, culling your tribe, and finally baiting you directly by taking your friend—who I am assuming was more than just a friend—to the processing plant. Maybe the eighth statue *is* in Brooklyn, maybe it is not; Harker would have been an imbecile to share its location with anyone, even his own progeny. He was many things, but never stupid. What is certain is that your friend was killed, if he or she was in fact taken to East 80th Street. The plant is a sort of living memorial to a crueler, more wasteful era, one that the rest of my tribe ended years ago. We allowed Xansati to continue to use the building as he wanted, as per our agreement, but we've kept a constant watch on it to clean up the trash, to cover for his people's sloppiness. We have found limbs dumped in or near the East River, bodies of humans who were deemed unfit for consumption. The last cleanup crew we had to send in found two castoffs who were still alive, a man and a woman, both O positive, both heavily sedated and badly injured. The man died in a matter of minutes, but the woman showed incredible fortitude. Early indications were that she would survive. We decided that she should have another chance, a fuller life, that she would make a welcome addition to the tribe. Vanessa, that woman is your newborn. We were waiting to tell you until she'd made it safely through the transition, which I trust she has."

"Oh my God." Vanessa swallowed hard enough for Ryan to hear it through the speaker. "Oh God," she repeated, "that's why she was so out of it when Brad and Randall brought her in. I thought it was part of the . . . Yes, yes, she's doing well, all things considered. She's done a great job."

"Good," Van Pelt said, nodding and smiling thinly. "That is excellent. Have you met her yet, Ryan?"

"I have," Ryan said, forcing a polite grin. "But I've tried to keep my distance. I remember what it was like to be a newborn. The, uh, lack of restraint."

Van Pelt nodded and snickered before taking another sip from the tube. He reached up and smoothed a misplaced lock of hair that seemed unnaturally wiry, as if it weren't his own.

Ryan tried to process everything he'd just heard. Nothing that Van Pelt had said contradicted anything in Derrick's research, even if he had left out significant portions. Vanessa, still audibly on the verge of hyperventilation, wasn't faking anything. And finding Jennifer discarded but alive was a plausible explanation for what had happened to her. She was a fighter, stronger than she appeared. It was one of the main reasons Ryan had been attracted to her, the biggest reason to think that she might have still been alive when he'd crossed the river to find her.

"I want to offer my condolences," Van Pelt said. "And I'm going to make you a promise. Xansati will be dead this time tomorrow. That's why I called this meeting. Vanessa will be part of a team of our most capable and seasoned warriors, a team that is going to go to the Cloisters, cleanse it, and lock the statues up for good. We cannot allow one insane misanthrope to jeopardize everything we have worked to build. Some of the other board members wanted to wait until next week, to do more in-depth reconnaissance, but after hearing you today, I am convinced that we need to strike as soon as possible, while we still have superior manpower and the element of surprise. While Xansati thinks there is still a truce."

Ryan looked at Vanessa. Her breathing had steadied and any shock she might have been feeling had been wiped clean, replaced with a calm, almost frightening resolve. The briefest mention of a mission had transformed her circuitry, switched her into full-on soldier mode.

She was ready to kill, no questions asked.

"I want to go with them," Ryan said.

Van Pelt frowned. "You're dying and you want closure," he said. "You want an eye for an eye from those who have wronged you. You have nothing left to lose. It's a natural response, a timeless one, one I deeply respect. But what could you hope to accomplish in going besides a quicker demise than the one you've already been dealt? No, I have a better idea. I want you in my tribe. I was prepared to offer you an invitation before I'd met you, but now that I have, I am even more convinced that it is the right course of action. Rodney, the strapping specimen standing outside this room, has been with us for twenty years. A little young, certainly, but we feel that he is ready to take on a parental role. Especially knowing that his new-born has already undergone the process, already understands the transformation and all that it entails. It will be easier for both of you."

Ryan sighed and shook his head. "Thanks for the offer," he said, "but I'm going to pass. I've made my peace with whatever's going to happen to me. I'm not scared of dying. And it just wouldn't feel right joining a new tribe after being in my old one for so long."

Van Pelt sat silently for a few moments before letting out a small chuckle. "You know," he said, "I believe that is almost exactly what Harker told me when we gave him the same option."

"You knew Arthur personally?"

"I spoke to him face-to-face only once, and briefly," Van Pelt said, "shortly after he left your tribe and shortly—he told us—after turning you. He seemed like a good man, intelligent, weary of the gift after so many years, confident that he had made the right deci-sion leaving Brooklyn, although he regretted that he had left behind a newborn as young as you were. But ultimately he was more Le-nape than Dutch, blinded by what the statues represented to him and not what they actually were. Though we have only just been acquainted, I don't see any of that part of Harker in you. You seem like your own person. You follow a lonely path, but a true one. That is more than can be said about most of us. On second thought, there is a part of tomorrow's assignment where you might be able to help us, if that is really what you want, if you are as selfless as you make yourself out to be."

"No fucking way!" Vanessa shouted. "He doesn't have any training. He's not healthy. What could he possibly—"

Van Pelt lifted a hand, silencing her instantly. "Ryan, I have enjoyed our chat," he said, "but you must be getting tired. You need to rest, to hydrate, to prepare your body to give whatever it has left in it. While Vanessa and I go over some of the more tedious details of the assignment, as well as a few unrelated matters, why don't you head back up to the lobby? They will get you something to eat while you wait. Vanessa will fill you in on your role later. I wish you the best of luck tomorrow and I sincerely hope to see you again."

Before Ryan could respond, the section of the chamber in front of him slid into the floor and he was assaulted by a rush of freezing air. He nodded at Van Pelt and glanced for a moment at Vanessa, who was looking at the floor, trying to hide her distress and doing a poor job of it.

When Ryan entered the hallway, Rodney, the muscular sentry, was standing in the same position against the wall, arms still crossed. He saw Ryan and grinned. "Well, are we going to do this or what?"

"Do what?" Ryan asked.

"You know, turn you. Make you my, uh, offspring, or whatever you want to call it. At first I was a little, like, iffy about the whole deal. I was hoping they were going to give me that tight little hottie who was all messed up when we dragged her out of the river. What a body on her, bro. I'm telling you. But then I thought about it and if we did end up doing anything, wouldn't that be kind of like incest? I'm probably better off with you."

Ryan felt his face flush, his body tense. "I decided not to take Van Pelt's offer," he said between clenched teeth.

Rodney looked confused. "Huh," he grunted. He shrugged. "No worries. They'll find someone else for me soon enough. You can count on that. Hey, you're staying with Vanessa, right?"

Ryan nodded.

"Do you have her number? I'd like to show her newborn around, when she's finished transitioning. I don't like them too feisty, you know?"

Ryan turned and headed for the elevator. The coldness he'd felt when Van Pelt had opened the glass chamber was replaced by a boiling irritation that seemed to be increasing in intensity with every step he took.

Instead of trying to stifle the heat, he embraced it, let the fury build so that he would be ready for the next day.

He needed to keep burning.

28

"I still don't see the point of you going with them," Jennifer said, massaging Ryan's chest while he recovered from a massive coughing spasm. "I've barely just got you back in my life, barely started to figure out who you really are."

They were intertwined on a mattress in the darkness of the containment chamber attached to Vanessa's apartment, which was functioning as Jennifer's bedroom until the tribe set her up with her own place.

Lying on his back, waiting for his breaths to slow and the ache in his chest to diminish, Ryan gazed through a large skylight at the cloud-dulled, orange-tinted night. "I want to see that the people who harmed you, the people who killed Seamus and came after the rest of my tribe, are going to suffer for what they did," he said. "I want to be there to feel their pain."

Jennifer sighed and withdrew her hand. She rolled over onto her back, parallel with Ryan, her right shoulder pressed against his left. "But isn't it enough to know that they're gone?" she asked. "Vanessa said that the job's going to be a relatively easy one, that the tribe's team will have strength in numbers, that What's-his-name and the other defectors won't expect anything. She doesn't anticipate any casualties on our end. Pardon the expression, but won't you just be dead weight?"

"One of the reasons there won't be any casualties, why we'll be able to catch them off-guard, is directly because of my role in the assignment, which is minimal. I'll be in and out before any real fighting starts. And, if something does happen, it's not like I have that much of a future to look forward to, anyway. I figure a couple months at the most."

Jennifer squeezed Ryan's forearm, hard enough to make him flinch. "What about the people who care about you?" she asked. "Don't you want to spend as much time with them as you can?"

"You mean the *person* who cares about me? I'm pretty sure Vanessa would have choked me out today if it hadn't been for the glass cages separating us."

"I *mean*," she said, rolling onto her side and pressing her forehead against his cheek, "wouldn't it be better to spend two more months together than just one night?"

Ryan sat up and put his arm around her. "I've lived a long, long life," he said, "and you're smart enough to live much longer than me. But you can't think like that. Extra time doesn't mean anything if you fill it with empty promises that might not ever materialize, if you spend it regretting the things you could have and should have done, if you're too sick to do anything about it. It took me almost a hundred years of near-isolation to break out of the shell that I'd constructed around myself, to be able to lose myself in a perfect moment with someone else. Trust your gut, no matter how many days you think you have left."

Jennifer rolled her eyes. "Okay, Dad," she said, teasing him. "Thanks for the words of wisdom."

"I know it's cheesy," he said, "but I just want you to know where I'm coming from, and why you aren't going to change my mind."

Jennifer smiled, sadly at first. As she pulled the blanket off them and climbed on top of Ryan, her expression changed to a mischievous grin.

"Well then, I guess I'm going to have to carpe diem the shit out of this moment right now."

She grabbed his arms, guided them to her thighs, and pulled him up by his beard toward her parted lips. Tongues intertwined, fingers fumbling, cupping, plying at warm skin that was collapsing in syncopated waves, the wetness between her legs. He slid inside and she mumbled stale heat against his neck, grunting, licking his ear, bucking, and he was looking up through the glass at the handful of stars that were pulsing, then dancing, singing, melting away the years, everything that had happened, everything he needed to do, transporting him to a place beyond his body, beyond pain, where there was only this instant, this heat, where there was only her.

He woke from a dream-free black hole, choking on the coppery sludge that had invaded his throat and nostrils, that was spilling from his mouth, running down his neck and chest and caking the mattress. The room's air was thick with its sickly sweet aroma.

Ryan frantically untangled himself from the sheets and shot out of the bed. He made it two steps before a spasm caused him to lean over and place his hands on his hips and he was spitting, vomiting, coughing violently. Tears streamed from his eyes and mingled with the growing puddle on the floor. He looked up and when his vision adjusted to the inky predawn shadows, he saw Jennifer crouching in the corner of the room, watching him intently, rocking silently back and forth, her knees pressed against her chest and her arms splayed in a pose of prostration. A foot-long gash ran vertically along one of her forearms, partially healed but still glistening. Arthur's knife, its blade stained black, rested a few feet away on the floor.

"I'm so sorry," she stammered, "I didn't know what I was doing. I thought that if I—"

But before she could finish, Ryan rushed past her and flung open the containment chamber's door. He staggered through the living room, naked, half blinded by the track lighting that had been turned up all the way, past the dining table where Vanessa was sitting with a large set of blueprints spread out in front of her. Her eyes widened and her lips parted in surprise. She started to get out of the chair, but Ryan waved her away and hurried to the bathroom that was adjacent to the kitchen. He slammed the door behind him and locked himself inside.

He turned the shower on, full blast and scalding, and scrubbed himself until his skin crackled, until it was on the verge of splitting. He watched the last of the smelly, viscous fluid congeal in the bottom of the tub and circle down the drain. After he turned the water off he stood for a few moments, gripping the rack that held the soap and shampoo, trying to slow his heart rate and combat the dizziness that made it feel like he would collapse at any moment.

When he emerged from the bathroom, a towel wrapped around his waist, Vanessa was sitting in the same place, concentrating on what Ryan now saw was an architect's layout of the Cloisters. There was a full glass of water on the table next to the blueprints. She looked up and motioned for him to take it.

"I never took you for the kinky type," she said. "Or maybe you were just trying out something new?"

Ryan slumped into an adjacent chair that had been pulled out, lifted the glass to his lips, and took a long chug. "She tried to turn me," he said. He groaned as a migraine formed out of nowhere and began to split his brain in half.

"Apparently she didn't do a very good job," Vanessa replied. "I guess her talents lie elsewhere. You going back for round two? If you are, you might want to take care of business now. The sun will be up soon. We only have a couple hours before we have to suit up with the rest of the team."

"I'm glad you find this amusing," he muttered.

"Aw, don't be so upset," she cooed, faux-affectionately. "I think it's cute. In a really sad, kind of fucked-up way."

Ryan tried to clear his throat, unable to completely shake the sensation of blood-related suffocation. "I need to go back in there and make sure she's not whittling her teeth into fangs and getting ready to suck me dry, or something worse. But while you're here, alone, I wanted to ask you why you lied about me to Van Pelt, about what happened at the processing facility, why you didn't tell him that your newborn was the reason I came to Manhattan. Doesn't that go against your code of ethics? I mean, Van Pelt does seem like your typical upper-crust scumbag. I wouldn't tell him anything, but he *is* your boss."

Vanessa began folding up the blueprints, as if she'd suddenly become nervous and her hands needed something to do. "After I'd been turned," she said, "and after I killed my maker, when I became a real part of the tribe, it was obviously a culture shock. It was hard enough trying to wrap my mind around the fact that I'd become something out of a comic book or a horror movie, without having to try to figure out what I was going to do, what my next step would be. The Committee made it easier, made me feel like I was a part of something special and sacred, the whole 'gift' thing. For the first time in my life, someone had given me a direction, a purpose. Of course I was going to do what they told me, undergo the training. I thought that was just the way it was, how the world I'd stumbled into had always operated. I wasn't going to ask questions."

"You had no frame of reference," Ryan said. "I probably would have done the same thing."

"When I became a maker and ran into you, that frame of reference shifted. The idea that you could survive and thrive as a blood-eater on your own, without the tribe looking after you and directing your daily life, it's mind-blowing. I started thinking back to some of the assignments I'd done, the lives I'd ended, things that I'd seen or heard that had seemed inconsequential at the time. Why all of us younger members of the tribe, out of nowhere, had been given humans to turn. I want answers, but I'm afraid of what will happen if I ask, if they think I'm no longer a happy drone. I don't want that for Jennifer. I want her to be able to make her own decisions. Also, I need to figure out what I'm going to do with this."

She picked up a clear plastic baggie that Ryan hadn't noticed and slid it across the table in his direction. Inside was a tiny, circular white capsule, smaller than an aspirin.

"What is it?" Ryan asked. He picked up the baggie and examined the pill closely. Its surface was smooth, like a candy shell, with no discernible markings.

"It's a tracking implant. You swallow it and it binds to your stomach lining instantly, at least that's what Conrad told me. He said that the Committee voted on a new protocol. All newborns have to swallow the implants, for safety purposes. So they can be easily located during the transition period. So they aren't a danger to— what did he say?—our species' anonymity. Maybe it's because of the whole Derrick Rhodes thing. Maybe it's something they've been discussing for a while. But if the Committee was so scared about disclosure, why wouldn't they give implants to all of us? Do they think that because they've beaten their dogma into our heads for so long, those of us who have been around a while are no longer threats? I don't like any of what's been going on. It smells like bullshit."

"You're right. It *is* bullshit," Ryan said.

He opened the baggie, lifted it to his mouth, shook out the implant, and swallowed. He washed it down with the rest of the water from the glass that Vanessa had given him.

She stared at him in silence for several moments, as if she were trying to figure out how to put together a puzzle where none of the pieces fit. "What the fuck did you just do?" she finally whispered. She was trembling, not out of anger, Ryan realized, but pure, uncontainable fear.

"I gave you another option," he said. "When we leave to go uptown, it'll look like you took her with you. When you get back, you can tell Van Pelt or whoever that you made a mistake, that you thought she was ready to fight, however you want to spin it. In reality, you'll be able to let her go off the radar. She'll be free to make her own decisions, whether she wants to stay or start again somewhere else as a human. It'll be her choice, not yours or the Committee's."

"What happens when the mission's over and you come back with us? How are we going to explain that? You going to throw on a wig and makeup? You're a decent-looking guy, Ryan, but somehow I doubt you'd be able to pull it off."

"I'm not planning on coming back."

Vanessa's demeanor immediately shifted to that of a senior officer about to berate a disorderly grunt. "The last thing I need is some suicidal cowboy to go in guns blazing and get the rest of us killed in the process," she snarled. "Whatever doubts I might be having about the leadership, the team is made up of other soldiers, people who are just following orders. I'm not going to sacrifice them because of your insane death wish."

"I'm going to do the job I've been assigned to do," Ryan replied, calmly. "I'm not going to jeopardize anyone else. Van Pelt may be lying to you about a lot of things, but you know he's right that my role will make it easier for the rest of the team, lower the risk of any casualties."

Vanessa nodded, grudgingly. "It's true, as much as I hate to say it. Do what you have to do, just don't fuck us over." She motioned contemptuously in the direction of the containment chamber. "Have fun explaining that to her. Karl's picking us up in three hours."

"Thank you," Ryan said, already heading back across the living room. He took a deep breath and walked into the containment chamber where Jennifer was still sitting on the floor, hugging herself.

It was time to say good-bye.

29

The so-called munitions warehouse wasn't as impressive as Ryan had expected. Although, if he was being honest with himself, those expectations were based solely on sixty years of half-watched science fiction and spy thrillers, the police procedural dramas that Jennifer had forced him to sit through, and the formfitting body armor that Vanessa had given him before they'd left her apartment: a moisture-wicking, Kevlar-reinforced compression suit that he was currently wearing under a black long-sleeve T-shirt and a pair of black track pants.

Ryan and Vanessa entered the side door of an abandoned, graffiti-covered gas station on East 2nd Street after Vanessa simply opened it with a metal key. There were no body scans and no chain-smoking doormen to impede their progress, just a vacant, dingy lobby. They walked through a set of unlocked double doors and into a large gutted room that had once been an automotive service garage. Two oil-smeared car lifts lined one wall, sharing floor space with dozens of cardboard boxes, rusted fuel drums, and random pieces of severed machinery.

Near the center of the room, four male figures sat at a table under an epileptic halogen ceiling lamp, similarly dressed in black athletic gear, the chunky outlines of their body armor suits clearly visible underneath. There was Rodney, Ryan's would-be maker; an even larger superjock with a bald head and a goatee; an identically sized—and equally follicularly challenged—Nordic monster; and a smaller, though no less fit Hispanic guy whose neck and hands were completely covered in floral tattoos. If this was a representative selection of the Manhattan tribe's muscle, Ryan thought, they could have done much worse.

All four of them had been silently fiddling with phones or tablets when Vanessa entered the room. As she and Ryan made their way toward the table, they put down their devices and noticeably stiffened their postures, like well-trained soldiers who had just been alerted to the presence of their commanding officer. Rodney stood up, nodded at Vanessa, and scowled at Ryan before heading toward a walled-off section on the opposite side of the garage that looked like it had once been an office.

"Troy, Gunter, Ramon," Vanessa said as Ryan shook hands with each of them and sat in an unoccupied chair. "Veterans of Normandy, Gettysburg, and the Mekong Delta, respectively, which they will tell you all about in excruciating detail if you spend more than five minutes hanging out with them."

"So you're the one who broke Rodney's heart," Troy said, grinning at Ryan. "He really was looking forward to being a father. But I think I speak for all of us, and—unfortunately—as his roommate, when I say that it would have been a major disaster. Unless you're really, like creepily, into Jason Statham movies and actually believe that you're a real-life version of the Transporter. Then you might want to reconsider."

"Or Justin Bieber," Ramon chimed in. "Remember when we were doing recon on that development near the Port Authority and he started lip-syncing to that shitty-ass song on the radio, how did it go, 'As long as you touch me,' or something?"

"'As long as you *love* me,'" Gunter corrected, "but I think for Rod the difference is insignificant." He broke into a belly-shaking laugh. The others joined in.

"You guys are fucking dicks," Rodney said from across the room, pushing what looked like a large laundry cart covered by a blue plastic tarp. He parked the cart next to the table and returned to his original seat, slapping the back of Troy's neck as he did.

Before Troy could retaliate, Vanessa cleared her throat loudly and every drop of levity in the garage evaporated. "All right, children," she said. "Playtime's over. Do we have a report from the scout team?"

Gunter opened his iPad and started scrolling. "They did a drone flyover twenty minutes ago, five minutes after the museum opened. Thirteen nonhuman thermal signatures, three of them located in the vault. One of those is different. It's, um, hotter. Xansati and all of his defectors, minus one or two. We can expect the same number of blood-eaters to be present at the close of business hours, in addition to maybe fifteen human hostiles, all of whom will most likely be armed, at least with DXT spray."

Vanessa nodded. "The building closes to the public at five o'clock," she said. "We'll be giving the museum visitors as much time to leave as we can afford, but we've got to get in there no later than five thirty. According to our intelligence, Xansati stays pretty close to the vault most of the time, but we need all of his people there, too. This is our best chance to erase the threat to our tribe, all of that threat's components, in one quick sweep without it making headlines. Anything you see moving once you're inside, regardless of age, gender, or species, you eliminate it."

The soldiers grunted affirmatively, without questioning anything Vanessa had said.

The naïve, artsy girl who had run crying into Ryan's arms forty years earlier was totally gone, he now saw. She'd been replaced by a stone-cold killer, made ruthless because of what she'd had to do to survive, but also because doling out death was in her nature as a dead warrior, just as it had been in his, as it was in everyone who had ever been turned. But Vanessa wasn't only a killer, she was a leader of killers, commanding the respect of people who had seen action in some of the most brutal conflicts in history. For Ryan, her transformation was as impressive as it was frightening.

"I know that all of you are at least moderately familiar with the museum's layout," Vanessa continued, "and hopefully you read the briefing we were sent. Are there any questions about what's going to happen, our team's specific role?"

"Seems straightforward to me," Ramon said, leaning back casually in his chair. "We have Ryan walk in, element-of-surprise-style. They won't smell him coming. Or at least they'll smell—no offense—a sickly dude with subpar blood. That'll be their mistake. Ryan will clear the entrance and then we'll come in and clear the rest of the museum's main level, make our way to the treasury vault from above while the other team—of whom I'm definitely not envious—digs through the tunnel system below the museum and enters the vault from below. Shouldn't be too much of a problem, unless Rodney goes full Michael Bay and starts blowing the bosses' family heirlooms to shit."

"That's a good point," Vanessa said, glaring at Rodney. "Try to limit damage to the exhibits."

"That all depends on what they're going to be coming at us with," Rodney said, a little defensively. "What kind of heat you think they'll be packing?"

Gunter looked up from his iPad. "Darts," he said, "same as us. Except theirs will be the old models, from the armory. Neither the scouts nor the drones have detected any signs of fortification or weapons shipments. As far as we can tell, they're operating under the conditions of the truce. We should be able to take out most of them before they realize what's happening."

"And even if they do realize, it won't matter," Troy said, standing up and flinging the tarp off the laundry cart, revealing the Hollywood-quality cache that Ryan imagined.

There were layers of small crates filled with pistols, rifles, flare guns, boxes of clear plastic ammo cartridges, and metallic grenade-like spheres. Troy reached under the weapons and pulled out black nylon utility belts with multiple holsters and compartments and distributed them to each member of the group, including Ryan.

Vanessa walked toward the cart. She picked out a handgun and two ammunition cartridges and tossed them to Ryan. The soldiers stood up and began zestfully rooting around the cart like bottle scavengers on recycling day, examining the firearms and shoving cartridges, spheres, and pistols into specific compartments of their utility belts with mechanical precision, as if this were an act they'd performed hundreds of times.

To Ryan, the pistol that was now in his possession looked similar to other semiautomatic handguns he'd owned, albeit a little more high-tech, made of polymer with a chrome lining and featuring an infrared sight and a twelve-round magazine. But the bullets in the cartridges were like nothing he'd ever seen. They looked like pointed oval shells made of clear glass that were filled with a brownish-yellow fluid.

"They aren't bullets," Rodney said, reading his mind. He was standing over Ryan, holding one of the spheres, his belt already fastened and loaded. "They're darts. The liquid part is a DXT concentrate. Strongest version they've come up with so far. When one of these little guys pierces the skin of a human, things tend to get messy real fast, we're talking seagull-eats-Alka-Seltzer messy. If your target's tribal, there might not be any combustion, but it'll have the same effect. Can you shoot?"

"I mean, I won't be trying out for the Olympic biathlon team anytime soon," Ryan said, twisting the pistol to make sure the barrel screws were tight. "But yeah, I can handle myself, especially if the targets are stationary and sitting two feet away from me."

"Let's hope so." He handed Ryan the sphere. "If shit goes severely bad, use this. A shard bomb. It's exactly what it sounds like. The shards have been dipped in, you guessed it, DXT. You activate it by pressing both of the small indentations on either end for three seconds. When you release it you've got another five before it detonates. Just make sure you duck behind something solid after you chuck it."

"Hey," Vanessa said, a note of concern in her voice as she strode over to them. "I don't think he's going to need that. He's only going to be inside for—"

She was interrupted by her phone, which started belting out a generic beeping ringtone. Gunter's iPad, resting faceup on the table, lit up at almost exactly the same time.

"Looks like the other team is uptown and ready to start setting up," Gunter said, checking the screen. "They're going to head into the park, canvass the area, figure out the best entry point into the tunnels. You want me to stay here and keep eyes on the entire operation, right?"

Vanessa studied her phone's screen for a moment, then nodded. "We should load the van," she said. "I'll have Karl pull it around."

"Don't want to go to work on an empty stomach," Rodney said, his voice quaking with sudden excitement as the soldiers stopped what they were doing and turned in unison, waiting for Vanessa to acknowledge them.

She rolled her eyes. "Fine, but make it quick," she said.

The rest of the team scampered off into the shadows toward the walled-off section of the garage. A few seconds later Ryan heard what sounded like a rush of air shrieking from a balloon, then the rip of fabric. Then a wet, gurgling noise.

"It's one of Xansati's disciples, or whatever you want to call them," Vanessa said disinterestedly as she touched something on her phone's screen and pressed it to her ear. "Rodney questioned him, tied him up, and left him in there. It's probably been three days. I'm surprised he's still alive. Or was. Must taste foul." She scrunched her nose in revulsion. "But it's their pregame ritual. God forbid we deny them of that."

There was a noise that sounded like several dozen sheets of bubble wrap being popped at once, followed by a testosterone-tinged cheer. Ryan tried not to visibly shudder, but he couldn't stop himself.

"You going to be ready to go when we need you to be?" Vanessa asked. "You still can back out if you want."

"I'm good," Ryan said.

"Good," she replied, heading toward the garage doors that faced the front of the building, giving Karl instructions in a low voice. She pressed a button on the wall, and one of the doors began to open electronically.

Ryan fingered the dart cartridges in his hand, visualizing a target for each of them, one in particular, older and stronger, who deserved the poison more than the rest.

Yes, he said to himself. *I'm ready to go.*

30

They sat in the tree-shaded, cobblestone parking lot, watching visitors exiting the arched wooden doors that functioned as the Cloisters' main entrance. The five-thirty bus arrived right on schedule. It swung around the circular stop that separated the parking lot from the moatlike walkway surrounding the museum while the last large group of stragglers took farewell pictures of the wide, citadel-style stone and stucco terraces and massive, centrally located medieval tower looming above them. The castlelike architecture was no less imposing than it had been during the previous three drive-bys the team had done in the last few hours. If the Committee had wanted to build a stronghold, they couldn't have picked a better location: one of the tallest hills in Manhattan, completely surrounded by a heavily wooded park that could only be traversed on winding, labyrinth-like trails, in a sleepy, out-of-the-way residential neighborhood that made Williamsburg look like Times Square.

But a stronghold was only as effective as its gates. And those were wide open.

Vanessa was sitting in the front passenger seat of the white eight-passenger van. She turned to look at Ryan, who was in the second row next to Ramon, closest to the sliding side door. "You're up," she said calmly, as if they were playing a board game and it was his turn to roll the dice. She motioned at the smartwatch on Ryan's left wrist. "Call when you clear the lobby. If we don't hear from you in two minutes we're heading in anyway."

He nodded and caught a glimpse of the soldiers in the rearview.

Their faces were similarly lockjawed, emotionless masks gazing no-where, exuding the calm of seasoned veterans. Karl was staring back at him from the driver's seat, his brow furrowed in contem-plation, probably analyzing the chances of Ryan fucking things up for his beloved Vanessa.

Don't worry about them, Ryan said to himself. *Don't worry about any of it. This will be over soon.*

He slid open the van's door and stepped onto the pavement. He crossed the parking lot, careful not to walk briskly enough to attract attention or to cause his shirt to fly up and expose his holstered pistol. To the handful of people he passed that were lingering at the bus stop or in front of the museum's entrance, whether they might be tourists or members of Xansati's entourage, he was nothing, or at the worst, another crazy (and sickly) aficionado of thirteenth-century tapestries hoping to snag a replica of one at the gift shop before it closed.

As he pushed through the doors, he found himself in an unoc-cupied, dimly lit stone alcove that had been constructed to resem-ble the bowels of a European monastery. He reached for the pistol and clicked the safety off, leaving it in the holster. To his left was a wide, upward-sloping passage. Opposite that was the closed-off entrance of a passageway that looked like it led to a subterranean section of the museum. Ryan visualized the blueprints of the build-ing that Vanessa had shown him and took the stairs. Before he'd gone ten steps, he saw the sallow, balding head of a man above him illuminated in the glow of a computer screen, sitting behind a desk on a wide landing. To the man's right, the stairs curved, narrowed, and continued ascending to a large entrance hall containing the information and ticket desk, Ryan's ultimate destination.

As Ryan climbed, he noticed that the man was wearing a navy-blue sports jacket with a security company's insignia. Paunchy, sixty-ish, much closer to dead than warrior. Ryan stepped onto the landing and was reaching for his pistol when the man looked up from his screen.

"Sorry, buddy," the man said, scrunching his nose a little, "we closed half an hour ago. You're going to have to come back tomor-row."

"I know," Ryan said, his fingers curling around the pistol's grip. "I was hoping that it wasn't too late to check the lost-and-found. I was here earlier and I think I might have left my backpack in one of the exhibits. It's got some stuff in it that I really need for work tomorrow. Look, I've got a picture of it on my phone."

Ryan lifted the pistol and fired in one quick motion. The dart lodged between the security guard's second and third chins, with seemingly no effect. He let out a confused grunt, plucked out the dart, and stared at it. Ryan was about to fire another round when the man let out a barely audible croak, began to convulse, and then shook so fast that it was almost seemed like he was vibrating.

His eyes widened, then rolled back, then turned a weird shade of neon pink. Then they melted into a thick sludge that oozed onto his face. A few more strands of the same substance escaped the corners of the man's mouth before he began deflating like a flesh balloon. Within ten seconds, there was nothing left of him but a chunky, leaking pile of skin and clothing where he'd been sitting. The chemical reaction hadn't necessarily been explosive; the security guard had simply been liquefied from the inside out. Meaning he was probably *Ànkëlëk-ila*, the first of his former species that Ryan had killed.

Before he could attempt to comprehend what had just happened, Ryan heard the sound of a conversation above him, echoing from the stairwell to his right. He jogged up the short flight of stairs and found himself in a cathedral-like, high-ceilinged atrium with three ornately carved archways—two large ones that led to exhibit halls and a smaller one that served as the entrance to the museum's gift shop, where soft flute music was wafting from unseen speakers.

The long, semicircular information-desk-slash-ticket booth was to Ryan's immediate left, manned by a pair of twentysomething girls wearing white collared shirts and sorting piles of earbuds used for audio tours. Before they looked up at him, Ryan fired two rounds in quick succession, hitting one of the girls in the side of the neck, the other in the shoulder. Instead of melting, they spontaneously disintegrated into puddles of sludge, coating the chairs they had been sitting in, the desk, and the wall behind them in splatter marks. It was an accelerated version of what had happened to Derrick Rhodes. The puddles had been human.

Ryan lifted the smartwatch he was wearing and swiped until he found the number he had been told to call. He found it and pressed the send button almost unconsciously; he was transfixed by the slime and the household-cleaner aroma it had begun to emit.

He heard a noise behind him, swiveled around, and saw a pale, middle-aged woman dressed in khakis and a navy-blue vest with a name tag. She was standing in the center of the gift shop, her mouth gaping in bewilderment. Ryan fired at her and she dove out of sight behind a stack of replica tapestries, lightning-quick, her reflexes much too fast for a mortal.

Before he could pursue her, he heard a voice echoing in the distance, getting closer. Three security guards were jogging toward him from the far end of the exhibit hall he was now facing, guns drawn, one of them barking into a phone. In the corner of his eye, Ryan noticed more movement, turned, and saw two figures, both dressed in black tracksuits, charging at him from the other exhibit hall to his left.

So much for the element of surprise.

One of the security guards got a shot off before Ryan had time to move. The sound was deafening in the hall's cavernous expanse. The bullet barely grazed the armor plate covering Ryan's shoulder, but the impact was strong enough to knock him back a few feet, into the side of the desk.

Ryan barrel-rolled across the desk counter and crouched behind it. The soles of his shoes struck the pink gunk on the floor, causing it to splash onto his pants and burn several small holes in the fabric. He fumbled around with his utility belt and found the compartment that contained the shard bomb Rodney had given him. As he gripped the smooth metallic sphere, the footsteps and voices got louder, closer, seemed to multiply and surround him. He pulled out the bomb and found the indentations that would activate it. Just as he was about to press them and toss the sphere, he heard two or three gunshots, then a series of muffled hissing noises followed by several thuds and the scattering of hard plastic on stone.

Then total silence, except for the gift shop music that had changed to a somber Gregorian chant.

"Whatever you're thinking about doing behind there," Vanessa said, "stop it."

Ryan put the bomb back in its compartment and stood up slowly, suddenly overcome with intense dizziness. He gripped the desk and tried not to cough, but it was impossible. Vanessa and Troy were standing near the stairwell, rifles lowered. Five steaming piles of mangled skin—in addition to random pieces of hair, clothing, and firearms—were scattered across the floor of the atrium. Rodney and Ramon were already moving silently and cautiously through the exhibit hall to the left, their rifles slung across their backs and their pistols raised, weaving around Virgin Mary statues and cruci-fixes in glass cases until they disappeared through a pair of open wooden doors.

Troy was grimacing, rubbing the edge of a hole in his cheek where a bullet had torn through the skin and exited the other side, healing much slower than it should have. "Fucking honey-dipped shells," he said to Vanessa, spitting blood. "Remember those?"

"You'll live," she replied, unsympathetically.

"I'm assuming the honey is DXT," Ryan said, hopping over the desk when he'd stopped coughing.

"Yup," Troy said. "Nowhere near as potent as what we're pack-ing, and our armor will stop them, but it still stings like a bitch."

"It'll do more than sting *you*," Vanessa said to Ryan. "You per-formed better than I thought you would, got us in the door without any problems, did what we needed you to do. Go back to the van and wait."

"No," Ryan said. He opened his pistol's magazine to refill the chamber. "I'm going with you. I read the mission briefing. I studied the blueprints. And I'm pretty sure I know how the statues work, if I make it that far. I can hold them without injuring myself."

Vanessa shook her head. "Out of the question. And when have you ever been close enough to a statue to know how your body would react to them? Unless you weren't telling me everything that—"

Ryan fired a shot over her shoulder. There was a high-pitched shriek that ended as abruptly as it started.

"What the fuck was that?" Vanessa stammered, physically shaken for the first time that Ryan could remember.

Troy jogged over to a jewelry display case near the entrance to the gift shop, reached behind it, and lifted a gelatinous corpse by the collar of its vest. The dart Ryan had fired was still lodged in its forehead. It was the shop's employee, or what was left of her.

"I'm surprised you didn't smell her," Ryan said to Vanessa. "Is that because of the, uh . . . job?" He lifted his fingers to his nose and made a pinching motion.

Troy's eyes widened as he walked back toward them. "*Dude,*" he exclaimed, trying not to smile, looking at Vanessa as if he expected her to strangle Ryan. "I can't believe you just went there. Based on the size of those balls alone, Vanessa, we should let him stay with us. He's not a bad shot either."

"*Fine,*" Vanessa muttered, her lips contorted into a fierce scowl. "We don't have time to argue about this anymore. But I'm not responsible for what might happen, what's *going* to happen. I'm done caring about you."

Though it wouldn't have helped to tell her at that moment, Ryan appreciated her concern for him more than she would ever know. She had given him a chance to die with the gratification of having avenged Jennifer, or at least knowing he had tried.

Vanessa's smartwatch flickered, flashing a message. "The other team is in the tunnels," she said. "Meaning they'll be losing service soon. Let's move."

The main level of the museum was modeled after a medieval abbey. It comprised eleven distinct chambers featuring Western European medieval artifacts that formed a rectangle around the museum's centerpiece, the Cuxa Cloister, an open-air courtyard and garden ringed by a series of arches that had once stood in a twelfth-century French abbey. The team's job, as Ryan understood it, was to split up and sweep the chambers, to clear it of any hostile elements, then converge and head belowground to the vault, eliminate Xansati, and secure the statutes, if the other team hadn't already completed their end of the mission or failed to do so.

To Ryan, it didn't matter who pulled the trigger, as long as he could see a body.

Rodney and Ramon had already headed south into the Late Gothic Hall, meaning the rest of the team would be going west, then south, eventually rejoining them and taking a descending flight of stairs adjacent to the Gothic Chapel. Vanessa lifted her rifle to her shoulder, turned on the sight, and stepped over the security guards' bodies and into the Romanesque Hall, trailed by Ryan, then Troy.

The room was largely barren and a good deal bigger than the atrium, its walls lined with giant, brightly colored frescoes and stone carvings of dragons, griffins, lions, eagles, and camels. The air was still, settled after the recent altercation, and almost totally silent, save for the echoing thuds of Ryan's feet against the stone floor that caused Vanessa to flinch a tiny bit every time he took a step. He'd forgotten how impossibly soundless dead warriors could be.

For a moment, he became self-conscious and a shred of doubt crept into Ryan's mind. He briefly considered whether he should continue, whether he was putting Vanessa and the team at risk. But he shook off the thoughts as she stepped cautiously through an archway bounded by the carvings of two sword-wielding kings and into a smaller room with an altar and a wooden and gold crucifix at its rear. She raised her hand and extended her thumb for the all-clear signal, or at least Ryan hoped that was what it was.

He followed her into a gallery illuminated by narrow stained-glass windows that shot kaleidoscopes of color onto carved statues of human heads, peering out from the walls that were composed of limestone blocks from a French church. Chairs had been set up in two parallel sections in front of an altar and were separated by an aisle-sized space. It was a beautiful—and at any other time, calming—scene. Not just this room, but the entire museum. If the situation had been different, if he hadn't had to worry about getting shot by chemically enhanced projectiles, Ryan would have enjoyed wandering the corridors, imagining himself lost in another place and era.

A hail of gunfire rang out nearby, shattering the chapel's contemplative aura.

"Let's go!" Vanessa grunted as she darted through a small doorway to left of the altar.

Troy and Ryan rushed in the same direction, weaving around the pillared boundary of a thirteenth-century monks' enclosure. When they caught up to her, Vanessa was situated in a large, naturally lit hallway facing the Cuxa Cloister, squinting into her rifle's scope, scanning the sundrenched, grass-and-plant-filled courtyard that featured two perpendicular walking paths and an ornately carved stone fountain at its center.

Directly across from where they were standing, on the other side of one of the gardens, Ramon was slumped in a sitting position at the base of one of the pillared archways that formed the cloister's border. His pistol was lying in the grass a few inches from where his left arm was extended as if reaching for the weapon. But he would never reach for anything again. Nearly a quarter of his head, mostly above the right temple, had been shot clean off, causing the skin around it to splay and peel back like a partially removed rubber mask. Still-steaming bits of skull and brain matter mingled with already-congealed fluids on his shirt and the pillar that was supporting him.

"Fuck," Troy muttered. "They had to have gotten right on top of him. How is that possible?"

"I don't know," Vanessa said. She lowered the rifle and nodded at an open doorway made of oak and iron, about ten yards past Ramon's corpse. "When I got here, I saw Rodney sprinting after someone into the tapestry rooms. He's sticking to the plan. We need to do the same."

"No updates from the other team?" Troy asked.

She looked at her smartwatch. "No."

They walked south for several yards along the edge of the courtyard, then took a right into a room whose floor space was dotted with sculpted bishops and gold-embossed angelic figures on cordoned-off pedestals, and whose walls were covered with paintings of saints in supplicating poses. There was no sign of movement. The room's southern boundary featured a nearly life-size statue of a pope or a cardinal, a three-foot-high stone barricade that separated the main level of the museum from the lower exhibits, a stone ledge overlooking those exhibits, and a narrow set of stairs that cut between the two.

Vanessa's watch lit up. "It's Rodney," she said. "He's at the Treasury entrance, about to rig the door. It's a straight shot for us through the crypts and the Glass Gallery, maybe sixty yards."

Troy slung his rifle over his shoulder, pulled his pistol out of its holder, and checked the magazine while Vanessa did the same. "These'll have to do from here on out," he said.

"So you're saying I'm ahead of the curve?" Ryan asked, checking the compartment on his belt that held the extra ammunition cartridges.

He got the slightest courtesy chuckle out of Troy, while Vanessa ignored him and headed quickly for the stairs. Her head disappeared behind the stone barricade. Troy nodded at Ryan to follow.

He'd gone down four or five steps when he felt the barrel of Troy's pistol pressing sharply into the center of his back. He stopped walking. "Easy, man," he said softly. "What's going on?"

There was no response. Troy pressed harder.

Ryan swung around and Troy's body tumbled past him down the stairs, collapsing in a disjointed heap near the stone tomb of a fourteenth-century Spanish nobleman. He convulsed in electric bursts, then began to shrink. An emptied dart was sticking out of the back of his deflated head.

A second dart zipped by, inches from Ryan's eye socket, and shattered against the ledge, burning an acid-rimmed cavity into the stone and releasing an overwhelming, sickly sweet hospital aroma.

Ryan didn't waste time trying to pinpoint the source of the shot. Instead, he sprinted down the remaining stairs and leapt over Troy's corpse, finding himself in the Gothic Chapel, a semicircular, vestibule-like room with brightly colored stained-glass windows and lined with the burial caskets of several important Catalan counts. Vanessa was frozen with her back to him, pointing her pistol at a mousy, gray-haired woman with a confused expression and a small metallic object in one of her hands. The two were standing four feet apart, separated by the eight-foot-long and three-foot-high tomb effigy of a famous crusader that was resting on the floor in the exact center of the room.

"Troy's gone," Ryan stammered, nearly out of breath as he pulled up even with her. "And they have darts. They have *our* darts. I thought they weren't supposed to have access to them."

"That's not all they have," Vanessa said softly, not breaking her gaze from the woman, who was shivering and mumbling to herself. She was clutching a shard bomb in her gnarled, arthritic fist, her unsteady fingers pressing the indentations that activated the detonator. If she let go, they'd have five seconds before the blast.

"He told me," the woman was muttering, "he told me to come here, said I could be one of them, that I would be, that I would, that I would be more than meat, that I would become one of them, that the pain would end, that the pain . . ."

She lifted the bomb as if she were preparing to throw it across the room. Vanessa put a dart in her chest and lunged at Ryan, pulling them both down to the ground, where they braced themselves against the side of the tomb. Ryan heard the clang of the bomb against the floor, then a soft popping noise. A burning hot mist settled on the back of his neck but before he could wipe at it, the bomb went off.

The detonation wasn't as loud as he had thought it would be, though he could still feel the blast's vibrations through several feet of solid rock and hear the rush of particles speeding in every direction, shattering the stained-glass windows, disfiguring the bodies that had been carved into the coffins that lined the walls.

Before Ryan could regain his composure and react to the situation, Vanessa grabbed him by the shoulders and pulled him up, dragged him across a section of the floor that was sticky with the woman's residue, down another set of stairs and into a long, rectangular room that contained dozens of rows of jewelry cases filled with gold signet rings, ivory and silver rosaries, and elaborate brooches. At the far end was a glass wall with the word *TREASURY* printed in bold letters above an open doorway, where Rodney was standing, fiddling with his watch.

He looked up, noticed Vanessa and Ryan, and did a double take, as if, for a moment, he didn't trust what he was seeing. He shook off his disbelief and motioned for them to hurry up and join him.

"Can you run?" Vanessa asked. She was still holding Ryan firmly by the collar of his shirt.

"Yeah."

She let him go. They sprinted toward Rodney and joined him in the smallest gallery that Ryan had been in so far. The section of the room where they were standing was only a few feet wide. After he'd put his pistol in its holster and spent a few seconds catching his breath, Ryan noticed that the room's walls were covered in woodcuts depicting the Crucifixion and the Passion. For a moment, he wondered why this part of the museum was called the Treasury. The artifacts didn't seem any more valuable than others they had passed. Was it a painfully obvious marker for anyone who knew what they were looking for, the tribe's version of an inside joke?

"I thought I was the only one left," Rodney said softly. "Troy?" he asked.

Vanessa shook her head.

"Shit," he muttered. "Well, at least your boyfriend's still with us," he said, his voice dripping with false enthusiasm.

Though Ryan didn't like the tone, he was glad to see a familiar face, even if it had taken a pretty good beating. Most of Rodney's shirt had been singed off, revealing the intact body armor underneath. There was a minor flesh wound in the side of his neck and a bullet-sized patch of scar tissue bubbling on the back of his right hand.

"What the hell happened back there?" Rodney asked.

Vanessa turned and looked back in the direction she and Ryan had come from, completely at a loss for words. Ryan shrugged, equally muted by what they'd just encountered. The old woman's face, right before Vanessa shot her, had been permanently etched into his brain.

"Were you able to get in touch with the team in the tunnels before the signal went dead?" Rodney asked, sounding more impatient with every word. "What's the next move? We can't just sit here. If you haven't noticed, Xansati's people are a little more prepared than we gave them credit for."

Vanessa turned and flashed her usual stone-faced glare. "We're finishing the mission," she said. "You have the battering ram?"

Rodney nodded. "Yup," he said, his somber expression suddenly shifting to a mischievous grin. "I think that's the right move, boss. I really didn't want to have to go back upstairs."

He reached into one of his belt's compartments and took out a gray plastic cube that was a little larger than a standard die. One of the sides was covered with a strip of black paper. He walked over to a recessed section of the wall that Vanessa and Ryan had run by when they'd entered the Treasury and ran his fingers along the edge of a nondescript, unmarked wooden door with no knob and no other way to conceivably open it. He pulled the strip of paper off the cube and pressed the newly exposed side onto the door near its right edge, about halfway up from the ground, where a hinge normally would have been. He began to fiddle with his smartwatch for a few seconds, then looked up at Ryan.

"You might want to turn around for this," he said. "Pretty sure your eyes won't be able to handle the glare."

"What is that device?" Ryan asked.

"Long story short," Vanessa said, "it opens things. Rodney's right. Turn around."

Ryan did as he was told and suddenly there was a grating noise, then several intense flashes that brightened the room to an extent that was beyond any kind of artificial light Ryan had ever experienced. He squinted, trying to focus on the woodcut in front of him, an image of Christ being struck by a Roman soldier, bleeding, while a woman knelt at his feet and an angel watched the scene from above, indifferent to what was happening. A plaque below the woodcut read: *Donated by the Van Pelt Family Collection.*

The noise ceased and the lights stopped flashing. When Ryan turned around, the door was flung open, revealing a narrow passageway that looked like it had been carved into the bedrock that formed the hill beneath the museum.

Vanessa ducked inside and motioned for Ryan to follow her. Rodney stood outside the entrance, attempting to extract a flare gun from his belt's holster.

"What are you doing?" Vanessa asked. "You can't use that in the passages. You'll kill all of us."

"Duh," Rodney said. "I just want to make sure that no one who wants to kill us will be able to follow us."

He lifted the gun, extended his arms, and aimed in the general direction of the stairs that led back to the upper level.

"The Committee won't be too happy about having to clean up after that," Vanessa said.

"Fuck the Committee," Rodney replied. "I didn't sign up for this shit."

He pulled the trigger and a screaming fireball exited the chamber. He dropped the gun and dashed into the tunnel where Ryan and Vanessa were waiting, slamming the door shut behind him. A few seconds later, there was a muffled explosion, then the sound of dozens of glass panes shattering.

"Only one way to go now," Rodney said, pushing past Ryan and heading briskly down the stairs.

The air in the passageway was damp and musty, and it was dark. The only source of light was a series of small antique lightbulbs that hung from the cavelike ceiling that seemed to increase in height the farther they walked. They descended for several minutes before the stairs ended and they were on level ground. The passage widened enough so that the three of them could walk side by side, but the lights were far more infrequent, so that Ryan could just make out each approaching glowing speck without seeing much of the passage itself. Something told him he wasn't missing much.

They continued for half a mile or so in the unchanging darkness before Rodney and Vanessa slowed their pace and began to sniff the air, their noses scrunched and their brows furrowed.

"What is it?" Ryan asked in a voice that was barely above a whisper. "Is it human? Xansati?"

Vanessa took a deep breath, then another. "I . . . don't know," she said. "I'm picking up several different blood types, but all of them are faint, washed out. Everything has been corrupted, consumed by a . . ."

"A burning," Rodney said.

He was right. Even Ryan could smell it. An intense odor of meat that had been left on a grill for a few days too long. And something else, a weird fungal aroma he'd never encountered.

The path curved sharply and for a moment they were bathed in total blackness. When they came around the bend they saw the vault—a massive stone-walled chamber whose entrance was a fifteen-foot-high archway like the ones in the Cloisters, but larger. The light from within bathed the remaining fifty yards of passageway in a soft golden glimmer.

The ground was covered in dozens of bodies, or, more accurately, the parts of those bodies that hadn't been totally vaporized.

There were compressed piles of leaking skin wrapped in security guard jackets and white museum shirts, pink splatter marks and puddles with shattered dart cartridges swimming in them. But there were also charred husks that had once been limbs, torsos, and skulls. A few intact figures, totally blackened, their arms raised in defensive poses, their scorched lips twisted in grimaces of pain and terror. It looked like they had been exposed to a heat so intense and sudden that they hadn't even bled from their injuries.

As overpowering as the smell was for Ryan, he knew that it was exponentially worse for Rodney and Vanessa as they zigzagged around the heaps of biological sewage, scanning the carnage through their rifle sights.

Rodney stopped moving. He lowered his rifle and groaned in disgust. "What happened here?" he asked. "How is it possible to fry someone like—"

"The statues," Vanessa cut him off. "We need to bury this place."

They were about ten yards from the archway, where the trail of bodies stopped. Except for one. Xansati was lying on the ground near the back of the chamber, his head slightly elevated on the bottom of a set of stairs that led to a raised stone platform, on which sat a small, semicircular hut. He was shirtless, caked in dust, his chest and neck covered in emptied dart cartridges, looking like the victim of a sham acupuncture session. In his hand he clutched a stone figurine, identical to five others that were scattered around him on the floor. Its gaping eye holes and bared fangs sent a tremor of anxiety through Ryan, one that he quelled by focusing on Xansati's permanently shuttered eyes.

Of all the corpses that he had seen, this was the only one that mattered, the one that would give Ryan peace when he'd have to confront his own swiftly approaching death.

It was over.

Vanessa clicked her smartwatch and raised her rifle. "We have confirmation of six statues and a body," she said into the device as she started walking slowly toward Xansati.

"Oh shit," Rodney exclaimed, softly, as if Vanessa had jogged something important in his memory. "I thought I was the only one left, I thought I was the only one," he muttered in a weird monotone stammer that made him sound like the old woman who had been clutching the shard bomb in the museum.

Ryan frowned at the hulking warrior-turned-moron standing next to him. Why was Rodney suddenly unraveling now? "You told us that already," he said, "when you, me, and Vanessa reconvened. Troy and Ramon and the other team are dead, but three of us made it. We're about to finish the job."

"No, you don't get it," Rodney said, snapping back to lucidity, taking a step forward so that he was between Ryan and Vanessa. "I fucked up. You shouldn't be here. This was supposed to be part of the cleansing. We're starting over, a new tribe. A younger tribe. One you could have been a part of if you'd let me turn you, but you gave up that chance. She never had one."

He lifted his rifle and fired. The dart hit Vanessa squarely in the back of the neck. She dropped her gun and swung around, unsteadily, staring back at them with the same look of confusion as the first security guard Ryan had shot. Her eyes melted out of her face and she crumpled to the ground, another quivering mound of waste.

Ryan reached for his pistol. His holster was empty.

Rodney swung around, grinning, pointing the rifle at Ryan. "Looking for this?" he asked, lifting up his shirt. Ryan could see the grip of his pistol hanging out of the compartment that had held Rodney's flare gun. "I took it after I shut the tunnel door and brushed past you. I'm surprised you didn't notice it was gone until now. Pretty slick, huh?" he added, proudly.

Ryan nodded, trying to combat the fight-or-flight tremors that were surging through his body. He needed to think. He'd come too far to throw everything away. But even if he could somehow lunge and wrestle the rifle out of Rodney's grip, there was no way he'd have time to fire it. Rodney could smash his face in without trying.

"So that's why the Committee has been making a point of turn-ing new members," Ryan said, stalling as he remembered some-thing, a possible way out if he could move fast enough. "That's what the tracking implants are for. They want a new generation that will be easier to control, made up of people that will be so psyched to be immortal that they won't question orders. And they're going to make you, what, like a general or something?"

"Something like that," Rodney said, moving closer to Ryan until they were less than a yard apart. "Pretty much. But now's not a great time to discuss politics. It's time for us to say good-bye. It's nothing personal, man."

Ryan took a deep breath, bent his knees, and lowered himself to a kneeling position, his hands at his sides. He began to slowly pull up his right pant leg while maintaining steady eye contact with Rodney, who grunted in annoyance. "Ah, come on, don't try to pull some begging shit on me," he groaned. "No matter what you say, I'm not going to turn you now. When has that ever worked? What crappy movie are you thinking of?"

Ryan didn't answer. Instead, he gripped the handle of Arthur's knife, which was strapped to his shin, and swung it in an uppercut motion that connected with Rodney's groin and burrowed into the soft gut above it. When Ryan removed the knife with a sharp twist, Rodney dropped the rifle. He stumbled backward, eyes wide, star-ing at the clumps of intestine that had begun to spill out of his ripped track pants and onto the floor. Ryan stood up and stabbed Rodney between the eyes, twisting the knife until he heard a crunch. He pulled the blade out and Rodney collapsed facedown into a puddle of pink slime.

"Nothing personal," Ryan said as he wiped the blade on his pants.

Before he could think about his next move, or about what had happened to Vanessa, a wave of vertigo overtook him, followed by a long coughing spell. He needed to sit down. He made for the cham-ber's glow and stepped under the arches that, he now saw, were carved to resemble a bear and a wolf baring their teeth at each other, frozen in precombat aggression. The chamber itself was circular with a domed, rotunda-style ceiling, where a pair of industrial floodlights shone down. The walls were natural rock, into which dozens of massive alcoves had been carved. He approached one of them that was near the chamber's entrance and saw thousands of bones—skulls, rib cages, femurs, vertebrae—stacked in no discernible order. Alongside the remains were arrowheads, carved wooden masks, pipes, and hatchets similar to the artifacts Ryan had seen at Natalia's house.

This wasn't just a vault. It was the original tribe's mausoleum.

Ryan heard a grunting noise and swung around, facing the hut—whose roof and walls, he now saw, were made of tanned animal hides—and the staircase. Xansati had hoisted himself up two of the steps, into a near-sitting position. His gray suit and white undershirt were peeling off him in shreds. Most of his hair looked like it had been singed off; his scalp was coal-black. His eyes were open and he was staring sideways at Ryan as if he couldn't move his neck. His brow and jaw were creased with muscular tension. The statue in his hand had turned a deep green color and seemed to be glowing, vibrating slightly. Something inside the jaguar was causing its eyes to pulsate, to shift in color from red to bright amber and back again.

Ryan walked over and ripped the statue out of Xansati's clenched fist. It was almost weightless, and hot and strangely sticky against his skin, as if it were covered in some kind of adhesive gel, even though its surface looked smooth and dry. A sudden surge of electricity shot into Ryan's fist and up his arm, a sensation that was both oddly invigorating and bewildering. Even after he dropped the statue and watched it land on the ground intact and upright, the tingling lingered.

He tried to ignore it and stood over Xansati, who seemed to be completely paralyzed. "You probably don't remember me," Ryan said, "and you don't know why I'm here. But believe me, you deserve this."

He raised the knife over his head, picking out a point of entry just above Xansati's sternum. Just before he plunged the blade into its target, Xansati croaked out a word.

"What?" Ryan asked.

"Jacob," Xansati said, a little stronger, stressing each of the syllables. "You're Jacob Arrington."

Ryan hadn't heard anyone call him by that name, his original name, in nearly a hundred years. It was a name that had been all but forgotten. He held the knife in the same position for a few indecisive seconds, then lowered it. "How did you know that?" he asked.

"Because you have my knife. The knife I gave to Arthur. He told me he'd buried it, left it for the young man he'd turned. A blond, pale man named Jacob who he said would be able to hold the *kwènishkwènayas*, just like I could."

"Hold the *what*?"

Xansati chuckled, then cringed in pain. "A long word, I know. In Lenape it means something like a cougar or a puma. The stone vessel you just took out of my hand. It's not the first time you've seen one."

"No," Ryan said, "it's not."

Xansati took a deep breath. "But you're no longer *Ànkëlëk-ila*," he said, "which means that you aren't carrying the vessel and haven't for some time. And you're wearing the uniform of my former brethren." His eyes widened in sudden trepidation. He gasped, trying to lift himself off the stairs. "Did you give them the jaguar?"

"That would really piss you off, wouldn't it?" Ryan asked, the old anger flaring up. "But no, I didn't. It's still in Brooklyn. Van Pelt would probably kill me as soon as I gave it to him. Or have one of the goon squad do it for him. That's how it works in Manhattan, right? You guys get other people to do the dirty work for you. It must have seemed so easy to find me, to attack my tribe, to destroy my girlfriend's life. All you had to do was shell out a few bills to someone, maybe promise them a place somewhere nice and gentrified, like you hooked up for Nicki."

"What reason would I have to try to find you?" Xansati looked utterly lost.

Ryan let out a bitter laugh. "You've been trying to collect all eight of the jaguars for years. You find out a few months ago that the second-to-last one has turned up at the Brooklyn Museum. Okay, easy enough, you'll pay to have it stolen. Now you're close, there's only one statue left, the one that belonged to your friend Arthur. You remember that he'd turned someone named Jacob. All you have to do is find me. You don't know how long it'll take but you know I'll turn up eventually, and you know that the Committee isn't going to be cool with you adding another weapon of mass destruction to your collection. So you give them some bogus excuse about why you can't be friends with them anymore and move everything up to the Cloisters, in preparation for whatever apocalyptic tea party you're planning on having with your eight stone toys."

Xansati cleared his throat violently. "If I wanted to take Arthur's statue, as you call it, I could have gone to Green-Wood Cemetery and dug it up myself. I know exactly where he buried it." He grimaced while his body twisted uncontrollably in a long spasm of pain. "Arthur and I never wanted to collect all of the statues to create a weapon," he said once he'd recovered enough to speak. "When he came to me with the first Brooklyn jaguar, it was because he'd been studying the statues for centuries and had grown to fear their power. This was during the First World War, when he'd seen the soldiers returning from Europe, in boxes or worse, and it became clear to him how humans would use the statues if they could figure out how to harness their energy. He sought me out because I was the last of the original tribe and he thought, correctly, that I would want to keep our relics out of the wrong hands."

"I know about Arthur's obsession," Ryan said, annoyed. "I know about the years he spent searching for the statues, before he disappeared. But I also know about the experiments. Why did you let that happen? Sounds like those were definitely not the right hands."

Xansati sighed. "I was curious. For six hundred years I'd just assumed the jaguars were magical, that they were infused with powerful spirits, like the medicine men would talk about. But after I lost contact with Arthur, a part of my mind became restless and I wanted to see if there was a technological explanation for what they could do. Why only some of us in the original tribe could touch them, why they could allow some of us to leave our villages and remain Ànkëlëk-ila. So I told the Committee about them. And at first, we did learn a great deal. But when I found out about the studies that were being funded by outside elements, what they were doing to our own species, the chemical by-products they'd isolated, I took the statues back. But it wasn't enough. I had to completely separate myself. That's why I brought them here. I thought they'd be safe. I never wanted to retrieve the seventh statue. The worst thing that could have happened was for it to resurface. All that did was stoke the Committee's desire to complete its ultimate goal of not only using the statues as a weapon, but of turning dead warriors into living weapons, ones that could be deployed whenever and wherever their masters see fit, whether those masters are the Committee or the American military. I didn't expect them to come after me so soon. I thought I would have more time to strengthen this place. I also didn't expect people whom I trusted, people whom I considered to be my friends to turn on me like this." He pointed weakly at the projectiles riddling his body. "I was stupid and I failed."

"So you're saying that if anyone took the seventh and came after me for the eighth, it was the Committee? They're the ones who found my girlfriend, tortured her, and destroyed both of our lives?" Ryan asked.

Xansati nodded, grimaced again.

Ryan tried to wrap his mind around what he'd just heard. What Xansati had said was in line with Derrick Rhodes's research, with what Rodney had said about a cleansing, with the tracking chip that Van Pelt had wanted to put inside Jennifer. Creating a legion of super strong, invincible mercenaries seemed right up the Committee's alley, as did buying off Xansati's followers.

But there was still one major point of contention.

"What about Nicki?" Ryan asked.

"Who?"

"Don't lie to me. I'm sure the Great Spirit, or your ancestors, or whoever you're going to be meeting in the next few minutes won't be happy with you if you do. Young girl, dark hair, curvy in all the right places, talks too much, B-negative blood. I saw you with her a few days ago, in an apartment on West 29th Street. You obviously found her attractive."

Xansati was silent for a moment, as if deep in thought. Suddenly his eyes widened. "Stella?" he asked. "How could you know about her?"

"I met her online, thought she was just a donor out to make a little money on the side. The second time I saw her she told me that the people she was working for had taken the woman I love and were going to kill her unless I gave Nicki—or Stella, apparently—the statue. So I followed her to Manhattan, tracked her to the building where you two were—"

"I ran into her on the street a couple of months ago," Xansati said. "Somewhere in Harlem. Or, I should say I *smelled* her. The scent was irresistible. I asked her if she might like to go to dinner, but she knew exactly what I really wanted. It clearly wasn't her first time dealing with our species. It was the best meal I'd ever had."

Ryan couldn't argue with that. Nicki's blood was how he imagined freebasing pure cocaine would feel.

"But she was only ever food to me," Xansati continued. "And maybe a little, what do you call it, stress relief. After a while I thought that providing the apartment on 29th Street for us to use might have been a bad idea, because she started coming on to me, strong, telling me she loved me, and that she was going to leave her fiancé in Brooklyn so she could be with me full-time."

"Her fiancé in Brooklyn?"

"Yes," Xansati said. "She said she lived with him there. A much older man. She showed me a picture of him. Didn't seem like her type. But what did I know?"

"What did her fiancé look like?" Ryan asked.

"A black man," Xansati said. "Salt-and-pepper dreadlocks. I think she said his name was Fred."

Not Fred, Ryan thought, *but close*.

Frank had been pimping Nicki out the whole time.

He thought back to the night in Prospect Park that now seemed like it had taken place in a different century, how he'd told Frank about Seamus, about how Frank had said he was going to make a few calls to some old contacts and try to figure things out.

Ryan now had a good idea who those contacts were.

Xansati groaned and coughed out a gob of pink fluid. "Do you know why Arthur turned you?"

Ryan shook his head.

"It wasn't by chance that he found you in the hospital. And you hadn't been exposed to a mysterious South American illness that had been brought to the city on that boat. There was a statue on board, the one that Arthur buried in the cemetery. It had activated during the trip. Its radiation killed everyone who came near it, except for you. You were immune to it."

"Then why was I so sick?" Ryan asked.

"Your cancer had taken a turn for the worse," Xansati replied. "It was as simple as that. Until he found you, Arthur and I thought I was the only one alive who could handle the statues when they started to glow, who knew how to channel their energy. There were some other *Ànkëlëk-ila* and medicine men who were able to touch them when I was young, but they're long gone. For everyone else, human or tribal, they're instant death."

Ryan nodded, picturing the burned corpses in the passageway.

"We still don't know whether it's genetics or environmental factors, but either way, you are among the rarest of the rare. And your purpose has come. You need to take the statues with you, get them as far away from Manhattan as you can. You need to find—"

Ryan felt a rush of air as a dart whizzed by him and struck Xansati in the forehead. Xansati's mouth shut and he trembled for a few moments and then went still. His eyes rolled back, then turned pink. But instead of liquefying they hardened and kept their shape, like two neon pebbles gazing into nothingness.

"God," a voice behind Ryan groaned. "Enough is enough. I don't have all day for this sob story. Oh, and drop the knife."

Ryan turned and faced Karl, who was standing a few yards away, wearing his usual sweatpants, his hair a disheveled mess, holding a pistol in one hand and a large duffel bag in the other. He tossed the bag and watched it land at Ryan's feet.

Although touching the statue had made Ryan feel stronger than he had in weeks, he wouldn't be able to get to Karl faster than Karl could get a shot off. Ryan dropped the knife.

"Pick up the statues and put them inside," Karl said.

"You were working for the Committee the whole time," Ryan said, trying to contain his fury so he wouldn't do anything rash. "Congratulations. You fooled me. And Vanessa. Did Van Pelt promise you the same thing he promised Rodney? A leadership role in the new tribe?"

"Vanessa was my friend," Karl said, his voice rising an octave.

Ryan saw that his eyes were bloodshot and wet. "She was more than that. I would have done anything for her. When I heard the explosion a few minutes ago, I ran here as fast as I could, to try to help her. It was like I could sense that . . ." He trailed off for a moment, tried to choke back a sob. "But now she's gone."

"Then why not just walk away?" Ryan asked. "Mourn her and move on. You don't know what you're getting yourself into."

"I read all of the documents you brought to Vanessa's apartment," Karl said. "I'm not stupid. Those rocks are worth a lot of money to a lot of different people." He motioned at Xansati with the barrel of his pistol. "I heard him say that you can touch them. So let's go. Put them in the bag."

"No problem," Ryan said calmly. He bent over and picked up the still-glowing statue that he'd taken out of Xansati's hand. As he did, he felt the same electric rush as before, coursing through his body with pharmaceutical precision. His mind was racing as he moved to place it in the bag.

How had Xansati been able to use the jaguar to scorch the bodies that were lying outside the chamber? Had he been able to focus the energy inside himself and somehow force it back out through the statue in a series of concentrated bursts? Or did the statue choose its targets at random?

An image flashed through Ryan's brain. He remembered the parchment that Vanessa had found rolled up in the handle of Arthur's knife. The drawings of figures holding the statues, the light radiating from their bodies.

Ryan slowly lifted the jaguar and held it with both hands a few inches in front of his chest. Two parallel bolts of energy raced through each side of his body, immobilizing him with their intensity, joining together with an audible clicking noise near the middle of his spine. The statue began to vibrate while turning a lighter shade of green.

"What the fuck?" Karl stammered, aiming the pistol at Ryan's forehead, his voice frantic. "What are you doing?"

Suddenly the statue became scalding hot and Ryan was forced to let it go. But it didn't fall to the floor. Instead, it hovered in the air and moved closer to Ryan's chest, as if it were drawn to him by some kind of magnetic attraction. Ryan and Karl watched in stupefied silence as the jaguar shrank to about half its original size, then flattened and changed from a solid into something supple and gelatinous as it pressed against Ryan's chest. It melted through his shirt and corroded his body armor before finally fusing to his flesh like melted iron in a mold. It cooled and hardened as quickly as it had heated up, so quickly he couldn't feel it.

But he could feel everything else.

He could smell each of the bodies in the passageway, whether they were human or dead warrior, every location on those bodies that chemicals had decomposed, the places where fire had met skin. He could taste the thick, badly circulating air, feel slight variations in the current with each of Karl's quickening breaths. He could see every bead of sweat that was pooling around Karl's temples, every one of his glistening pores.

The only thing that Ryan could compare the sensation to was when he had been turned, but this was on another level, and without any of the corresponding terror and disorientation. Whatever the statue was doing to him, it felt right. Better than right.

He took a step toward Karl, who fired all of his remaining darts at Ryan's face and neck. They glanced off Ryan's skin as if they'd been made of paper. Karl threw the gun down and turned to run, but Ryan grabbed his wrist before he could take a step. Ryan felt the adrenaline inside him manifesting as heat that quickly spread from his chest and down his arms, collecting in his hands.

The skin on Karl's arm where Ryan was holding him began to bubble, then fall off in wet clumps until Ryan was gripping bone. Karl let out a feral screech that was cut short by the index and middle fingers of Ryan's free hand jabbing through his neck and out the other side.

Ryan let go and Karl fell to the ground with a dull thud.

He stood still for a moment while warm blood puddled around his feet, waiting to be overcome by a coughing spell, a spasm of vertigo, or an anxiety attack, but nothing materialized. He felt stronger and more focused than he'd ever been, and he didn't care why or how it had happened.

There was no moment of indecision as he calmly strode to the platform where Xansati was lying, collected the remaining statues, and put them in the duffel bag, as he walked out of the chamber and briefly paused in front of Vanessa's corpse before heading back up the tunnel toward the museum.

He knew what he needed to do.

He needed to go *home*.

31

He watched the familiar shoreline flash by across the East River as he sped southward on the FDR Drive—the mouth of Newtown Creek that separated Queens and Brooklyn, the crumbling industrial yards of Greenpoint and Williamsburg being swallowed by under-construction residential towers and office buildings, the Williams-burg Bridge looming thirty blocks ahead of him, a landscape that Ryan never thought he would see again. But now he found himself returning to it with the same sense of urgency as when he'd left.

He slammed on the van's brakes as the traffic suddenly began to bunch up near the East 23rd Street exit's off-ramp and swerved a little into the adjacent lane, where he was greeted by the fierce horn blasts of a cab and a small Toyota coupe as they maneuvered around him. He instinctively reached for the duffel bag on the pas-senger seat next to him. Its contents had shifted but seemed intact.

"Focus on the road," he mumbled, reminding himself that he'd never been behind the wheel of a vehicle as large as the eight-passenger Ford E-150 that Karl had left running in the Cloisters parking lot, that he hadn't driven a vehicle of any kind in more than a decade, that a traffic stop would result not only in a major delay but also the unnecessary loss of life for any officer who tried to de-tain him.

Though he still felt physically rejuvenated by the statue that was affixed to his sternum, the adrenaline-laced certainty that had con-sumed him had been replaced by the problematic reality of the paths he might choose to take.

More than anything, he wanted to retaliate. But as strong and unbreakable as he felt, he knew that if he walked into Van Pelt's office, there was a good chance that he wouldn't walk back out alive, and if he did, it would be with a target on his back. Putting any legitimate dent in an organization as formidable and connected as the Manhattan tribe would take weeks or months of preparation, time that he might not have. He had no idea whether the statue's effects were temporary, and if they were, how long they would last.

Then there was Frank. The ancient hustler always looking for his next scam, the next big payday, always at the expense of anyone he knew he could use, as Ryan had learned the hard way. Whatever hand he'd had in helping the Committee bring down Xansati and in trying to locate the eighth statue, it was almost certain that it had been monetarily motivated. Ryan was motivated to separate his former father-figure's spinal column from his body, but that might involve a significant manhunt through Brooklyn, which also meant time.

The most prudent move, he decided, was to retrieve the eighth statue from the bridge. Derrick Rhodes had talked about traveling to Iceland. Maybe Ryan would go there and dump the duffel bag into a mile-deep fjord. Maybe he'd do the opposite of Arthur and scatter them across the vastness of a continent.

Instead of continuing to the bridge, as he'd originally planned, he got off the highway at the next exit and drove onto the Houston Street off-ramp.

Before he disappeared, he needed to make a quick stop.

32

When Ryan stepped out of the elevator, Jennifer was standing in the doorway of Vanessa's apartment, arms folded over her chest. As he approached, her facial expression changed from one of relief, to confusion, to complete disbelief. Her eyes narrowed and her nose wrinkled as she tried to make sense of what she was seeing and smelling.

"Where's Vanessa?" she asked. "What is that on your—"

"Shut the door," Ryan said, cutting her off as he walked past her and into the apartment. He made his way through the kitchen and into the dining area, where a laptop sitting on the table was open with a Twitter news feed live-streaming on its screen. He scanned the ceiling and the walls and crouched under the table, looking for any object, obvious or discreet, that might be a camera or a sound recording device.

Jennifer had followed him into the room and was watching him. "Okay," she said firmly, "you need to stop and tell me what happened. From how weird you're being, I'm assuming it's bad, but there hasn't been anything on social media, which has got to be a plus. Also, why is there a Batman logo tattooed onto your chest? And why do you smell so . . . amazing?"

"Where's my backpack?" Ryan asked, standing up and placing the duffel bag on the table.

Jennifer rolled her eyes, unsatisfied with his evasion. "It's in my bedroom, where you left it," she muttered.

Ryan hurried through the apartment and came back into the

dining room a minute later wearing the T-shirt and jeans he'd had on before Vanessa had given him the body armor. He placed the backpack on the table, opened it, and rifled through it until he found the flash drive. He glanced up at Jennifer, who was still hovering in the entranceway. "You might want to sit down," he said.

As she did, Ryan slid the flash drive across the table in her direction. He tried to explain, as succinctly as he could, what had happened to him, going back to being turned by Arthur, his years in Brooklyn and his relationship with Frank, everything he'd gone through after meeting Nicki, up to Karl's death in the vault. Ryan told Jennifer all that he knew about the statues, what Derrick Rhodes had discovered about them, his own firsthand experience of their unpredictable nature and how the Committee wanted to hijack that energy, how they were going to use her and the rest of the newborns as test animals once they'd sufficiently thinned the herd.

Unlike Vanessa in the coffee shop, Jennifer's stone-cold expression didn't change to one of discomfort or fear as he talked. Her eyes remained fixed on his, unblinking, an icy blue barrier that made it impossible to know what she was thinking. Maybe she'd been exposed to so much life-altering outrageousness in the past few days that she was numb to any further, slightly more absurd-sounding developments; for her, it was simply par for the course. Or maybe the story, especially the death of her maker, had shocked her into stoic silence. Either way, Ryan had no idea how she would react to the plan he'd crafted on the way to Vanessa's apartment.

"I'm going to take the last statue and then I'm driving as far away from the city as I can," he said. "I'm not sure where, but I can't stay here. Even if the tracking implant I swallowed was somehow disabled by the energy surge, the tribe has resources that extend far beyond Manhattan. When I leave here, take the flash drive to the nearest copy store, or anywhere that has Internet access. E-mail its contents to the address that's written on the drive and destroy it. That should keep the tribe occupied for a few days. Go somewhere safe, maybe your old apartment, maybe somewhere uptown, somewhere you can disappear until things settle down a little."

Jennifer frowned and looked at the flash drive. "I'll e-mail the files," she said, "but once you grab the statue, you're coming back to pick me up. I'm going with you."

"Absolutely not. I don't know how to control these things," he said, motioning at the duffel bag. "They're unpredictable. And one of them is stuck on me like a giant leech. What happens when it falls off? What if it doesn't? What if I'm a human IED?"

Jennifer's expression changed for the first time as she flashed the vaguest hint of a smile. She shrugged. "I don't know," she said, "but one thing's for sure. You aren't human anymore. But even if something *does* happen to you, I want to be there. If what you're saying is true, there's nothing for me here. I can't hide on a thirteen-mile, two-million-person island for very long, even with my . . . um, abilities."

Ryan nodded. "You'll have to leave. Which means you'll return to your original, mortal state. You'll be even more vulnerable, which is why it would make even less sense to be anywhere near me." He sighed. "Please trust me. Everything I've done has been to try to protect you."

Jennifer's eyes came to life, flashing angrily. She leapt up and sent the chair she'd been sitting in careening across the hardwood floor. "It's been about *me*?" she growled. "Are you sure? To me, this just seems like more of the same suicidal martyr crap that made you decide to go to the museum. I didn't want you to go. You'd already found me. I'd forgiven you and thanked you for what you'd done. All I wanted to do was spend time with you. But you were too wrapped up in the emotional thrill ride you'd been on since you left Brooklyn. It wasn't about me anymore. It was about how good it had felt for you to break free from the boring drudge of your lonely existence, for your life to finally have meaning. I thought that the reason you were so jacked up was because you'd been confronted with your own approaching death. But even now, when you've made it back from the Cloisters, when it looks like you've been given a third chance, when you should be curious about what you've become, you're still hoping to play the fatalistic hero. I mean, Jesus, you're talking about the possibility of literally going out with a bang."

Ryan sat in silence for a long time. "If that's how you feel," he managed, finally, "then I respect that."

Jennifer's frown disappeared. Her shoulders sagged as if they'd been weighed down by a sudden sadness. She walked over to Ryan and took his hand in hers. "It's not that I don't appreciate you," she said softly. "I do, way more than when I thought you were some kind of commitment-phobic weirdo who was too scared to sleep over at my place." She laughed, then turned serious. "But you need to let me make my own decisions. This is about both of us."

"Of course," Ryan said. "If that's what you want."

"It is," she replied. "Oh, and I'm going to need to eat you."

"What?"

Jennifer gripped Ryan's wrist, lifted his forearm until it was even with her face, and inhaled deeply like she was smelling a warm baguette fresh out of the oven. "You told me that something in your DNA, in your blood, is what allows you to hold the statues. And maybe the jaguar that's bonded with you has amplified those genetic traits. What if I were to drink your blood? Wouldn't it be possible for me to sort of absorb your abilities, at least temporarily?"

Ryan thought back to the meals he'd had—the varying degrees of freshness, the rarity of the types, the age of the donors. It was true, the quality of the meal did make a huge difference. Her idea was a little odd but it was worth a shot.

"Might as well see what happens," he said.

He bent over and rolled up one of his pant legs until he could remove his knife from its holster. He laid his left arm on the table, palm facing up, and made a deep incision in his wrist, slicing through the ulnar artery.

Before the blood had a chance to spurt, Jennifer was on her knees, her lips clamped tightly around the wound, gorging herself. Ryan gasped at the urgency of the fluid leaving his body, though he felt no pain after the first few seconds. Instead, there was only the sensation of being totally joined to someone else, of reciprocation instead of draining, of sharing life instead of taking it. The longer he let his guard down, the more he let her take, the deeper the connection felt, until it got too deep. She wasn't going to let him go until he was dry.

"That's . . . that's enough," he stammered, suddenly feeling like he was on the verge of passing out.

She started sucking harder, as if she hadn't heard him, her eyes narrowed in greedy concentration.

"Stop!" he shouted. He grabbed the back of her neck with his free hand and ripped her off him with the last bit of strength he had left. She gulped as blood spilled across the table and onto the front of her white V-neck T-shirt. Still kneeling on the floor, she began rocking loosely, back and forth, as if she were somewhere else, in a profound trance or a drunken stupor.

"Oh my God," she murmured when she eventually came to her senses. "I'm sorry, but that tasted . . . incredible."

As Ryan's wound closed and his light-headedness began to clear, Jennifer stood up and unzipped the duffel bag.

"Don't—" Ryan started.

But before he could move to stop her, she quickly picked up a jaguar, one that was giving off a lime-green glow. Its eyes burned like two tiny orange flames. She rolled it around in her fingers, then gripped it tightly for several seconds. She put it back in the bag. "A little hot, but nothing I can't handle," she said, smiling, wiping excess blood from her upper lip.

Ryan looked down at his wrist, expecting it to be bubbling with scar tissue. It was already healed, nothing but smooth skin, no sign of an incision. He stood up and reached for the duffel bag.

"I'll keep an eye on these," Jennifer said, putting her hand on his arm. "If they're still able to track you, they'll do it sooner rather than later. You don't want to be caught with all of the statues. It'll be better if we split up. You drive to the bridge, pick up the last jaguar. I'll leave here, e-mail the files, and head to my apartment. I found my keys and phone in Vanessa's room."

"What happens if you run into someone from the tribe?" Ryan asked.

Jennifer shrugged. "Between the massive cover-up that's probably taking place right now at the Cloisters and the information we're going to be releasing into cyberspace, I think that most of the tribe will be preoccupied for the foreseeable future. And if someone stops me, I'll tell them the truth. I'm a newborn who's stopping by my old place to pick up a few things that I'll need for my new life. I mean, I *am* going to need to pack some clothes. Vanessa may have been a badass, but her fashion sense had a long way to go before it caught up with her killer instinct. Do you have a phone?"

"Yeah." Ryan opened a small pouch on the side of his backpack. His phone had been turned off, for how long he didn't know. When he powered it up, he saw that the battery was at fourteen percent. "It's got enough juice," he said, pressing the airplane mode icon.

"Okay. Call me when you're on your way back to Manhattan," Jennifer said.

"I will," Ryan agreed, slinging his backpack over his shoulders. "We shouldn't leave here at the same time. I'll go first."

Jennifer leaned in and kissed him. She pulled back and grabbed the front of his shirt. "You're coming to my apartment tonight," she said forcefully, her shining eyes belying her stern expression. "No more excuses."

"I'll be there," Ryan said.

33

He parked the van near the corner of Wythe Avenue and South 6th Street, on a part of the block that was located almost entirely under the eastern terminus of the Williamsburg Bridge. He got out and walked to a fenced-in commercial parking lot bounded by two large pillars and a stone abutment. It was well past sunset and the permanently shaded area was almost entirely obscured by shadows. The parking lot and its attendant booth were vacant and there were no nearby pedestrians to welcome Ryan back to the borough of his birth, which was exactly how he wanted it.

He leapt easily over the eight-foot fence and jogged across the cracked, sooty pavement to the abutment, a massive wall that supported both the bridge proper and the walking path that ran alongside it. It was composed of large, identically sized bricks that were each about two feet wide and a foot tall. He ran his hand along a row of chest-high bricks until he found one that was loose. Using his knife as a wedge, he pried the brick out of the wall and reached into the space behind it. He pulled out the shoebox from Urban Outfitters and opened it.

Inside, wrapped in tissue paper, were a pair of small rocks identical to the hundreds that were scattered among the parking lot's debris piles. The statue was gone.

One word flashed across Ryan's brain: Frank.

He reached in his backpack, picked up his phone, and took it off airplane mode. There were no new voice mails. The only new text message was from Jennifer: *Sent the e-mail, back at my place. See you soon!*

He turned the phone off to conserve its battery and started walking back to where the van was parked.

Jennifer wouldn't like it, but he had to make a detour. If Frank still had the eighth statue, Ryan needed to take it from him. Even if he'd already gotten rid of it, it was time for Ryan to finish things with his old mentor, to break him the way he'd broken the Brooklyn tribe, to return him to dust.

There were only so many places Frank could hide. And Ryan knew where to start looking.

34

The clock on the van's dashboard read 2:14 A.M.

Ryan glanced across the street from where he was parked, at the dilapidated, three-story brick building with busted-in windows, graffiti-covered walls, and scrubbed-out early-twentieth-century signage—only the word *CHEMISTS* was completely legible. Someone had tacked up an advertisement for bedbug removal services on a garage door that was as cracked as the pavement that surrounded the building and its similarly desolate neighbors lining the street. The area had gained some notoriety for being one of the hardest hit during Hurricane Sandy, but Ryan had seen it crumbling for far longer, since he'd shoveled coal at the now-abandoned shipyards that were a stone's throw away from where he was sitting.

He opened his phone to text Jennifer the address, as he'd done for the previous three locations he'd visited.

545 Columbia Street. Hopefully last stop.

The screen went black as the battery died. Ryan opened the glove compartment and dropped the phone inside.

In hindsight, he told himself, he probably should have started here, at the safe house in Red Hook. But it had seemed too obvious, so he'd gone to the last two places that Frank had called home (or the last two Ryan had known about), a white-shingled row house in Canarsie and the bottom floor of a brownstone in Bensonhurst. The first had been empty and the second had been occupied by a Cantonese family. And when he'd stopped at Natalia's house in Flatbush, it was as ruined as it had been the night he'd left it, devoid of life.

Ryan checked the magazine of the dart pistol he had taken from the Cloisters. There were four cartridges left. He tucked the pistol under his shirt, got out of the van, and walked across the street, touching the jaguar that had fused to his chest and scanning the building for security cameras. None were visible. He shoved aside a concrete traffic barrier that was blocking a smaller door next to the garage. The door looked like it had been partially torn from its hinges. Ryan pressed it lightly and it swung open, releasing a strong, musty waft of stagnant air.

Inside, the ground floor—illuminated by orange streetlight glow—looked exactly as it had the last time Ryan had seen it forty-five years earlier, shortly after Frank had bought the building. Besides a few large chemical drums, discarded pipes, and metal rods that had been piled into a corner, the space was empty, its walls covered in grime and mildew, its floorboards warped and rotting. Across from the industrial debris, a set of metal stairs led to both the upper levels of the building and the basement. Ryan walked slowly across the room, deciding whether to go up or down, when he heard the sharp hiss of air followed by an earsplitting shriek somewhere below him. Then the equally sweet and bitter aroma of chemically corroded flesh, like what he'd smelled in the tunnel beneath the Cloisters.

Ryan reached for his pistol and rushed down the stairs. At the bottom, he found himself in a gutted, laboratory-like space lit by weirdly flickering blue light tubes that lined the ceiling. The outer walls and floor were covered in filthy gray ceramic tiles that might have once been white. There were stainless-steel shelves attached to a wall near the stairs that held dozens of glass beakers and graduated cylinders. Ryan was standing in what had once been, he guessed, a kind of reception area connected to a long hallway with multiple rooms on either side. Those rooms' walls had been knocked down during a half-assed remodeling effort and had been replaced by semitransparent plastic sheets.

Pistol raised, Ryan headed into the hallway and was immediately confronted by three impossibly tall and immobile humanoid shapes behind the sheet to his right. He paused, watched for signs of movement, listened for heartbeats, smelled the air for sweat, but he couldn't discern anything. *Fuck it*, he said to himself as he ripped the sheet from the ceiling and stepped back, ready to fire.

The bodies had only appeared tall because they were suspended in the air, hanging from long meat hooks that had been inserted between their shoulder blades. They were naked. Their skin was almost completely charred, covered in a layer of alligator-scale scar tissue that looked like it had healed and been reopened hundreds of times until it had finally petrified. Their faces, blackened and contorted into grimaces of pain and terror, were barely recognizable. Two were young, barely adults, a guy with high cheekbones and shaggy, port-colored hair, and a blond girl with full lips who was missing both of her eyes that Ryan remembered being dark brown and almond-shaped.

Asher and Fiona.

The third corpse looked exactly as it had in the picture Ryan had been sent. Seamus's neck was bent forward at an unnatural angle, his long hair draped over his eyes, his mouth slightly open and circled with a crusted-over pinkish fluid.

The last of the Brooklyn tribe, minus two.

A hiss of air like the one Ryan had heard earlier echoed from somewhere down the hall, followed by another scream, weaker than the first. Ryan left the bodies and returned to the hallway. He'd gone maybe twenty yards when his nostrils filled with the now-familiar sickly-sweet aroma of DXT coupled with the stench of mutilation. There was something moving slightly behind a curtain to his left. He ripped the plastic aside.

The room—or what had once been a room—was smaller than the space where Seamus, Asher, and Fiona were hanging. The only piece of furniture was a large stainless-steel table that had been set up near the back wall. An open laptop rested on top of it. Natalia hung from a meat hook a few feet away, flanked by a pair of industrial chemical spray guns on tripods that were connected to the laptop via USB cables. Her entire body was covered in bubbling pink scar tissue urgently trying to heal itself before the next blast of what Ryan assumed was DXT vapor. She hung as flaccidly as the others, arms at her sides, eyes closed, but her fingers and toes were twitching involuntarily. She opened her charred lips and let out a low groan.

Ryan rushed across the room to the table and ripped the USB cables from the laptop. He shoved the spray guns away and gripped Natalia by her torso, carefully hoisting her up until the meat hook slid out of her back with a low slurping noise. Her eyes opened, widened in fear, and her muscles tensed. She tried to struggle, feebly, for a few seconds until her vision focused and she recognized Ryan. She relaxed, went completely limp.

"Thank you," she whispered before her eyes rolled back into her head.

"He came back to my house a few hours after you left," Natalia said, hugging herself under an emergency medical blanket that Ryan had found tucked under some rubble. "He didn't say anything, just doused me in that—what did you call it?—DXT, tied me up with bungee cords that must have been coated in the same substance. There was a girl with him. Dark hair, red earrings, fantastic-smelling blood. I remember watching her snoop around my foyer as Francis carried me to his car. Then that bastard brought me here. It's been more than a week, hasn't it?"

They were sitting on chemical drums in the shadow-strewn darkness of the ground floor, where they'd been for twenty minutes waiting for Natalia's body to heal. Though there were still patches of wet, oatmeal-like clumps on her neck and cheek, they were diminishing. She was beginning to look more or less like she always had. The fire was returning.

"Were they dead when you got here?" Ryan asked.

Natalia shook her head, staring at the floor, her hands forming tight fists. "Seamus definitely," she said, "and maybe Fiona. I was never in the same area as the rest of them. The first night I heard Asher and Frank talking, arguing, then several voices I didn't recognize. The spraying wasn't as frequent at first, but I was still in and out of consciousness. I know that I smelled the girl with the remarkable blood at some point. There were sounds—the wailing of machinery, Asher screaming, begging them to stop whatever they were doing to him, to get it over with and kill him. Then it got quiet for three or four days, maybe more. Then it was my turn."

Ryan listened to a vehicle on Columbia Street as it drove slowly by the building. He waited for the sudden squeal of brakes, the click of doors unlocking. But the car never slowed down. "What do you mean, your turn?" he asked.

"Frank came into the room, turned off the spray guns. He was smirking like usual, like we were friends, like he hadn't been lying to my face for God knows how long. He said that he'd made friends, powerful friends. I assumed he was talking about the Manhattan tribe, but he wasn't really specific about anything. Except that who-ever he had linked up with had inspired him to revamp our tribe, to modernize it, to expand. He rambled for a long time, some hogwash about it being our species' time to take control of what was ours, that he finally had the right tools for a major purge, or something to that effect. He was so calm, like we were having a bloody chat over tea."

For as long as Ryan had known him, Frank had always been disgusted by humans, something Ryan had chalked up to Frank's childhood as a slave. But as much as Frank regarded his former spe-cies as inferior, he knew he needed them to survive. He'd never seemed like the type to start spouting revolutionary rhetoric, let alone spearhead a revolution. This was about money, plain and simple.

"He said he would give me the opportunity to join him," Nata-lia continued, "to sit next to him on a new tribal committee—I think that was what he called it—but that as a show of good faith, I'd need to help him replenish our numbers and become a maker. I asked him what the rest of the tribe had said, what had happened to them. He didn't say anything, only that you'd fled Brooklyn, followed in the same cowardly steps as Arthur Harker before you."

"He wasn't lying about that part," Ryan said.

Natalia's brow was now able to wrinkle again, and she made full use of her rebuilt facial muscles to stare at him in disbelief. "But if you're human," she said, "how did you lift me? How could you—"

"What did you say when Frank offered you his terms?" Ryan said, cutting her off.

Natalia scowled. "I wanted to say no, of course. I'm quite content with the life I've carved out for myself. I have been for a very long time. I imagined we all were. A parent is the last thing I've ever wanted to be. Frank had made it clear that refusing him wouldn't be an option, so I told him I would turn whoever he wanted, but I said I didn't want any part of a new tribe, that I would leave Brooklyn peacefully once he no longer needed me. He agreed and left the room. He came back a few hours later, pushing a man strapped to a hospital stretcher, a great lumbering goon whose rotten liver I could smell from across the room. I think he was drunk. Frank wheeled him close to where I'd been strung up, cut me open with a scalpel I assume he'd dipped in DXT. I turned the man, or, more accurately, bled onto him until Frank was satisfied and wheeled his new freak out of the room. Instead of coming back to let me down, Frank turned the spray guns on again and left me. I don't know how long it's been. Days, a week maybe. I wouldn't have lasted much longer if you hadn't found me."

Ryan's mind raced. Frank was mirroring the Committee's protocol, which confirmed that he was in direct contact with them. If he was creating his own tribe of lab rats, and if he hadn't sold the two jaguars that had come into his possession, then there had to be a base of operations, somewhere relatively accessible but still off the radar. But if not here, then where?

"You said that Frank hasn't been here in days," Ryan said. "Where would he have gone?"

Natalia had slipped off the emergency blanket and was pulling on the leggings of a blue plastic hazmat suit that had been lying folded in a box nearby. "Down the street, I suppose," she said, matter-of-factly.

"Down the street?"

"At one of his warehouses on the Erie Basin."

The Erie Basin, when Ryan had worked there, had been a major commerce center of New York Harbor, a mandatory stop for commercial ships and barges on their way to the Erie Canal. Now, save for Ikea, it was as decrepit as the rest of the surrounding neighborhood, a hodgepodge of broken docks and storage facilities that made the safe house look sturdy by comparison.

"If this had been two weeks ago I would have been surprised if you'd told me you didn't know about them," Natalia continued, "but now that we've had a glimpse into what Frank truly is, it's not all that shocking. A few years ago, he bought properties on the water, three or four at least. They were purchased without incident, except for a grain elevator that got him involved in a lengthy bidding war with Ikea. I never asked him where he got the money, or why he wanted to keep boosting his real estate profile with ghastly fixer-uppers when he hadn't even done any work on the safe house in three decades. Quite frankly, I didn't want to know. Frank had always been paranoid; I thought that maybe he was just getting worse in his old age."

"He *is* worse," Ryan said. "But this ends tonight."

Natalia chuckled bitterly. "And how do you propose to do that?" she asked. "You don't know what he's got in those buildings, how many people he's turned. Even if both of us were at full strength, it would be suicide to walk in there. You're better off calling the police, though it's likely they'd doubt the validity of your claims."

"I'm beyond full strength," Ryan said. He lifted up his shirt.

Natalia's eyes widened as they fixed themselves on the jaguar. She lifted her hand to touch it, but Ryan grabbed her before she could.

"You probably don't want to do that," he said.

She nodded, still mesmerized. "You knew where to find it," she said. "And you know how to use it."

"I've found all eight of them," Ryan replied. "Frank has the last two. I know how to use them enough to get them out of his hands. Or at least I'm betting on it."

"We have a lot to talk about," Natalia murmured.

Ryan reached into his pocket, fished out the van's key, and handed it to her. "And we will," he said, "as soon as I finish things here. It'll be safer for you if you go back to your house and wait for me. Then we'll have a nice, long chat."

Natalia nodded and stood up, slowly, trying to remember how to balance herself. "How will you know what building he's in?" she asked.

"I'll know."

"Good." She passed Ryan and began walking in the direction of the stairs.

"Where are you going?" he asked.

She turned and smiled sadly. "There's an incinerator on the third floor. I'm going to give our friends downstairs a proper burial. It's the least I can do."

Ryan watched her disappear belowground. He had some flames of his own, burning through his veins, begging to be released. But unlike the cold corpses hanging in the basement, Frank would be alive to suffer their full intensity.

35

Ryan leaned against a metal railing in the shadows beyond Columbia Street's dull orange lampposts, observing the long, peak-roofed and otherwise nondescript commercial facility across the street that was completely encircled by a large parking lot and a chain-link fence. Behind him, the black water of the Erie Basin lapped gently against the concrete seawall. He could feel the after-hours energy of Manhattan and hear its pulse across the harbor, an incessant buzz that seemed light-years away from the silent industrial desolation he now faced.

He heard something approaching. A bicyclist came into view, pedaling around a sharp bend where the road curved to match the contour of the harbor, moving at a brisk pace and humming along with the music in his earbuds. The man was heavily bearded, wearing a beanie, a neon tank top, and bathing trunks. A fishing rod was strapped to his backpack, bobbing above his head like a CB radio antenna.

Keep going, keep going, Ryan said to himself.

The bicyclist noticed Ryan, slowed, and pulled up next to the sidewalk. He took out an earbud and waved. "You looking for something?" he asked, with a loud but friendly Southern accent that cemented his identity as a non-native, if casually stopping to speak to a stranger at three in the morning hadn't already made it excruciatingly obvious. "You know Ikea doesn't open for like five hours, right?"

"Just taking a walk," Ryan replied, brusquely.

The man craned his neck and scanned the dimly lit street and the totally obscured waterfront. He shrugged. "Whatever floats your boat, man. Just make sure you keep an eye out. There's been some weird stuff happening around here."

"Like what?"

"Couple days ago my buddy caught a catfish with three eyes in the Gowanus Canal. I'm not shitting you! He took a video, you can look it up. It's gone viral. Anyways, that's where I'm heading. I figure if he can catch something like that in the middle of the day, who knows what kind of critters will be lurking now."

Ryan noticed a light go on above the entrance to a loading dock across the street. "Good luck," he said absently, focusing on the building to see what would happen next.

"Well, okay, have a good one." The bicyclist reinserted his earbuds and took off into the night, leaving behind a thick aroma of sweat and recently imbibed weed.

Ryan didn't have to wait long. Two young men dressed in black tracksuits exited a door to the left of the loading dock and lit cigarettes. An identically clad woman joined them a few seconds later. She said something and the men laughed. The three of them took out their phones and began scrolling around.

They didn't hear Ryan as he entered the parking lot through a traffic barrier several yards away, bending a metal rod so he could slip through the gate. They didn't notice anything until he clicked off the safety of the pistol and fired. A dart hit one of the men in the shoulder. Another nestled near the woman's throat. By the time the second man looked up from his phone, his colleagues had already liquefied. The cigarette fell out of his mouth. He turned to run but slipped on the slick ground. Ryan walked over and stepped on the back of the man's neck, keeping his face pressed into the steaming puddle until his muffled screams turned into wet gurgles and then silence and his body stopped twitching.

Ryan wiped his shoe on the pavement and walked inside the building, through the door that the group had left open when they'd started their cigarette break. A narrow, unlit hallway led to the bottom of a cramped stairwell, with no place to go but up. At the top of the stairs, Ryan found himself on a wide landing area that seemed to run along the entirety of the building's four walls. The ceiling, only a few feet above where he was standing, was covered in rows of ultra-bright halogen tube lights, giving the space the same sense of clinical sterility as Conrad Van Pelt's office.

Walking to the edge of the landing and leaning over a safety railing, Ryan looked down at the facility's lower level, a massive patchwork of white-walled, rectangular enclosures with Plexiglas ceilings and no discernible entrances or exits. It looked like a human-size rodent labyrinth, or an ultra-sanitized version of the slaughterhouse pens Ryan had seen on a television documentary. Whether the space would be used for experimentation purposes or as holding cells for newborns, it was impeccably (and expensively) built, a testament to years of planning, and a disturbing reminder of how deceptive Frank had been.

About fifty yards down the landing, a broad-shouldered figure obscured by a royal-blue hooded sweatshirt was sitting at a stainless-steel computer station with multiple monitors, adjacent to the safety railing and overlooking the enclosures. As Ryan approached, the person—who appeared to be male—kept watching the monitors, oblivious to everything around him, occasionally typing something on a wireless keyboard, or sipping from a metal, canteen-style water bottle. When Ryan moved behind the computer station, he saw that three of the four screens were occupied by various sports-betting websites, showing the lines for several NBA playoff games that would be played the following evening. The fourth screen looked like a typical Facebook news feed.

"Andy, you back already?" the man at the desk asked in a crackly, booze-soaked drawl without swiveling around in the black leather chair he was sitting in. "That was fast, bro. You sure you smoked the butt or just ate it? Well, since you're back, what do you think about Denver at Golden State? I was going to take the under but now I don't—"

The man stopped in midsentence, made several loud sniffling noises, and swung around in his chair. It was James Van Doren. He was still plump but looking healthier than he had in years. He was clean-shaven and his skin was smooth and pale, with no trace of circles under his widening eyes. Ryan could see his muscles tensing under his Knicks sweatshirt and too-tight track pants, closer to the athlete he had once been than to the obese slob he had become.

"You've got some food on your upper lip," Ryan said. "You must still be pretty hungry."

After a few moments of paralyzed silence, James shook off the shock of seeing his former client and reached up to wipe the blood mustache off his face. When he removed his shirt sleeve, the surprised grimace had been replaced by his standard shit-eating grin. "Hey, man," he said, trying, as always, to inject levity into the situation. "Uh, welcome home. Never thought I'd be seeing you again. To what do I owe the pleasure?"

"How long have you been working for them?" Ryan asked.

"Who? Frank? The Committee? Right now things are kind of confusing. I guess it's been about a year, just after I'd been diagnosed with hepatitis and just before they found out I also had pancreatic cancer." He sighed. "Looks like I'm going to be working for, um, whoever, a little longer, too, though that wasn't originally part of the deal. I was planning on my life turning out kind of like yours. You know, chilling, watching movies, taking down the occasional new-in-town twentysomething who doesn't know any better."

Ryan took a step forward, his right index finger curling around the pistol's trigger. "Like Jennifer?" he asked.

"Who?"

"The twentysomething brunette you—or someone using one of your phones—strung up and photographed in a basement on East 80th Street. The reason I came to Manhattan."

"Oh right," James murmured. He hoisted himself out of his seat with minimal effort, raising his palms in a placating motion. "If it's any consolation, we never hurt her. Drugged her, sure. We had to make it look real so you would take the bait. Nicki must have sent you the pictures while she was buttering up that Indian dude, what's his name, Xander? He had a place on the Upper East Side."

"I saw the basement," Ryan growled. "I know Jennifer was there."

James frowned. "Bro," he said. "Frank took the pictures. I know you don't get out much but there are a lot of grimy, horror-movie-quality rooms all over the city. They aren't hard to find. Maybe he used that spot back up the road where the rest of the old tribe is hanging. Maybe Nicki took some background pics of the basement you're talking about and used Photoshop to superimpose your girl into the shot. What I do know for certain is that he could have killed her, but he didn't."

"Frank knew she was strong," Ryan said, "so he wrapped her up and gave her to the Manhattan tribe as a gift. A sign of his good-will to let them know that he was on board with the purge they've been planning, that he was willing to supply them with whatever they needed."

James shrugged. "I don't know about all that," he replied. "But at least she'll live forever. That's good, right? That'll give you some closure?"

"I'm sure you loved playing the middleman," Ryan said, ignoring his questions. Frank had picked a perfect lieutenant. As long as he made James think he was in a position of power, if he gave him employees to boss around and created the illusion that his responsibilities were actually important, he would do anything for him. And Frank had done more than that. He'd given James the only thing that was more precious to the financial advisor than money—a way to permanently prolong his wretched existence.

"I had nothing to do with the girl," James barked, suddenly becoming defensive. "My job, the main thing I had to do so Frank would turn me, was to find Derrick Rhodes and lead him to the Manhattan tribe. I did that, and did it well. I even turned well. I could control my appetite almost immediately. Frank said he'd never seen anything like it. That's why he's put me in charge of, um, whatever this place is, whatever projects the tribes are planning. They know they can trust me."

"Where's Frank?"

"Close," James said. "At the old place on Beard Street."

Beard Street intersected with Columbia Street, a quarter mile back in the direction from which Ryan had come. Was James talking about the safe house, or did Frank own another building nearby? Ryan shook his head. "That's not particularly helpful," he said. "Where on Beard Street?"

"Of course there's a live feed," Frank said, ignoring him. "He knows what's going on here. Which is why you showing up tonight, killing my staff members, smelling like you've been chugging from the fountain of youth, it's not a good look for me. I don't know how you did it and it doesn't matter. It needs to end. I feel bad having to end our conversation, and I'm sure a part of me will feel bad while I'm eating you, but you've got to understand where I'm coming from. I'm not going to die because of you."

Ryan raised the pistol. For a moment he felt a twinge of pity for his former donor. For all his manipulative traits, James really was just an oblivious moron, a giant pawn in a game he would never understand. Then the moment passed.

James snorted. "What are you going to do with that?" he asked. The grin had returned, spreading from cheek to chubby cheek.

"What I should have done to your grandfather."

"My grandfather? What does he have to do with—"

Ryan fired. James looked down at the dart protruding from his still-sizable belly.

He plucked the empty glass casing from his gut and rolled it between his fingers. "What kind of bullet is . . ." He trailed off and looked up at Ryan, ashen-faced. The grin was gone. "Oh fuck," he mumbled as his body started to spasm wildly. He wheeled backward onto the computer desk, shattering two of the computer monitors with his flailing arms before completely losing his balance and tumbling over the safety rail. A second later, the sound of rubber thwacking against Plexiglas echoed throughout the building.

Ryan checked the pistol's magazine. There was one dart left.

36

Beard Street's cobblestones looked exactly as they had the last time Ryan had walked over them, but everything else—the rows of boarded-up and decaying buildings that had once serviced the previous century's maritime industry, vacant lots littered with rusting construction equipment, a small marina and docking area for water taxis, the expansive blue and metallic façade of Ikea's main building—was a disconcerting juxtaposition of advanced urban decay and modern retail, with nothing in between.

Of more immediate concern to Ryan was that he couldn't find Frank, even after walking the entirety of Beard Street's five blocks several times. He could still feel the statue's energy surging through him, felt his senses amplified to the point where he could smell someone sautéing leftover linguini and clam sauce a quarter of a mile away, but there was no sign or scent of his former mentor. He could start systematically breaking into every building on the street, but besides the obvious alarm-triggering issues, that might take hours. The sun and the eyes of morning commuters would be upon him soon.

The doubts began creeping into Ryan's mind. He should have kept James alive long enough to show him where Frank's office was. He should have tried to see if he could have learned anything from the remains of James's computer display. Maybe he shouldn't have trusted Natalia. Maybe she was just another cog in the fucked-up wheel he'd gotten himself wrapped around. She and Frank might be watching him now, waiting for the perfect moment to strike.

Stop it, he told himself. It did no good to think about what he couldn't control. The past was the past. People were who they were. He forced himself back into the present and decided to start over, to head back to the safe house and see if there was anything there that might be of use.

As he began walking east, the sky shifted from black to murky gray, illuminating the harbor and the trash-covered shoreline to his right. But a minute and two blocks later, it was something in the darkness to his left that caught Ryan's eye. Sandwiched between a pair of nondescript two-story brick buildings was a narrow alley that was fenced off from the street. Between the fence's metal grates, he could see the rear end of a black BMW, its bumper glowing with a freshly waxed sheen.

He wasn't entirely sure, but it looked like the same year and model as the car Frank had torched. Moving closer to the alley, he caught the faintest whiff of vaporized marijuana and remembered the device that Frank had been using in Prospect Park. He pulled out the pistol from under his shirt, clicked off the safety, and walked up to the front entrance of the building on the left.

He tried shouldering into the rust-covered door, but as weak as it appeared, it wouldn't budge. It was as if some kind of blockade had been set up behind it, or it had been reinforced with an uncommonly resilient alloy. Ryan looked up from where he was standing. There was no fire escape and the windows on the second floor had been barricaded with the same metal as the door.

As his frustration began to mount, he felt the statue's heat surge through him, the same heat that Xansati had used to burn his enemies, the same heat that had dissolved Karl's skin and muscle when Ryan had grabbed his wrist. He had an idea.

He gripped the door's handle, closed his eyes, and tried to corral his anger and anxiety, to focus all of it down his arm and into his hand. A second later he felt the handle getting hot, hotter, boiling and finally liquefying. He heard a loud clicking noise, followed by the release of air. Ryan gasped from exertion and uncurled his fist. He opened his eyes and glanced down at his hand. It looked like it had been doused in silver spray paint, the same color as the shallow hole that had been scorched into the concrete near his feet.

He pushed the door and it swung open easily. Stepping inside the building, Ryan was immediately overcome by the stench of human decay that permeated every corner of the room, a brightly lit, windowless space with blood and excrement-stained walls that looked like they were made from the same material as the ones in Conrad Van Pelt's office.

There were corpses everywhere. On the floor, slumped against the wall, bodies stacked on bodies. Men and women, an entire spectrum of ages and ethnicities. Most of them had been stripped of clothing, and none of them were intact. There were cavernous, gangrene-colored gashes in chests, throats, and torsos, leg and arm bones that had been cracked and partially detached from sockets, thighs covered in smaller incisions that looked like they'd been gnawed into the flesh.

And there was something else. Something breathing.

Ryan saw her leap from the periphery of his vision, so fast that he didn't have time to react. She was on top of him, ripping his pistol away and crushing the barrel with her bare hand, clawing at his chest, gnashing at his shoulder blade. Her eyes were bright but unfocused, animal-like, her black hair falling over her face in wild ringlets. Pink foam was dribbling from her mouth and had left large stains on the front of her tattered T-shirt and gym shorts. She was strong, stronger than anyone he'd had to fight off. But not strong enough.

Ryan kneed Nicki in the gut as hard as he could. She flinched and howled and in that moment he wrapped his fingers around her neck, channeling the fire that had re-ignited inside him. He stood up, continuing to hold her as she writhed in agony, the smell of her boiling skin filling the room. She tried to kick and lash out at him a few times, weakly, before slumping to the ground, completely subdued by the pain.

"Where is he?" Ryan asked, wiping her drool off his face with his free hand.

She stared at the floor and let out a bloodcurdling moan.

"Where the fuck is Frank?" he shouted, gripping her tighter, but Nicki only screamed louder. She was useless, totally consumed by the hunger.

Ryan looked around the room. There was a door on the far wall, nearly identical to the one he'd just come through. As he walked toward it, dragging Nicki, her screams became more intense, almost inhuman. Clearly she wasn't fond of what was on the other side.

"Please, not again," she groaned, her voice hoarse, lacking any trace of the snarky self-assurance she'd displayed when they'd first met. "No more, not him, not, no . . ."

Ryan ignored her pleas and gripped the handle, mentally preparing himself to liquefy it, but the door swung open easily. It had been unlocked. *Just like with Jennifer,* he said to himself, before quickly erasing her image from his thoughts. He needed to focus on the task at hand.

The room he and Nicki entered was identical in size and shape to the previous one, only it was spotless, almost like it had just been constructed, and there was a spiral staircase in the far corner that led to the second floor. The air was pure except for a hint of the vapors that Ryan had smelled outside the building. The Ramones' "Rockaway Beach" was blaring from unseen speakers.

"Stand up," Ryan commanded.

Nicki cringed and made another weak attempt to crawl back toward the entryway. She shook her head. "No," she whispered, the same pink spittle caking her lips.

Ryan clamped down on her, harder than he had before, until he touched bare spine. She shot up immediately, yelping in agony. They walked to the stairs, Ryan holding Nicki an arm's length in front of him. As they started climbing, the music got louder, then suddenly shut off.

Nicki stopped in midstride. She tried to turn her neck to face Ryan, but he wouldn't let her. "I'm sorry for what I did to you," she said softly, sounding more like her old self. "Just let me go. You don't know what he'll do to us. You can't stop it. You can't—"

"Whatever choices you had, you've already made them," Ryan said. "Walk."

Her shoulders slumped, but she didn't try to resist. They made it to the top of the stairs and entered a small, loftlike space, no bigger than Ryan's living room in Crown Heights, illuminated by several rows of dimmed track lights. The walls were completely covered in papers. There were several maps of Brooklyn, many depicting the streets of various neighborhoods. Others were topographical and showed the borough as if the images had been plucked from Google Earth, covered in red permanent-marker scribbles made by a maniacal, childlike hand. There were yellowed, older drawings showing other regions and parts of the world that Ryan recognized—Nevada, Scandinavia, Indonesia—and others that he didn't. A small desk with a large computer monitor sitting on it rested against the back wall, which was covered by what looked like star charts, depictions of various constellations outlined with paragraphs of the same red writing. Ryan didn't see any sketches or photographs of the statues, but there were numerous pictures of seemingly random monolithic structures, most of which looked like natural formations.

Besides the desk, the only other piece of furniture was a stainless-steel table in the middle of the room that Frank was standing behind, perusing an open leather-bound manuscript and smoking from a vaporizer pen. He was wearing a black tracksuit. A jaguar statue sat on the table an arm's length away from him, not glowing, its eyes black and gaping.

Frank exhaled a faint cloud of vapor, looked up from the book, and smiled at Ryan, who was still holding a cowering Nicki.

"I see you tamed my guard dog," he said calmly. "And it looks like you had a bit of a falling out with your financial advisor." He motioned at the image on the computer screen behind him. It was a video still of the facility on Columbia Street that Ryan had infiltrated earlier, shot from an angle above the glass-ceilinged enclosures, and focused on a splattered mess of flesh and clothing that had once been James Van Doren.

"Tonight feels like a teachable moment for me," Frank continued, placing the vaporizer pen on the table. "If you want something done right, you need to do it yourself. I mean, look at you. The lone-vigilante role seems like something you were born for, something I certainly never saw coming. I mean, that kung-fu grip and that complexion. Wow! You really need to tell me your secrets. Is it a new diet? A new workout routine?"

As jovial as his old friend seemed, Ryan understood that there was a purpose to the banter, that Frank would use his prolific bullshitting ability to gain some time, to feel out the situation. Frank had been around at least one of the statues. He would have some understanding of their magnetic properties and sense that Ryan was in possession of one, that Ryan was able to wield it. If Frank had been contacted by the Committee, he would also know what had happened at the Cloisters.

Frank knew he was trapped; his darting, unsmiling eyes told Ryan as much. But a hunted animal was always at its most dangerous when it had been backed into a corner. Though he felt nearly invincible, stronger than he ever had, Ryan had come too far to make any kind of rash decision on how to deal with his former mentor. He needed to do some feeling out of his own.

"Seems like it would have been smarter for you to follow my lead," Ryan said, "instead of leaving whatever you're trying to accomplish in the hands of a bunch of cracked-out Run-D.M.C. fan club members. Seriously, what's the deal with those jumpsuits? You have to admit that they're a little cheesy, even for you."

"You know, you're really dating yourself with that reference," Frank replied, the old joke sliding from his lips as easily as it always had. "I bought the warehouse—the one you made a mess in tonight—from a group of Korean businessmen who were running a bootleg sportswear operation that had become less than profitable. They threw in the suits as part of the deal. Everyone likes a uniform. People want to feel like they're a part of something bigger than themselves. The members of my little, um, militia seem to like them."

Ryan snickered. "From what I've seen, the junkies in your *militia* would do anything you told them for a few nickel rocks. Is that how you're paying them? Or did you promise them something else? Maybe they think you're going to turn them."

Frank shrugged. "Everybody wants something. Luckily most of the people whom I've taken under my wing are relatively simple souls. Their vices are easy to procure."

"What do you want?" Ryan asked. "Money, right? But you're smart enough to realize that Manhattan is just using you. What was their offer? To make you CEO of a satellite branch of their tribe? As soon as the experiments are under way, as soon as they've made a deal with the military, they'll take the statues from you, whether you let them or not. Then what's your play? You can't stop them."

"The military?" Frank asked in between bursts of laughter. "Is that what Xansati told you? No, it was probably Derrick Rhodes, regurgitating all of the crap I . . . Ha! Oh man, that's too funny. Of the vague network of interconnected organizations that might be described by the average Joe, collectively, as the *military*, maybe half of them know about the Manhattan tribe. They certainly don't have any real idea about the statues. The members of the Committee are imperialists, always have been. By joining the tribe and cheating death, they've trapped themselves on an island, literally, unable to expand to a degree that they find satisfactory. Basically, they're a bunch of old, rich, and bored white dudes who haven't had anything better to do in two hundred years. They aren't creating super soldiers for the government. They want to build an army for themselves, ego-less enforcers who can impose the Committee's will wherever they see fit. It's all very predictable, very blasé if you ask me. I was only humoring them until I had the opportunity to pry every last one of the statues from Xansati's dead hands—an opportunity that was apparently taken from me, according to the frantic e-mail I got from Van Pelt an hour ago. Oh well. Long story short, the last thing I want to do is spend my time training newborns for a cause I don't care about. I like being on my own. Let's be serious. We both know I'd never be a good father."

While Frank was talking, Nicki had started rocking back and forth, staring at the floor and whimpering softly. The noise got progressively louder until it became a high-pitched whine that wouldn't stop regardless of how hard Ryan squeezed her neck. Frank glared at her, his lips curling in utter disgust. Then he smiled.

"Oh, sweetie," he said, looking at her, "this is isn't what you had in mind when we started hanging out, is it?"

She shook her head, still staring at her feet.

"I get it. It's my fault for not explaining things as carefully as I should have. It's a problem I have sometimes. But listen, if you want to leave, if you want to end this, just say the word. Ryan will release you and you can go."

She muttered something under her breath, too soft to make out.

"What was that?" Frank asked.

She looked up at him. "Do it," she growled between clenched teeth.

Frank lifted his arm, closed his eyes, and cupped his hand over the statue's head. It immediately began to turn neon green. Instead of injuring him, its energy seemed to surge harmlessly through Frank, giving his skin a radiant glow. His facial expression was one of absolute calm and focus.

Before Ryan could do anything, Nicki's body began to vibrate and then heat up to a temperature so extreme that he was forced to release her. She collapsed onto the floor in a writhing heap, her mouth gaping, straining to scream, but all that came out was a plume of foul-smelling smoke, as if her esophagus had scorched itself from the inside out. Her hair turned to ash and her skin went from brown to black as her limbs contorted unnaturally and finally stiffened after one last major spasm. She looked exactly like the bodies Ryan had seen in the tunnel beneath the Cloisters. Frank opened his eyes and removed his hand from the statue, which continued to shine, its eyes golden and pulsing.

"Well, that's a shame," Frank said. "I liked her. She was no Arianna, though she did have her moments. But like I already said, I'm no father."

While Ryan stood frozen in disbelief by what he had just seen, Frank walked over to the computer desk and grabbed the chair that was next to it. He slid it across the floor in Ryan's direction. It skidded to a halt a few inches away from Nicki's charred remains.

"Take a seat," Frank said. When Ryan didn't move, he sighed, walked back to the table, picked up the vaporizer pen, and tapped it against his chest. It made a clacking noise, the sound of two hard objects coming together—the second Brooklyn statue. "Think carefully before you decide to do anything stupid."

Ryan slumped into the chair, shell-shocked.

Frank took a pull from the vaporizer pen, walked over to the wall to his left, and stared at a three-foot-by-five-foot map of Brooklyn, the largest in the room. "What do you know about the geographical features of Long Island?" he asked.

Ryan didn't say anything. He stared straight ahead, unblinking.

"I'll take that as a 'not much,'" Frank said, looking at Ryan and chuckling softly. "Basically it's a bunch of loose rocks and soil that were deposited by glaciers as they retreated during the last ice age, meaning that not only is it extremely young by geographical standards, but it also has a unique mineral composition. There are numerous areas where interesting magnetic anomalies occur, where objects that are already magnetically charged seem to change, to increase in strength. You're sitting over one of those areas now."

Frank walked back to the center of the room and picked up the statue, juggling it briefly between his palms before returning it to the table. "One of the most essential parts of survival is knowing where you're from, understanding your environment. But it doesn't end there. You need to know who you are on the inside. It's just as important. I take it you're wondering how I'm able to handle the statues?"

"It did just cross my mind," Ryan mumbled. As hot as the energy surging through him had become, and as much as he wanted to charge Frank and attack him head-on, he understood that his only chance of walking out of the building alive was to wait for a better option to present itself. He needed to appeal to Frank's penchant for rambling for as long as he could.

"My mother was born a slave," Frank said, "but she didn't die one. As far as I can tell, she was brought to New Amsterdam on a ship from the Caribbean and sold to one of the first merchants in New Netherland, a man named Christiaensen who needed someone to feed, bathe, and clothe his invalid daughter. When the girl died a few years later, my mother escaped and traveled east for several days until she stumbled upon a Lenape hunting camp, where she was brought before the son of the local tribe's chief. Apparently they hit it off right away because I was born nine months later. I don't remember my grandfather's name or what he looked like but I know that he wasn't a big fan of me, because when I was five and he sold the tribe's land to the Dutch, I was part of the deal. My parents didn't even try to stop him. That was probably the start of some very serious mommy and daddy issues, but I'd like to think it all worked out in the end. I inherited the only gene that matters, the one I share with you, the one we used to share with Xansati."

While Frank talked and stared at the maps, Ryan tried to glance around the room without making it too obvious, desperately searching for a way out. He noticed a sudden movement in the corner of his eye. It had come from the image on the computer screen, which Ryan now realized was a live video feed. The reflection of a face appeared in the glass ceiling next to James's splattered corpse. A few seconds later, it was gone.

"Are you upset that you couldn't kill Xansati personally?" Ryan asked, suddenly feeling like it was even more important to keep the conversation going as long as he could. "Would it have brought you closure?"

Frank shrugged. "There might have been some symbolic justice, but really I just wanted to get the jaguars out of the hands of someone who doesn't appreciate them for what they are, who doesn't understand their true mechanics."

"I don't know, Xansati seemed like he had them pretty well figured out," Ryan replied. He motioned at Nicki's body. "He made a lot of people look like her."

Frank turned to face Ryan head-on. His smile was gone. "He was part of a culture that worshipped the jaguars literally as spirits, and believed that the ability to create dead warriors was a gift from the gods. Any knowledge that Xansati had about the statues would have been the same basic information that had been passed down by his tribal elders for thousands of years, a very small fraction of what the artifacts can do. A visually impressive fraction, but a fraction nonetheless."

Ryan could see that his former friend was starting to get visibly agitated. He needed to keep prodding, to get Frank worked up enough that he would let down his guard, if only for a moment.

"What about the Committee?" Ryan asked.

"What about them? The Committee didn't do half of the tests that Rhodes's information said they did. They probably wanted to, but Xansati took the statues back and hid them before they could. This was years ago. They'd lost interest until I started fanning the flames." Frank snorted out a bitter laugh.

"Another aspect of survival is understanding the people in your life," he continued. "The ones you do business with, your friends, the ones you want to become your friends, the ones you simply need to take something from. You need to uncover their desires, what motivates them, what scares them, how to make them move in the direction of your choice. And when an opportunity arises, you need to take advantage of it. I fed Derrick Rhodes, just like I fed Xansati, just like I fed the Committee, just like I fed you. I gave Van Pelt the idea to start the purge and told him I'd do the same, started building the facility on Columbia Street so that he'd think I was serious, when in reality it's a sham setup made of Plexiglas and cheap drywall. I sent Xansati a version of the information I was sending to Rhodes, made him wary enough of the Committee's intentions to get him to leave the tribe and gather his statues in one location. When the seventh statue showed up at the Brooklyn Museum, I got you to give up the location of the eighth."

Ryan bit his lip, tried to stay outwardly calm. He listened as a car passed by the building, slowed, but didn't stop. "Seems like a lot of work for a few old pieces of rock," he said. "What were you planning on doing with the statues once you got them? World domination? A tea party at the safe house? You must have something figured out."

"A few old pieces of rock," Frank repeated, chuckling. "I guess that is what they are. A composite of numerous elements, some of them without names. And they play host to numerous colonies of bacteria—the stuff that causes the glowing effect and makes the statues deadly for most people—that predate, well, almost everything."

"I never took you for someone who was interested in microscopic organisms."

"I'm interested in a lot of things. I was interested in Arthur Harker's research, not only his handwritten observations, but also the collection of ancient maps and manuscripts that he deposited at Natalia's house when he left Brooklyn. I was interested in the progress that Arthur and Xansati had made before Arthur abandoned their project, which is why I made contact with Xansati years ago, convinced him that I was an acolyte of Arthur's."

"I mean, you kind of were his student," Ryan replied in a smartass, matter-of-fact tone, trying to get a rise out of his former mentor, prodding at his less-than-stable emotions in the hopes that Frank might let his guard down for a moment. "You basically just absorbed everything Arthur—and later, Xansati—discovered and are using it for yourself. The only thing you added to the equation, as far as I can tell, is your penchant for manipulation, which you've been kind enough to share with me."

"The only thing," Frank repeated slowly and softly, his lips curling into a self-assured grin. But Ryan could see his muscles flexing involuntarily, his body glowing from the heat that was surging underneath, the heat that Ryan was pretty sure would be difficult for Frank to control no matter how much time he'd spent with the statues. The jaguar on the table next to him shone brighter, pulsing in time with the surges under Frank's skin.

"There are more than a few things," Frank said after a few moments of silence, his smile gone and his voice slightly increasing in volume. "But you're partially right. Manipulation is at the top of the list. And not just people. I manipulated the research of others to suit my own needs, manipulated the Internet to further my own investigations. Arthur and Xansati never discovered how to manipulate the magnetic currents that travel through the statues, that surround us, that possess the power to influence everything we do, to subvert gravity. They never figured out how to merge their brainwaves with the statues' energy. But I did. My predecessors were obsessed with studying the history of the Lenape, thinking they'd find their answers in the oral traditions of mushroom-addled shamans, but they should have gone back much further in time. They should have ventured way beyond the scope and experiences of one tribe. Have you heard of the Coral Castle in Florida?"

"You'll have to excuse my fourth-grade education," Ryan said dryly. "Don't think I ever made it to geography class, or spent as much time online as you clearly have." He took another quick look around the space. The computer screen on the desk behind Frank went black, switching to power-saving mode, he assumed.

Frank, seemingly unaffected by Ryan's impudence, riffled through the papers on the desk in front of him, pulled one free, and tossed it to Ryan. It was an eight-by-ten photograph of several carved stone structures—a crescent moon, a massive obelisk, a spherical object that looked like a planet encircled by rings.

"In the early twentieth century," Frank said, "a Latvian immigrant named Edward Leedskalnin built a monument to his ex-fiancée on a stretch of rural land that bordered the Everglades. He quarried more than a thousand tons of coral and used it to construct a house for himself, a megalithic castle, and a sculpture garden. He built it alone, with no heavy machinery or other modern equipment. For years he worked at night; no one ever saw how he'd managed to do it except for a few local kids who said he lifted fifteen-ton blocks like they were hydrogen balloons. When people would ask him how he'd managed to complete his seemingly impossible project, he'd tell them that he'd *discovered the secrets of the pyramids,* or something that sounded equally insane."

"But it wasn't insane, was it?" Ryan replied. "He was using a statue the whole time."

Frank shook his head. "A man who came directly from Eastern Europe with no possible trace of Native American genetics? No way. An activated statue would have destroyed him before he had the chance to lift a pebble."

"I'm European, too."

"Like most people born on this continent, Ryan, you're a mutt. Do you know who all of your great-grandparents were, where they were from? What about your grandparents? You don't have any idea what you are. The point I'm trying to make is that the statues aren't unique. There's a much larger world of artifacts and objects with similar properties, spread throughout the world, able to be accessed by more than just the descendants of one ethno-cultural group. Something Harker would have understood if he'd just opened his eyes. If he hadn't wasted his time on pointless exercises like turning you."

Frank stood up and backed away from the table slightly. *If he moves another two or three feet,* Ryan thought, *I might be able to make a jump for the statue and grab it before he can do anything about it. I need to keep him talking.*

"Arthur turned me because I survived exposure to a jaguar,"

Ryan said. "He knew I'd be able to handle the statue he buried in case something happened to him."

"Arthur?" Frank snickered as he took another step backward. "Arthur wanted your blood for himself. Nothing more, nothing less. Lacking any real knowledge of hereditary science, he thought that if he could eat enough of you, your physical attributes might somehow transfer to him. Maybe he didn't drain you all the way because he thought he'd taken enough to effect a change within himself. Maybe he just couldn't stomach that much A positive. I know I couldn't." Frank paused. "Whatever the case, once he'd taken what he wanted from you, that was it. He was done with you. He was done with his tribe. Didn't care that he'd left us with the burden of raising a bastard."

Frank, his face now contorted into a weird, quizzical expression, took another step backward. His ass was nearly resting on the computer desk.

"So what are you going to do with your jaguars?" Ryan asked, softly. "Going to build a monument for your mother? Maybe your grandfather?"

As soon as Ryan finished speaking, Frank closed his eyes and Ryan felt a heat welling up inside him, a heat that wasn't his own. Suddenly it ignited with the force of a hundred bullets fired at once, a searing that tore through flesh and bone, rendering him immobile and, for a few seconds, unconscious.

When Ryan's senses came back to him, Frank was sitting at the table, calmly taking a hit from the vaporizer pen. The outline of the statue glowed faintly under his shirt. "To answer your question," Frank said, "I'm leaving. I'm finally getting out of this city, then the country, freeing myself from a three-hundred-year-old yoke of oppression. That is, once I get my hands on the statues you took from Xansati."

"It seems to me that you only need one statue to travel and keep your immortality intact," Ryan said, trying to buy more time that he didn't have, trying to shake off the shock of whatever Frank had just unleashed. "What would be the point of keeping the rest of them? Are you planning on selling them to Van Pelt? Maybe some shady character in the military?"

Frank chuckled as he put down the pen and glared incredulously at Ryan. "Again with the military? No, they'd be much more interested in strapping me onto a laboratory table. They'd probably just lock up the statues. They have bigger and older toys to play with. Like I said, the statues aren't unique. Now if I happened to take a trip to Syria, Moscow, or Pyongyang, I'm sure that I'd receive a much different welcome than I would in Washington."

"You'd sell the statues to terrorists?" Ryan asked.

"I'm not selling anything to anybody," Frank replied. "Not yet. The only thing I want is what I've always wanted, the one thing I've never been able to buy or steal: the freedom to do whatever I want, whenever I want, wherever I want. If I have to start out in a desert or a godforsaken tundra to achieve that freedom, then so be it."

"I don't have them."

"Well, duh. I wouldn't expect you to be that stupid. Where did you stash them? Your apartment in Crown Heights? The cemetery? The Williamsburg Bridge? No, those are all too obvious."

Ryan stared straight ahead, unblinking.

Frank looked down at the papers in front of him for a few moments, then looked up, his eyes wide in surprise. "Ooh," he murmured, "I see what's going on here. Jennifer's alive. You destroyed her tracking implant. She never went to the museum with you. I'm assuming she's still in Manhattan."

Ryan stayed silent. He felt beads of sweat pooling, then streaking down his cheeks.

Frank clicked his lips in disapproval. "She's still a newborn, Ryan," he said. "She has no idea what she's doing. How long do you think it'll be before the Committee finds her? We need to get to her before they do, before they take the statues."

"Why would I help you do anything?" Ryan spat.

"Because I don't want to kill you. I think I've made it abundantly clear in these last few minutes how little I care about you. I feel even less toward your girlfriend. Take me to the statues and I'll be on my way. You'll never have to see me again. You and Jennifer can leave the city, start a life together in a small town with ample parking and a good school system, have two-point-six kids like a couple of normal Americans, forget that any of this happened to you. Or you can wait around for Van Pelt to put your heads on spikes above the Corbin Building. It really doesn't matter, as long as you give me what I want."

Maybe Frank was being sincere, Ryan thought. Maybe escaping the circumstances he'd been dealt had always been his motive, even before he'd been turned. But after everything that had happened, the lies and bodies that had piled up for years, Frank's promises meant nothing.

The conversation was going to end now, even if the best possible outcome of facing Frank head-on was giving Jennifer a longer head start, a better chance at getting away from all the assholes who would be pursuing her.

He needed to test the limits of Frank's powers, to hold on for as long as he could.

"I'm not giving you anything," Ryan whispered.

Frank sighed. "Okay," he said.

Ryan suddenly couldn't move his arms or legs—or anything else below his neck. But he wasn't paralyzed; he could feel his muscles straining against whatever gravitational ties were binding him, the dead weight of his torso slumping toward the ground.

Frank closed his eyes and placed one of his hands on the statue.

Another magnetic shock wave, much stronger than the first, burrowed under Ryan's skin and into every one of his cells, causing them to expand until his entire body seemed to be on the verge of a violent collapse, until Frank pulled back and Ryan blacked out again.

When he came to, eyes open but still shuttered in darkness, Ryan braced for another molecule-shattering round of pain, but nothing happened. As his vision cleared, he heard a series of urgent electronic bleeps, like a smoke alarm going off. He saw that the computer screen had reactivated and was streaming a live feed of Beard Street, directly in front of the building. A gray Audi sedan was in the process of parking near the adjacent curb.

"Is that the fucking . . . ?" Frank was standing up, muttering to himself, watching the screen, his back turned to Ryan and the statue.

Ryan collected all of his remaining strength in an attempt to move himself, but the strain was unnecessary. He watched as his arms lifted easily, as his fingers curled into fists, then uncurled. Whatever control Frank had been exercising over him had been lifted, at least temporarily.

He leapt forward, sending his chair clattering across the floor, reaching for the statue as Frank quickly swiveled back around. Just before he could grab it, a shock wave went through him, as if he'd touched a high-voltage electric fence but far stronger. He fell to the ground as the now-familiar foreign presence began to work its way through his body, absorbing and spoiling the energy he'd been gathering and sending out excruciating shards of radiation that sent him into a seizurelike trance, distorting his vision in paralyzing bursts.

After what felt like a long time, when the light patterns in front of his eyes cleared a little and the throbbing decreased, he saw Frank standing over him, holding the statue, mouthing, *You shouldn't have done that*, the words echoing over and over until they seemed to amplify and blend together into an earsplitting cacophony that latched on to Ryan's skull and wouldn't let go. Frank's jacket had begun to separate and fray around the chest area; the jaguar that was attached to him was burning through the black fabric, revealing its green skin and yellow eyes that glowed with a brutal, inescapable intensity.

Ryan tried to focus, tried to force himself up for one last desperate lunge, but as soon as he lifted an arm, Frank closed his eyes and a fourth tidal wave of agony shot through Ryan's limbs and gathered in the space beneath his rib cage. He watched helplessly as his T-shirt ignited and the unseen force began prying at the statue that was fused to his torso until it broke free and rolled onto the floor, leaving a messy tangle of skin and tendon. Ryan's sight became kaleidoscopic, a blaze of colors and fuzzy outlines, as his body went into shock and his conceptions of time, space, and consciousness blurred into dreamlike chaos.

He gradually became hyperaware of his molecules aching, shifting, then breaking apart, of sinking into a mudlike substance that enveloped him and stung his already-festering wounds, of a blank starless sky opening up above him, ready to swallow. He was in a large open space and Frank had been replaced by hundreds of dark creatures with amber eyes and animal-like faces shuffling toward him from a distance, howling from twisted black mouths.

As they approached, their voices got louder and Ryan could see them salivating, froth pouring from their mouths and dribbling down into the dirt. They surrounded him, chanting in a strange, guttural language, creating a whirlwind of noise that accelerated Ryan's disintegration until something changed and they suddenly went silent.

Two figures seemed to rise from the ground and approach from the opposite direction. One had chocolate-brown hair, the other blond, neither with any discernible facial features or even visible bodies, but Ryan somehow knew that they were feminine. Each carried something in her hands: impossibly bright and undefined objects that wreathed everything around them in a golden warmth that caused the dark creatures to scream, to shudder in pain, to hurl themselves into the sky's abyss until there was only one remaining, older and bigger than the rest, his hair long and matted, his eyes wild with anger. The creature tried to continue the chant but the women were stronger, combining and focusing their light until the ground shook and the sky erupted and rained down shards of acid.

Ryan forced himself to focus, to shake off the darkness that was threatening to consume him and everything around him, and began moving toward the women. Just as he was almost close enough to make out the details of their faces, the creature howled from where it crouched a few feet away, lashing out against whatever force was emanating from the objects.

A second later, it tensed up for a final attack, its muscles taut and gleaming, foam dribbling from its gaping mouth. It leapt past Ryan, leaving in its wake a thick, exhaust-like substance that began to fill the air, seeping into Ryan's mouth and nostrils, clogging his ears and shrouding his sight. In the moment before he lost complete control of his senses, he watched as the creature collided with the brown-haired woman, creating a massive shock wave that sent daggers of lightning and chunks of debris flying in every direction.

Then nothing.

When Ryan finally came out of his deafblind stupor, he was

back in the building on Beard Street, or what was left of it. Most of
the western wall had been totally blown away, leaving an unobstructed view of the seawall and the sunlit Erie Basin. The floor
was covered in a thin layer of foul-smelling soot. Spiderweb cracks
were expanding across the ceiling, causing flakes of paint and drywall to rain down on the center of the room, where a naked and
badly burned Frank was straddling the woman's motionless body.
He was strangling her, a series of subhuman grunts exiting his
mostly singed-off lips and the gaping hole in his chest. Four of the
jaguar statues lay on the ground a few inches away.

Ryan's adrenaline spiked and he charged forward, automatic
reflex, grabbed Frank by the shoulders, and pulled him off the
woman like he weighed nothing, ripping off two large chunks of
Frank's gelatin-like flesh in the process. Frank looked up from the
ground where Ryan had tossed him, his face twisted in a grimace
of shock and anguish.

"You can't . . . you can't be—" he started to gargle, but before
he could finish, Ryan was on top of him, punching him in the head
and neck again and again and again until Frank's windpipe was
sticking out of his throat and his face resembled that of a boxer who'd
been left in the ring twenty rounds too long. His one remaining eye
was open and unmoving.

Ryan pulled himself up and immediately doubled back over.
With his bloodstained hands balled up on his knees, he began dry-
heaving from the pain, from utter exhaustion, from the smell, from
everything.

When he lifted his head a few moments later, he saw to his surprise that Frank was still alive, more or less. Both of his arms were
flailing weakly, his gnarled fingers searching for the statues.

Ryan walked over and stomped on one of Frank's hands. The
crack of bone wasn't as sharp as it should have been, more of a rubbery crackle. He reached down and picked up one of the jaguars.
He bent down and held it over Frank's face, feeling the heat surging
through his body as the statue began to glow.

Frank's only response was a twitch that might have been in-
voluntary, a silent, toothless whimper.

"You want this, motherfucker?" Ryan snarled. "Then take it."

He plunged his clenched fist through Frank's stomach and deep into his gut. Fighting to stay conscious, channeling the statue's energy with everything he had left, Ryan watched as the jaguar got brighter, more intense, until it became too hot to hold, until it ignited.

Until Frank was a pile of ashes.

Ryan rolled over and closed his eyes.

After some time—how long, he couldn't say—he felt a pair of hands grip both sides of his head above his temples and heard a familiar voice whisper, "Relax, it's almost over." He tasted a harsh, steaming hot liquid being poured down his throat until he choked and sputtered, unsuccessfully trying to break free of the hands' grip. A numbing warmth shot through him and he was spinning, sweltering, floating up and out of his body before everything went yellow and then shut off.

"I think he's waking up," Jennifer said. Her voice was muffled, as if she were speaking behind a wall or at the far end of a long tunnel. "Come on. We can't stay here much longer."

Ryan opened his eyes. He looked up and saw Natalia standing a few feet away, wearing a lightly stained jacket and jeans. The skin on her face had returned to a smooth, pale sheen. Ryan's duffel bag was unzipped and lying in the rubble near her feet. The heads of the statues he could see inside the bag weren't glowing.

He ran his fingers across his naked torso, felt the undamaged skin that gave no indication it had ever played host to an ancient and mysterious version of an Energizer battery, as if that part of the last few days had been nothing more than an elaborate nightmare from which he was only now waking.

A pair of hands lifted him to his feet, steadied him, and spun him around. Jennifer looked tired. There were circles under her eyes, as if she hadn't slept for several days, and the skin on her neck and cheeks was pink and scaly—the remnants of a burn that was quickly healing itself. She was wearing one of Vanessa's white T-shirts, covered in splatter marks of various hues and at least two sizes too big, making her look even more worn out. Shrunken.

She was one of the women who had been holding the glowing objects, the one whom Frank had almost managed to choke out.

He stared at her in amazement. "How did you—" he started before she cut him off by placing a palm over his lips. Her hand smelled strange, vaguely chemical, like the bodies in the vault below the Cloisters, the debris that was currently covering the floor of the room. The scent caused him to shudder involuntarily.

Jennifer seemed to sense his discomfort and drew him in for a long embrace. "Thank you," she whispered.

Natalia lifted her head from the tattered, leather-bound book she'd been perusing. "Yes, thank you," she repeated. "When that wanker blew me clear out of the room, I thought I might lose both of you. It seems I almost did."

"How did you know where to find me?" Ryan asked, still more than a little shell-shocked as he tried to piece together everything that had happened.

"I found your phone in the van and charged it when I got back to my house," Natalia replied. "I didn't know if Jennifer was another part of Frank's bullshit campaign, but I took a risk and contacted her anyway. I'm glad I did."

"When she called, I'd already e-mailed the files on the flash drive you'd given me and crossed the bridge into Brooklyn," Jennifer said, taking her phone out of her pocket and checking something. "I thought Natalia was a trap, but I went to meet her when she called me. Maybe in hindsight it was kind of stupid, but I'd retained all of my . . . uh, tribal abilities since I'd left Manhattan and I felt that whatever power was in the statues would protect me, would activate if I came into any danger. That they would show me how I could use them."

Ryan scanned the room again, zeroing in on the wall that had been partially destroyed. "It looks like they did," he said.

"Ahem," Natalia cleared her throat. She bent over and picked up the duffel bag. She put the documents she'd been reading inside and zipped it up. "I don't want to toot my own horn," she said, lifting the bag by its strap and handing it to Ryan, "but any sort of 'activation' that you may or may not have recently witnessed was due to the efforts of yours truly."

Ryan slung the bag over his shoulder. "How is that possible?" he asked. "Did Frank show you how to—"

"Frank didn't show me anything. Over the years, we only talked about the statues in the vaguest terms. But I knew Frank was far more interested in them than he ever let on. I knew that Arthur was wary of that interest, which is why I never told Frank about the messages Arthur sent to me, about the knowledge I received. I saw how you looked up to Frank as a kind of surrogate father figure, knew how close the two of you were, so I couldn't very well tell you about any of it if I wanted to keep it from him."

"But Arthur disappeared," Ryan said, suddenly annoyed at what was beginning to sound like another instance of him being left out of the tribal loop. "How could he send you anything?"

Natalia frowned. "Arthur left," she said. "Leaving isn't the same as disappearing. It's certainly not the same as dying. There were letters throughout the years, phone calls, faxes—if you can believe it—and later, e-mails. Arthur forwarded me everything he knew about the properties that govern the statues and other objects like them. He sent me a vial of a concentrated serum that contained the same unique genetic markers that allowed you and Frank—and now Jennifer and me—to handle the statues. I daresay I know more about what we're dealing with than Frank ever did."

"*E-mails?*" Ryan sputtered, incredulously. "A serum? Frank said he lost contact with Arthur in the forties or fifties, and by that point he'd already been out of the tribe for almost thirty years. If he's still alive, that would mean he'd be—"

"Incredibly old?" Natalia interjected. "I'm not entirely sure myself how it's possible. But he may not be alive. The last message I received from him was about seven years ago. I believe he was somewhere in the Southwest, New Mexico, Nevada, something with an *N*. I'll show you all of our correspondences once we get out of here."

"Which we need to do *now*," Jennifer said. In one hand she was holding the extracted hard drive from Frank's desktop. In the other, an unused road flare. "You can continue the chitchat later."

Natalia nodded and started heading for the stairs. "You're right," she said. "We still need to sweep the other warehouses, dismantle a few more computers and one or two more bodies. Torching this hellhole should give us enough time to do it."

Ryan paused as Natalia disappeared down the spiral staircase, still trying to process everything that had happened, where they were going, what would happen next. He looked at the vaporizer pen lying a few inches from a gnarled hunk that had once been a fist. He watched Jennifer spark the flare and fling it across the room, watched the corpses and the floor around them ignite in a massive blaze.

As the flames consumed the room, and as Jennifer shouted and motioned frantically at him to make for the exit, Ryan braced for a rush of emotions that never came. There was no lingering anger, no cathartic release, no pang of survivor's guilt. There was only a hazy disconnect, like the first seconds after waking, when the boundaries between the dream world and your own are uncertain, when you don't want to pinch yourself because you're unsure of what might—or might not—happen.

The statues in the bag began to glow. Jennifer grabbed Ryan's arm.

He woke up and ran.

37

Ryan took one last scan of the apartment, making sure that there was nothing he'd missed that he might want to take with him. But the space in Crown Heights he'd called home was as barren as it had been the night two weeks before when Frank had woken him up, as it had been for years, the last in a long line of temporary, white-walled Brooklyn hideouts.

He was standing in the kitchen near Luis, who was hunched over the island countertop wielding an electric drill. Luis was trying to reattach the false bottom to the torn-apart drawer that had once held Ryan's gun, humming a merengue tune that Ryan had often heard him blasting on his boom box, drowning out the MS-NBC news report on the TV screen.

When Ryan had shown up at the building's doorstep a few hours earlier, the normally jovial superintendent, sitting in a folding chair with his usual cerveza, tensed up like he was ready to bolt, as if he'd come face-to-face with a ghost. After Ryan assured him that he was very much alive, Luis's expression shifted to one of uncharacteristic disappointment.

Luis explained that since Ryan had disappeared on the same night as the shooting on Nostrand Avenue, he and his buddies from the neighborhood figured that Ryan had been involved, that he'd been—based on their assumptions about Ryan's career—the victim of some kind of white-collar shakedown gone wrong. It would take at least another month for the apartment to be declared abandoned, and in the meantime, the men decided to mourn Ryan's unfortunate demise by holding a dominoes tournament to see who would get to claim his stuff. Luis had won the rights to Ryan's couch and television, the two most valuable items in the apartment, and he'd outfitted Ryan's front door with a new padlock to protect his future plunder.

When Ryan had informed him that he was, in fact, leaving, that he had only returned to pick up a few articles of clothing (and some documents that he hoped were beyond Luis's comprehension), and that Luis could have anything he wanted, the portly old man had perked up right away. He'd even offered to fix any structural damages in the apartment so Ryan wouldn't lose his security deposit. Ryan had tried to politely decline, but Luis insisted, possibly because of a guilty conscience over intending to steal Ryan's property.

Luis finished reassembling the drawer. As he picked it up and turned to place it in its slot, he stubbed his slipper-clad toe on the camouflage duffel bag near Ryan's feet, the bag from the Cloisters that was now overflowing with T-shirts, boxers, and socks Ryan had taken from the bedroom closet. Luis howled, handed the drawer to Ryan, and hopped around the kitchen as gingerly as his rotund frame allowed, cursing in Spanish.

The instant that Luis had made contact with the statue at the bottom of the bag, Ryan thought he felt something like a cold magnetic tremor surge through his body. Or maybe it was just a normal muscle twitch. Whatever it was, it was gone in a second.

"What do you have in there, underwear and . . . dumbbells?" Luis muttered, rubbing his foot.

Ryan shrugged as he slid the drawer into its slot, trying not to laugh. "More like a rock collection. Sorry."

"Fucking loco white boy." Luis shook his head, grinning through clenched teeth. He glanced across the living room, Ryan assumed, to remind himself that while pain was only temporary, leather upholstery and high-definition screens were forever.

As Ryan bent down, he heard a familiar name amid the otherwise negligible drone of a TV newscaster. For a second, he thought he'd imagined it, but when he looked across the room at the TV, he saw a screenshot of Conrad Van Pelt's Wikipedia page juxtaposed with a photograph of him walking outside the Corbin Building, an image Ryan immediately recognized from Derrick Rhodes's papers.

It was followed by a sequence of nearly identical split screens featuring several other members of the Committee. Then a press conference led by an exasperated-looking Cassius Van Pelt, the current president of the family company and a fatter, older, and less mangled version of his great-great-great-grandfather. Even if the Manhattan tribe weathered the media storm, which it probably would, the elders would have their hands full for the foreseeable future.

Before the newscast cut to a commercial break, there was a preview of an upcoming segment that promised an interview with a man who claimed to be part of a "clandestine vampire syndicate." An accompanying photograph appeared on the screen—a quasi-homeless-looking, middle-aged guy with long greasy hair plastered to the side of his face, a half-smoked cigarette pressed between his scowling lips.

It was Sean, Van Pelt's longtime doorman. Finally able to get back at his boss, to take the freak show public.

Ryan snorted in amusement.

"*¿Los vampiros?*" Luis scoffed, looking up at the TV. He was messing around with his toolkit that was spread out on the kitchen island, taking apart the drill. "What are they going to come up with next? You should have been here in the eighties, *papi.* I saw plenty of vampires and zombies, only we called them base-heads. You would need more than a stake to take one of those *culeros* out."

"Must have been wild," Ryan said, not really paying attention as he read the news ticker on the bottom of the screen. *Cloisters museum closed to public for second straight day due to gas leak. Yankees win 9–8 nail-biter in Houston. No fatalities suspected in Red Hook waterfront fire.*

Lying partially hidden in the crevice of two couch cushions, Ryan's phone began to vibrate, then blast a familiar, obnoxious ringtone. He crossed the room, turned the TV on mute, and picked it up.

"I know I'm late," he said. "I got sidetracked by my super, saying good-bye to the place. It's harder than I thought it would be. But I got everything I needed. I'm leaving now."

Jennifer sighed dramatically. "If you want to hang out and drink Modelos with Luis, that's fine with me," she said. "I mean, I've only waited seven or eight months for you to come over. What's another couple hours?"

She was joking, but Ryan knew that a couple of hours or even a couple of days would be nowhere near enough time to sort through the chaos that had occurred and the possibilities of what might happen next. The fact that Arthur might still be alive. That the Manhattan tribe, once they weren't preoccupied with the fallout from the files Jennifer had leaked, would probably make him public enemy number one. That he wasn't sure if he was human or *Ànkëlëk-ila* or something in between. His apprehension about Natalia staying in Brooklyn and his thankfulness to her for giving Ryan and Jennifer her car. What they were going to do with the statues once they'd left the city, where they were going to go, how they were going to stay off the radar.

He took a deep breath and cleared his head until the only thing that remained was Jennifer's face creased in laughter, her big eyes beaming back at him.

Everything else could wait, at least for a little while.

"No," he said, walking back toward the kitchen, "I'm done here." Luis patted Ryan's shoulder and winked as he headed in the opposite direction, out the front door and back to his stool and his bottomless cooler of beer. "I'm a little hungry. I was thinking that before we take off, maybe I could park Natalia's car in your garage and we could check out that ramen spot near your place that you always wanted me to try. Is that cool with you?"

"I don't know if I'm in the mood," Jennifer replied. "I had a pretty satisfying liquid lunch today. B negative. Why don't you just pick something up on the way?"

"Well, I guess we're on different sides of the double helix again. Talk about a role reversal."

She laughed. "There have always been differences between us. We've made them work before. Why sweat it? I know I won't, because . . . well, I can't."

Ryan smiled. "I'm leaving now," he repeated, the words sounding even better the second time around. "I mean it."

"I know you do," she said before hanging up.

He picked up the duffel bag, slung it over his shoulder, and walked out of the apartment, closing the door behind him.

Acknowledgments

Much gratitude goes out to my editors, Brendan Deneen and Peter Joseph, as well as the rest of the staff at Thomas Dunne Books and Macmillan Entertainment. Thank you for having the faith to bring me onto this project and trusting me from day one. Your unwavering support, encouragement, and positivity made writing the book a hell of a lot of fun.

To all the teachers, mentors, early readers, and workshop-mates who have helped me shape my words over the years, especially Josephine Humphreys, Brian Henry, Jonathan Dee, Binnie Kirshenbaum, John Reed, Garrett McDonough, Stephen Cicerelli, Jobie Hughes, and Jonathan Maberry—and anyone else who's bothered to spend time with my stories. You are the reason I continue to plod stubbornly along the literary path.

To my Richmond and Loomis people, the Little Branch crew, the Third Stall, the Burger Bashers, and everyone else who keeps me (in) sane and reminds me that an occasionally decent world exists outside my writing cave—I couldn't have done this without you. Special shout-outs to my 2015 roommates—Sean, Len, and Anthony—and my parents, Lodia and Charles Vola, who heard the worst of my grumblings about vampires and supernatural conspiracies, and who delicately—and sometimes emphatically—told me to suck it up. And to Sandra Morrow, whose Facebook skills are much appreciated.

And finally, to the City of New York, without which this book couldn't exist, and without which I couldn't, either: thank you, thank you, thank you.